PRAISE FOR *DIVINE JUSTICE*

"Comforti details twists and turns in this riveting crime thriller that will have you tearing through the pages toward the climactic conclusion."

—Wayne Miller,
author of *Burn Boston Burn*

"*Divine Justice* is a deftly plotted and intricate story that weaves disparate threads together in a compelling tale. There is plenty of full-on action to satisfy any adrenaline junkie."

—Reader's Favorite
– 5 stars

"Stan Comforti delivers crime thrills with a level of emotional resonance that makes us yearn for more Sam Caviello stories to come."

—John Brewer,
author of Coldiron's Cure

"*Divine Justice* is a well-crafted maze of morality, murder, and the blurry edge of justice, which drives the momentum and tangled plotlines that makes this thriller so hard to put down, keeping the pages turning even faster."

—Self-Publishing Review

"Fans of murder thrillers will find *Divine Justice* fast-paced and highly readable."

—John Gilchrist,
author of Law for the Layman

DIVINE
JUSTICE

DIVINE JUSTICE

A SAM CAVIELLO FEDERAL AGENT CRIME MYSTERY

BOOK 4

STAN COMFORTI

DIVINE JUSTICE

Copyright © 2025 by Stan Comforti

This book is a work of fiction. Names, characters, places, events, or incidents are used fictitiously. The story is a product of the author's imagination. Any similarity to actual persons, living or dead, actual events, or locations is coincidental and not intended by the author.

Editor: Erin Clyburn
Proofreader: James Abbate
Cover Designer: Zizi Iryaspraha Subiyarta, ziziiryasse@gmail.com
Interior Designer: Amit Dey, amitdey2528@gmail.com
Publishing Consultant: Geoff Affleck, authorpreneurbooks.com

ISBN 979-8-9928892-0-8 (paperback)
ISBN 979-8-9928892-1-5 (eBook)
ISBN 979-8-9928892-2-2 (hardcover)

FIC022020   FICTION / Mystery & Detective / Police Procedural
FIC031010   FICTION / Thrillers / Crime
FIC030000   FICTION / Thrillers / Suspense

DEDICATION

In memory of my two friends and ATF colleagues, Larry Doster and Sal Petrella, who passed in 2023. They are sadly missed and quietly remembered every day. They are two special friends who will never leave us. Rest in peace, my friends.

PROLOGUE
JANUARY 2014

The chilling winds off Long Island Sound lashed against the Compo shoreline, slicing through the upscale Westport neighborhood like a ghost's whisper. The family had just cleared the dinner table at the Donnelley estate, a gleaming symbol of wealth and privilege perched above the restless waves. Their picturesque home, towering windows, and modern stone facade seemed to glow faintly in the dim light, a beacon against the deepening night.

The sea breeze carried a tang of salty air and a scent of cedar that lined the manicured lawns. Outside, the waves surged higher, slamming against the rocky shore as if trying to claw their way onto the pristine land. Above, the half-moon wove in and out of thick, brooding clouds, casting fleeting, silvered shadows that danced across the home's sleek exterior.

Inside, all appeared tranquil, a curated image of comfort and success. Jon Donnelly's wealth was almost mythical in town whispers, thanks to his prestigious jewelry emporium. JD hid his precious stones, bearer bonds, and cash in a high-tech, practically impenetrable vault in his sprawling estate. Its contents? A fortune, kept closer than any bank vault, for reasons no one dared to question.

However, the house's serene exterior contradicted the storm brewing outside and within. The air seemed charged with the kind of tension that makes animals skittish and turns shadows into menacing shapes. Nightfall had shrouded the neighborhood, yet it felt like something or someone was watching.

Among the hum of holiday tunes and the joyous chatter, JD, his wife Alexis, and their three teenage children had just finished dinner. The teenagers, home during the school vacation, enjoyed playing games on their new iPads and calling friends on their new iPhones. The kids looked forward to gathering around the Christmas tree, removing and boxing dozens of ornaments and a slew of multicolored tree lights. Alexis abstained from joining the teenagers with the family tradition. She was not feeling well and retired to the bedroom to rest. Upbeat holiday tunes played as the kids sang along with the melodies, passing the ornaments to each other before handing them to their dad, who filled the storage boxes.

When the tree stood bare, the kids congratulated each other with fist pumps. Alexis, dressed in a robe, returned to the dining room to remind JD about scheduling an appointment with their accountant in the morning. But before she spoke, a security alert sounded, shattering the fragile festivity. JD's face turned pale as he glanced at the security monitor, seeing four masked figures advancing toward the front door.

"Safe room now!" JD's command snapped through the room with urgency and fear.

Alexis, unsteady on her feet, felt a surge of nausea as the weight of impending danger pressed upon her. "This is a mistake. Not tonight," she mumbled, then yelled, "Hurry up, children! In the bedroom!"

The Donnelley kids' laughter, now silenced, began moving with fear and determination, except for Daniel. The holiday melodies provided an eerie backdrop to the unfolding chaos as the other two kids scrambled to obey their father's orders. The once-merry atmosphere now echoed with a distant ring of doom.

"What are you doing, Danny? Get into the safe room!" screamed JD.

Daniel, defiant, stood by his father's side with resolve. "I'm staying here with you, Dad.

JD was about to take hold of his son's arm and pull him to the safe room when the four masked home invaders entered the room with guns drawn. JD immediately began to yell in anger at the intruders.

"What's the meaning of this? The house is alarmed, with instructions for the police to respond immediately without calling first!"

In the dimly lit family room, the apparent leader, obscured by a sinister mask, confronted JD with a gun pointed at his face. "Yeah, well, that's not gonna happen. Do what I tell ya. Open the safe, and nobody will get hurt."

Alexis heard the commotion from the family room while pressing the hidden release button and pushing a narrow dummy wall into a secure, small, safe room. She shoved her youngest kid inside with instructions to be quiet and not to come out until told to. The youngster sat before a large split-screen monitor, allowing those in the safe room to see the bedroom and the family room from the undetectable security cameras. Alexis tried ushering her middle child, Kylie, into the room, but she refused shelter.

"I'm staying with you, Mom." Her eyes blazed with defiance, starkly contrasting the terror felt by the intruders invading their sanctuary.

"No. These men are dangerous," warned Alexis. "I want you in the room now. Please."

Kylie refused and moved further back into the bedroom. Hearing feet shuffling on the wooden floors, she saw two men about to enter the room. "Mom, they're coming into the room."

Alexis quickly closed the wall and moved toward Kylie to protect her as two invaders entered the bedroom, with one grabbing Alexis's arm.

"Relax, lady. Stay calm, and nobody will get hurt. We'll be out of here in a few minutes."

In the family room, the vocal leader told JD to open the safe. JD refused and repeated his warning.

"The police will be here any minute now."

"The cops ain't coming, man. I turned off the alarm when I came in. So open the frigging safe now, before I hurt you."

JD didn't believe the guy could have had the alarm code. More so, he was disturbed that the alarm company hadn't called about the intrusion. The company always called if someone hadn't turned off the alarm within sixty seconds. He refused their request again, claiming he kept his valuables in a vault at his downtown business in Greenwich.

"You're lying, and it's pissing me off. I warned you nobody would get hurt if you did what I told you. If you had opened the safe, we'd be outta here already. Now I have to get nasty." The leader put a gun to Danny's head. His silver pistol ominously glittered in the subdued light. The room pulsed with heart-pounding fear; the odor of breath and sweat in the air gave a scent of impending violence.

"If you don't open the safe in ten seconds, I'm gonna blow your son's head open. One, two, three, four—I'm not fooling around, man. Do ya want your son dead?" The guy paused to give JD time to reconsider. "Okay. His death will be on you. You'll regret it forever. Where was I? Oh, yeah. Five, six, seven, eight . . ." The guy pulled the gun's hammer back. "Nine . . ."

"Stop! Okay! I'll open the safe." JD couldn't chance the guy wasn't crazy enough to kill his son. He slowly stepped to the wall cabinet and the door handle on the right side. He placed his thumb on the handle, allowing the security eyelet time to recognize his fingerprint. He turned the handle down to open it. Inside was a heavy steel high-security burglar safe with a facial pad. JD placed his face in front of it to unlock it.

"Wow, man, that must have cost you some bucks." He winked at his comrade and said, "Bones, watch the kid while I keep an eye on the safe."

JD didn't open the door. He stood his ground.

"Hey. Open the friggin' door and get out of the way, or your kid is dead." JD hesitated, then he opened the door halfway and stepped back.

When it opened, Bones took his eyes off Danny, anxiously glancing into the safe and seeing a mother lode of jewels and money inside it.

Danny saw his only chance as Bones looked away from him. With anxiety streaming through his body and his heart fluttering like a hummingbird's wings, he quietly took two steps toward the fireplace. Danny grabbed the fireplace iron poker and foolhardily stormed at Bones. Bones' peripheral vision caught Danny's movement. He whipped his gun hand toward Danny, but not fast enough before the teenager rammed the poker down on Bones' arm. The impact caused a cracking sound, inducing an angry cry from Bones while dropping his gun to the floor. Danny pushed Bones to the floor, kicked his weapon away, and turned to attack his cohort, but not quickly enough. The ringleader turned around in desperation with his gun aimed at Danny's boyish face. With strained facial rigidity, he pulled the trigger. The blast sound bounced off the walls, followed by the thud when Danny dropped dead to the floor.

Furious, JD, a military warrior in another lifetime, circled his left arm around the ringleader's neck, grabbed his gun wrist with the other, and forced the arm hard against the corner edge of the cabinet.

In the bedroom, Alexis became terrified when hearing the gunshot. Concerned about her son, she tried to escape the clutches of the two men. She didn't get far when one intruder caught her arm and threw her onto the bed. Alexis surprisingly bounced up and slammed her fist across the guy's face, causing his mask to fly off to one side, hanging from his ear.

"Ahhh! You stupid woman. That was a big mistake," said the angry guy she hit. He reached for his gun, whispering, "It's the last one you'll ever make."

Defiant, Kylie screamed and slammed into the guy. He temporarily lost his balance as Kylie punched him, hitting him across the cheek and knocking him backward. The guy exploded with chaotic anger as he aimlessly shot two rounds at Kylie, which echoed with the roar of screams and a rasping tang of blood as she crumpled to the floor dead.

"Jesus, Zee, whataya doing, man?" shouted his cohort.

Shocked and shrieking, Alexis, with glazed-over, swelling eyes, began flailing her arms with closed fists at Zee. He fell to the floor on his back with his gun hand up, haphazardly firing twice at her but only hitting the ceiling. Alexis feverishly jumped on top of him, swinging wildly at the guy's face, breaking his nose as blood spattered down on his face and the floor.

"Get her off me, Tonio!" yelled Zee.

Tonio gripped Alexis under her armpits and lifted her off Zee. Zee swiped the blood from his nose, scrambled to his feet, and pointed his gun at Alexis.

"Don't!" shouted Tonio as he moved back to avoid getting shot.

Zee fired two rounds into Alexis's chest, forcing her back, hitting the edge of the bed, and sliding down to a sitting position on the floor. Her body weight slowly leaned right until her arm and head hit the floor.

Inside the safe room, Alexis's youngest teenager was traumatized, frantically trembling in fear at what happened in the bedroom. The child's lips were so tightly bound it caused the cheeks to bloat. The youngster cleared both eyes from sobbing and glared with hatred at the guy called Zee. Terrified, with clenched fists and inflamed eyes, the teenager glared at him, permanently ingraining the killer's face into memory, never to be forgotten.

In the family room, JD, still struggling to get the ringleader to drop his gun, slammed the guy's gun hand against the cabinet again, causing the weapon to fall to the floor. JD shoved the guy to his left and reached for the gun. Back on his feet, holding his broken arm, Bones stepped on the gun, shouting, "Gil, get the guy!"

Gil sprang back and corralled JD, forcing him to the floor and leaving the once-proud veteran at their mercy. Using all his strength, JD rolled to his back, trying to bounce up, but Gil had his gun back, pointing it at JD's head.

"You should've let us get what we came for and left. But no, you had to be stupid. Big mistake, asshole. You give me no choice." JD tried swinging his arm at the guy, but Gil slapped it away and then shot JD dead. Although Gil was furious that he had to kill JD and his son, he remained content.

Gil gazed at the open safe jammed with bearer bonds, thousands in cash, and precious jewelry. "Bones. Find out what happened in the bedroom. Then get back here to help me load up our bag so we can get outta here. I think we struck pay dirt. The safe is loaded."

Minutes later, Bones returned. "Zee killed the woman and her daughter,"

Zee followed behind, shrugging his shoulders. "Hey. The woman slugged me and tore off my mask! I couldn't let her identify me to the cops. Could I, Gil?" Zee wiped blood from his face, saying, "The punk kid punched me in the mouth. She had it comin', man."

Gil shook his head in disgust. "We told them to cooperate, and they wouldn't get hurt. But they didn't listen. So be it. Let's finish up and make sure we didn't leave anything behind. Zee, you and Tonio clean up everything in the bedroom, especially your blood. Do it quick so we can leave. Someone probably heard the shots and called the police."

Five minutes later, the four men rushed out of the Donnelly home. They heard police sirens in the distance. They ran to their white-colored van, which they made up to look like a FedEx vehicle. They drove off at the posted speed limit, away from the sounds of the emergency vehicles. Amid the turmoil, the sirens drew closer, a contradictory symphony heralding the arrival of justice, only not in time.

The youngest teenager remained silently in the safe room for several minutes, gathering the courage to exit. Finally, leaving the safe room, the youngster refrained from looking at the bodies on the bedroom floor, only stiffly moving toward the family room like a zombie.

A moment later, police rushed into the home's open front door with guns drawn. They momentarily froze at the sight of the family room.

"Guys," uttered one officer, pointing at the young teenager standing motionless in the dining room, white as a ghost in total shock, standing like a small figurine.

"Call for an ambulance!" shouted the sergeant.

The intruders, their loot in hand, fled into the night, leaving behind a scene of shattered lives and a fourteen-year-old child forever scarred by the intensity of that fateful night.

CHAPTER
1
SEVEN YEARS LATER

I t was seven-forty-five in the morning. The bedroom was dark and whisper quiet. The window shade was open about five inches from the top. The sunlight from the morning sun peered through the space, radiating sunbeams on ATF Agent Sam Caviello's face while he slept. Distracted but absorbed in sleep, Caviello turned away from the sun's rays. The radiation and the warming breeze against the swaying tree branches brushing against the building caused creaking sounds outside the window. The breeze muffled the swishing sounds and clatter across the window. The sounds were too subdued to disturb Caviello's deep sleep. Now and then, Caviello moaned, visualizing past horrors on the job. It wasn't until an incoming cell call abruptly awakened him.

With his eyes still anchored shut, he mindlessly searched for the phone on the nightstand. His hand carelessly searched for the phone but fumbled with it as it slipped from his fingers onto the floor. Aggravated, he shifted to the bed's edge, searching for the phone with closed eyes. Sam swayed his fingers back and forth on the floor, hitting the cell phone and knocking it further from his reach. Impulsively, with his eyes partially opened, he stretched his arm to latch onto it with a tight grip, bringing it to his ear.

"It's not even close to nine o'clock yet," Sam griped.

"What?" said the puzzled caller.

Then, realizing it wasn't the senator or her representative, Sam changed his tone. "Sorry, who's this?"

"It's Gabbi, Sam. Did I wake you?'

"Uh, yeah, kind of. Sorry, Gabbi. I didn't see who was calling. I thought it might be the senator who wanted to see me this morning."

"The senator? Why would a senator be calling you? Is it because you rescued the little girl, Ena?"

"Not exactly. When Ena and I landed at the Boston airport, a crowd of reporters and agency heads were waiting to welcome her back home to her mom and grandma. It was an amazing site. My son, Drew, was part of the welcoming committee at the airport. When the state police guided Ena and her mom out of the terminal, with the reporters tagging behind, Drew and I stayed way back to avoid them. A Secret Service agent was waiting for me at the terminal exit. He told me a US senator wanted to meet me at a nearby hotel. Remember, you and I participated in that early morning raid at the commune before Ena and I flew to Boston. I was dead tired."

"How can I forget that? We had to get up at three in the morning."

"I wasn't going anywhere to meet with anyone other than to the apartment and crash in bed. I told the agent to have the senator call me in the morning but not until after nine o'clock."

"Oh, that's why you were so cranky when you answered my call."

"Yep. I looked at the alarm clock rather than the phone, expecting it to be the senator."

"I didn't know Secret Service agents protected senators."

"They normally don't. However, the agent mentioned that the senator was the favorite to win her party's nomination to be the next President of the United States."

"Oh. That might have gotten me to go with the agent."

"I didn't care. I was fighting to stay awake and leave the terminal without sleepwalking." Sam's phone sounded off again. He looked at the cell's screen and saw Donna Ranero, the Supervisory Assistant US Attorney in Boston, was calling.

"The US Attorney is calling me. I don't want to take it, but I should. Call me any hour, even to say hi, and I'll do the same."

"Okay, I miss you."

"Miss you, too." Sam ended the call, noticed it was not close to nine o'clock, but answered the US Attorney's call.

"Good morning, Donna. I hope it's not too important. I'm still in bed."

"Sorry. I suspected you might be, but I'm under pressure to arrange a meeting between you and Senator Alvarado-Thornton."

"Oh, that. What's this all about anyway? Why is it so urgent for a US senator to meet with me? Does it have anything to do with me bringing Ena back to her mom?"

"No. It has nothing to do with Ena's kidnapping but about the possible abduction of the senator's son."

CHAPTER

2

Sam glanced at the exquisite blue sky with the sun's rays reflecting off the ocean waters surrounding the backside of the federal courthouse in Boston's Seaport District. The salty air from the harbor filled his senses, a nostalgic reminder of his childhood, where his uncle, a lifeguard at their town's private beach, frequently took him there for the day. Sam loved the beach and soon planned to enjoy the ocean's salty breeze while vacationing on a Caribbean Island. Hopefully, the job wouldn't once again interfere with his time off.

As he approached the federal building, he studied the bustling Seaport District, alive with restaurants, retail shops, hotels, and condos, still growing into a mini-metropolis. Foot traffic was heavy as people hurried to work or wherever they were going. Passing through the court's security, he glanced at the picturesque courthouse lobby with its vast floor-to-ceiling rear windows reflecting the sun glittering off the harbor's water outside. Sam took the elevator to the US Attorney's Office floor.

The receptionist greeted him with a warm smile. "Morning, Sam. You can head down to Donna's office. She's waiting for you."

Sam knew the way to Ranero's office. Walking down the hall, he noticed Secret Service Agent Hadley sitting on a side chair, wearing dark-rimmed glasses. He was engrossed in reading something on his cell phone. Ranero's office door was open, so Sam tapped it, walked in, and greeted her as she sat behind her desk.

"Morning, Sam. Did you get enough sleep?"

"I would have gotten a lot more if you hadn't called for me to come here."

"Well, you're here now, so let's head to Lucas Stewart's office and join the others."

"The others? How many are we meeting with?"

"Lucas, Austin Taylor, the FBI Agent-in-Charge in Boston, Dell Haskins, his supervisor, and Alan Davies, the new FBI Agent-in-Charge in New Haven. You know Debra Durrell, the US Attorney for Connecticut. She'll be monitoring the meeting via a Zoom video, and of course, Senator Alvarado-Thornton will be there with her assistant."

"Oh, great. That's seven against one. Why do I feel this may not be good for me?"

"The senator is on your side, and she's the one who counts. Not to mention, Deb and I are also in your corner."

Sam followed Donna Ranero to the Office of the US Attorney for the State of Massachusetts, Lucas Stewart. They entered his office and into an adjoining conference room, where Stewart was seated at the head of the long conference table. FBI Agents-in-Charge Taylor and Davies and Supervisor Haskins were sitting to his right. The senator and her assistant were seated to his left. Stewart asked Ranero and Sam to take a seat.

Sam, dressed in a short-sleeved, black-collared polo shirt, a navy sports coat, and casual khaki trousers, studied the more formal, well-dressed ensemble seated around the table.

"Sam, why don't you sit next to Dell, and I'll sit across from you?" said Ranero.

Stewart was the first to speak. "Sam, this is Senator Evelyn Alvarado-Thornton," he said, pointing to the senator, "and her assistant, Brittany Tanner. About four weeks ago, the senator's son, Travis, went missing. As of yet, we don't know what happened to him or why. We haven't had any ransom demands or heard from him since then. The senator and her husband, Wesley Thornton, have called their son's cell numerous times, leaving messages for him to call back, without success. The FBI in New Haven began an investigation, interviewing his classmates, roommates, friends, and professors at Yale University, where he was a student. So far, we have no leads as to what happened to him. The senator has heard about your success in finding the kidnapped young girl, Ena, and rescuing a state police detective's kidnapped daughter. She has asked if we could have you join the investigative team in hopes you might add a new perspective to the investigation."

Sam sat there, consumed by it all, not wanting to get involved with another kidnapping investigation. Kidnapping was the FBI's responsibility, and he didn't want to get immersed in another long-term investigation, especially since the FBI preferred he didn't. He needed a vacation that he hadn't had in over a year. Sam considered all the approvals he'd need internally and the necessity to familiarize himself with the mandates he'd have to follow working with the FBI.

Stewart saw Sam reflecting on the assignment. "Sam, are you with us? Any questions, comments, or concerns you'd like to bring up?"

Sam paused to gather his response, then spoke. "How's this going to work? Have you received authorization from ATF for me to work with the FBI? Who will I be answering to, someone from the US Attorney's office or the FBI, and who will I work with during the investigation?

"We've taken care of the authorization for you to work with the FBI. You'll be temporarily assigned to the FBI under their supervision and oversight by Debra Durrell, the US Attorney for Connecticut."

"We'll assign a Connecticut FBI agent to work with you. That agent will be responsible for all written reports and updating our office daily on the progress of any significant events or pending actions. In addition, the assigned agent will enlighten you on all FBI procedures and protocols," stated New Haven FBI Agent-in-Charge Alan Davies.

Sam considered what both men said and reflected on his preferred input before accepting the temporary assignment. "If that's the case, I'd prefer to work with Agent Kiara Rivers, whom I worked with when we brought Ena back to Boston, and FBI supervisor Dell Haskins, to be our contact person.

I've worked with both and feel comfortable working with them instead of someone I don't know. I work a little differently than most agents. I don't want interference from anyone telling me I'm not allowed to follow my hunch as to who to interview or where to go to collect what may be needed to find what happened to the senator's son."

Debra Durrell spoke before Stewart or Davies did. "I've worked with Sam on a previous case and appreciate his investigative talent. Although, at times, I wondered why or how he conducts his search or inquiry, he has proven to be very savvy in getting results. It would be counterproductive for Sam's peers to question how he works. If there is a need to question how he conducts his probe, let me be the deciding official to approve or disapprove his undertaking."

"I understand Mr. Caviello has inserted himself in three previous kidnapping investigations. I'm sure we all know that kidnapping is the FBI's jurisdiction. As Mr. Caviello said, he works differently than most agents, and I assume he includes FBI agents in that category. Speaking for all FBI agents, we follow the agency's high standards of investigative procedures, principles, and policies, and we expect that Mr. Caviello follows them to the letter of the law as all FBI agents do," said Alan Davies.

This meeting was the first time Sam had met Davies. He wasn't impressed. Sam didn't appreciate Davies addressing him as mister rather than as an agent and lecturing him on investigative procedures. He thought it would be better not to join the investigation if the FBI treated him as a rookie agent just hired.

"Thank you, Mr. Davies, for pointing out the FBI's high standards. Based on your remarks, I take it you're not supportive of me joining the team. I want you to know I'd put my investigative standards to the test of any federal agent, including those in the FBI. So you know, I didn't insert myself into this investigation, and since you apparently prefer that I didn't participate, I'd like to go on a much-needed vacation."

"Wait, what's happening here?" said an irritated Senator Alvarado-Thornton. "I requested Agent Caviello to be a part of the investigation, and you assured me he would."

"Agent Caviello will be a part of the FBI's investigation. I cleared it with the Directors of the FBI and ATF," said the US Attorney for Connecticut, Debra Durrell. "You are aware of that, am I right, Alan?

"I never said he couldn't be a part of the investigation, but he has to follow the FBI's guidelines and not his own."

"My investigative principles are the same as yours," said Sam.

"Okay, so that's settled," said Durrell, anxious to end turf disputes. "We should provide Agent Caviello the support he requested regarding his choice of a partner, and I believe Dell to be an excellent choice to supervise them." Durrell looked to Davies and Austin Taylor for their agreement.

Taylor nodded in agreement. Davies preferred that Caviello be supervised by him or a New Haven supervisor. However, he nodded in agreement but stipulated that his New Haven office would continue to have overall control of the investigation to find Travis.

"I request Agent Caviello to have the freedom to use his investigative talent without the burden of bureaucrats looking over his shoulders hampering his efforts," said the senator sternly."

"I agree," said Durrell. "Agent Caviello has proven he's an exceptional investigator. We don't want anyone to micro-manage his search. I'm sure Sam will inform Dell of his progress and receive authorizations where policy requires it. If there's an issue with Sam's conduct or practice, I will decide the matter. I hope there won't be any for me to decide." She looked to see if there were any further comments, then added, "I think we settled everything. If there's no further discussion, let's adjourn."

Before the meeting adjourned, Sam had additional requests. "I would first like to review all the reports on those interviewed, all investigative progress reports, and critical intelligence. Then I'd like to start the interviewing with the senator."

"That won't be necessary. We already interviewed the senator and her husband, and it will be part of our reports that you'll review," said Davies.

"I appreciate that, but I need to conduct my own interviews. Interviewing a person a second time sometimes can be effective in obtaining additional information that could be helpful."

"Well, it won't be necessary in this case," repeated Davies.

"I have no issue with Agent Caviello interviewing me," said Senator Alvarado-Thornton.

There was a quiet moment as Davies first looked at Austin Taylor for support, then the senator. He was not pleased that he didn't get the support.

Sensing another oncoming dispute, Donna Ranero spoke before someone else did. "I guess that's settled then. Agent Caviello will interview Senator Alvarado-Thornton. Any further questions or comments before we adjourn?" She waited a second for a response and noted none, adding, "Okay, Alan, when could you have the files ready for Sam's review? The sooner, the better."

Davies lowered his head to conceal the scowl on his face before answering. "I'm sure Dell could retrieve them from our system and have Caviello and Agent Rivers review them here in Boston."

"I could have them ready for review by the time Sam and Kiara are available if that works for them," said Dell Haskins. "Sam, you'll need my approval before making any copies to take with you."

Sam nodded his approval.

"Great. Sam, I suggest you review the FBI's report of their interview with the senator as soon as you get it," said Ranero. "The senator will be in New Hampshire tomorrow and return to Boston the following day. Arrange a time to meet with her at her convenience when she returns to Boston."

Lucas Stewart, Austin Taylor, Alan Davies, and Dell Haskins left the conference room, leaving Ranero, Sam, the senator, and her assistant, Brittany Tanner, remaining.

"Evelyn, you're welcome to use this room for the interview when you return to Boston," said Ranero.

"That won't be necessary, but thank you, Donna. You've been a great help. I'll have Brittany contact Agent Caviello when I return, and we will agree on a place to meet."

"Sam, would you wait in my office? I need a moment with the senator to see her out. It'll only be a few minutes."

CHAPTER

3

Fifteen minutes had passed while Sam waited patiently for Donna Ranero to return to her office. He began scanning through a Boston Magazine that was on her desk. As he did, his phone buzzed. Sam answered the call from FBI Agent Kiara Rivers.

"Morning, Kiara."

"Well, I never thought I'd see you again, let alone get assigned to work with you. Where are you?"

"I'm in Donna Ranero's office awaiting her return from escorting Senator Evelyn Alvarado-Thornton out of the US Attorney's Office."

"Can we meet somewhere for lunch?"

"Yeah, right after I finish meeting with Ranero. Where do you want to meet?"

"I'm in town, but finding a place to park in the city is impossible. I prefer not to meet at my office or the courthouse. I'll head north on 1A toward Revere. There's a 99 just before the traffic circle. Let's meet there."

"I know the restaurant. I don't know how long I'll be, but be patient, and I'll meet you there."

As Sam hung up, Ranero walked into her office and sat in the chair next to him.

"Sam, I know you wanted to take some well-deserved time off, and I'm sure you didn't want to get involved with another missing person investigation."

"You got that right, Donna. What puzzles me is how the senator came up with my name."

"She read the news story about rescuing Ena after two men abducted her from her school. She was impressed that after the child's mother asked for your help, you took it upon yourself to make inquiries, realizing the wrong guy got arrested for the abduction. As usual, you followed a hunch, found Ena in Nashville, and brought her back to her mom."

"That's it?" questioned Sam.

"No. That piqued the senator's interest. She had her aides provide further background information on you. Her aide's research learned that you, on your own, found the abandoned van the terrorists used after shooting a state trooper. In addition, you were instrumental in discovering where the terrorists were holding two abducted teenage girls who you rescued. The senator also learned you saved a state police detective's daughter, whom the terrorists had kidnapped. Long story short, the FBI's four-week-long investigation was not progressing fast enough for the senator. Evelyn and I met and became friends while attending Yale Law School. She called me for help. I contacted Deb in Connecticut, and we thought her request to assign you to the investigation might be productive."

"So, I have you and Deb to thank for getting me involved with this investigation instead of enjoying a quiet, stress-free vacation on a beach sipping piña coladas. Not only that, I also have four people to answer to. Dell, Davies, Debra, and you."

"I'm sorry, Sam. I promise Deb, and I will go easy on you." Ranero chuckled, "When you discover what happened to the senator's son, I promise I'll do all I can to ensure you can take a well-deserved vacation."

"Not necessary, but thanks."

* * *

Thirty minutes later, Sam entered the 99 Restaurant, searching the bar and nearby dining booths for Agent Rivers. She should be easy to spot even in a crowd. She had mentioned that her dad was a tall, handsome black man who married a spirited, younger Hispanic gal from Colombia, South America, home of many beautiful women. Kiara was no exception. Although not tall, she was a feisty, young agent in her late twenties who Sam respected when they worked together on the Ena abduction case.

"Are you looking for Kiara?" asked the hostess.

"I am. Is she hiding from me?" Sam said jokingly.

"No. She asked that I watch for your arrival and take you to her booth in the back, where it's quieter this time of day." The hostess escorted Sam to a rear booth near a window, where most booths in the section were empty.

"Well hidden, Kiara. This must be a covert meeting," said Sam jokingly.

"It's better to talk privately and avoid others overhearing our conversation."

"Yeah. I'd do the same."

"So, when my boss called and said he had a special assignment for me, I was apprehensive. I was concerned whether special meant the investigation was in recognition of my good work or the opposite. I was pleasantly surprised when he told me it was to work the case of the senator's missing kid. I thanked him for considering me for the assignment. He told me I should thank you since you asked for me. You must have reached the celebrity stage as an investigator. Not only did you get handpicked by a US senator, maybe even the next president, but you picked my boss to oversee the investigation and chose me as your partner. That's some doing, Sam."

"Sorry, your boss took you away from whatever investigation you were involved with. I hope you don't mind working this case with me."

"No. On the contrary, I would prefer to work on this case. The one I'm currently involved with was closed for lack of prosecutive merit. I'm just surprised how I was selected to work with you."

"By how do you mean you're surprised how I got involved?"

"You could say that. The FBI has been working on this case for weeks now. I guess the senator wasn't happy with how it's going, so out of the blue, she wants you involved, hoping you will miraculously find her son."

"I didn't want to get involved with another case, especially this one. I planned on taking a long vacation."

"So, couldn't you have told her no?"

"Not really."

"Why not?"

"Because her son is missing. I see this job not only to put bad guys in jail but also to help the victims of crime, especially young kids. Law enforcement should do all they can to do both. At least I do. Not to change the subject, but when we discover what happened to the senator's son, you'll get the recognition from your boss and a US senator for doing an outstanding job."

"What are you talking about? We'll be working on this together. If we find him, we'll both get the credit."

"Yeah, but this is an FBI case, and when we find him, the news headline will read, 'FBI finds the senator's missing son.' That's fine with me. I'll immediately disappear and enjoy a few weeks on the beach. You, however, the FBI agent spearheading the investigation, will be congratulated for doing what others couldn't do."

Kiara remained quiet but understood what Sam was saying about who would subsequently get the credit in the news. "Why did you pick me, Sam?"

"Partly because I wanted to make it up to you after I got involved with Ena's kidnapping without informing you earlier. We later worked well together with you, helping to get Ena home. Anyway, when someone asks for help finding a missing child, I can't refuse, and I'm sure you wouldn't either."

"We can't save everybody that goes missing, Sam."

"Everybody hasn't asked for our help. The senator did, and we'll do our best to find her son."

Kiara believed Sam was not an average agent. He responded to an Asian mother's plea for help to find her daughter Ena, who was kidnapped from her elementary school in Boston. Alone, he found her in Nashville after the FBI had arrested the wrong person for the abduction.

"So what's our plan to find Travis Thornton and bring him home to his mother?"

"Let's review what the FBI agents did so far. Time passed, so some of those interviewed may have remembered something they didn't mention during their initial interview. We need to dig deeper and ask those we interview who else knew Travis. The more people we interview, the more likely we'll gather new clues. Too often, if agents don't ask the right questions, they miss critical information."

"What if the agents asked all the right questions?"

"It's possible but unlikely. Have you ever been on a long surveillance at night, and there's no movement by the bad guys for hours? You're tired and close your eyes for a few seconds, or you and your partner look at each other while talking instead of watching the target. Perhaps one of you goes for coffee, or you start reading your email on your phone. Surveillance can be boring, causing all of us at one time or another to glance away from focusing on our target, if only for seconds."

"Okay. What's that got to do with interviewing?"

"My point is that conducting several interviews on the same day sometimes becomes boilerplate. As a result, agents tend to ask the same questions and occasionally don't fully absorb the answers without asking follow-up questions. What I'm getting at is we don't want to miss anyone who might provide the one key piece of information we need to put us on track to find out what happened to Travis. Like a long surveillance trying to stay focused on a target, we must focus on the answers during interviews. A follow-up question could clarify, expand, or identify something important omitted the first time. It's like squeezing the last drops out of a lemon."

"Wow. Here, I thought I would indoctrinate you on FBI procedures. Instead, you're coaching me to extract as much as possible from those I interview. I'll remember the squeezing a lemon reference you made when I conduct interviews," said Kiara, jesting. "What do you suggest we do first?"

"First, get all your agency's reports, including any intelligence they have, for us to review. We dissect the answers of those interviewed and explore what could be missing from their responses, like what wasn't asked or followed up on. From that, we decide who we should reinterview. It may be tedious, but it might give us better insight into what happened to Travis."

"You seem sure that by redoing what other FBI agents have done, we'll generate leads to finding Travis."

"I do. I'd be surprised if we didn't come up with others to interview, resulting in new leads to follow."

CHAPTER

4

At the Boston FBI office, Sam reviewed half of the twenty-four interviews and the intelligence reports collected during the FBI investigation. Kiara studied the other half. They then swapped the files and made personal notations to decide who to interview again. Kiara identified two persons to interview a second time. Sam selected four persons to interview again. The two Kiara picked for a second interview were two of the four Sam had identified. So, they agreed to reinterview four persons at Yale University.

"I should hear from the senator's assistant tomorrow for a time and place to interview the senator. After the interview with the senator, we should drive to New Haven and start the interviews at Yale," said Sam.

"Sounds like a plan, Sam. Let's get out of here."

"I don't know about you, but I'm hungry. Do you want to get a quick bite here?"

"I got very little sleep last night. I'm drained, Sam. I want to get home and get some sleep. Besides, I have leftovers in the fridge. I'll call you in the morning. As you said, we should know where to find the senator's son after we finish all the interviews. Right?"

"Ha. I wish it were that simple, but who knows what could turn up?" Sam humorously followed it up, saying, "If the senator's son doesn't greet us when we arrive in Connecticut, plan on staying a while."

Sam stopped at a takeout restaurant close to his son Drew's apartment for a sandwich and arrived at the apartment ten minutes later. He sat on the couch and stared out the large floor-to-ceiling windows overlooking the Mystic River and the beautifully lit-up Boston skyline. Sam thought of his son and decided to call him. Drew, a Diplomatic Security Service Special Agent, was on a thirty-day assignment to relieve colleagues at the US embassy in Ukraine.

Drew answered, saying he could only talk for a few minutes. He said things were fine but hectic, with warning alerts sounding off frequently in the war-torn country throughout the day and night. Drew said he now slept at the embassy for security reasons and was learning a lot about embassy operations, which would help when he eventually got assigned full-time to one.

"Dad, I'm getting a call I need to take. I have to go. I'm glad you called. I'll call you when I can. Love you."

"Love you, too. Take care and be safe."

Sam placed the phone beside him on the couch. He stared at the city skyline again, praying his son would remain safe during his tour in Ukraine. Sam closed his eyes, visualizing his son was returning home tomorrow. He started to doze off when his phone's ring snapped him back into consciousness. He checked the phone's screen, seeing it was the senator's assistant, so he answered it.

"Sam, it's Senator Alvarado-Thornton's assistant, Brittany."

"Hi. How are you?"

"I'm fine, Sam. The senator asked me to call to let you know she would be available to meet with you tomorrow morning at eleven at the Boston Harbor Hotel. I'll text you the room number by nine tomorrow."

"That's fine. I'll inform Agent Rivers, and we'll be there at the designated time."

"The senator prefers that you come alone."

"Agent Rivers and I are partners in the investigation. We interview as a team."

"The senator knew you would feel that way, but she prefers you come alone. She won't change her mind."

"I see." Sam thought perhaps he should cancel but changed his mind. "I'll be there, but I would have..."

Before Sam could say anything further, Brittany hung up.

Sam put the phone down, thinking tonight's calls could have ended better. He set the alarm and climbed into bed, hoping he'd have better success tomorrow.

CHAPTER
5

It was a gloomy evening on a cloudy mid-March night in 2021. The moon peeked through eerie clouds with light rainfall falling in a New Haven neighborhood plagued by crime. A local tavern off Whaley Avenue had become a favorite hangout for unsavory individuals. At two o'clock in the early morning hours, one such repugnant character, Geno Alonzio, known as Zee by his criminal cronies, stumbled out of the establishment. He slipped on the slimy water spewing from a broken section of the rain gutter above the front door, which angled toward the sidewalk. The middle-aged, intoxicated Zee wore ragged blue jeans, a long-sleeved crew shirt stained with paint, and a New York Mets baseball cap. While trying to cross the street to his two-year-old Dodge Ram, he stumbled and smacked into the back of a parked car.

Parked a short distance from the pickup was a dark-colored Toyota sedan with heavily tinted windows preventing anyone from seeing who sat behind the driver's wheel. The driver purposely scrutinized the saloon that night. The driver, Alex, sat up in the seat, peering through binoculars to identify the guy who had exited the bar. Alex's gut churned when confirming it was Zee. His heart hammered in his chest. His body went cold with dread with flashbacks to when he was only fourteen years old, hiding in the family's safe room while four men invaded their home shouting obscenities. What Alex witnessed that harrowing night caused unbearable nightmares that never ceased and remained until this day.

Zee and his three comrades had invaded the home, stole millions in cash, bearer bonds, and diamonds, and then murdered his entire family. Following that night, Alex was left alone with one set of foster parents after another until the state awarded Alex's uncle guardianship. Although his uncle and wife provided support and care, it was never the same as his loving parents and siblings. For seven years, Alex prayed religiously for one thing—retribution against the killers and justice for his family. He had made that solemn promise to his mom and planned to keep it.

Alex snapped out of a stupor when Zee barked in pain while struggling to straighten up from leaning against the parked car. Alex guessed Zee was fiftyish and about six feet tall when he could stand up straight on two steady feet. Alex wiped the tears rolling down both cheeks as he focused on Zee stumbling across the street without looking for oncoming traffic on a dimly lit street.

Halfway across the road, a car came from around the bend and slammed on its brakes, skidding to a stop. The fear of seeing the vehicle heading at him caused Zee to fall to one knee, leaning as if he were about to collapse.

The car obscured Alex's vision as to whether it had hit Zee. He prayed the car had crushed Zee dead under its wheels, eliminating one less murderer to deal with. That thought ended when the car's driver backed up and drove around Zee, yelling obscenities. With bulging eyes and flared nostrils, the hammered Zee swore while giving the finger to the driver as he sped away.

Zee labored to stand, but both wobbling legs gave way, causing him to fall face down on the hard pavement. While straining to push up to his knees, Zee slurred profanities. Alex couldn't help chuckling at such a pathetic sight, knowing it would be easier to deal with a drunk.

It took minutes for Zee to get back on his feet and finally stumble to his truck, leaning on its door to prevent falling to the pavement again. Zee slowly reached into his pants pocket for his truck keys but cursed when he didn't find them. He checked other pockets with similar disdain, then angrily shouted out f-bombs.

Inside the bar, Zee's three comrades were chugging beer, laughing about their successful hit on another home the night before.

"You think Zee will be able to make it back here to get the jacket he left behind?" said Bonarz.

"I doubt it. We don't call him Zee for zero brains because he has any smarts," said Acosta. "He's probably trying to remember where he was and if he even had a jacket,"

"I bet his truck keys are in his jacket. I'll check," said Bonarz. "Yep. Here they are." The three men laughed while Bonarz, nicknamed Bones, twirled the keys around his finger. "I'll bring his jacket and keys out to him."

"Screw him. Let him find his way back if he can," said Gil, the group's self-appointed leader. "I gotta piss. One of yooze get another pitcher."

When Gil weaved toward the restroom, Bonarz whispered, "I don't give a crap about what Gil says. I'm gonna bring his coat to him. If it were up to Gil, he'd dump Zee to keep an even bigger share of the money for himself."

"Well, do it before Gil comes back," said Acosta.

Outside, Zee was still leaning against his truck, babbling to himself, when he heard his buddy shout his name.

"Hey, Zee, you left your coat behind, man!" shouted Bonarz, exiting the bar. Bonarz skidded and stumbled on the slippery sidewalk before straightening his stance to trot across the street with the coat.

"Man, you look like shit, Zee. Maybe you shouldn't drive. Give me a minute, I'll get one of the guys, and we'll drive you to your place."

"Uh, no way, Bones. I'm okay. We made a good hit last night, so go back inside and celebrate."

"Yeah, well, Gil's bullshit with you hitting on another woman. He warned you about that before."

"Shit, man, it looked like she winked at me, you know. I can't help it if I get a little frisky. I thought she wanted me."

"She wasn't winking. She was scared shitless and kept closing her eyes. You should stick to Gil's plan to go in, take what we can get, and leave. Just between you and me, Gil's had it with you. He'll dump you from the crew if you don't follow the rules. Get it? Now, wait here. I'll get one of the guys, and we'll drive you to that dump you call home."

"No, Bones! Damn it! I'm driving myself!" Zee shrugged his shoulders like he didn't need help. "I did it many times after drinking pitchers of beer. Besides, my place is not that far from here anyway."

"You can't even stand up straight, asshole. You live, what, five, maybe six miles from here? You'll be lucky to make a hundred yards. Think of this truck you just bought. Do you want to crash into a tree or head into another car? Use your head, man."

"Nah, I'm okay. I don't need no chauffeur."

"I'm calling Gil. He won't let you drive in your condition. The last thing he wants is for you to get arrested after the hit we made. Your name has probably been in the system since the cops brought you in for questioning years ago. So let us drive you home."

"Come on, Bones. Yooze guys drank as much as me, and some of yooze can't even see at night. I'll be okay. I'll go slow. If I have a problem, there's a shithole motel down the road from here. I'll stop there and sleep it off. Okay?"

While the two men argued, Alex took photos of both, noting the names Zee, Bones, and Gil mentioned. Alex remembered their nicknames the night when they invaded the family home.

Zee finally shoved Bones away, unlocked his truck's door, and struggled to get into the driver's seat. He wiped his blurry eyes to clear his vision, lowered the window, and spit the phlegm stuck in his throat. It landed on Bones' shoe.

"What the hell, Zee? Screw you! You're frigging crazy! You better not get arrested—otherwise, Gil will kill you!"

Zee started his truck, shifted it in gear, and spun out, leaving Bones standing there, shaking his head in disgust. He watched Zee's vehicle sway from one side of the road to the other before miraculously straightening it and disappearing around the curve.

Bones shook his boot, trying to get the spit off before crossing the street. He headed to the bar as Alex slowly drove by the tavern, getting a closer look at him. He was sure he was one of Zee's accomplices that night years ago. Alex then stepped on the gas to catch up to Zee's pickup. He followed a distance behind, amazed that Zee had avoided an oncoming vehicle, missing it by inches. At this point, Alex hoped Zee would make it home so he could take revenge against his first target.

CHAPTER
6

After swerving erratically between the lanes several times, Zee somehow managed to make it home. He turned sharply left onto his dirt driveway, crashing into the mailbox at the entrance. The already battered mailbox, held together by bungee cords from previous encounters with Zee's truck, now leaned precariously close to the ground.

Alex drove past the entrance, watching Zee navigate the narrow driveway before turning left. Alex made a U-turn and returned to the leaning mailbox. Seeing no movement or lights down the driveway, Alex shut off his headlights and slowly drove toward the house. He stopped where Zee had turned left and saw an old cottage. Alex glanced at the house surrounded by nearby overgrown brush, invasive live plants, weeds, and trees. It seemed to Alex that Zee lived like a hermit hidden in an uncared-for shanty. A single light flickered inside. Alex grabbed a small black bag from the passenger seat, exited his vehicle, and quickly put on protective clothing, gloves, boot covers, and a baseball cap. He adjusted a voice distortion device over his head as he quietly stalked toward the front door. He studied the worn, wood-sided cottage with its fractured side window as he approached the front stairs.

The first wooden step squeaked under Alex's foot. He paused and tested the second step before stepping on it. Reaching the landing, he peered through the window and saw a light in the rear room, likely the bedroom. Alex pulled back from the window when Zee entered the front room to turn off the light. Alex figured Zee was heading to bed. He grabbed the doorknob, pushing slightly on the door. He was surprised when the door effortlessly slid open.

Alex quietly moved inside. He moved away from the door when he saw another light near the rear adjacent room. Alex reckoned it was the bathroom when he heard water running. Careful not to make any noise, Alex slithered behind a wall close to the hallway leading to the back rooms. He pulled a 9mm pistol from the black bag, waiting for Zee to come out.

Zee burped several times as he peed into the toilet. He turned off the bathroom light without flushing and stumbled into the bedroom. Alex seized the moment. He snuck behind Zee and shoved him hard toward the bed, forcing him to his knees.

"What the hell?" Zee murmured, trying to stand. Alex pushed him down again with his foot. Sitting on the floor with his back against the bed, Zee slowly faced his assailant. Alex intentionally struck him across the face with the butt of his gun, snapping Zee's head back.

"Ah, that frigging hurt, man!" shouted Zee, with glossy eyes and blood dripping from his nose. He struggled to focus on Alex, who pressed a handgun against his forehead.

"What do you want, man?"

"I'm here to pay you back for killing my mom and sister, asshole. I want to know who was with you when you robbed our house and killed my family. I want names and addresses. If you answer truthfully, you live. If not, you're a dead man."

Even in his stupor, Zee trembled. He squinted at the intruder with long gray hair, a beard, and a four-inch scar across his left cheek. "Uh, man, I don't know whatcha talking about. I neva killed anybody. You got the wrong . . ."

Alex cut him off by hitting him across the face again.

"Damn, that hurt! Come on, man, no more. I'm no killer."

"Yeah, you are. You, Gil, Bones, and the other guy broke into my home in Westport. You stole money and diamonds from my father's safe and killed my family. You killed my mom and sister in the bedroom. I'll give you one more chance. Tell me the truth, or I'll hurt you worse if you lie. I've got all night, but you don't, so talk."

"If you mean the guys I was drinking with, I don't know their names. Only their nicknames: Gil, Bones, and Tonio."

Not wanting to drag this out, Alex grabbed a pillow from the bed, pressed it against Zee's forehead, and pressed the gun against the pillow.

"The pillow will muffle the sound of the gun when I pull the trigger. This is your last chance to tell me the truth. I'll count to three, then pull the trigger."

Terrified and trembling, Zee pissed his pants.

"Phew. What's that smell?" said Alex, sniffing a foul odor. He then looked between Zee's legs. "You pissed your pants? You're a dead man now."

"No, no. I'll tell you what you want to know."

"You better be telling the truth," said Alex, pressing the gun harder against Zee's head. "Start with Gil. His name, where he lives and works, and his girlfriend's name, if he has one." There was only silence. "Start talking now."

With a hoarse, slurred voice, Zee spilled the details. He named his partners, what town they lived in, and where they worked. Zee only knew Gil's girlfriend's first name, Maggie, who worked at a salon.

"That wasn't so hard, now was it? You wouldn't have suffered if you had told me that from the start. Now, tell me about the detective, Leon Mackey, who got you off the hook for murdering my family."

"I only know Gil paid off the detective."

"Who told you which house to hit and gave you the alarm codes?"

"I don't know. Only Gil knows. He neva told us who they are."

"I will kill you if you don't tell me what I want to know."

"I only know Gil's brother worked for an alarm company. The owner wanted the codes from him. Gil found out about it from his brother and went to the guy, wanting in on the operation. I don't know the guy's name."

"Was Gil an alibi for you?"

"Yeah, so was his brother Stevie and Maggie, Gil's girlfriend."

"Is Gil's brother still working for the alarm company?"

"No. Another guy is doing it, but I don't know him."

"You did good, Zee. Now, where's your safe?"

Zee hesitated, then lied, "I don't have one. I spent all the money."

Alex slammed the gun's grip across Zee's left knee. They both heard the sound of shattering knee bones. "Don't lie to me, Zee. Where's the safe?"

Zee cried out, his eyes glossy and teary from the pain. "Okay, okay! There's a metal case under clothes in the closet."

Seeing Zee's pistol, wallet, and cell phone on the end table, Alex snatched the gun and cell and placed them into his black bag. He searched the closet for the container under the clothes. Inside it, he found cash and a black pouch containing diamonds. The pouch had his father's jewelry store's logo embroidered on it.

"What an idiot," mumbled Alex. *I'll make sure the police know about this.* He left the diamonds in the bag but pocketed the money. He opened the wallet and found Zee's license and several photos, one with four other guys and a woman. Alex held the photo to Zee's face and asked him to identify them. Alex pointed to each person while Zee named them; from left to right: Peter Gilinsky, whom they called Gil; Gil's girlfriend, Maggie; then his brother, Stephen; Frank Bonarz, nicknamed Bones; and Antonio Acosta, whom they called Tonio.

"Remember, Zee, if you bullshitted me about your buddies, I'll be back. You won't see me or hear the bullet coming. I'm leaving now. Tell your friends I'm coming for them one at a time."

Alex exited the house, removed his disguise and protective wear near the open car trunk, and stuffed them into a plastic bag. On his drive home, he grumbled and whispered, "I despise that bastard. It would have been more satisfying to kill him, but I'm no killer. Anyway, I need Zee to warn his buddies they're next." Alex wanted the killers to feel the fear that his family felt, knowing a nemesis would drop in on them when least expected. Alex had become spiritual like his mom, promising retribution for the killer's sins and giving them everlasting punishment witnessed by the heavenly souls who suffered at their hands.

Several miles ahead, Alex slowed the car to a stop, glanced up at the heavens, and whispered to his mom, "Please guide me in keeping my promise to you; the killers have to pay for what they did to our family."

*   *   *

The next day, Alex started at the salon where Zee said Gil's girlfriend worked. He found the modest salon on the street Zee had mentioned. He waited and watched the place until closing time. When Alex saw the interior lights get turned off, two women emerged from the salon, one taller with dark, wavy hair, the other a blonde with gray streaks. He tailed the dark-haired driver, following her for ten minutes to an old apartment complex in New Haven, where she dropped off the blonde. The driver then went to a more upscale complex, where she parked in a side lot and entered the building. Alex noted both addresses.

Over the next few days, he would snap photos of Gilinsky, Bonarz, and Acosta and their vehicles when leaving their workplaces. He would shadow them to their homes. The easiest to follow to his residence was Detective Leon Mackey. With their faces and addresses locked in his memory, Alex was ready for the next uninvited visit.

CHAPTER

7

S am woke up early. He received the text from Brittany before nine with the hotel room number. He called Kiara to inform her of the senator's request for a solo interview.

"Good morning. The senator's assistant called late last night. The senator wants me to interview her alone at the Boston Harbor Hotel at eleven."

"Why alone?"

"She didn't give a reason. It's her preference. I tried to insist, but her assistant said the senator wouldn't change her mind."

"That's odd. What do you make of that?"

"Maybe she's just cautious and wants to control the narrative. Regardless, I'll do my best to get what we need and meet you afterward. I'll fill you in on our way to New Haven."

"All right. We'll play along if that's what the senator wants. Call me when you're done."

Sam spent time formulating questions for the senator. He left his apartment early and took the T, the transit subway, as the Bostonians call it, to the Boston Harbor Hotel. He breathed in the crisp morning air, sharpening his senses as he walked to the hotel. The luxury of the hotel was undeniable, reflecting the senator's status. Debating whether to knock on the senator's door ahead of the scheduled time, Sam chose instead to be courteous and called her room. It took five rings before the senator answered.

"Good morning, senator. This is Agent Caviello. I'm in the hotel lobby. Is it all right for me to come to your room now?"

"I appreciate your punctuality. Give me five minutes, and come on up."

Sam figured that getting to the top floor would take that long. He glanced at his watch, waited three minutes, and then made his way to the elevator. The ride was smooth; the ding announcing each floor passed like a countdown to an uncertain engagement. Upon exiting, he faced a long corridor, the end room beckoning. He knocked softly, expecting Brittany. Instead, the senator herself opened the door, draped in a long, light blue silk robe.

"Come in, Sam. Please, have a seat on the sofa."

Sam crossed the plush carpet to an almond-colored three-cushioned sofa, his gaze drawn to the floor-to-ceiling windows framing a breathtaking view of Boston harbor. The deep blue sky was cloudless, and the sun's reflection danced on the ocean below. He concealed his awe, focusing on the task at hand.

Senator Alvarado-Thornton settled into a matching almond-cushioned club chair on Sam's left. The senator's posture was poised, her legs with model-like tanned skin elegantly crossed. At fifty-two years old, she looked much younger, her movements fluid, reminiscent of a catwalk strut. With long, wavy light brown hair and sparkling hazel eyes, she could easily pass for a model rather than a politician. Sam kept his gaze locked on her eyes, determined not to be otherwise distracted.

Sam had read the FBI's report on the initial interview of the senator, which was extensive, reflecting answers to standard boilerplate questions. He planned on asking only several questions that the FBI didn't ask or avoided asking.

"Before we begin, I sensed tension regarding protocol between you and the FBI. I want you to know, Sam, you have my complete backing to employ whatever talent, technique, or method you have to find my son, even if it falls outside what the FBI mandates."

"Senator, I assure you my investigative standards, although they may differ from others, are above reproach and have been very effective."

"Donna Ranero convinced me you were the best person to find my son. I'm counting on you."

"I'll do my best, senator." Sam's questions aimed to learn more about the relationship between Travis and his parents. He'll learn more about Travis from his friends and roommates at Yale. He first asked if the senator and her husband had different opinions on what school Travis should attend, what he should study, and what career he should pursue.

"Well, I didn't expect that question. My husband and I certainly recommended schools and career goals for Travis. I wouldn't say he rejected any of our choices."

"Other than Yale University, did Travis consider other schools?"

"We recommended Harvard, Princeton, Georgetown, and Yale. My husband graduated from Fordham and Yale Law School. I graduated from Wellesley and Yale Law."

Sam questioned if Travis mentioned other schools he would prefer to attend or enroll in studies he favored other than those the senator and her husband recommended.

"Yes, but what does that have to do with Travis being missing?"

"I'm thinking out of the box, wondering if Travis preferred a different educational path and career than what you and your husband chose for him."

The senator said that they didn't choose any path for him. Travis had a few other schools in mind but decided on Yale. He chose his major course of study and would choose a career of his choice. The senator added that most kids who graduate from high school are unsure of what they want to do in life. Parents try to give them options for a financially rewarding and respected profession.

"Did you and Travis discuss what he wanted to do after high school? Did he mention he'd like to take time off and travel before deciding to attend college? Did you have disagreements outside education or careers?"

"No, other than a few friends suggested they travel before starting college. Travis is a very bright kid, but he lacks self-assurance about his ability to attain the status of his parents. I sometimes thought he worried about having to live up to our success. Travis said he wanted to learn more about who he was before starting college. Wesley and I tried guiding him in making the appropriate decisions. He chose to attend Yale. We only wanted the best for him."

Sam asked if Travis had male and female friends and was happy or depressed about anything.

"He had several male and female friends who were good kids. He had a girlfriend during his sophomore and junior high school years. They broke up the summer before his senior year."

"How did that affect him?"

"He seemed like it was for the best. I never got any indication that it bothered him."

"Are you aware of any disagreements Travis had with anyone, maybe a classmate or someone at the university?"

"None that I'm aware of. Travis gets along with most people but can be intense about his studies."

"Have you noticed any changes in his behavior or mood leading up to his disappearance?"

"He seemed a bit more withdrawn the last few times we spoke. I chalked it up to stress from his studies."

"Senator, do you have any reason to believe someone might want to harm your son?"

The senator paused, her eyes welling up with tears. "No, but I fear the worst. He's a brilliant young man, but sometimes brilliance attracts envy and malice."

Sam nodded, taking notes. "We'll do everything we can to find Travis. Your insight is invaluable. Do you have any other information that might help us?"

"I feel so helpless, not having anything concrete to help you find Travis."

"You have helped, senator. You helped me understand Travis from your point of view rather than from others."

"Thank you for saying that. Remember what I said. Continue what you do best in your investigations, even if it doesn't fit the FBI's protocol. Most importantly, promise me you'll find my son."

"I promise we'll do our best to find him."

The interview wrapped up. Sam thanked the senator for her time and left the hotel. He called Kiara and asked her to pick him up outside the hotel.

"On my way. How did it go?" said Kiara.

"I'll fill you in when we meet."

Kiara arrived about fifteen minutes later and began their drive to New Haven.

"So, what did the senator say?" Kiara asked as they hit the highway.

"She's worried sick, as expected. She mentioned Travis was more secretive and withdrawn lately."

"Did she give any specifics?"

"None." He briefed Kiara on what he had learned from the interview, then recommended they stop for lunch and focus on the interviews at Yale with the hope of discovering something new that leads them to Travis."

CHAPTER
8

Zee went to the hospital emergency room, enduring fascial stitches and surgery to repair his shattered knee. He fabricated a story about falling from a ladder onto a concrete sidewalk to avoid any police scrutiny. Zee insisted on rehabbing at home, so the hospital released him. He hobbled on crutches to his truck, cursing Alex, the old guy who did this to him.

He called Gilinsky, who seethed while Zee embellished his story. "A crazed guy broke into my place and demanded the names of all of us who robbed and killed his family. I tried fighting him off, but he broke my nose and my knee and then held a gun to my head."

Gilinsky's voice sizzled with fury. "Meet me and the crew at my brother's café. Now."

"No way, man. I can't even walk. I'll call you back in a few days when I can walk with crutches."

* * *

Sam and Agent Rivers arrived in New Haven, Connecticut, at two-thirty that afternoon. The city welcomed them with a mix of old-world charm and modern hustle, with the architecture in the city in stark contrast to the Gothic design within the Yale campus. Yale takes up sixty percent of the city's property. As they cruised through the campus and drove by the downtown square, Sam suggested they pay a courtesy visit to the local police department, a gesture of respect and collaboration. Rivers, nodding in agreement, steered their car towards the PD.

Navigating the crowded streets proved challenging. Street parking near the PD was scarce. After circling the block, Rivers finally found a spot a block away. The initial sunshine of the morning had given way to a gloomy, gray blanket of clouds. The air carried a calm, persistent breeze that prompted them to zip up their lightweight jackets as they briskly walked to the police department.

Inside, the front desk officer, a grizzled veteran with eyes that had seen too much, regarded them with a practiced indifference. They flashed their badges, the polished metal catching the dim light, as they requested directions to the detective's unit. After a quick call upstairs, the officer directed them to the fourth floor, where Lieutenant Cassidy Dawson awaited their arrival.

Lieutenant Dawson was a woman of alluring presence, her gaze sharp and calculating, yet her demeanor exuded a cautious warmth. She led them to her cluttered office, the scent of stale coffee hanging in the air. After introductions, Sam explained their purpose in the city, the case that had gripped the attention of more than just the local law enforcement.

Detective Matt Kendrick, a tall, lanky figure with a perpetually furrowed brow, joined them at the lieutenant's request.

"I'm aware of the investigation," Lieutenant Dawson began, her tone edged with skepticism. "But why is ATF involved? We never received any information that guns were in play."

Agent Rivers remained silent, a faint smirk playing on her lips as she awaited Sam's explanation.

"It's complicated," Sam replied, his voice steady and assured. "The student's mother, Senator Alvarado-Thornton, specifically requested my involvement due to my history with missing person cases."

Dawson leaned back in her chair, her expression shifting from skepticism to intrigue. "What history are you referring to?"

Rivers stepped in, her voice smooth and authoritative. "The senator read about Agent Caviello's unique record in finding and rescuing missing persons. Given the high-profile nature of this case, the FBI thought it prudent to have him join our investigation."

A smile broke across Dawson's face, her skepticism giving way to reluctant admiration. "Wow. This is a first on two counts. First, the FBI invited an ATF agent to assist, and second, an ATF agent known for finding missing persons. We could use an outside perspective on some of our long-standing missing person cases."

Sam chuckled, a deep, resonant sound that filled the room. "I don't have a magic wand, lieutenant. It's about digging in, being persistent, and following your hunches."

Dawson nodded, her eyes narrowing thoughtfully. "Detective Kendrick has done plenty of digging, but we've yet to have any luck on those cases I mentioned. So, what can we do for you?"

"We wanted to introduce ourselves and let you know we'll be conducting several interviews in the area, mainly at Yale," Rivers explained, her tone professional yet friendly.

Dawson handed them her business card along with Kendrick's. "Feel free to reach out if you need anything. Let us know if you find any leads on the senator's son, especially if it points to something sinister."

"Absolutely. Thank you, Cassidy," said Kiara.

"Call me Cassie," Dawson corrected with a smile. "Thanks for the heads-up."

As they left the PD, the city around them seemed to pulse with a muted energy; the anticipation of their task added an edge to their steps. They headed back to Kiara's government-issued vehicle, affectionately dubbed a G-car by agents. They mapped out their plan for the day.

"Let's start with Addison Holmes, Thornton's girlfriend," Sam suggested. "We might get more from her. Then we'll talk to his roommate, Timothy Blake, and gather names of others in the dorm."

Kiara nodded, the wheels of their mission already turning in her mind. She called Blake, who agreed to meet them at his dorm on Hardy Street in twenty minutes, while Sam arranged to meet Holmes at the law school café at four-thirty. Blake was available sooner, so they headed to his dorm. They drove along the historic old Yale campus, its Gothic architecture casting long shadows on the cobbled paths.

The dorm's cornerstone, etched with 1871, hinted at the countless stories and secrets that passed through its walls. Timothy Blake was waiting in the entrance lobby, a nervous energy about him as he greeted them. Blake led them to a study room; the air inside smelled of old books and the faint mustiness of aged wood.

Kiara introduced herself and Sam, her badge lending an air of authority that seemed to comfort and intimidate Blake. She recapped his previous statements, then began with a straightforward question, her tone gentle yet probing.

"Have you heard anything new about Travis Thornton since our agents last spoke with you? Any rumors or whispers, even if they seemed unimportant?"

Blake shook his head. "No, nothing."

Kiara leaned in, her eyes searching his face for any flicker of doubt. "I want you to take your time with my next questions. Who else did Travis have regular contact with? Friends, classmates, professors, even casual acquaintances?"

Sam added, "Think about anyone you've seen him with, even in passing. We need to know everyone he might have interacted with."

Blake's brow furrowed as he thought. "Uh, well, there's Ryan Norwood across the hall, Addison Holmes, of course, and Lauren Kimbrough, but she transferred to another school. Travis and Russell Chandler were buddies. Travis once mentioned possibly joining a film and media group, but I'm not sure he followed up on it."

"Can you show us around your floor?" Sam asked. "We'd like to talk to anyone who might know Travis."

As they climbed the creaky wooden stairs to the third floor, the building seemed to hum with the faint echoes of its storied past. Blake knocked on Norwood's door and pushed it open after hesitating.

"Hey, Ryan, these agents want to talk to you," Blake said, his voice echoing slightly in the narrow hallway.

Norwood, startled, looked up from a book he was reading. He was a tall, slender student with a mop of unruly hair and a perpetually distracted expression. Kiara and Sam entered the room.

"Tim mentioned you saw someone he doesn't know with Travis recently," Kiara began, calm and reassuring.

Norwood nodded, his eyes widening slightly. "Yeah, I saw him with a guy a couple of times. Once at The Bow Wow and another time at Starbucks on Chapel Street."

"Can you describe him?" Sam asked, pulling out a notepad.

Norwood thought for a moment. "African American, tall, about six feet, with medium-length twisted hair. Both times, he wore black workout pants and a black and gray windbreaker. I also saw Travis with another guy, Raffi. I think he's a grad assistant here."

Sam got nothing further from Norwood. Norwood claimed he didn't know either student. He and Kiara spent the next hour talking to students on the floor, but none had much to add. Most described Travis as a quiet, solitary guy who kept to himself and didn't socialize much. Kiara left her card with those they spoke to, urging them to reach out if they remembered anything else.

Kiara and Sam then strolled to the law school café to meet Addison Holmes. They both felt Travis's girlfriend would tell them something new, like she had heard from Travis recently, or would reveal a new lead.

CHAPTER
9

A s Sam and Kiara entered the law school, Kiara, who had a law degree, gave Sam a little history about the school she had learned online. "I didn't know that years ago, the law was learned by clerking as an apprentice in a lawyer's office. Yale Law School evolved from one of these apprenticeship programs, specifically from a New Haven law office of a practitioner named Seth Staples. Staples had an exceptional library of law books that were hard to find anywhere else. He established the New Haven Law School, began training apprentices, and later became affiliated with Yale. I could go on about the school's history, but I see Addison Holmes waving to us from a rear table. So, let's get back to work."

Kiara introduced herself and Sam before sitting across from Addison. Before asking a question, Addison said, "I'm worried about Travis. Is he okay?"

"We're still trying to find that out and need your help," said Kiara.

"I don't know what else I could add. I haven't heard from Travis even though I've called him several times. Do you have any further information about what happened to him?"

Sam took the lead in questioning Holmes. "We don't know what happened to Travis, but we're conducting additional interviews, hoping we learn the names of others who might have a connection to Travis. I read your previous statement and hope to clarify some of your answers and perhaps learn something new from you."

"You could call me Addi. I'll answer your questions, but I don't have much time. I have an appointment that begins in forty minutes."

"I'll do my best to speed this up. Am I right in saying that you and Travis were close friends?"

"Yes, we dated until he went missing."

"How did you guys meet, and how long did you date?"

"We sat near each other in one of our first-year classes. We got to know each other and studied together for exams. We hit it off from the start. We dated for several weeks, eating at cafes, watching movies, and attending school plays together. Travis was fun to be with; I liked him a lot."

"You said in your previous statement that Travis seemed bothered by something. Did you notice something was wrong immediately when you were together, or did he say anything about what concerned him?"

Addi didn't respond immediately. Her lips quivered, and her eyes became glossy. "Things seemed okay at first. We watched a movie after returning from a café. It was a romantic movie that had a great ending. At the end, we looked at each other, and we kissed. We embraced and began kissing with passion. My hands began to, uh, you know, feel him. He let me for a moment, but then his demeanor surprisingly changed. He looked at his watch and said he was sorry but hadn't slept well the night before and needed to get to bed early. I asked if everything was all right and if I had done anything wrong." Addi paused and appeared uneasy. "Travis didn't answer at first. He looked confused like he didn't know what to say. I told him I liked him a lot and thought he felt the same, so I asked him to talk to me about what was bothering him. Travis stood there staring at me, shaking his head until he answered that he liked me, too, but wasn't sure who he was or wanted to be."

"What do you think he meant by that?"

"I asked him that, but he didn't answer other than saying he had to leave. I thought about that every day since. I couldn't come up with any reason why he would say that. I only knew Travis as a genuine, honest, thoughtful guy."

"I'm sorry that happened, Addi," said Sam. "Did you two talk again after that night?"

"Only on the phone. Travis said he needed some time to get his head straight. He mentioned he planned to talk to someone at the law school whom his professor suggested he speak to for counseling."

"Did Travis mention the person's name at the law school?"

"No. I didn't ask, thinking it was personal between Travis and his counselor."

"Did Travis mention the professor's name who suggested that Travis seek counseling at the law school?"

"I'm fairly sure it was a professor who taught a political science ethics class. I think his name was Reed."

"Does Travis have anyone he considers a close friend here at school?"

"I thought I was his closest friend. I'd guess it might be his roommates Timmy Blake, Ryan Norwood, and Chris Randell at his dormitory. He once mentioned another guy he met, a guy named Julian. I think he is a student studying theater."

Sam turned to Kiara for any further questions, but she shook her head no, so Sam asked a final question. "We talked to Travis's roommates and learned that Travis recently was seen dining with an African American student, six feet tall with braided hair and wearing workout attire. Is this the guy Julian you mentioned, or do you know who that person might be?"

"No. I don't have a clue."

Sam thanked Addi and asked her to contact Agent Rivers if she learned anything new about Travis or the student, Julian. He then asked what Addi was studying.

"Chemistry. I want to be a doctor."

"Great choice."

"Can I call you and ask if there's been any progress on finding Travis?"

"You can," said Kiara, who gave Addi her business card.

Addison Holmes looked at her watch and then quickly left the café. Sam suggested they find Professor Reed. He looked up the location of the political science program on the school's website. They then left the café.

"Well, we're making progress. We learned that Professor Reed, Raffi, and Julian knew Travis, and they were not interviewed or mentioned in the FBI reports. The campus map shows the political science building is within walking distance. Reed might know the name of the counselor Travis went to see. If he does and we find the counselor, we might have a missing piece of the puzzle that tells us why Travis suddenly disappeared."

CHAPTER
10

iara and Sam entered the political science building, scanning the directory in the lobby for Professor Reed's office number. They navigated through the dimly lit hallways, finally finding his office toward the rear of the building. The door was open, and a woman was feeding paper into a large copier tray.

"Good afternoon. We're looking for Professor Reed," Kiara said.

The woman glanced at the clock on the wall. "Professor Reed is lecturing a class on the second floor. His class should be finishing up just about now. Take the elevator down the hall to the second floor, turn right, and the classroom is the first room on the left."

Kiara and Sam followed her directions, taking the elevator to the second floor. They arrived just as a stream of students rushed out of the classroom toward the elevator and nearby stairs. The two agents pressed themselves against the wall to avoid being trampled by the students. Once the hallway cleared, they entered the classroom, spotting an older gentleman they assumed was Reed, conversing with a younger African-American student.

"Professor Reed, do you have a moment?" Kiara said, displaying her FBI identification.

Reed looked puzzled and instructed his assistant to give them privacy. The assistant retreated to a small adjoining alcove.

"What's this about?" Reed asked.

"We're here about Travis Thornton," Kiara began.

"What about Travis?" Reed's brow furrowed.

"He's missing. No one, including his parents, has seen or heard from him in weeks. He's no longer here at school."

"Yeah, I heard some rumor about that. So, what's that got to do with me?"

"We understand that Travis came to you seeking counsel," Kiara said, her tone firm.

"Who told you that?" Reed's voice edged with defensiveness.

Sam stepped in. "It's not important how we know. Tell us why he reached out to you, what counseling you gave him, or who you suggested he see for counseling."

"Any counseling I might have given to a student is private between the student and me."

"Well, you're not a priest or an attorney who has privileged conversations under state and federal law. So, if you prefer that we subpoena you before a federal grand jury, we can get that done this afternoon and have you report to the federal courthouse tomorrow. Or you can talk to us now and answer our questions truthfully so we can be out of here."

Reed sighed, clearly weighing his options. "Ask your questions."

Sam nudged Kiara with his knee, prompting her to continue. Meanwhile, Sam noticed the younger man in the alcove staying within earshot.

"Why did Travis come to you for counseling?" Kiara asked.

"Travis was troubled by what others expected of him and his self-identity. It's complicated and digs deep into his emotions and psyche. He was skeptical of his sexuality, career goals, and their impact on his family and friends, not to mention the prejudice that comes with it. I'm not a psychologist. I advised him to seek counsel from Jonathon Martin, who volunteers as a counselor. I made an appointment for him."

Sam cut in again. "Thank you, professor. Is Professor Martin a therapist, and where can we find him on campus?"

"He's an adjunct professor, who I understand had a strong curriculum in counseling. I can look up his location and number in the directory," Reed turned toward the alcove. "Raffi, could you find the directory on the desk and bring it to me?" The young assistant retrieved the directory. Reed wrote down the location and telephone number on a slip of paper and handed it to Kiara.

"We appreciate your help, professor. Have a good day," Kiara said.

Kiara and Sam walked to the elevator and waited for it to arrive. Sam kept an eye on the classroom door. As the elevator door slid open, the young man, Raffi, emerged into the hall.

"Going down?!" Sam called out to him.

Raffi hurried to join them in the elevator, and the three rode down to the first floor. When the door opened, Sam asked Raffi if he would walk with them. Raffi agreed and stepped out onto the front porch.

"Raffi, you know Travis, right?" Sam asked.

Raffi, clearly uneasy, nodded. "Yeah, I know him."

"You guys have a mutual friend. I don't know his name, but students saw you walking with him and Travis. He's taller than you, wears workout pants and a jacket, and has similar braided hair like yours."

"You must mean Julian Jarrett. He's cool. Very smart."

"Does he play sports here at school?" Sam asked.

"Nah, Julian is into the arts—music, theater, and filmmaking. He loves the theater."

"So, Julian and Travis are close friends?"

"Uh, yeah. Real close, if you know what I mean."

"Not exactly. How do you mean?"

"More like, uh, I guess, like lovers."

"They show that how, holding hands, kissing, or hugging each other?"

"Not really. I'm only assuming they are friendly like that from how they act with each other."

"I see. Agent Rivers and I would like to talk to Julian about Travis. Do you have his number or know where we can reach him?"

"I haven't seen him in a few weeks and don't have his number. We bumped into each other here and there, but we're in different programs and circles of friends. Like I said, he's into acting. I'm into computers and economics."

"Any idea what happened to Travis?"

"None, other than he was in Professor Reed's class, and I saw him a few times with Julian. I saw them once in the dining hall, sitting next to each other at a table for six. The other time, I bumped into them walking on campus with another guy. That's all I can tell you."

"Who is the other guy?"

"He's a friend of Julian. I only know his first name is Tyrese. Julian never mentioned his last name."

"Describe him."

"He's a big guy, a little overweight, not flabby but hefty, like a football tackle."

"What else? How tall is he, what's his hair color, does he have any tattoos or scars? Anything you can remember about him."

"He's maybe six-three, with bushy hair and streaks of blonde. He wears black-framed glasses, tattoos on both arms and a small scar on his forehead, right—no, left side. I only saw him twice. Both times, he wore old baggy blue jeans and a T-shirt."

"Do you know Julian's major or where he lives?" Kiara asked.

"No. It could be the theater or music department. Check the school directory. I have to run. I'm late for class."

Kiara handed her business card to Raffi. "If you see Julian again, please call me."

Raffi examined the card. "Okay, uh, Agent Kiara Rivers." Raffi grinned and added, "Can I call you? Maybe we can get together for coffee or a drink."

"How old are you, Raffi? Are you even old enough to drink?"

"Oh, yeah. I look young, but I'm twenty-four and a grad assistant here at the school."

"Well, I'm much older than you and have someone in my life, but thank you."

"Lucky guy. Nice talking to you guys."

As they walked, Sam bumped shoulders with Kiara. "Hey, I didn't know you had someone in your life. Tell me how you two met and a little about this guy."

"Gee, Sam. I don't have to tell you anything about my love life. It's private."

"Come on, Kiara. We're partners. I want to know more about you. When can I meet him?"

Kiara stopped and looked Sam straight in the eyes. "First of all, it's not a he but a she, and I don't want to get into it. It's still evolving."

"At least tell me a little about her. Is she an FBI agent, a cop, a doctor, what?"

"Please. She's not FBI or a cop. I don't date anyone in law enforcement."

"I think you're itching to tell me more. I saw the glow on your face when you told Raffi you have someone in your life. That was a first step; now take the second and let it all out."

"Okay, okay. I guess I have to tell somebody. It might as well be you. Her name is Mariela, and she graduated from Harvard as a medical biomaterials engineer. She works for a high-tech biomaterials company in Boston that manufactures replacement medical devices and implants, such as pacemakers and joint replacements. She frequents hospitals to meet with doctors who use her company's instruments. She's a brainer, very smart, and very hot."

"Whoa. I have to meet this remarkable woman. How did you guys meet?"

"Forget it. You're not meeting her."

Not wanting to discuss it further, Kiara changed the subject. "Don't we have work to do? You promised we'd find Travis, so let's find him so we can get back to Boston."

"Yes, ma'am. It's a short walk to the law school, so let's find Professor Martin. I feel he has the answer that will help find Travis."

CHAPTER

11

The law school receptionist's office was a short distance down a long hallway. Before entering the office, Sam scanned the directory on the wall for Martin's room number. They glanced into the office and saw the receptionist typing on a computer.

"Can I help you?" asked the woman, her voice tinged with polite detachment.

"Yes, we're looking for Mr. Martin's office," said Kiara, trying to sound authoritative but nonthreatening.

"Professor Martin is in with someone and asked not to be disturbed. Do you have an appointment?"

"No, we don't," said Kiara, displaying her badge. "I'm FBI Agent Kiara Rivers, and this is my partner, Agent Caviello. It's urgent we speak with Professor Martin."

"Professor Martin gave me strict orders not to disturb him. He won't be available for another hour. I could make an appointment if you'd like, or you could return later."

"That won't be necessary. Thank you," interjected Sam, his impatience barely masked.

"I'll let him know you were here," said the woman, collecting papers from the copier before walking out of the office and up the stairs.

Sam remained silent while waiting for the receptionist to reach the second floor.

"You want to come back later?" asked Kiara, her frustration evident.

"No. Let's find Martin's office and knock on the door."

"Wouldn't that be kind of rude?"

"You wanted to find Travis and get back to Boston, right? You're the FBI. I'm sure Martin would understand. Maybe he could cut his meeting short and see us now."

"Well, it's worth a shot," Kiara conceded, though her hesitation was evident.

They walked down the first-floor hall, searching for Martin's office.

"Here's number seven, so I bet his office is the first one around the corner," said Sam.

"You're brilliant, Sam," said Kiara teasingly, trying to lighten the mood.

They passed by an unnumbered door and then came to the door numbered seven.

"Hey, I guessed right. Here's where we get some answers," whispered Sam, the excitement in his voice failing to mask his bravado.

Kiara lightly pushed Sam's arm and whispered, "Funny, Sam. Should we knock or walk in?"

Sam held up a finger, signaling to wait a minute, and put his ear to the door.

Annoyed but curious, Kiara whispered, "What's that, your listening device? Is this what you use in your investigations?"

"Listen," Sam whispered back, his expression serious.

Uneasy, she put her ear to the door and was disturbed by what she heard—raised voices, arguing with threats.

"What the hell is going on in there?" she whispered, her heartbeat quickening.

"Sounds like an argument." Sam tried the doorknob, but it was locked.

"We can't barge in like that," Kiara said, her mind racing through the possible repercussions.

"Okay, so we knock."

Kiara thought it was a bad idea. "Let's come back later."

Sam, curious and impatient, knocked brazenly. He then put his ear to the door again. This time, he heard footsteps.

Kiara appeared embarrassed and slapped him on the shoulder. "Let's get out of here."

"Who's there?" shouted someone from inside the room. "I'm in a meeting!"

"FBI, Mr. Martin. We need to speak with you," said Sam, his voice firm.

"Can't you come back later?"

"It's important. We need information that we believe only you can provide," Kiara added, her tone softening slightly.

There was no immediate response. Sam put his ear to the door again. He heard whispers between two people, then a door closed, followed by footsteps coming closer. Sam backed away from the door as it opened.

Kiara studied the man briefly while he stood at the open door with a hostile glare, narrow, hardened eyes, and clenched jaw. Kiara guessed he was about five-ten, in his late thirties, and of average build. He had wavy light brown hair graying on the sides and a stubble beard, portraying what many believe is cool or masculine. Martin's cheeks were flushed, the anger evident in his eyes.

While displaying her badge, Kiara identified herself and Sam. Sam peered down the hall and noticed an embarrassed student peeking at them from an adjoining room. The student quietly exited and hurried around the hall corner toward the exit.

"Didn't the receptionist inform you I was unavailable and not to be disturbed?" Martin's voice barely contained his anger simmering beneath the surface.

Sam answered before Kiara could speak. "No one was in the receptionist's office. We saw a woman walking up the stairs carrying a stack of papers, so we found your room number from the directory and came to your office."

Exasperated, Martin took a deep breath and blew it out, shaking his head in disgust. Then, without speaking, he opened the door wider and motioned for them to enter.

"Now, tell me what's so urgent that you couldn't wait to ask me for information that only I could provide?" His sarcasm was biting, and his irritation was evident.

"We're investigating the disappearance of a young student here at school who went missing after seeking counsel from you," Kiara said, her tone steady but respectful.

"Do you have a name?" Martin's eyes narrowed further.

"His name is Travis Thornton," said Kiara, watching for any reaction.

"Many students seek my counsel. I can't remember every one of them." Martin's voice was dismissive, suspiciously secretive.

"I assume you keep a record of those students you counsel," said Sam, his patience wearing thin.

"I'll check my calendar. Do you have a time frame?" Martin's movements were deliberate, almost as if he were stalling.

"Within the past two months," said Kiara.

Martin looked down at his desk calendar, then, with a frown and pursed lips, stared at the two agents in defiance. "As you should know, any counseling I give a student is private."

Thinking he'd heard this before, Sam stepped closer to Martin, his presence imposing. "You're counseling Agent Rivers and me right now, and I assure you it wouldn't be considered private counseling. Like most teachers, you advise students here in your office, similar to any teacher in a classroom. So your counseling is not protected like a doctor or priest in a confessional booth where a person's confession is considered sacramentally sealed."

"I disagree." Martin's voice was steady, but there was a flicker of doubt in his eyes.

"You'll lose any standing you think you have in court and with the administrators at Yale when it's known that you and that young student you left in the adjoining room didn't sound like counseling but a heated argument behind closed doors. There was a lot of foul language that didn't sound like professor-to-student counseling." Sam's tone was ice-cold, his eyes locked on Martin's.

"How dare you," Martin sputtered, his face reddening.

"Dare me all you want. Before I entered the room, I noticed the young student leaving the room next door. I recognized him as the same kid who only yesterday gave us directions to a café nearby," It was a ruse often used by Sam to get answers. "We talked along the way, and he gave us his name. He'll be the next person we interview."

Martin no longer stared at Sam in arrogance but bowed his head in thought, his defiance draining from his posture.

"Thornton's mother is a US senator if you don't already know. She hasn't heard from her son Travis in weeks. She's afraid that someone kidnapped him or maybe he's dead. We only want to know if he is all right. That's all we want, nothing else. Give us what we want, and we'll leave and consider our visit private." Kiara's voice was softer now, almost pleading.

"Well, I can tell you he's not dead."

"We need to verify that personally. Is he somewhere with Julian?" Sam's question hung in the air, heavy with implication.

"You know Julian?" Martin's surprise was genuine.

"Yes, we know," pretended Sam.

Martin's anger subsided. "What I tell you must remain anonymous."

"Okay, it'll remain between us as long as you tell us the truth," said Kiara firmly.

Martin explained that Travis suffered from internalized fear of being ostracized for preferring to be with a man. "Travis claimed his parents, sister, and friends would not understand his feelings for Julian. In addition, Travis's mother and father pressured him to be a lawyer. He has no interest in being a lawyer."

"Where is he staying?" Kiara's question was direct, her eyes searching Martin's face for any sign of deceit.

"I don't know. He didn't say."

"Well, how do you know if he is all right?" asked Sam, suspicion lacing his words.

"He calls me, but he doesn't have a phone. He removed the SIM card from his phone, shut it off, and left it in his campus room so no one could track his whereabouts. Travis doesn't want anyone to know his location."

"That doesn't seem likely unless he's in trouble. We need to verify this by talking to him. How do we do that?" said Kiara.

Martin raised his hands. "I can't give you Julian's phone number."

"Really?" Sam said, incredulous. "We can subpoena you before a judge? How do you think a judge will rule on your refusal to provide the location of a US Senator's son who is missing?"

Martin didn't think long about appearing before a federal judge, so he shook his head, repulsed, saying he would call Julian.

"We need the number," Sam demanded. "Call Julian and have him put Travis on the line."

Martin wrote Julian's phone number on a Post-it and handed it to Sam.

"What number will you be calling him from?"

"My cell."

With both numbers Martin provided, Sam took Kiara aside and whispered, "Call your office and have them trace the call from Martin to Julian. Tell them it's urgent because it may lead us to Travis's location."

Kiara stepped out of the office and called her Boston supervisor. Moments later, she reentered Martin's office and nodded to Sam, acknowledging she had made the request.

"Call Julian," Sam instructed, his eyes fixed on Martin.

Martin hesitated but dialed Julian's number. The resentment shown by Martin was evident as the phone rang. When Julian answered, Martin told him the FBI was back on campus asking questions about Travis. Travis's mother was pushing hard to get answers about her son. "They want to talk to Travis," Martin said, but when asked if he was alone, Martin played along to get rid of the feds. "Oh, he went for a walk to clear his head. Okay. Tell Travis to call me when he gets back."

Julian understood the FBI was in Martin's office. Martin ended the call and said, "Travis went for a walk."

"Oh, how convenient. So it looks like we can't verify Travis is alive and well," Sam said, his frustration barely contained.

"He is alive. I can attest to that," Martin insisted, but his voice lacked conviction.

"Not good enough. We need to attest that Travis is alive and well. We'll wait for him to call back."

"I have a class in five minutes. I have to go upstairs to the classroom now."

"We'll leave a business card. Have Travis call Agent Rivers when he finishes his walk."

"I'll have him call. But I can't force him to. I did as you asked. I'd prefer you don't return here," Martin said, his voice irritating.

"We won't return if Travis calls us back, but if he doesn't, because you call and warn him, all promises are off, and we'll be back for you. We'll have a subpoena with us and bring you to a federal judge," Sam warned, his eyes fixed on Martin.

"I wouldn't do that," Martin said in defiance.

"Right. Tell him to call us, and he better, or we'll see you again very soon."

Leaving the office, a dissatisfied Sam shook his head, saying, "I should have had Martin call on speaker so we could listen to the conversation. Bad on my part."

Kiara called her Boston office to determine if they had tracked Martin's call. She got her answer and hung up.

"Let's get back to the car, Sam. We have a general area. Let's head there now," said Kiara.

CHAPTER

12

Kiara informed Sam that her agency tracked Julian's cell to the New Fairfield area, but the call wasn't long enough to pinpoint an address. Sam pulled out a Connecticut map and directed Kiara to New Fairfield.

"Do you think we'll find Travis there?" Kiara's voice held a note of uncertainty.

"Your guess is as good as mine, "I don't trust what Martin told us that Travis was out walking." Sam flipped through the interview files on the senator and her husband. "Wesley Thornton lists a New York address, and the senator lists an address in Washington, DC. There's nothing in New Fairfield. I'll call her and ask if they have other properties."

"For all we know, these guys might have their cell phone in one location that automatically transfers the call to another cell somewhere else miles away."

"You could be right, Kiara. The FBI trained you well. I'm glad we're working together."

"Me, too, Sam," she said with a smile. "But I have to say I've never worked with anyone like you. How you handled Professor Reed and Martin was mindboggling. I would never have confronted them in the manner you did, but it surprised the hell out of me that it worked. The more I see how you work, the more I understand how successful you are in finding people."

"Uh-huh. There's more to it than that." Sam never wanted to disclose that he received weird feelings throughout his body that helped him find what or who he was looking for.

"Oh, there's more. What else helps you besides the ill-mannered approach you take with people?"

Sam said nothing further about it. The strange sensations Sam received were a mystery to him. He couldn't explain why he received the feelings, so he kept it to himself. No one would believe him anyway.

Kiara followed the directions, which brought her to Route 37, heading north toward New Fairfield. While driving, Sam called Senator Evelyn Alvarado Thornton's cell, which she answered after three rings. "Sam, what is it? Any news about my son?"

"Not yet, but Agent Rivers and I are following a new lead, and I need your help."

"Yes, of course. How can I help you?"

"I've looked through the interview reports on you and your husband and saw you listed a residence in New York and DC. Do you or your husband have any properties in Connecticut?"

"Wesley's dad has a property in Connecticut that he rarely uses anymore. How does that help you? Do you think Travis could be staying there?"

"It's one of several leads we're following, no matter how minor they seem."

"Well, hold for a second while I find the address."

"Whoa! What's that up ahead?" said Kiara.

Sam assessed the situation as they drove towards a state police cruiser with its flashing strobes lighting up the scene. "It looks like a state trooper pulled over a van," said Sam. As they passed the trooper's vehicle, they witnessed a lone female trooper confronting three men outside a van with assault rifles strapped to their shoulders.

"Whoa, we need to circle back and support the trooper. She's all alone, facing three armed men."

While Kiara searched for an area to turn around, Sam couldn't wait for the senator to find the addresses. "Senator, Agent Rivers, and I need to stop and assist a state trooper on the side of the road. Could you text the addresses to me?"

"Yes, but call me back with an update on your progress?"

"Will do. I have to go. Sorry." Sam ended the call.

He then searched for the closest state police troop and dialed the number.

"State police, Southbury, you're being recorded."

Sam identified himself and described the scene at a mile marker on Route 37 northbound. He requested backup for the trooper, who was confronted by three armed men. The desk officer was aware the trooper had reported pulling over a van minutes earlier, so he immediately alerted other nearby state officers for assistance and contacted a SWAT leader for additional backup.

Kiara found a designated dirt road to cross the median grass strip separating the two opposing lanes. Once on the other side, she drove past the trooper's cruiser, searching for another crossover pathway. She went nearly a mile before finding one.

"Kiara, pull over so we can throw on our vests and grab more ammo. Then put on your emergency lights and pull up behind the trooper's car."

"Sam, it's dark out here, surrounded by woods and very little traffic on the road. Let's try not to get into a confrontation with those guys?"

"That's the last thing I want, but we have to prepare for anything. You go to the trooper's side, and I'll cover from the other side of her car. Identify yourself loud enough so they all hear you're with the FBI."

"I'm a little nervous about this, Sam."

"So am I. Maintain a grip on your holstered gun. There could be more than three men, so stay alert. If any of them make a move with their weapon, order them to stop with your gun aimed at them. You cover the guy near the driver's door, and I'll do the same on the other two. If they force you to fire your gun, make sure you hit them, then find cover."

"I'm well-trained, Sam, but unlike you, I've never experienced being in a gunfight."

"Your training is your advantage. Do as the FBI taught you instinctively; don't think about it first. I'll back you up."

Kiara, still apprehensive, pulled up in the back of the trooper's car.

"Kiara, the trooper's a young female. Sound confident when you meet her and tell her I'm on the right side of her car."

It was nighttime, but a nearly full moon provided enough light to make out those holding weapons. Kiara advanced to the trooper's side, identifying herself as FBI, loud enough for the three men to hear her. Sam moved to the opposite side of the trooper's vehicle with his hand on his holstered semiautomatic pistol.

Sam spoke immediately. "Gentlemen. Relax, please. We don't want anyone to get hurt. Let's talk this through."

"Yeah, well, we told the lady cop we just want to go on our way. We haven't done anything illegal. We only pulled over to relieve ourselves. It's been a long ride, and we didn't pass any rest stops."

"I understand. I'm Sam. What's your name?"

"I go by JJ. Why is the FBI here?"

"My partner and I were heading north for a scheduled interview. We passed a lone trooper facing three men with guns, which got our attention. We thought we could help to settle things peacefully, JJ."

"We're not looking for any trouble. We're heading north for training with legal guns that belong to us. We're all legal and want no problem with the police."

"What kind of training? Are you part of some unit?"

"We're Americans simply trying to keep the peace. You could call us peacekeepers if you need a name."

"Okay, then, let's stay calm and keep the peace here, JJ. I'm sure the trooper stopped after seeing you guys with guns and needed to check things out. If what you say is true, that the guns are legal and you have the proper gun-carrying permits, everything should be fine."

"We're already late and would like to get on our way. We don't have time to—" JJ stopped talking when interrupted by one of his men.

"JJ, I see two police cars moving fast on the other side of the median strip. I'm sure they're heading here."

JJ's rifle slid off his shoulder.

Sam drew his gun and aimed it at him. "JJ, please. Let's stay friendly here with no trouble. Please slide your AR-180 back onto your shoulder. Okay?"

"You can tell it's a 180, huh?"

"I'm an ATF agent."

"Hey, guys, he's ATF."

"What are we doing, JJ?" said his comrade near the van. "More cops will be here in seconds."

JJ turned back, facing Sam. "You're bringing in more help. You can't convince me you will let us go on our way. Right now, we outnumber you five to three. We have two guys inside the van."

"That's three to three, JJ."

"How do you count? Look around you, man. There are three of us outside and two more inside the van."

"Yeah, but you'll be dead before your gun moves another inch, and your buddy behind you will join you on the ground. I'm an expert shot, especially at this close range."

With her gun drawn, Kiara said, "We got the other one in our sights, Sam."

Sam heard the van's side door slide open and glanced at the guy who came out. Sam smirked, saying, "One of your guys in the van just jumped the guardrail and disappeared into the woods, JJ."

Two state police vehicles pulled up at the scene with their blue emergency lights flashing.

JJ's gun remained off his shoulder. The guy behind him slid his rifle down his shoulder.

"I have my sights aimed at your face, JJ. Unless your weapon falls to the ground in three seconds, your face will split open, as will your buddy's behind you. One, two . . ."

Of the two police vehicles that had stopped, both troopers exited their vehicles with assault weapons pointing at the militia members.

JJ, realizing the police outnumbered them, dropped his gun after Sam shouted the number two. His companion behind him hesitated but did the same after seeing Sam shift his aim at him.

"You did the right thing, JJ," said Sam. "Tell your buddy on the side of the van to do the same so he'll live another day."

JJ looked at his brother-in-arms on the side of the van. He saw five guns aimed at him. He knew it was over for them. "Okay, Mo, let's not test this. Lay down your weapon."

The two troopers that arrived collected the guns and cuffed the suspects. Sam checked the van. The guy inside raised his hands, saying he didn't want any trouble. Sam escorted him to the troopers, who handcuffed him. Kiara joined Sam, gently pushed him away for privacy, and whispered with a breath of calmness. "Phew, that was tense, Sam. I need a drink, maybe two."

Two additional troopers arrived. One trooper saw the suspects were under control and called out, "Agent Caviello, where are you?"

"I'm over here with Agent Rivers."

The trooper, showing sergeant stripes on his sleeve and the name Franklin on his shirt above his badge, held out his hand for them to shake. The sergeant thanked them for supporting their young officer and asked if they would come to the barracks to provide a statement. "The troop commander, Ed Reyes, wants to meet and thank you both."

Walking back to Kiara's G-ride, Kiara handed Sam the car keys. "I'm still a little shaky. Would you drive?"

While driving to the Southbury barracks, Sam suggested she call their supervisor, Dell Haskins, and report their assistance to the state police. He also asked her to have Haskins notify his boss. While Kiara made the call, Sam took a deep breath and sighed with relief, thankful that the confrontation with the militia guys had ended well. Ongoing guilt remained with him after losing his former partner and lover, Detective Juli Ospino, during a previous police raid. He felt responsible for watching over Juli that tragic morning so both would go home safely that day. Instead, he had to attend her funeral days later. He didn't want a repeat occurrence with Kiara.

"I guess this means we won't find Travis tonight," said Kiara.

"Let's play it by ear until we finish our statements. I'll check if the address the senator sent me is nearby."

"You okay, Sam? You look like you're in a trance."

"Yeah. I'm alright." Sam gave Kiara an unsettled smile. "I was thinking back to the female trooper alone, facing three men with weapons. We did a good thing, partner, helping a colleague in a pickle, and left a tenuous scene with no one getting hurt. When we finish at the state police facility, I'll ask for a good place to eat. If we have to stay the night, we'll have that drink—or two—that we both need. Then, hopefully, we'll find Travis in the morning."

Kiara reported the incident to her boss, who commended them for their heroic support. When the call ended, Kiara's eyes were glued on Sam as he drove. Although nervously worried about confronting trained militiamen, Kiara was in awe of how Sam took command of the situation. She had heard rumors about Sam that described him as reckless, but now that she had worked with him, she knew otherwise.

Sam noticed she was staring at him. "What?"

"Hmm, nothing," said Kiara with a blushed face. She looked away, knowing Sam was somewhat unconventional, but his tactics worked. She was impressed by how Sam felt duty-bound to back up the lone trooper and take charge of the tense situation. She liked working with him. His casual bantering was in fun, and he was overly respectful.

Kiara smiled and looked his way again. When he glanced back at her, her words came out spontaneously. "I like working with you, Sam."

"We make a good team, Kiara."

*   *   *

Zee was ready to meet his cronies after Gil had called, insisting he meet him at his brother's café. Gil, Bones, and Tonio were already seated at a table, pouring beer from large pitchers. Alonzio was mockingly called Zee by his cronies because they believed he had no smarts and caused security concerns whenever they committed robberies.

As Zee hobbled into the bar, Gilinsky sneered, drawing the crew's attention. "There he is, the idiot who gave up our names. Sit down, airhead. Tell them what you told me."

Zee sank into the booth, wincing. "This freak broke into my place, put a gun to my head, and threatened to pull the trigger. What was I supposed to do?"

"Let him blow your brains out, stupid," Bones sneered. The crew laughed harshly.

"Screw you, Bones. You woulda shit your pants if he had a gun to your head."

"Enough," Gilinsky snapped. "We got to deal with this guy before he gets to the rest of us. What'd the guy look like, Zee?"

"Older guy with long, scraggly gray hair, blackish beard, scar on his face. Bigger than me and mean-looking," lied Zee. "He wore a Yankee baseball cap and something like a microphone to disguise his voice."

"Why didn't he kill you, Zee? You gave him what he wanted," said Tonio harshly.

"He wanted me to deliver a message that he's coming after all yooze guys one-on-one to pay you back for what we did to his family."

"Shit, this guy is serious. It behooves us to bury this guy before he gets to the rest of us," Bones growled.

Gilinsky's face darkened. "From now on, be on guard. Vary your routes. Check your car mirrors for anyone following you. Put extra locks on your doors and lock all your windows. Carry your gun everywhere. Think of traps to use. We'll finalize a plan to put this guy down hard."

The three men pounded the table. "Yeah, let's kill the bastard!" they chorused, their voices dripping with malice.

CHAPTER

13

After leaving the state police barracks in Southbury, Sam followed the navigation directions to the family restaurant recommended by the troopers. Inside, Kiara ordered pecan-crusted salmon with a honey Dijon sauce, potato puree, and seasonal vegetables. She yearned for a martini but settled for coffee. The restaurant didn't have lattes. Sam chose a four-ounce filet, medium with seasonal veggies, and a glass of water.

While waiting for their dinner, Sam read the text message he had received from the senator. It contained an address at Candlewood Lake in New Fairfield.

Knowing the address and the town wasn't far, they decided to drive there rather than wait until morning. They chatted about what they had learned from the state police sergeant and lieutenant.

"It turned out to be a great bust. I wasn't surprised the troopers arrested the guy who disappeared into the woods," said Sam. "I laughed when the trooper said the guy ran back to the road after hearing a bear growling nearby. The police recovered eight similar assault rifles, some converted to fire fully automatic, and six 9mm Glocks, each with an attached Glockswitch. I knew the device was popping up nationwide, but the lieutenant said it's the first they came across in Connecticut."

"How does the switch work, Sam?"

"It's a small metal piece, about three-quarters of an inch by a half inch, attached to the back of a 9mm Glock. It functions like an auto sear, applying pressure to the trigger bar and allowing the gun to fire fully automatically. Anybody could buy them online, mostly from Russia and China. These switches are illegal under federal law and have become a huge problem in the US."

"What also surprised me was that three of the militia guys had felony convictions, and all but one had fictitious identification. I think these guys were up to no good, don't you?" said Kiara.

"Yeah, I'm sure of it. We did good, Kiara," said Sam. He held up his water glass for a toast as Kiara raised her coffee cup and clanged them together. "Here's to staying safe on our job and having success in finding Travis Thornton."

"Salute," responded Kiara. "I hope we didn't jinx finding him after getting sidelined to deal with the militia guys."

"No way. Here comes dinner. Let's enjoy the meal and get a hold of Travis so we can go home."

"Touché," Kiara giggled.

When leaving the restaurant, it took less than half an hour to drive to Candlewood Lake. Although nighttime, the nearly full moon shone brightly, enhancing the visibility on the dark road.

"I've got the navigation set for the address, so take my phone and guide me to the house," said Sam.

Still jittery about the skirmish with the armed militia, Kiara constantly babbled while heading to the lake. "I'm glad we didn't spend the night in Southbury. I'm not sure I would have gotten any sleep. I still think about our confrontation with those guys. We're lucky it didn't become a real nightmare, thanks mostly to you, Sam. We could have been injured or killed tonight."

"Not a chance. We had them covered."

"I've been with the FBI for nearly seven years but have never faced such a hostile situation. On the other hand, I've heard you've had similar, and even more dangerous, situations. We had them covered, but it still haunts me that we were on a dark, isolated road outnumbered by five trained guys with assault weapons."

"Mmm. I'm not making light of the situation. It was a horrific experience, but it ended with no one getting hurt. We had a plan, and we saw it through. Chalk it up to a learning experience on how to handle a similar situation. Remember always to outnumber the bad guys, and if the shit hits the fan, take cover, and that doesn't mean hiding behind a sheet metal car door."

"Thanks for the basic instruction."

"I was being facetious and hoping to get a little laugh from you. We did a good thing, and nobody got hurt. You were a hero out there."

That made Kiara laugh and helped her unwind from the confrontation she had experienced. Sam wanted to keep it going, so he laughed along with her.

"Thanks, Sam. I needed that to get my mind off that situation."

The road on the west side of the lake was narrow and winding, with many twists and turns. At one point, the road traveled high enough to see the lake with the moon reflecting off the water.

"Sam, let's pull over and gaze at the moon glittering off the water."

"What, is this going to be a romantic moment?" Sam said with a smirk.

"Funny, Sam. I enjoy beautiful settings, such as the moon reflecting over water at night. Even you must appreciate its artistry."

"Is that why so many artists paint this scene?"

"You're hopeless."

Sam pulled off the road, which widened for cars to stop and view the scenic lake.

"Wow, this lake looks massive," said Kiara.

"It sure is. While waiting for the check at the restaurant, I looked up Candlewood Lake on Wikipedia. The lake was man-made, measuring approximately eight square miles, and reportedly the largest in Connecticut. It borders five towns, including New Fairfield. During that time, a power plant company decided to clear the valley where the lake is now and pump water from the Housatonic River into it.

"It had to be a big job," said Kiara.

"Yeah. Over a thousand men, including hundreds, involved in cutting down all the trees and burning them. The idea was to build a dam and a power plant to produce electricity for the resort area during summer heat waves. What amazed me from the article was that the water that flooded the valley caused a small island village to sink. I hope they got all the people out first," Sam said jokingly. "The settlers named the lake after Candlewood Mountain, which they named after the Candlewood Tree, which they took saplings from to make candles."

"That's a mouthful of candles if I ever heard one. Is that an island in the middle of the lake?" asked Kiara.

"Yeah, one of twelve, according to the article. Let's head to the house and get this interview done. I've had my fill of artistry for tonight."

Sam drove further past a fork in the road and wondered if he had taken the right way. "Do I make any turns up ahead?"

Kiara studied the phone's navigation. "Oh, crap. I wasn't paying attention. Sorry. We should have stayed left at the fork."

"I'll turn around in this driveway." Sam turned around and drove back to the fork in the road.

Studying the navigation, Kiara indicated that the fork was approaching, and it was a sharp turn to the right.

As Sam approached the fork, he had to stop at the sign before turning. When he stopped, a car came through from the other road. Unfortunately, with the car's tinted windows, Sam couldn't make out the driver, Julian Jarrett, who headed south toward New Haven.

CHAPTER

14

Alex watched the Morrison Mill Works, a machine shop on the outskirts of New Haven, where Peter Gilinsky worked. Alex waited patiently, his eyes fixed on the exit, while the turmoil churned inside his gut. The overcast sky swallowed the sun, casting a dull gray light over everything—a fine drizzle tapped Alex's windshield. Fog crept in, shrouding the area in a thick, ghostly veil, reducing visibility to a mere whisper of distance. Alex glanced at the time every few minutes, the tension in his chest coiling tighter with each glance. It became twenty past five. "Maybe the guy's working overtime," he mused. "Doesn't matter. I've got all night to visit him."

Ten minutes later, the side door of the Mill Works creaked open, and a group of men spilled into the parking lot. Alex squinted through the fog, trying to match faces to Gil's photograph. The distance and fog made it difficult, but he knew Gil's silver Chevy Equinox and kept a watchful eye for the vehicle.

Soon enough, Gil's SUV emerged from the lot and turned left, heading south towards the inner city. Alex followed a careful distance behind, his heart thudding in time with the windshield wipers. Gil navigated through the maze of city streets, finally turning onto the street where his girlfriend worked at the salon. Alex's grip tightened on the steering wheel as he watched Gil pull over and beep his horn. A woman, assumed to be Maggie, emerged from the salon and slipped into the passenger seat.

The SUV merged back into traffic, with Alex trailing two cars behind. As luck would have it, Gil sped through a yellow light, leaving Alex fuming at the red. He slammed the steering wheel in frustration as the SUV disappeared around a corner. The light finally changed. Alex honked at the car in front of him, urging it to move. He swerved around the sluggish vehicle and tore down the street to make the turn. He noted the street name as he did, recognizing it as the same street where Gil's girlfriend lived.

Gil's SUV pulled into an apartment complex parking lot, with Alex not far behind. Alex parked on the roadside, his mind racing. Not surprisingly, Gilinsky followed Maggie into the apartment complex. Alex decided to wait. He had all night. He reclined his seat, closing his eyes to calm his nerves. It was only six o'clock.

As his eyes closed, the never-ending memories flooded back. The horror of the night Gil and his followers murdered his family played on a loop in his mind. His throat tightened, heart pounding as he relived the brutal scene, his families' faces forever etched in his memory.

A sudden slam of a car door snapped Alex awake from dozing off. Gil's SUV headlights flickered on, driving out of the lot and heading north. It was after ten o'clock, and the streets were mostly empty. Alex waited a few moments before following, a cold smirk forming on his lips. Tonight, retribution was within his grasp.

Gil merged onto Route 15 North, with Alex trailing behind. Apprehension intertwined with anticipation as Alex followed the SUV onto Route 8, heading towards Shelton and Derby. His pulse quickened, knowing he was nearing the moment of confrontation. Gil exited for Derby, weaving through the town before turning onto Deepwood Drive. Alex hung back, careful to avoid suspicion.

Alex stopped with his lights off at the crest of a hill, where he saw Gil's SUV pulling into a driveway. He remained at the curb, giving Gil time to enter his house. Ten minutes later, Alex drove slowly by Gil's house, taking in the surroundings. Gil's tan cape house was modest, sitting on the corner of Deepwood Drive and Parker Lane. A light glowed in the first-floor living room. Tall cedar trees bordered his backyard, offering some concealment. Alex drove to the end of the road, saw a nearby CVS Pharmacy, and parked in its parking lot, biding his time.

An hour passed before Alex returned, creeping along Deepwood Drive. He drove by the house where he saw the first floor was now dark, but a second-floor light was lit, assuming it was the bedroom. It was eleven-thirty. "Perfect," whispered Alex. He moved onto Parker Lane, seeking a discreet place to park. At the end of the street, Alex turned onto Chester Drive, where he saw an abandoned home on the corner with its front door plastered with notices. He entered the driveway and parked behind a shed, obscuring his car from the neighborhood view.

He grabbed his black go-bag and moved stealthily along the back of the houses on Parker Lane, which were dark and silent at the late hour. Alex squeezed between the cedar trees onto Gil's backyard. The second-floor room was now dark. He waited several minutes before surreptitiously advancing to the house's side door next to Gil's SUV. Using the vehicle as cover, Alex picked the doorknob lock and the two deadbolts. He slid foam covers over his shoes to muffle his steps and donned his night vision device.

He cracked the door open, scanning for any booby traps. Finding none, he silently crept inside the house. He delicately moved towards the stairs, but something gave him pause. Knowing Bones and Zee must have warned Gil, Alex sensed it was too easy and inviting when entering Gil's home. Using the night vision device, Alex studied the stairs from the bottom to the top. What he saw at the top troubled him. He stepped back, concerned that Gil had set a trap.

CHAPTER
15

Kiara provided directions to the senator's house. "It's just ahead on the right. Let's hope Travis is there so we can finally close this case." Minutes later, they arrived, but the darkness of the night shrouded the house.

"I don't see any lights on in the house, and there are no cars in the driveway," Sam remarked as he parked in front of the garage. He stepped out and used his phone's flashlight to check for any cars in the garage. "No cars in the garage and no sign of life," he said.

Kiara's frustration bubbled. "Let's ring the doorbell."

They approached the door. Kiara pressed the button twice and then knocked forcefully. Silence greeted them.

"What now?" said Kiara, her voice tinged with disappointment.

Sam rechecked the address obtained from the senator. "It's the right address, but I'll call to confirm."

A call to the senator's assistant yielded confirmation. "We're at the right place, Kiara."

"Dammit! I hoped we'd find him," said Kiara, with frustration.

"I bet Professor Martin called and warned them we were coming."

Sam scanned the neighboring houses, his eyes settling on one atop a hill across the street. He pointed to the house and said, "Let's pay them a visit. Maybe they saw something here."

They drove up the steep driveway, exiting the car to a breathtaking view. When they walked to the front door, an outdoor spotlight lit up the front entrance from a high rafter. Sam pressed the doorbell. Seconds later, a disembodied voice asked, "Who is it?"

"We're with the FBI. I'm Agent Rivers with my partner, Agent Caviello."

"How do I know you're with the FBI?"

"You could come to the door, and I'll show you my identification."

"No one is here. I'm talking to you on my phone from New York. You could hold your identification next to the doorbell camera and tell me why you're here."

Kiara complied, saying, "We were to meet your neighbor across the street, but we're surprised that no one was home. We thought that perhaps you had seen him or a car leaving earlier," said Sam.

"The owners are usually there during late June or early July."

"Yes, I understand, but we arranged to meet their son, Travis, who was staying at the house. However, no one is home. We hoped your security cameras might have seen him or his vehicle at the house earlier."

"Our security cameras point toward the immediate grounds in front of our house, but not as far as the house across the street."

"Okay, thank you. Can you please tell us who we are speaking with?" asked Kiara.

"I'm Attorney James Brennan."

"Well, thank you, Mr. Brennan."

Kiara and Sam went back to their car and drove away.

"Is it possible for your office to ping the towers for Julian's and Martin's phones to get calls made or received today?"

"I'll call and find out. It may take a while."

"Let's drive back to New Haven. I want to stop at the ATF office tomorrow and prepare a brief report on tonight's encounter with the militia group. Then, a short stop at the PD's detective's unit. If you get feedback from your office on the cell phones by then, it might tell us we need to revisit Professor Martin and give him an incentive to cooperate."

"You're not going to handcuff him, are you?"

"Hey, that's a great idea, Kiara. Thanks."

"Wait. I didn't mean . . ."

Sam interrupted her. "I'm joking, Kiara."

CHAPTER
16

A lex wiped the sweat from his forehead, his heart pounding like a war drum. His breathing quickened, and his stomach churned with disturbing sounds. He took a moment to decompress, forcing himself to remember why he was here. Determination fueled him, pushing aside his gnawing anxiety. He pulled out a charged Taser. Using his night vision scope, he took a deep breath before cautiously climbing the stairs with his back pressed to the wall. He stepped lightly, each creak underfoot heightening his senses until he reached the top step. Hearing Gil's snoring offered a fleeting sense of relief.

The next step was critical. Alex had spotted a wire stretched across the landing, one end connected to a buzzer. He lifted his leg to step over it, then carefully elevated the other, ensuring he didn't trip the alarm. Gil's snoring continued a rhythmic, almost mocking sound.

Alex feared Gil might be faking, ready to ambush him. He edged to the bedroom door, dropped to one knee, and peered low around the door frame. Gil lay on the floor, his head propped on pillows against the bed's end table and a quilt covering his body. A gun lay beside him to his right. Alex backed away, slowly standing as he formulated his next move. Taser in one hand, the pepper spray in his back pocket, he stepped into the room. Gil didn't stir, his snores unwavering.

Alex grinned, quietly grabbed Gil's gun, and slipped it into his other rear pocket. He moved back, studying Gil with long-lasting hatred before flicking the light switch on. The sudden brightness made Gil squint and shield his eyes, blinking rapidly. When he saw Alex, he frantically searched for his gun, but his hand came up empty.

"If you make any sudden moves, I'll Taser you into a heart attack," Alex said, his voice distorted by a voice enhancer. "Keep your hands on the quilt. I'm going to cuff you for my protection."

"I know why you're here," Gil stammered, his voice gravelly. "Zee told me about you, but I swear I wasn't there that night, and I never killed anyone."

"Shut up. Does the name Danny ring a bell? You shot him and his dad after he opened the safe. Zee was in the bedroom, assaulting and killing Danny's mom and sister. Now, we'll replay that night. I'll be you, and you'll be Danny. I'll shoot you dead, just like you did to him."

"Wait, wait," Gil pleaded. "I wasn't there. Zee is a psycho. If he told you about a robbery, it was him and his friends, not me. I swear."

"Liar. I was there, hiding in a safe room. I saw you, Bones, Zee, and Tonio. I heard everything, including Zee calling you by your name, Gil."

Gil became numb, realizing that this guy had witnessed the entire atrocity. Gil's eyes widened while sweat beaded on his forehead.

"Put your hands together, asshole," Alex ordered.

Now trembling, Gil brought his wrists together, knowing he had to make a move or die. Alex put away the Taser and then made his first miscue. When leaning over to cuff Gil, he left himself open. Gil swiftly shifted his cuffed hands away and up over Alex's head and grabbed the back of Alex's neck, pulling him into a crushing embrace. Alex's right arm became pinned between them, his left arm struggling to push away. Alex's legs flailed to find leverage, but Gil's vise grip tightened around his neck. Gil was a bigger, muscular guy who outweighed Alex by over forty pounds. Gil forced Alex's head to his chest, giving Alex's nose and mouth little room for breathing. Alex felt his strength waning, panic rising as his air supply dwindled.

"I got you, you bastard," Gilinsky growled. "I'm going to bury you where no one will ever find you."

Alex, desperate, reached for Gil's gun in his rear pocket. His hand searched, but his arm frantically swayed around his backside. He finally tightened his arm muscle to control its swerving and clutched the gun. He felt faint, knowing he had little time before passing out. Alex yanked the gun halfway out, but it slipped from his quivering fingers. Before it dropped, Alex caught the weapon against his thigh and gripped the handle tightly. With a surge of adrenaline, he brought it to Gil's thigh. He slid it to Gil's knee. Feeling pressure on his knee, Gil pressed harder on Alex's neck. With barely enough strength remaining, Alex squeezed the trigger.

"AHHH!" Gil screamed. His grip on Alex slackened as pain shot through his whole body. Alex managed to push away onto his knees, gasping for air. Anger flared within him. He labored to straighten up, whipped out the Taser, and shot Gil at close range in the chest. The jolt caused Gil to convulse for several seconds before collapsing into a heap of inert flesh.

Panting, Alex spun aimlessly around the room, dizzy and confused. "Gotta find his stash. Wait, wait, no time. The neighbors. Shit. Got to get outta here fast," he stammered.

Alex took a deep breath to compose himself. Knowing neighbors might have heard the gunshot and called the police. He has to leave the money behind. He peeked out the window and saw lights on in two houses across the way, one of which had a neighbor peering out a window. Alex collected his bag and rushed to the doorway when Gilinsky stirred. In a swift, brutal move, he struck Gil across the face with the gun, breaking his front teeth and knocking him out. The payback wasn't enough, though, so with a mighty blow, he smashed the pistol into Gil's other knee, ensuring his walking days would never be the same. His hands covered with tight-fitted latex gloves, Alex placed the gun in Gil's hand, pressing his index finger on the trigger.

Satisfied, Alex shut the light, carefully stepped over the trip wire, and descended the stairs, gripping the handrail. He locked the inside doorknob, stepped outside, and quietly closed the door. He locked the deadbolts with his pick, leaving no sign of a break-in. Alex hid behind Gilinsky's SUV, glancing at the houses across the street. Sirens wailed in the distance, shaking his very soul.

Not seeing anyone watching, Alex crept across the backyard. Blue lights glistened in the sky, and louder sirens gave Alex increasing anxiety. He ran to the last two cedar trees and hid between them. He peeked at the houses that stood between him and his car. Lights were on inside the first two homes. The second house's rear spotlight lit up the backyard. Seconds later, police cruisers arrived at Gil's house with officers shouting instructions to search around the outside. Alex's anxiety heightened, and his heart pounded against his chest, knowing he had no way to escape.

An officer with a flashlight scanned the cedar trees with a bright flashlight beam, searching for any movement. Alex trembled, causing the tree branches to flutter. The officer hovered near where Alex hid. Alex stiffened to stop his trembling. Suddenly, he felt the heat of the flashlight glare, realizing he was about to be caught. Alex had no choice now. He slid his leg out to the neighbor's backyard and was about to make a break for it. The glow of the light beam intensified. Alex's left cheek felt warm, as if someone's hand had touched him. He closed his eyes while touching his cheek. It felt like someone touched and squeezed his hand. He thought it was the officer who was about to pull him from between the trees and handcuff him. But, unexpectedly, the light beam suddenly vanished from his face. Alex opened his eyes, filled with repulsive emotion of being apprehended by the police. But seconds later, Alex heard the officer calling out, "All clear in the back!"

What? Alex whispered as relief slowly washed over him. He felt bodiless, not knowing what had happened. Internally, he felt weird, like something spiritual took hold of him. He shook his head, trying to wake himself from a dream. He looked up at the sky in a dreamlike state, seeing a bright light disappearing into a dot. He closed his eyes and saw a glowing faint image of a woman smiling before dissipating into thin air. "Was that my mother?" Alex murmured. The sound of an ambulance arriving woke him from his surreal state. He heard the officers mention that the detectives were minutes away. Alex glanced at the line of houses he would have to pass. No one was peering out the windows on the first two houses, and the spotlight was now off. Not waiting for another second, he scampered across the back lawns, panting like he was running a marathon. His eyes remained glued on police movement, apparently getting ready to interview neighbors.

When he reached the abandoned house, a police cruiser stopped at the nearby intersection. Its floodlight swept the street and the house on Chester Drive. Alex hit the ground as the floodlight swept above his head. The light then shifted to the first two homes on Parker Lane. Alex scrambled to his feet, made it unseen to his car, and hid behind it. He removed his disguise and gear and placed them quietly into the trunk. He waited until the officer approached a neighbor's residence. Alex backed out of the driveway with his car's lights off, creeping onto Chester Avenue. He avoided the brakes, easing to a stop before driving off. He turned left at the next intersection, put on his lights, drove to Deepwood Drive, and turned right.

As Alex ascended the hill, he saw blue lights flashing from the other side of the hill. Anxiety set in as Alex gripped the steering wheel, fearing the police detectives might pull over vehicles leaving the area of the crime scene. As Alex reached the crest of the hill, an unmarked police cruiser sped past him. Alex watched in the rearview mirror, his heart racing, hoping the cruiser didn't make a quick turnaround. When the police sedan faded into the distance, Alex wiped the sweat from his neck as beads dripped down his back. His heart continued to accelerate as he realized he nearly got caught by the police. He craved a more potent drink than water to calm his nerves.

"Two more to go," he whispered, hoping to survive them.

CHAPTER
17

It was late morning when Kiara called the New Haven FBI office to secure parking in the federal garage. An agent stood by the open garage door, waving her in as she arrived. Kiara parked the G-ride and followed the local agent to the FBI office. Sam headed to the ATF office on the second floor. The field agents greeted Sam warmly with handshakes before his supervisor and colleague, Jordan Toliver, welcomed him into his private office.

"When are you returning to Hartford, Sam? It's been, what, a year or so? I thought your assignment with the Massachusetts State Police was temporary."

"It was, but the US Attorney's Office requested I assist the FBI in investigating the disappearance of a senator's son."

"That's a first—an ATF agent assisting the FBI. It's usually the other way around."

"Right. But the Assistant US Attorney made it happen, leaving me little choice. Anyway, it's good to see you, Jordan. I wish I could stay to chat, but I have to cut my visit short. I'd appreciate it if Claire would type a report regarding my assistance to the state police last night and get it to the SAC. I already prepared it for the state police. I only need Claire to scan it to an ATF report form and send it out."

"No problem. She'd be happy to assist."

Sam and Claire greeted each other with a hug, having known each other for years. Claire always had a pleasant smile and was receptive to helping him. It took a few minutes for Claire to finish the report and send it to the Boston Office. Sam left the ATF office and met Kiara in the lobby. They returned to Kiara's car and drove to the PD. Kiara identified herself to the front desk officer and was allowed to take the elevator to the detective's unit. As they entered the squad room, Sam noticed a mass of detectives and uniformed officers bustling around an easel pad in preparation for an operation.

"Sam, come in and shut the door!" yelled Lieutenant Cassie Dawson. "I'm sorry, I don't remember your partner's name."

"It's Kiara Rivers from Boston. It looks like your office is ready to serve a warrant."

"Right. Sorry. This fax arrived a few minutes ago from the DA's office. Are you aware of it? It's a sketch of a guy who broke into a house and assaulted another guy with a gun. The District Attorney's Office distributed the wanted poster to all Connecticut police departments."

The lieutenant handed it to Sam. Sam and Kiara studied the sketch of the assailant and his description.

Sam handed the fax sheet back to Cassie, saying, "We haven't seen it before. Is your unit ready to serve a warrant?"

"Yeah, but it's not regarding the guy in the sketch. We're about to start a briefing for searching a suspect's home in another matter. We visited him previously, knowing he had a registered AR-15. He reluctantly allowed us to take the AR for ballistic examination but refused to let our guys inspect all the drawers in his secure gun cabinet."

"Is this the same case where someone killed two workers at a beverage distribution company?"

"It's the same, Sam."

"I guess your ballistic exam didn't show his AR was the weapon used."

"Right. However, our background check on the suspect's military service showed he served two tours in Afghanistan. It's known that soldiers return home with souvenirs lost in battle. We suspect he may have another weapon in his gun case. Hopefully, the suspect wasn't smart enough to get it out of his house and bury it where we wouldn't find it."

"Did he have ammo in his cabinet?"

"He did, but examining the striations in the recovered bullets used in the murder did not match those fired from his AR."

"Hmm. So, if you don't recover another weapon during your search, what are you left to charge the suspect?"

"If the search doesn't find another weapon, we'll bring him in for intense questioning, hoping he cracks."

"Did you find any expended shells from where the shooter positioned himself?"

"No. The shooter was smart enough to collect them. Do you have any ideas, Sam?"

"How many shots did the shooter fire?"

"He shot three times, hitting the owner's son twice and the woman once."

"So, you're sure it was your suspect?"

"Yeah. The owner, who planned on retiring, was grooming the suspect, Mark Callahan, to run the business. The owner's son, who for years wanted no part of the business, unexpectedly decided to work for his father. The owner had Callahan train his son to take over his job while Callahan ran the business. After learning the job, the son convinced his father that he could handle both jobs. His father was more than pleased to have his son manage the company with his guidance and approved his son's suggestion to let Callahan go with a less-than-worthwhile severance."

"What about the woman? Did anyone have a motive to kill her? Was there a romantic connection between the son and her?"

"We ruled that out. Any other ideas from either of you?" asked the lieutenant, eyeing Kiara.

"Callahan would have to be stupid to kill the owner's son, knowing he'd be the prime suspect."

"We couldn't identify anyone else with a motive and an AR."

"How sure are you that the shooter shot from the location you searched?"

"We're reasonably certain. The state police used a laser and what they called the properties of the right triangle to determine the shooter's location across the parking lot and up a slope to the woods. We searched the area they calculated as the spot from where the shooter fired. He brushed the ground clean in the area to cover any footprints."

"The shooter might have covered his cartridges if he brushed the entire area. I'd recommend another search with a metal detector and expand the search area. It's worth another look."

Lieutenant Dawson considered Sam's suggestion regarding a second search. She said she'd be in touch. After leaving the PD, Sam and Kiara visited the Yale admissions office to determine Julian Jarrett's status at Yale.

CHAPTER

18

Kiara and Sam entered Yale University's Admissions Office. A receptionist directed them to the proper student records office, where Kiara identified herself and requested verification of Julian Jarrett's student status. The records representative typed the name into a computer but found no record of Jarrett.

"It's Jarrett with two r's and two t's?" the representative asked.

"I believe so, but could you check for spelling variations by searching names beginning with JA?" Kiara replied.

"I found nothing for a Jarrett spelled differently."

Sam added, "Jarrett was into artistic studies like theater and music. Do different colleges have their separate directories?"

"If he were an enrolled student, his name would be in our database."

"Can you check if he was a former student?" Kiara asked.

"I can check the past three years." After a moment, the representative found a match. "Julian Jarrett was permitted to monitor a Theater and Performance Studies class last year but left without completing the semester."

"Does it say why he left?" Kiara inquired.

"Only that it was disciplinary. Our administrator would have more details. Let me see if she's available."

Minutes later, a woman in her mid-forties, wearing a navy dress and a green cardigan, approached.

"Good afternoon. I'm Marjorie Greenberg, Undergraduate Admissions Director. May I see your identification, please?"

Kiara displayed her FBI credentials and introduced Sam as her partner. Greenberg explained, "Julian Jarrett voluntarily left the program after violating school rules. Other student's parents complained to campus police about Jarrett, leading him to leave campus. You might want to check with the campus police for additional information."

After thanking Director Greenberg, Kiara and Sam drove to the campus police department. There, they met Police Chief James Hoskins, a tall, well-built African American in his early fifties with short gray hair. Hoskins, impeccably dressed in his uniform, was personable and mentioned several FBI agents he had met over the years.

Kiara explained their purpose, and Hoskins chatted about his department, which comprised over ninety officers patrolling the campus. "We provide security for over fifteen thousand students, over five thousand faculty, and eleven thousand staff members. It's a city within a city."

Kiara and Sam exchanged glances as the chief kept talking while looking for Julian Jarrett's file.

"Ah, here it is," Hoskins said, reviewing the paperwork. "Jarrett conned money from two students. He romanced them for a few dates, then claimed poverty and asked for help with tuition. He only monitored a theater class, but the students gave him money—one gave him twelve hundred dollars, the other a thousand. When their parents found out, they complained to the administration, which turned it over to us. We questioned Jarrett, who claimed he had no money for restitution. The students didn't want to testify, so the administration barred him from campus, and we warned him we'd arrest him if he returned."

"Did you check his record, Chief?" Kiara asked.

"Yes. Jarrett had a North Carolina driver's license. We found he had three shoplifting arrests, possession of fentanyl with intent to sell, and conning an older woman out of money. The prosecutor dropped the fentanyl charge after the buyer recanted his identification, the older woman refused to press charges, and the prosecutors decided to drop the misdemeanor shoplifting charges after a school employee, their name not reported, paid the store for the goods taken."

"Can we get a copy of his record, photo, date and place of birth, and last known employment?"

"No problem. Jarrett claimed to work as a short-order cook in West Haven. I'll give you the name, but we determined the place doesn't exist."

"Do you know the name of the professor who let Jarrett monitor the class?" Sam asked.

The chief provided the name and everything he had on Jarrett. Kiara thanked him as they left.

Walking back to their car, Kiara and Sam had to move aside on the sidewalk for students rushing to class. Sam marveled at the scores of students rushing to their classes, many walking in groups, talking about their classes or sports. It reminded Sam of his college days. Sam's parents couldn't afford college, so he worked two summer jobs and part-time during the school year to pay his way. Graduating from college turned out to be the best decision of his life. While the classroom shaped his intellect, college life taught him independence and the value of interaction with others. Friendships with diverse classmates broadened his perspective, deepening his understanding of cultural differences and the struggles others face. Collaborative study sessions challenged him to embrace ideas and viewpoints unlike his own, fostering empathy and open-mindedness that would later define his approach to life and work.

"Sam, are you with me? You seem focused on all the students heading to their classes."

"Yeah. Thanks for the wake-up. I was thinking back to my college days. It was a worthwhile experience. If I hadn't decided to go to college, I wouldn't have this job working with you. I'd probably be working a lower-paying job trying to make ends meet like my parents. Anyway, let's locate the professor who allowed Jarrett into his class. "It might lead to something. After that, we could revisit Martin."

Using the campus map, they found the School of Drama. While waiting for assistance, Sam admired the names and photos on a wall of the school's alums, including Paul Newman, Meryl Streep, Sigourney Weaver, and Bill Clinton.

"Sorry for the wait," said a staff member, taking Sam's attention away from the alumni wall. "How can I help you?"

Kiara showed her credentials and asked for Peter Cambridge.

"His office is on York Street. Take a right, cross Chapel Street, and take a left on the walkway near the newspaper office. The building will be straight ahead. The directory will provide his room number."

Following the directions, they found Cambridge's office. The door was partially open, so Sam knocked and walked in.

"Mr. Cambridge?" Sam asked.

"Yes. Can I help you?"

Kiara introduced herself and Sam. "We're investigating the disappearance of a Yale student connected to Julian Jarrett, who monitored your class."

"Ah. I remember Julian. How can I help?"

"We understand you permitted him to monitor your class at a staff member's request. Who made the request?"

"Jonathan Martin from the law school. He's an adjunct professor and a member of the student disciplinary board, and he counsels students with various issues."

Kiara glanced at Sam, who didn't seem surprised. He asked, "Did Martin mention why he recommended Julian?"

"Only that he mentioned knowing a family member of Julian, but I don't recall specifics."

Kiara thanked Cambridge, and they left his office.

"Let's confront Martin," said Sam. "He better cooperate fully this time."

"Be careful, Sam. Don't do anything that can get you in trouble. Remember, you're supposed to follow FBI protocols. No harassing or threatening anyone."

"I don't harass or threaten witnesses. I convince them it's better to cooperate or face the consequences. Martin is hindering our investigation into Travis's disappearance. It's time to convince him to cooperate or face charges."

CHAPTER
19

The late afternoon haze began fading as Alex took the entrance ramp from New Haven onto I-95. The weight of his mission caused continuous apprehension and impatience. Every mile closer to Milford, where Frank Bonarz, known as Bones, worked at a tire company, intensified the drum of anticipation in Alex's veins. With grim determination, Alex had meticulously charted the route to Bones' workplace. He parked in the shadowed recesses of a nearby liquor store, waiting for Bones to emerge from his workplace.

Alex held back when Bones left the parking lot, allowing ample distance between them. He was keenly aware of the possibility that Gil had forewarned Bones and might be on the lookout for a tail. With deft precision, Bones stopped at a liquor store and walked out moments later with a paper bag tucked under his arm. Back in his vehicle, Bones drove to his apartment, continuously looking in his rear-view mirror, fearing the vigilante was following to terrorize him.

Alex trailed discreetly behind, like a phantom, biding his time until the cloak of darkness enveloped Bones' arrival at a dilapidated apartment complex. The structure loomed like a forgotten relic, the oldest building constructed in the complex, with its decrepit façade a testament to the bleakness within its walls. With a weary sigh, carrying his bag of bourbon,

Bones locked his truck and shuffled towards the entrance. He used a key to unlock the flimsy doorknob. Anyone using a credit card or screwdriver could easily slide the latch bolt open to enter the lobby. Bones' apartment was on the basement level. There were fewer apartments in the basement, which also housed the shared laundry room and the electrical and boiler rooms. The rents for the basement units were the cheapest among all the units in the complex.

Bones entered the unkempt one-bedroom unit. He removed the leftover dinner from the refrigerator, warmed it in the microwave, and then set it on the dining table where he had placed the bourbon. Bones washed a used fork and dinner knife, ripped a section from the paper towel rack, and sat at the table. He took a long swig of the liquor before reaching for the TV remote. Bones found an adult movie to watch, ate a lukewarm dinner, and continued downing the bourbon. After dinner, he moved to an old upholstered armchair with faux leather and duct tape, covering a few rips. The chair's frame, made of natural wood, was set on a reclined angle.

Alex waited from the shadows outside, his gaze unwavering when Bones disappeared into the dimly lit lobby of the building. As the night deepened its hold, Alex slipped into the role of the hunter, his senses honed like a razor's edge. Disguised and shrouded in darkness, he quietly went unseen into the apartment lobby, easily bypassing the lock with a credit card. Alex checked the names on the apartment's numbered mailboxes and quietly moved down the stairs to the basement level. He found apartment number one, the first unit on the left. Alex heard the low humming sound coming from the boiler room. The hall felt clammy and musty. He waited until the humming stopped before putting his ear to the apartment door and listening for any sound inside the apartment. He heard the sound of a television and heavy snoring, likely coming from Bones. Alex smirked, seeing Bones was security conscious, with two recent deadbolt locks added to the key-locked doorknob. He thought to check for other warning traps after picking the locks and cautiously opening the door. Alex quietly entered the apartment that permeated the mildewed, dingy air.

Inside, Bones slumbered in a haze of bourbon, a fallen titan entangled in the web of his own making. Alex's eyes narrowed with grim resolve as he beheld the sorry spectacle before him. With steady hands, Alex loosely bound Bones in a web of rope around the chair. He placed duct tape across Bones' lips, knowing it would awaken the boozer.

"Good evening, Bones," Alex's voice cut through the stillness like a blade, cold and unforgiving. "I'm Alex, but I'll be Danny tonight, a name you probably remember."

Bones' muffled protests fell on deaf ears as Alex laid bare the sins of the past, each word a damning indictment of Bones' complicity in the tragedy that had befallen Alex's family. With steely determination, Alex demanded a reckoning for the debts owed in blood and sorrow.

"Mmm, mmmm," crooned Bonarz, trying to yell through the obstructed mouth as he squirmed in his chair.

"It won't do you any good to yell. No one will hear you mumbling. I prefer that you remain quiet, or I will knock you unconscious. Think back seven years ago when you, Zee, Gil, and Tonio broke into a family's home in Westbrook. It's where Gil shot my brother, Danny, and my father. It's the robbery that Zee got held as a suspect by the police but was set free and not charged because of a corrupt cop, Detective Mackey. I'm here to get the details of the payments paid to the detective for getting Zee off scot-free. I also want to collect back your share of what you guys stole."

"Mmm, mmmm," screeched Bonarz, shaking his head no.

"Are you trying to tell me that you'll give back your share and tell me everything about how Detective Mackey helped you guys? Did he always get a cut of the action?"

"Mmm," Bonarz squealed again, shaking his head in denial.

"Well, if you're answering no to my questions, I have no further need of you." Alex took Bones' gun from the side table and aimed it at his forehead. Bones' feeble denial rang hollow, his fate sealed by the weight of his own guilt. Alex gave Bones a final ultimatum: cooperate or die, his finger trembling on the gun's trigger against Bones' forehead.

"Mmm," shuddered Bones, shaking his head up and down affirmatively.

"You're saying yes now?"

Bones bobbed his head up and down again.

"That's smart, Bonesy. I'm going to remove the tape from your lips. I want you to whisper answers to my questions. If you try shouting out for help, you're a dead man. Understand?"

Bones nodded yes.

Alex put the gun to Bones' forehead while slipping off the tape about halfway. "Where's the money and diamonds?"

"What's left is hidden in a locked metal box in the bedroom under the dresser," mumbled Bonarz.

"That's too loud. Whisper more softly. What deal did you and your crew have with Detective Mackey?"

"Gil took care of that. Me and the other guys never met him."

"Did Mackey get a full share?"

"I don't know."

Alex pressed the gun hard on Bones' forehead, causing his head to push back forcefully. "That's bullshit, Bonesy. You guys were friends, calling each other by made-up nicknames. The three of you had to know how Gil split the goods. It's time for you to pay the price. I let the others live, but I'm going to pull the trigger on you."

CHAPTER
20

Bones trembled so violently that the chair quivered beneath him. Perspiration streamed down his cheeks. But that wasn't all that drained from his body.

"What's that smell?" Alex's nose wrinkled in disgust as he examined Bones' pants. "Jesus, Bones, did you piss your pants?"

"You're scaring the shit out of me, man."

"You shit your pants, too?"

"No, but I had to piss, bad. I couldn't hold it."

"Your whole body stinks. I got a whiff of you when I walked in. Do you ever take a shower?"

"Hey, man. I worked all day. It's hard work."

"Yeah, right, of course you do," said Alex, repulsed. "Are you ready to talk, or should I put a hole in your head?"

"Okay, I'll talk. Gil told us he gave Mackey twenty percent of the cash but no diamonds. But one time, Mackey demanded a share of the diamonds. Gil joked that he gave him only two diamonds out of the three bags, which held a lot more."

"How did Mackey get the prosecutor to drop charges against Zee?"

"Gil told Mackey that Zee was with him, his girlfriend, and Gil's brother at a bar. Gil's brother owns the bar. The three swore Zee was with them the night of the robbery. Mackey told the prosecutor that a young kid would be a weak witness against three adult witnesses who said otherwise. Gil had to pay Mackey off big-time for his help, but he didn't tell us how much."

"Did Gil pay off the prosecutor, too?"

"No. Mackey handled that end by not giving him enough to charge Zee."

Considering how easily Bones gave up information, Alex wondered if he should change tactics, figuring Bonarz might tell all and snitch on his buddies. Alex always carried notes on the dates and places of their suspected robberies. So, after reflecting on it further, he decided to try something new on Bones.

"I answered all your questions. You're not going to kill me, are you? You didn't kill Zee or Gil."

Alex glanced around the small, dark apartment. The combined living room, dining room, and kitchenette took up no more than six hundred square feet. Two small basement hopper-type windows opened at the top for ventilation. The place needed it. Alex looked disgusted at the torn, beat-up old couch and the cheap dining table with only two chairs—however, Bones spent willingly on a relatively new brand-name, sixty-five-inch TV and a new pick-up truck. Alex stepped toward the open bedroom door, where he saw a messy, unkempt twin-size bed and a four-drawer dresser used as an end table with a desk lamp on top. Bones' used clothes were spread on the floor instead of in a laundry basket.

"For a guy who steals money and works a full-time job, you sure live like a homeless guy," said Alex. "What the hell do you spend your money on, Bones? Certainly not for a nice apartment, furniture, and clothes."

"Hey, I bought a new truck, and I like booze and women," muttered Bones.

"Women go out with you? You smell like you haven't showered in weeks."

"Yeah, well. I pay 'em good."

Alex figured as much. He scanned the room again and eyed a white-lined paper pad and a pen on the untidy dining table. It gave him an idea, thinking it might get the cold case on his family's murder reopened and solved.

Bones was drenched in sweat, causing a waterfall onto his brow and cheeks. His body trembled like quivering branches swaying in a swirling wind. Alex couldn't stand the sight of this creep, who reeked of booze and stunk worse than a horse's turd. Alex remembered Bones acted like a big bully, frightening unarmed victims with a gun in their faces. Now that Alex had reversed the situation, Bones was just another frightened coward. He despised Bones, wishing he could pull the trigger on him. But Alex couldn't kill a fly, never mind a person, even a killer. Alex only wanted justice for his family and other victims who had suffered at the hands of this cowardly bunch.

"I'll give you a choice, Bones—die here right now or continue to live by doing what I tell you to do. You've got ten seconds to decide."

"What do I have to do?"

"You won't like it, but it'll save your ass. You agree to write a letter to the state prosecutor describing all the robberies and murders you and your buddies did over the last ten years. Name your buddies and who was responsible for the killings. You won't have to sign it. You'll refer to yourself as 'me' instead of your name."

"Shit, man, they might figure out who wrote it. That would put me in prison forever."

"That's where you and your crew belong. Besides, it's better than dying in your chair tonight."

"I'll be dead anyway, man. The other guys will kill me for talking."

"We can fix that. Your best chance to survive is making a deal with the prosecutor. The fact you don't sign the form is a plus. They'll be eager to find out who you are, have you come forward, and make a deal to get your cooperation. After all, you'd help them clear many unsolved robbery and murder cases and bring closure to the victims' families after all those years. In your letter, demand the prosecutor guarantee a deal of a lighter sentence with protection from your buddies in writing and to appoint a top-shelf attorney for you, paid for by the state. A lighter sentence for what you and your friends have done is a bargain. Plus, with good behavior, you'll serve even less prison time. That's the best deal you'll ever get."

"Hey, man, there's no way I could remember all the places we hit."

"I bet you could remember a lot more than you think. I'm sure you and your friends laughed and bragged among yourselves about the scores you pulled for weeks after." Alex walked around the back of the chair Bones was tied to, put his gun against Bones' head, and asked, "So what's it going to be, Bonesy? Be the first of your buddies to die, or do you want to continue to live?"

Petrified when Alex cocked the pistol, Bones yelled, "Okay, okay, man, I'll write whatever you want me to!"

Alex slapped Bones hard across the side of his head with his hand.

"Ah! That hurt, man!"

"I told you to whisper, Bones. No speaking loudly. The next time, I'll quiet you for good."

Bones breathed heavily, as if out of breath, but didn't say another word.

"I'm going to untie the rope around your chest. Don't move an inch when I do, or I'll zap you with a Taser."

After untying the rope, Alex had Bones bring his hands together in front of him, where Alex cuffed them with plastic handcuffs. He then cut the cord, releasing Bones' feet. Alex got behind Bones and ordered him to sit at the dining table. As Bones staggered to the table, Alex pulled out the chair and pushed Bones onto it. He pulled notes from his back pocket, placed them on the table, and set the white-lined pad and pen before Bones. The notes prepared by Alex listed suspected home invasions that Bones and his crew had carried out over the last ten years. He had Bones read them.

"Man, some places on the list we didn't do."

"Don't bullshit me, Bones. There might be a couple, but you guys did most of them. Check the ones you guys didn't rob."

Bones studied the list of twelve homes in western Connecticut, checking off four he claimed they didn't rob.

"I'll help you write the letter." Alex took hold of Bones' hand, painted his thumb with a magic marker, and then had him begin writing what he dictated. Bones started with the date, then the DA's name and address at the top. He continued writing from the earliest date forward, naming the locations of the robberies. Bones identified his buddies and himself as me, what they stole, and who they killed at three different homes. Alex secretly scribbled a note while Bones wrote the letter.

Alex continued dictating the rest of Bones' confession, telling him to request a deal for his cooperation, a state-paid high-profile attorney to represent him, and guaranteed protection from his crew members. He dictated the DA's address for the envelope and carefully read the letter to ensure Bones' accuracy.

"You did good, Bones. A few misspellings and some address numbers transposed, but all in all, pretty good."

"Why did you blacken my thumb?"

"Oh, that. Let me see the thumb." Alex held Bones' thumb out while folding his other four fingers and then pressed the thumb onto the bottom of the letter.

"Hey, for chrissake, man, you said I wouldn't have to sign the letter."

"I kept my word, Bones. You didn't sign it."

"Well, my thumbprint is the same as my signature."

"You never told me the cops have your fingerprints on file, so how would I know?"

"Shit, man. Gil and the other guys will kill me."

Alex folded Bones' letter and placed it and the note he wrote into the envelope. Alex's note described where the police could find the money and diamonds they stole. "You asked for protection, and I'm sure the DA will protect you if you cooperate. You'll get the best deal of any of your buddies. I will leave now, so relax while I tie you to the chair."

Alex tied a rope around Bonarz's arms and chest to the dining table chair's backside, but not as loosely as he promised. He then tied his ankles to the chair legs.

"You should manage to untie yourself when I leave."

Alex quickly entered the bedroom, pushed the dresser out, and lifted the two loose boards. He found a metal container, forced it open, and took all the money except fifty dollars but left the diamond pouch. Alex stuffed the money, Bones' gun, and cell phone into his go-bag and scanned the room to ensure nothing was left behind. He ensured Bones didn't have a wired phone. Alex didn't cut the plastic ties around Bones' wrists to make it harder for him to get free. Before leaving, Alex left a final message for Bones. "Tell your buddy, Tonio, he's next. Oh, I almost forgot. Be smart. Don't tell your friends you ratted on them."

Alex left the apartment, drove out of the complex, and then pulled off the road to remove his disguises and clothing covers. He then went by a post office in Bridgeport, where he dropped Bones' letter into the outdoor mailbox, still wearing a latex glove. Alex slammed his fist on the steering wheel in celebration, knowing the night turned out perfectly. He drove off, talking to himself. "How stupid Bones was for writing the letter. Those four guys would make the Three Stooges look smart."

* * *

It took a while for Bones to calm his jitters and figure out how to get loose. His jacket hung over the other dining table chair. He always carried a switchblade knife inside the inner breast pocket.

He wiggled the chair closer to his jacket. He took more deep breaths before pulling the jacket to his chest and the knife from his pocket. With the knife, he cut the plastic ties to release his cuffed wrists. Getting his arm around the chair wasn't easy with the tight rope around him. Reaching and pulling the tangling robe string to undo the shoestring knot took a while. He pulled the rope away from his body and untied his ankles. He wiped the sweat from his eyes and took a couple of deep breaths to calm himself.

Without thinking, Bones grabbed his truck keys and scrambled to his truck to warn Acosta. He looked at the time before starting his vehicle. It was late. Antonio would be home sleeping. He could call him but remembered the vigilante took his cell. Frustrated, he sat in his vehicle, muttering, "What the hell do I do now?" He considered driving to Acosta's place but didn't remember the address or how to get there. He'd only been there once before.

It was too late to do anything. Bones grudgingly returned to his apartment, sat on his cushioned chair, and took several swings of bourbon. He knew Acosta started work at seven-thirty. He figured it was better to get some shut-eye, buy a burner phone in the morning, and warn Acosta at his job. Knowing who the vigilante was visiting next would give the crew the best chance to set a trap and nail the bastard.

CHAPTER
21

Kiara and Sam had stepped into the bustling corridor of the law school, where Sam spotted a man leaning against the wall at the bottom of the stairs to his right. The man, likely in his fifties, wore a casual black jacket, khaki trousers, and a fedora hat reminiscent of old mobster films. He gnawed on a toothpick, his gaze fixed unyieldingly on Sam.

"Let's go straight to Martin's office," Sam whispered to Kiara.

They walked past the receptionist station without stopping, but the receptionist's voice rang out, "May I help you?"

Kiara and Sam exchanged glances before returning to the office, asking for Professor Martin. The receptionist, a stern woman in her forties, informed them that Professor Martin was not in his office.

"Where can we reach him?" Sam inquired, his patience thinning.

"He didn't say, only that he wouldn't be in for several days."

"Does he live on campus?" Sam pressed.

"I don't know where he lives. Some grad students and professors reside at a residence building managed by a private concern on York Street. Would you like to leave a message for him to call you?"

"No. I tried calling several times today but got no answer. Did he recently change his number?"

"He did, but I'm not allowed to give it out."

"Do you maintain a visitor or appointment log for Mr. Martin?"

"No. He keeps his own appointment log."

Determined, Sam asked if she would call his office to check if he returned without telling her.

As Sam spoke, he heard heavy breathing behind him. He turned to see the fedora man leaning over him, projecting the look of a bully.

"I doubt he's in his office, but I'll dial his number," the receptionist said, eyeing the stranger behind Sam uneasily. She dialed the extension and listened to a voice. "Is that you, professor?" she said surprisingly. "The two FBI agents are here again." She received an answer and hung up, looking perplexed. "Uh, I guess he's in his office."

Sam thanked the receptionist and glanced at the fedora man, who was back at the bottom of the stairs, signaling someone at the top. Sam saw the bottom of a man's trousers at the top of the stairs. He and Kiara advanced down the hall, tension mounting with each step.

At Martin's office, the door was closed. Sam knocked while turning the doorknob. The door opened, so Sam walked in with Kiara close behind. They both froze at the sight of a stranger sitting at the desk, his feet propped up, puffing on a cigar.

"How can I help you two?" the man drawled.

"We're here to see Professor Martin, and you're not him," Sam stated, his voice cold.

"Mmm. What do you want to see Gian—uh, Jonathan about?"

"That's private between Professor Martin and us," Kiara interjected firmly.

"And who are 'us'?"

"I'm FBI Special Agent Rivers, and my partner Agent Caviello."

The man lowered his feet, stood about six feet, two inches tall, and walked around the desk toward Sam. He wore a dark suit with a black T-shirt. As he approached Sam, his suit coat slightly opened, revealing a gun tucked into his belt. He got too close for comfort, forcing Sam to step back. The man's breath reeked of cigar smoke.

The office door closed behind them. The fedora man and another similarly dressed thug entered, looking like nightclub bouncers, their hostile glares fixed on Sam.

"Cavello, huh?" said the man from the desk, mispronouncing Sam's name. "An Italiano working with a black female fed. Whataya think of that, boys?"

The two thugs snickered. "Not good, boss," one of them sneered.

"Yeah, not good at all," the boss man smirked. "Jonathan is my little brother. I understand you two have been harassing him. That's a problem. I don't like anyone making trouble for my kid brother."

"We're not bothering your brother. We're looking for a missing kid; your brother could help us find him," Sam explained.

"He doesn't know anything about any missing kid. He doesn't want you guys busting his chops and threatening to take him to court."

"We don't want any trouble," Kiara said, her voice wavering slightly.

"Well, we're here to make sure you don't come around pestering my brother again."

Sam knew this guy was trouble. He felt his body tense up, with fists clenched, ready for anything. He anticipated the bully was about to do something stupid.

The boss man had to weigh over two hundred twenty pounds. Sam saw him bring his right arm back with a closed fist. Sam acted quickly. He pivoted one hundred eighty degrees around with his left elbow high, slamming it into the guy's face, breaking his nose. The blow sent the boss man staggering backward, slamming his back into the desk. He screamed in pain, crumpling to his knees.

"Sam, behind you!" Kiara shouted.

The fedora thug charged at Sam. In a swift motion, Sam blocked the guy's sucker punch with his left arm and struck the man's throat with his right fist, dropping him to the floor.

"Sam, gun behind you!" Kiara yelled.

Sam crouched and grabbed his gun while swiveling around toward the boss man, who reached for his gun. Sam pulled the trigger, hitting the man squarely where he aimed—in the groin. "Ahhh!" yelled the guy as his arm dropped while pulling the trigger. The gun blast was low and to the right of Sam, missing Kiara's leg by inches. The guy toppled to the floor, writhing in agony.

The third thug lunged at Kiara, snatching her gun as she reached for it, holding it to her head.

"Sam!" she bellowed, struggling as her assailant tightened his grip around her neck.

Seeing Kiara in peril, Sam kicked his attacker's gun away and, not wanting a standoff, immediately shouted back to Kiara, "Force him to your right!"

Kiara grappled with her attacker, managing to twist to the right, forcing her attacker's view away from Sam. In seconds, Sam rapidly circled behind them, putting his gun to the head of Kiara's attacker.

"Drop your gun now, or I'll blow your brains out!"

The gun held by the thug immediately clattered to the floor. Sam holstered his gun and grabbed her attacker's wrist. He pulled his arm from Kiara's neck and firmly forced it against his back. He shoved the man toward his companion, who was still croaking while clutching his throat on the floor. Sam ordered them to lie face down. With Kiara's help, Sam handcuffed them and pocketed their guns and IDs. Sam quickly moved to the guy holding his crotch, cuffed him, and secured his wallet and gun.

Sam moved back to Kiara, asking if she was okay.

"I'm a little shaken, but I'll get over it," Kiara replied, her face bleached, her voice unsteady.

"I'm calling the US Attorney and the campus police. Would you call Davies and request backup for the arrests and an ambulance for the one I shot?"

Sam called Attorney Debra Durrell but was transferred to Brian Murphy. Sam briefed him on the incident. Murphy said Durrell was unavailable but ensured she would get back to him. Sam then contacted Lieutenant Dawson and the campus police chief, who agreed to respond to the scene.

Shortly thereafter, Campus Police Chief James Hoskins and two officers arrived. Sam briefed the chief. Twenty minutes later, FBI agent Alan Davies and three agents entered. Davies immediately approached Kiara, demanding a thorough account of what happened. He didn't hide his anger, wanting to know why she hadn't reported a potential confrontation beforehand. Kiara explained, but he rejected it as unacceptable.

Next, Davies stormed toward Sam, his face tight with frustration. His voice was strained as he demanded, "We need to talk privately. Now." He didn't wait for a response as he headed for the hallway. Sam, visibly irritated, sighed and rolled his eyes, knowing what was coming—a lecture. Reluctantly, he followed Davies but stepped aside at the door to make room for EMTs wheeling in a gurney. The office buzzed with tense energy, agents on edge, the hum of police radios, and the metallic clink of the gurney wheeling in the room. Once in the hall, the echo of the chaos softened, but Davies's voice was sharp as ever.

"Explain why the hell you didn't contact me before anticipating a confrontation!" Davies barked, his eyes burning into Sam.

Sam's expression remained flat. He already knew Kiara explained the situation. At this point, trying to explain again was like talking to a wall. Davies had already passed judgment.

"Listen, Alan," Sam said, his voice calm but firm. "We'll file a full statement. You'll see we followed procedure."

Davies's eyes narrowed. "What procedural book were you following?"

"The same one we both do," Sam shot back without missing a beat.

"I highly doubt we're operating under the same standards."

Sam opened his mouth to respond, but the EMTs interrupted, wheeling the gurney into the hall. The man on it, bruised and bloodied, was the one Sam had shot. Sam's eyes focused on the gurney, then back to Davies.

"You're in charge now, right?" Sam asked, his tone edged with sarcasm.

Davies bristled. "Unquestionably."

Sam pointed to the gurney. "Then why isn't the arrestee cuffed to the gurney and escorted by your agents? That's not FBI protocol."

Davies's face twisted in frustration, his jaw clenching as Sam called out to the EMTs, "Stop. That man needs to be handcuffed and escorted by the FBI."

Turning back to Davies, Sam added, "You're in charge, Alan. You should start following FBI procedures. This never happens when ATF is in charge." With that, he left Davies standing there, his frustration boiling over in silence.

Back in the office, Sam headed straight to Kiara. "Did you say something to set Davies off?" he asked, his tone half-joking but still curious.

Kiara shook her head, exasperated. "He was already fuming before I even got a word in. I told him the truth—the guy and his crew threatened us. He pulled a gun on you, and his buddy put one to my head. We'd probably be dead if you hadn't acted as you did."

Sam's jaw tightened, and for a brief second, the reality of how close they both came to being killed hung over him like a heavyweight. Before he could respond, Cassie entered with Detective Kendrick in tow, both radiating concern.

"What the hell happened here?" said Cassie.

Sam quickly filled her in, his mind racing through the details. Together, they walked to the spot where the bullet meant for him had lodged in the wall's wooden base molding. They removed it and bagged it for evidence.

"This is huge, Sam," Cassie said, her eyes wide in awe. "I overheard one of the agents say the guy you shot is the son of Santo Lamartino's—the New Jersey Mob boss. You really stepped into something big."

Sam's brow furrowed as her words sank in. "Lamartino, huh? He said he was Professor Martin's brother." A moment of realization flashed in Sam's eyes. "If he's Lamartino's son, it makes sense that Martin must be his son, too."

"Hmm. Martin—Lamartino. Do the names sound similar?" said Kiara. "I'll call Dell to run a check on the names of Santo Lamartino's sons?"

Before Sam could process the revelation further, his phone buzzed—it was US Attorney Durrell. He quickly filled her in, his voice steady as he mentioned Martin's connection to the Mob boss. Durrell didn't hesitate. "Get to my office immediately. Bring Kiara. This is big."

Sam ended the call and turned to Cassie. "You and Detective Kendrick should come with us. This is far from over."

CHAPTER
22

Kiara and Sam were the first to arrive, meeting with Attorneys Durrell and Murphy in their conference room. The attorneys manifested tension as they listened to Sam's threatening encounter with the mobsters. Cassie and the detective arrived five minutes later. Kiara also recounted the harrowing confrontation with the three men, detailing every moment of the nonfatal shooting that left Nuncio Lamartino, son of the notorious New Jersey Mob boss Santo Lamartino, wounded. Durrell and Murphy meticulously questioned Sam, ensuring his answers would be airtight in his official statement. Once satisfied, Durrell had her assistant type up the statements for Sam and Kiara to sign.

Minutes later, Alan Davies stormed in with another agent, confirming that the man shot was indeed Nuncio Lamartino, accompanied by two known felons from the Lamartino crime family. Durrell couldn't hide her satisfaction. The arrest of three Lamartino Mob members was a significant triumph. She insisted the FBI continue their investigation to gather evidence against Santo Lamartino.

"I'm still not satisfied with how Caviello got into this situation," Davies fumed. "He should have reported a potential confrontation so I could have sent agents to handle it properly."

"That's bullshit!" Sam snapped, his eyes blazing with resentment. "Kiara and I went to Professor Martin's office, not some Mob hideout. We had no idea Lamartino would be there. When his henchmen trapped us, we acted as any federal agents would—appropriately and effectively. We arrested three mobsters without a scratch on us."

Kiara nodded fiercely. "We did our job better than anyone else could have under those circumstances."

Davies glared at Sam. "I'm your superior and don't appreciate your tone."

"You're not superior to anyone in this room," Sam shot back, his voice ice-cold.

"Okay, that's enough!" Durrell's serious tone relieved the tension. "Alan, Kiara, and Sam have given their statements. Brian and I commend their performance under such duress. I want your office to find out if Santo Lamartino is culpable in the assault. Conduct a fingerprint comparison on the guns used so we can prosecute all three assailants. In addition, investigate if Professor Martin is a Lamartino in disguise."

Stung by Durrell's rebuke, Davies nodded curtly with squinted eyelids and a tense jaw. He left the office dejected with his assistant.

"Sorry about that, Sam," Durrell sighed. "You told me Davies had it in for you. I see it now."

"Thanks for the support. If there's nothing else, Kiara and I should get back to finding Travis Thornton."

With nothing else required, Sam and Kiara exited the federal building with Cassie and Kendrick following.

"Why do you think Davies is so uptight with you?" Kiara asked as they stepped into the sunlight.

"I haven't the faintest idea. Maybe it's because the senator requested I work on the case, causing Davies to feel his office should oversee the investigation without my help."

"Whatever," Kiara said, taking a deep breath. "What a day. It's great to inhale the fresh air after the stench that reeked in Martin's office. I don't know about you; I need a latte and something to eat. Let's head to that Starbucks we passed on our way here. Would you drive, Sam?"

Sam drove to Chapel Street. He spotted a vehicle leaving a parking space across from the café. "Perfect timing," he said, maneuvering into the spot.

"Good job. I'd be here all day trying to park in that tight space." Kiara laughed. "Are you joining me for coffee?

"I need to return a call. Are you dining inside or doing a takeout?

"I need to relax after dealing with those Mob thugs."

"I'll wait in the car. When you finish, could you bring me a coffee, cream, no sugar? My treat."

"I think I could afford to treat you to a coffee," she said jokingly. "I'm taking money but leaving my gun in my bag under the seat. Keep an eye on it?"

"I'll guard it with my life."

Kiara darted across the street and into the bustling Starbucks. She found the last empty table and quickly claimed it, leaving her jacket on the chair before heading to the counter. She ordered her favorite latte and a cinnamon coffee cake, then returned to her seat, taking a moment to decompress. She glanced around at the Yale students engrossed in their laptops. She looked out the window and saw Sam with his phone in his ear. The server soon brought her order. Kiara sipped her latte and sighed contentedly. "Mmm, that's good."

Sitting in the car, Sam hadn't had time to return the calls from Gabbi Walters, the Nashville Detective he partnered with to find the kidnapped eight-year-old Asian girl, Ena. Her phone rang five times before she finally answered.

"Sam. I'm glad it's you. How are you, and what have you been up to?"

"Everything is fine, just busy. I'm in New Haven, Connecticut, working with the FBI, looking for another missing person."

"You mean the senator's son?"

"Yes, but I don't want to discuss it on the phone. How are you doing with those big cases you made in Nashville? I wish I were there helping you get them ready for prosecution."

"I got a lot of help from the detectives and ATF Agent Aliyah Mayfield. Most of the suspects are pleading out, as are the two bikers we had the confrontation with at the church. Most are getting a deal but will serve time. Billy Lomax agreed to plead guilty, providing his sister, Angela, got no jail time for pleading to a misdemeanor charge."

"That's great. I thought you'd be tied to that case for a year or more, preparing for multiple trials. So I'm happy for you that it's almost over, and I hope you can take some time off to visit me in Boston."

"I have news for you. I can't come to Boston now, but I promise I will when I can. I decided to accept an offer to join ATF. In three weeks, I'll start training at the ATF Academy in Glynco, Georgia. I want to ace the training. Aliyah mentioned that the student who finishes first in the class gets awarded their choice of office assignment. I want to work in Boston with you. I miss you, Sam."

* * *

Kiara took a bite of her coffee cake, savoring the taste with a smile. Her eyes caught an older man with scraggly gray hair wearing a baseball cap entering the café. He seemed oddly familiar. Her eyes narrowed as he approached the counter, wondering where she had seen him before. It revealed itself when the guy reached for his wallet. His jacket swung open, revealing a gun tucked into his waist.

That's it, she thought. *It's the guy in the sketch that's wanted by the DA.*

Keeping a sharp eye out for the police, Alex appeared edgy. He glanced around the tables as he paid. Taking his change and coffee, he turned toward the exit and caught Kiara's stare.

Kiara's heart raced as she watched him hasten towards the exit. She gazed out the window, seeing Sam's phone still at his ear. She wished she could get his help telepathically, but couldn't, so she left her drink and cake and followed the wanted man outside.

When outside, Kiara called out, "Sir, hold up!" When he ignored her, she shouted, "FBI, stop!" She reached for her gun but remembered she had left it in the car.

Hearing the command to stop, Alex thought of running but impulsively turned to face the agent with a gun in hand. For a moment, he seemed puzzled. The agent had no weapon. Alex figured she wasn't alone and he could get arrested. He impulsively aimed only to wound her so he could escape. He pulled the trigger and quickly ran from the scene.

Kiara stood frozen, with her mouth open and eyes wide, watching the fiery blast from the gun. The bullet tore into her left shoulder, twisting her to the ground with searing pain.

CHAPTER
23

With the car window open and Sam on the phone with Gabbi, he felt a sudden jolt of fear when hearing a loud pop.

"What was that, Sam? It sounded like gunfire." Gabbi's voice trembled slightly.

"It was. I gotta go. Talk later."

Sam's response was abrupt, his body already in motion. He dashed out of the car, his eyes scanning for any sign of danger. A man was hurrying toward York Street, and Kiara was nowhere in sight. Sam sprinted across the street, his heart pounding against his chest. An oncoming vehicle's horn blared, startling Sam and narrowly smacking him into a parked car. Sam scrambled faster onto the sidewalk and pushed through a group of students to get within steps of the assailant.

Alex glanced back, his eyes squinting, with sneering lips concerned about getting caught by his chaser. He reached inside his waistband the second Sam sacked him to the ground. They both hit the pavement hard. Sam's mind reeled as the assailant's wig shifted, revealing short, darker hair underneath and his faux beard now covering his nose.

Alex instantaneously swung his arm towards Sam, the butt of his gun connecting with Sam's head above his right ear. Pain exploded with stars dancing in his vision, interrupting his scuffle momentarily, but he managed to cling onto the assailant's leg as Alex tried to pull away. Sam's grip slid down Alex's leg, freeing the black canvas sneaker and gray sock into his hand. Alex yanked the shoe away from Sam, but the sock remained in Sam's control.

Dazed, Sam watched Alex hobble away, straightening his disguise and replacing his hat. Sam staggered to his feet, stuffed the sock into his pocket, and regained his balance to chase Alex to York Street, where Alex had darted across. Not far behind, a delivery truck drove between them, blocking Sam's view. When the truck passed, Sam saw Alex enter a vehicle across the street and sped from the curb.

In the middle of the road, Sam pulled out his cell phone to capture the fleeing vehicle on video. As he steadied his camera, a loud horn blared, startling him. He twisted around to see a massive truck suddenly screech to a halt just feet away.

"This is a road, not a sidewalk, stupid!" the driver yelled.

Sam hurried to the sidewalk with a rapid heartbeat and breathing heavily. He momentarily stood dazed before realizing the guy he chased may have shot someone near Starbucks. He rushed back toward the cafe, a sense of dread growing as he approached a crowd gathered around a body on the ground. A siren wailed in the distance. Sam began running, praying it wasn't Kiara on the ground.

When he reached the scene, his heart sank. Kiara lay wounded, a woman kneeling beside her.

Sam yelled, "Police! Someone call an ambulance! Push back to give us room, please!" Sam's voice tinged with panic. He felt his heart thumping against his chest.

The woman assisting Kiara mentioned she had called for an ambulance.

"Sam," Kiara gasped, clutching her shoulder and whispering, "It was the guy, uh, . . . from the sketch . . ."

"Don't talk, Kiara," Sam urged, his voice shaking. "Help is on the way."

Sam looked at the woman assisting, saying, "Help me turn her toward me, lift her blouse, and check for an exit wound."

The woman followed Sam's instructions and confirmed there was an exit wound.

Sam retrieved QuikClot bandages from a pouch on his back belt, handing one to the woman. Without instruction, the woman expertly applied it to the exit wound while Sam addressed the entrance wound.

A police car arrived, followed by an ambulance. The officer pushed the crowd back, making way for the EMTs.

Sam flashed his badge, saying, "Secure the scene. Get a forensics team here and call Lieutenant Dawson, Major Crimes Unit. The victim is an FBI agent." He turned to the EMTs. "She's been shot in the left shoulder. Get her to the best trauma hospital in the city."

"That'll be Yale-New Haven Hospital," one EMT responded.

"I have to get to my car. I'll be right back. I'm riding with her to the hospital." Sam turned to the woman who had helped. "Are you a doctor?"

"I'm a nurse," she said, handing him her card. "I work at Yale-New Haven."

"Thank you." Sam sprinted to Kiara's car, securing the investigative files in the trunk and taking Kiara's bag with him before returning to the ambulance. As he climbed in the rear with Kiara, his phone rang.

"Sam, what's going on?" Lieutenant Dawson's voice was urgent.

"Agent Rivers was shot. They're taking her to Yale Hospital. Meet me there. I've got a photo of the shooter's getaway car." Sam's voice was steady, but concern was increasing inside him.

The ambulance sped away, its siren wailing. Sam held Kiara's hand, silently promising he wouldn't rest until he caught her shooter.

CHAPTER
24

Sam sat tensely in the emergency waiting room at the hospital, his fingers tapping an anxious rhythm on his thigh. He had already called both the local and Boston FBI offices to inform them of Kiara's injury. The Boston FBI supervisor, Dell Haskins, promised to drive to New Haven and arrive as soon as possible. Sam had also contacted Debra Durrell to brief her on the shooting incident.

"Do you think this has anything to do with the confrontation you and Kiara had with the Mob boss's son?" said Durrell.

"I'm not sure. I briefed Dell Haskins, who will be here soon, and I'll discuss it further with him."

"Do you have any further information on the shooter?"

"Not yet. I was in my car on the phone when I heard the shots. I saw the shooter leaving the scene and chased him. He got away in a car, but I recorded the vehicle and license plate. I'll have the New Haven detective I'm working with run the plate."

"That's great work, Sam."

"Thanks. I know finding Travis is our top priority, but I'm going to find the guy who shot Kiara. I can do both."

"I know you can. Keep me informed."

"Will do. The lieutenant just arrived. I have to go."

Lieutenant Cassie Dawson arrived with a blend of authority and calm. "What do you have for me, Sam?"

Sam played the video he obtained on his phone, zooming in on the license plate on the shooter's car.

Studying it closely, Cassie said, "It's a rental. I'll get it traced."

Cassie called her office, requesting that the officer run the plate number. Minutes later, the officer reported it was rented at a local car rental shop.

"Okay, the car rental shop is not far from here. But, before we leave the hospital, let's get you stitched up; you're bleeding." Cassie stepped away briefly, returning with a doctor who examined Sam's wound. Sam followed the doctor to an examination room, where he stitched the wound closed. Once finished, Sam asked the doctor if he could find out how Kiara was and if he could see her.

The doctor inquired and told Sam that Kiara was okay but still under anesthesia. "It may take a while for her to awaken."

Sam felt he was partially to blame for Kiara getting shot. He believed Kiara would never have gotten shot if he had been there to deal with the guy. When Sam entered Kiara's room, she was still unconscious, her face a canvas of pain. He held her hand while watching her intently, willing her to awaken so he would know she was all right. Cassie sat quietly, glancing at her watch periodically. Minutes later, FBI Agent Davies and a female agent entered.

"What's Kiara's status?" Davies asked.

Sam repeated the doctor's update. "The bullet damaged her shoulder. She'll need extensive rehab."

"How does this affect the Thornton case?"

"It's a minor setback. I'll continue working the Travis case once I find her shooter."

Davies rolled his eyes, showing displeasure. "Leave finding the shooter to us. You should focus on the Thornton case."

"Kiara is my partner. Let's work together on finding her shooter."

"Your mission in New Haven is the Thornton case. That's it."

Before Sam could respond, Kiara stirred, her eyes fluttering open. "Sam, you're here," she whispered, her voice weak.

"Yeah. How are you feeling?"

"Like I got hit by a truck," she replied, tears welling up. "Thanks for being there."

"What's important is that you'll be fine and back working soon. I'm going to find the creep that shot you."

Davies looked irritated with Sam's remark about finding Kiara's shooter but remained silent.

"I have to get back to work. I called to update Dell and Durrell," said Sam. "I brought your bag." He jokingly added, "I'm keeping the important item until you leave here. Do you want me to call anyone for you?"

"No, I'll handle it," she said, her voice still shaky.

As Sam left, Dawson mentioned that Davies wasn't very tactful with him.

"Yeah, well, I was going to turn over the sock to him, but I think the state can analyze it faster. Can you help with that?"

"Absolutely. I know someone who can expedite it. Let's head to the car rental place first, then we'll go to the lab."

"Thanks, Lieutenant. I appreciate it."

"It's Cassie, Sam. Let's work together on this case."

"Sounds good. Let's take two cars in the event you get called back to your office."

Sam followed the lieutenant after having her drop him off at Kiara's G-ride. Despite Davies's request that he not get involved, Sam was determined to find and arrest her shooter.

CHAPTER
25

The rental company office was a relatively gray stucco building on Route 5, a busy two-lane road in North Haven. It contained an office and a garage used for car cleaning and inspection.

Sam parked alongside the lieutenant's black sedan in front of the office. Exiting his car, Sam felt the bright sun peering from a cloud in the sky. A quick thought of being on the beach in the Caribbean passed Sam's mind as he followed the lieutenant into the office.

Dawson displayed her badge, asking for the manager, who was expecting her. Audrey appeared from a side door, waving Dawson and Sam to her office. After pleasantries, Audrey sat at her desk and pointed to her computer screen.

"I brought up the video from when the person who rented the car came into the office to sign the paperwork. Watch the screen as I start to play it."

They watched the shooter arrive to pick up the rental car. He wore sunglasses and a baseball cap pulled down to hide his face. The cap covered long, wavy gray hair. The guy wore similar clothing as he had on when Sam chased him from the shooting scene at the Starbucks. Sam could make out a beard as the guy completed the rental paperwork before leaving the office and driving away in the rental car.

Audrey said the renter, Elliot Townsman, rented the car for three days. It is supposed to be returned today, but he has not returned it yet.

"What do you want to do, Sam?"

"I'm going to wait until he shows up."

"I'll wait with you."

An hour passed before a similar vehicle pulled into the car return area near the open garage door. The driver exited the car facing away from the security camera on the building's front. He handed the rental paperwork to the outside attendant. The guy wore a different coat with a hood pulled over his head. Sam could make out the beard but not the guy's face. He was carrying a backpack on his right shoulder. He appeared to be a little shorter and thinner.

"I can't confirm it's the same rental until the attendant scans the return sheet," said Audrey.

The attendant studied the paperwork and began inspecting the vehicle for any damage before signing off on the car's return. In the meantime, the driver was on the phone. The attendant took his time with the examination. When he completed it, an SUV entered the parking lot and drove to where the suspected shooter was waving. The attendant scanned the return and provided a copy of the receipt to the guy, who immediately entered the driver's side backseat of the SUV. The SUV then left the lot, heading north on Route 5.

"Give me a second to check the vehicle numbers," said Audrey. "Let's see…yep, it's the same car."

"Let's follow them," said Sam, who rushed to his car, drove off, and caught up to the SUV. He tailed the Hyundai for three miles before it pulled into a hotel parking lot and around to the back lot.

"That was quick," said Dawson on her cell phone.

"I'd say. The question is, will the guy spend the night or check out to head home? I'm going to wait. Can you? It might be a while."

"I'll call my office and tell them I'm on surveillance."

"I'll take the back exit, and you watch the front. Stay on the phone so that we can talk."

The lieutenant called her office, took a message, then told Sam she had to return to her office and left the parking lot.

At the back of the hotel, Sam stayed in the first row of parked vehicles and saw the SUV had stopped in the second row to his right. A large delivery van blocked his view of the suspect exiting the SUV and entering another vehicle. Sam backed up and spotted the top of a black sedan leaving from behind the delivery truck. Watching through his rearview mirror, he saw a black BMW driving toward the front of the hotel and turning right on Route 15 South.

Sam backed into the space between two parked cars and sped toward the road. Traffic was heavy, causing Sam to wait more than he wanted to turn onto 15 South. When he had the chance, Sam stormed onto the road and passed a couple of vehicles until he saw the BMW. He slowed, staying behind a van. Ten minutes later, the BMW took an exit. Sam followed the sedan onto Route 67. He continued following through the towns of Seymour and Oxford, then crossed I-84 through Southbury, Roxbury, and into Washington.

They drove past a boutique inn and spa in Washington before stopping near the town's green, where the BMW pulled into a café parking lot. Sam pulled over to an open space on the street and walked to the café, a faded, white, historic two-story building converted into a quaint local café. Standing at the café entrance, Sam took a few seconds to admire the beautiful white steepled church across the street, a typical site in many old New England communities. There was little foot traffic in the business district, but many vehicles were parked outside several business fronts. When Sam entered the coffee shop, he first scanned the tables for the suspect but didn't spot him.

The café resembled a combination general store and a coffee, pastries, and sandwich shop. It immediately brought back memories of his teenage years in his hometown, meeting friends at a similar sandwich eatery. Sam sat at a small six-seat counter, gazing at the people seated at the dining tables. He guessed most were locals enjoying a meal with family or friends. He smiled, watching two joyful toddlers with big smiles feeding themselves with their fingers and bits of food dripping down their mouths. It was obvious to Sam that the elderly gentleman and woman at the table were the kids' grandparents, loving every minute with the youngsters. Sam ordered a coffee while studying the menu for something to eat until he saw the display of pastries across from him. Some looked so delicious they appeared to cry out, "Try me."

When the waitress delivered a cup of coffee, Sam took a sip while glancing back at the dining area. He saw a person who wore a jacket similar to the guy who returned the rental car entering the dining area from a rear hallway. A sign above pointed to the restrooms.

That person stared at him with a puzzled look. Now looking irritable, that person marched directly toward him. Sam turned away, pretending to look at the menu.

CHAPTER
26

S am remained looking away from the person who stormed toward him. He wanted to avoid an altercation. He continued drinking his coffee, staring at the menu.

"Who are you, and why are you following me?" asked the person.

Sam pretended whoever spoke wasn't talking to him.

"Hey, you at the counter. I'm talking to you. Answer me."

Sam turned to face the person. He was captivated but not surprised by who he saw. He sat speechless, unable to immediately respond to a beautiful, slender young woman standing before him. He immediately thought he might have followed the wrong person.

"Answer me. Why are you following me? Are you a cop?"

Sam, thinking fast, stood, faced her, and shook his head, no. "I'm a reporter."

"A reporter. What could you be writing about that concerns me?"

"I'm a crime reporter. I travel anywhere there's a crime of interest to readers."

"What do crime stories have to do with me?"

"I have no idea. I left New Haven a short time ago. I was there interviewing a Yale University professor for a story I'm doing. When I left his office, I heard a gunshot and a commotion nearby. I headed in the direction of the shot and learned that someone had shot an FBI agent. I took as much information as possible at the scene, but the police detective in charge would make no statement until they completed an investigation. I plan on interviewing her tomorrow."

"So you just happened to be where a crime occurred. Lucky you. There must have been a lot of people to interview who might have witnessed the shooting."

"I did interview three women at the scene, but I have an appointment to meet a friend near Waramaug Lake. I'm joining her to hike the scenic trails and photograph the beautiful sunsets she bragged about. I plan on returning to New Haven in the morning. I apologize if it seemed I was following you. When I drove by this café, I stopped to grab a coffee and have something to eat."

"Was the FBI agent all right? Was she seriously injured?"

"Do you mind if we sit and chat? I'm short on time. I need to grab something to eat with my coffee in a hurry. I want to get to the lake soon. Coffee and a sandwich are on me."

The young woman agreed only to hear what the reporter had to say about the shooting in New Haven. She led Sam to a far table. The waitress asked if they needed a menu. The woman said she only wanted a coffee to go.

Sam brought his coffee from the counter and said, "I'll have the white lemon-filled pastry that called out for me to taste it."

"Good choice," said the waitress.

"Having pastries with their coffee seems more like something cops would order," the young woman said suspiciously.

"I, uh, always heard it was donuts the police ordered with their coffee."

"What paper do you work for?" asked the woman.

"I guess you could say many. I'm a freelance reporter."

"What's your name again?

"It's Sam. What's yours?"

"I prefer not to give my name."

"Can you tell me why?"

"I don't want my name mentioned in your stories."

"Well, I'm not planning to—"

The waitress brought a coffee for the young woman, who sipped it before asking, "Can you answer my question? Was the FBI agent all right?" she asked in a concerned tone. "Was she seriously injured?"

"The police kept everyone back from her. I saw a woman and an officer in plain clothes giving aid before the ambulance arrived. Do you know anything about it or know who was involved with the shooting?"

Suddenly, the woman frowned, her lips rigid and eyes narrowing, as she looked intensely at Sam. "What? Why would I know anything about the shooting? I just wanted to know if the agent was okay. I'm done here." The woman started to walk by Sam without her coffee but stopped to gaze at him as if she had seen him before, then said, "Don't follow me. If you do, I'll call the police and have them arrest you for stalking me."

Sam looked around the dining area, seeing others in the room looking his way. He took a large bite of the small pastry and then stuffed the rest into his mouth. He washed it down with his coffee. Sam scanned the café again to ensure no one was still looking his way. He then poured the woman's coffee cup left behind into his cup. Sam held the bottom of the cup, wrapped it in a napkin, and left the café with it. He took her cup to have it analyzed for fingerprints and DNA. He left money to cover the cost of the two coffees and pastry before hurrying to the side door. Sam watched the young woman exit the parking lot and turn right.

He rushed out the door and jogged to the G-ride half a block away. He floored the car, squealing the tires, as he left the parking space, trying to catch up to her. Once he spotted her vehicle up ahead, he allowed a car ready to pull out of a driveway to drive out in front of him. Sam didn't want the young woman to see his car behind her. They traveled north on Route 47 until they approached Route 202, where she turned toward the village of New Preston. Sam slowed to allow another vehicle to pass him and remained a reasonable distance between them. A short way south on 202, the BMW turned right. The car in front of Sam continued on 202, so Sam slowed before taking the right turn onto Lake Road, where he maintained a greater distance behind the BMW. He continued driving toward Lake Waramaug State Park when his cell phone rang. He saw the call was from Detective Dawson, so he answered it.

"Hey, Sam. Any luck at your end?"

"I'm not sure. I'm still tailing the person, hopefully, to a residence. I have the plate number and ran it through the ATF office, and I should get a call back soon."

"Sorry, I had to leave you," said Cassie. "I got a call from the office and needed to respond to a scene. Call me later, and we can meet."

"Listen, Cassie. I have a coffee cup the suspect drank from. Can we give the cup and sock to your friend at the state lab for DNA and fingerprint analysis soon?"

"Let's get it to the lab tomorrow."

"Okay, great. Talk soon." Sam ended the call and continued tailing the BMW from afar until it turned left. He slowed to a crawl when he realized it had turned into a dirt driveway. Sam pulled over to the side of the road to study the area. Trees and brush covered a good part of both sides of the road he was on. Pressing the gas pedal slightly, he inched closer to the driveway. Trees blocked the house at the end of the long driveway. Sam could only make out the roof line. He drove further and turned off the road into a space between a few trees and overgrown weeds on the opposite side.

Sam wanted a closer look at the house and its surroundings, so he crossed the road into a treed property on the right side of the driveway to get a clearer view. When deep enough into the trees and brush, Sam estimated the house sat about sixty yards from the road. It was an aged rustic cape with worn brownish wooden shingles and original windows. He didn't see the BMW parked near the house. As he crept slowly toward the rear of the house, he heard a dog bark.

Oh no, not a dog. I better not get too close, thought Sam apprehensively. He advanced ten more feet before seeing a barn behind the cape. The woman had parked the BMW between the cape and the barn. Sam hid behind a vast tree, peaking at the old barn with only one wide door that slid open. Sam heard the woman call for the dog from inside the barn. He watched the woman at the barn door with the dog at her side. She crouched, petted, and talked to the dog as it licked her face. Sam guessed the dog was a Rottweiler, and he had no desire to be seen and confronted by it. The woman stood up and walked the dog to the rear of the house, presumably to enter it. Sam decided not to press his luck. He gave her enough time to enter the house, then began trampling back to his car. His cell began to ring. He quickly lowered the volume. Seeing it was the ATF office, he answered it by whispering.

"Hi, Sam. I have the registration info for you. Are you ready to copy?"

"Give me a second," he said as he reached his car and retrieved a pen and notepad. "Okay, I'm ready."

The Intelligence Assistant (IA) reported that the black BMW was a White Plains, New York rental. The IA gave Sam the name of the current renter, who contracted the vehicle two weeks ago. "I did a wants and warrants check on the owner, which came back negative. I also searched nationally for the owner's name and found nothing locally; there were several similar names, but not with the same DOB or description."

"I'm going to try to get an address of a residence I'm watching. Once I have it, I'll call you back. Thanks."

Sam decided to drive back to New Haven and meet with Lieutenant Dawson.

CHAPTER
27

Bones woke up at nearly nine the following day. He was groggy from drinking the night before and needed time to remember what he had to do this morning. He washed his face with ice-cold water and drank coffee before realizing he had to warn his friend Acosta. He grabbed his truck keys and drove to a small shop that sold burner phones. He purchased two burner phones in case one got compromised. He then arrived at where Acosta worked as a security guard in Bridgeport. He entered the building and approached Tony, who sat behind the security desk.

"What are you doing here, Bones?"

"I have to talk to you, man. That vigilante guy who popped in on Zee and Gil broke into my place last night and threatened to kill me for chrissake. The guy means business. He wanted information on us, but I made most of it up. If I didn't give him something, he'd kill me."

"What information did you give him?"

Bones hesitated before lying, saying he had heard rumors that Gil and Zee robbed some rich people's homes in Connecticut. I said nothing about you and me."

"What? Gil and Zee will kill you if they find out you ratted them out. You know that, right?"

"I had to tell the guy something. He had a cocked gun against the back of my head. I came to tell you we gotta do something about this guy. You know what I mean?"

"Any idea who this guy is?" Hearing the front door open, Acosta looked to see who the visitor was. "Bones, someone's coming to the desk. Move away until they leave."

Bones walked over to the building directory, pretending to look for a name. He glanced at the security desk until the visitor walked to the elevators. He then returned to the desk.

"So, do you know who this guy is? If you don't, how do you figure us getting to him?"

"The guy didn't leave his calling card. He's not stupid, you know. He said his name was Danny, thinking we'd remember the name from a hit we made. Anyway, he's been to Zee's place, Gil's, and now my place. So that leaves only you, man. He's coming for you next. Maybe we watch your place to get him when he shows up."

"We better call Gil and get everybody together on this."

"Gil could hardly walk, so he can't help us other than give orders. So let's you, Zee, and me talk it over and make a plan to nail this guy."

"We should let Gil know what we're planning to do."

"I'm not calling Gil. You can if you want to."

"When do you think we should do this?"

"This prick is not taking his time getting to us. So let's start after work. I'll call Zee and have him meet us if he's not hiding somewhere. We could meet at a pub near your apartment. After we agree on a plan, we set up at your place and wait for this guy when he shows up. When he does, he's in for a big surprise."

*   *   *

The following day, an unsettling itch drove Sam back to New Preston Village, a quaint hamlet nestled in rolling hills and whispering pines. He couldn't shake the mystery of the woman in the sleek BMW from his mind.

Her enigmatic presence pulled at him like an invisible thread, compelling him to uncover if she was the shooter and why.

Sam's first stop was the local post office, nestled within a modest strip mall—a small cluster of shops located only a quarter mile from the woman's residence on the same side of the winding street. The strip mall was a microcosm of village life, featuring a stationery shop brimming with quaint greeting cards, a cozy café exuding the rich aroma of freshly brewed coffee, a liquor store, and the post office, where an elderly clerk presided over the counter like a guardian of village secrets.

Inside, Sam introduced himself to the clerk, who's wrinkled face revealed creases with the lines of time. He inquired about the address just down the road.

"I don't do the mail route in town. I only work behind the counter," replied the clerk. "You'd have to talk to the delivery carrier who delivers the mail on that road."

"Who is the carrier, and is he delivering mail there now?"

The clerk glanced at a clock on the back wall, its ticking the only sound punctuating the silence. "His name is Walter. He should be delivering on that road somewhere. He usually brings his lunch and might have stopped at a friend's house to chat."

"Does his friend live on the same road, and would I be able to spot his postal vehicle from there?"

"Walter is a contract carrier and drives his car. I think it's an old gray Chevy. I don't know his friend or where he lives," she responded.

"Okay. Thanks for your help, ma'am," muttered Sam.

Outside, Sam threw up his arms in exasperation, feeling like he was chasing shadows in a fog. He climbed back into his car and drove past the young woman's house, his eyes scanning both sides of the road for any sign of the elusive gray Chevy, but the road stretched empty before him. Disappointed, he turned around and parked behind the strip mall, deciding that the wooded area separating the mall from the house was short enough to traverse on foot. The only obstacle was a chain-link fence, its dull metal gleaming in the sunlight at the tree line.

From the trunk, Sam retrieved a fanny pack stuffed with essentials, including tools, gloves, and a baseball cap. He walked along the five-foot tall fence, searching for something to boost him over it. He walked about twenty yards, where he found a large boulder, its surface rough and weathered, standing about two feet high. Sam donned his gloves, stepped onto the rock, and scaled the fence with a grunt of effort.

He crept through the woods, each step crunching softly on the fallen leaves until he found cover behind a broad tree. He could see the open front barn door from this vantage point, but the property was eerily silent. He assumed the woman and her dog must be around since the barn door remained ajar.

Patience became his ally as he waited until the sound of an engine startled him. A woman's voice called to the dog, followed by the thud of a car door closing. A midnight blue Mustang convertible backed out of the barn, its top down, revealing a flash of the driver's dark reddish hair whipping in the breeze. Sam guessed the convertible was a 2015 model, its glossy finish gleaming under the sun. The woman exited the car, slid the garage door shut with a metallic clang, locked it, and drove off, the dog a silent sentinel in the passenger seat. The car disappeared down the road towards the business district. Sam breathed easier, happy the dog didn't catch his scent and started barking.

Relieved, Sam edged out from behind the tree and approached the BMW, his curiosity piqued by the barn. But the sudden crunch of gravel under tires made his heart leap into his throat. *Damn. She's back already?* Sam thought. With no time to find a proper hiding spot, he crouched low and shuffled around the BMW, taking cover behind the front grille. The vehicle stopped. Sam heard footsteps like someone walking, then pausing, then walking again before a car door slammed shut echoed through the air.

Remaining behind the grille, Sam heard the vehicle drive toward the barn—his heart rate quickened. He worried that the dog would sense him hiding behind the BMW. When the car stopped, he ducked lower. His knees ached from the prolonged crouch, and his breaths came shallow and quick. The vehicle seemed to move, maybe making a turn, and drove forward again, heading toward the road. He peeked to get a look at it as it went past him. *Phew* signed Sam as relief washed over him. He felt a twinge of foolishness for being spooked. It wasn't the Mustang he saw. It was the postal carrier, Walter, in his Chevy delivering the mail. Sam shook his head in disbelief, amused by how he thought the woman had returned, worrying about the Rottweiler, the real threat.

With the Chevy gone, Sam straightened up and pushed aside his uneasiness. He hustled to the house's front door, knowing Walter held the key to the house's address. Sam searched for the mailbox, finding it near the front door. He pulled out four letters: one addressed to Alexis Townsend, one to J. Townsend, and two to E. Donnelley, all marked with the address 44 Shore Hill Road. Sam snapped photos of the letters and replaced them, his mind swirling with questions about the names. At least he knew the address now. He could investigate the names later.

Wasting no time, he dashed toward the barn, eager to uncover its secrets. As he passed the BMW, he glanced back and realized something he had overlooked. He moved to the passenger side and tried the door handle. To his surprise, it opened. He rummaged through the glove box, finding a car rental document. The rental documents listed the renter as TJ Realty, with a Scarsdale, New York address, and the renter's name was T. James Townsend. Sam quickly photographed the documents, heart thudding with the thrill of discovery.

He approached the barn cautiously, glancing over his shoulder to ensure the woman hadn't returned. The barn's exterior was a patchwork of old and new, with two freshly installed windows and skylights on the east side casting soft light into the dim interior.

He spotted a dark-tinted double window in the back beside another sliding barn door. Peeking through the windows, he saw a modest living space—a kitchen, a small dinette, a love seat, and a desk cluttered with papers. It looked like the young woman lived there rather than the house in front.

Sam examined the sliding barn door, secured with a heavy padlock. To the right, an original small window, high off the ground, seemingly the most accessible entry point. The window was about six feet up, making it difficult for him to reach and open. He spotted two wooden pallets nearby that could serve as a makeshift ladder. He dragged one over, leaning it against the barn like a ladder, and climbed up. The window was stubborn, probably sealed shut from years of neglect. Sam pulled a mini pry bar from his fanny pack, wedged it under the window, and forced it open just enough to grasp and push it up far enough to slip through.

Inside, he landed softly on the floor, taking in the barn's interior—a mix of storage and a cozy living space. One side was cluttered with garden tools, a rusty old lawn mower, and a snow blower, while the other housed the woman's living quarters. A new wooden door with a standard doorknob and two deadbolts marked the entrance to her apartment.

Sam made quick work of the locks with his picks and stepped inside. The room was a testament to meticulous care, with light-colored walls and neat arrangements. An L-shaped kitchen counter held a stovetop, microwave, and small dishwasher. A sink beneath the double windows overlooked a small garden and an open, overgrown field. A small couch sat beside a wall beneath the east side window. There were two doors on the opposite wall from the kitchen, one leading to a closet and the other to a narrow hallway.

In the center of the room, a dinette table stood against the wall, surrounded by three chairs. To the left was a desk cluttered with a laptop, papers, and a cup of pens. Against the desk, Sam saw two guns: a 12-gauge Remington shotgun and a .30-30 Winchester rifle. Sam, wearing surgical gloves, inspected them, finding both were loaded. He unloaded the guns and then returned them to their places. He placed the ammo under a stack of paper on the right side of the bottom drawer. He knew he'd return here and didn't want to face the woman with one of these loaded guns.

The desk drawers held more secrets: a loaded Glock 9mm, a family photo album, and another album filled with newspaper clippings about robberies and murders in southwestern Connecticut. Sam skimmed through the articles. Sam found another folder with notes on four robbery suspects, a police detective, a prosecutor, and a photo of three men and a woman. Someone had hand-printed the first name of each person in the photo.

There has to be a connection between what happened near the Connecticut shore and the young woman, thought Sam. He searched the other drawers and found a zippered travel wallet holding two motor vehicle licenses with the young woman's photo and names Sam hadn't expected. *Maybe I followed the wrong person from the hotel,* wondered Sam. However, Sam was curious about why the woman kept the newspaper articles, so he took pictures of them, the notes, and the photo to study and interpret later. Sam saw a Smith and Wesson Equalizer 9MM pistol in the last drawer. He heard what sounded like a dog barking outside. He closed the drawer and carefully listened for a car driving to the front of the barn.

Not hearing anything, he moved on to the two doors by the wall. The first opened into a narrow room with the furnace and AC units. The second door led Sam into a narrow hallway with a washer and dryer behind slatted closet doors. Past the laundry, he entered a small bedroom, its double bed neatly made and an end table with a lamp, an alarm clock, and a family photo beside it. Sam studied the photo. *Interesting,* Sam thought. He snapped a picture of it and returned it to the end table. The room was a serene haven, painted in soft blue, with a royal blue curtain hanging on each side of the single window. A door led to a tiny bathroom with a white sink, vanity, mirror, and shower stall.

Sam returned to the main room when he heard the sound of a car stopping near the barn. It sent a jolt of panic through him. He scanned the room to ensure he hadn't left any traces of his presence, then turned the doorknob to its lock position and shut the door softly. He then heard someone unlocking the front sliding barn door. Not having time to lock the deadbolts, Sam dashed to the exit window to escape before he got caught.

CHAPTER
28

A t the rear window, Sam searched for something sturdy enough to support his weight. An old carpentry horse caught his attention—weathered by time but still worthy. Sam dragged it against the inside wall, its wooden legs scraping softly against the earth. He cautiously stepped onto the horse, placing his hands on the still. The horse wobbled under his shifting weight.

Sam put one leg over the window sill. Crouching down and using his other foot to thrust himself through the window, the horse buckled and clattered to the ground. The noise echoed through the silence like a gunshot in the night. Sam panicked, his heart pounding against his chest.

Outside, the young woman paused at the barn door, her ears pricked by the sudden commotion. Rusty, the woman's Rottweiler, paced and growled from the Mustang's front seat. The dog's sensitive scent detected a threat and barked. The woman's fingers trembled as she struggled to open the barn door. Sensing an opportunity, Rusty leaped from the car and bolted into the barn, its barks reverberating off the wooden walls.

Sam's foot groped blindly for the wooden pallet he'd placed earlier. His foot hit the loose top board, causing it to break loose. Sam slid down the pallet, crashing to the ground. The impact knocked the wind from his lungs. Pain seared through his hip and shoulder. He let out a strangled cry.

Rolling onto his stomach, he grimaced, clutching at the dirt, his body protesting each movement. The dog's snarls grew closer on the other side of the barn's wall. Fueled by adrenaline and a primal fear, Sam grabbed the pallet and placed it where he found it. He heard the dog's growl from the open window. He instantly bolted for the woods, glancing over his shoulder for the dog, every step a painful reminder of his fall.

Inside the barn, the young woman followed the dog's barks to the open window. Realization dawned on her, and she rushed outside, her heart racing like a horse. The dog, agitated and growling, trailed her as she scanned the barn's backside, her eyes desperate to catch sight of the intruder.

Sam heard the distant barking growing louder sixty yards deep into the woods. He pushed himself to move faster, each step a struggle against the low branches clawing at his face and the roots eager to trip him. Apprehension clenched his stomach when looking back repeatedly, expecting the dog to appear at any moment. In his panic, he didn't notice the fallen branch ahead. His foot caught the branch, sending him airborne, crashing into the wet, leaf-strewn ground with a thud.

The cold earth pressed against his skin. He could feel sweat trickling down his face. His heart raced, the pounding in his chest almost drowning out the sound of the dog's persistent barking. He pushed himself up, his body aching, and continued his desperate dash towards the fence. Anxiety gnawed at him, his thoughts a jumble of escape and urgency.

Sam saw the fence yards ahead. He glanced back, his blood running cold as he saw the dog—a blur of fur and fury—chasing and getting close. "Shit," he whispered, his voice barely audible over the sound of his ragged breathing. Desperation fueled his legs, propelling him forward. By chance, he spotted a low-hanging tree limb that partially overhung the fence and made a beeline for it.

The dog's snarls were close enough to send chills down his spine, its hot breath almost tangible on his heels. With a burst of strength, Sam leaped, his fingers grasping the rough bark of the limb. His left hand slipped as he hung by one grip. The dog was near and ready to grab at his feet. Sam struggled for breath, stretching his left arm to grip the tree. The dog jumped, his teeth catching the heel of Sam's sneaker, knocking it off his foot. Concerned that the dog might gnaw at his shoeless foot, Sam swung back and forward, throwing both legs high. As he did, the dog's jump missed snatching a foot by a hair. With all his strength, Sam swung his legs high enough to clear the fence while letting go of the limb. He hit the ground hard on the other side, the impact jarring his bones.

The dog hurled itself at the fence, shaking it like it was trying to knock it down. The dog growled, filled with frustration and rage. Sam stared wide-eyed, panting at the sight, his chest rapidly heaving. Slowly, he pulled himself up, his legs trembling as he limped toward his car. Sam opened the truck and pulled out a pair of shoes from his go-bag. He slid into the driver's seat, his ego bruised and body aching. He slammed the door behind him. Sam momentarily stared back at the dog, still growling with its front paws halfway up the fence. The dog settled down, grabbed Sam's sneaker with his mouth, and rushed back to show his owner the trophy he got.

"Oh, sure. Steal my sneaker. You owe me a new pair, pal." Sam whispered. He put the car in gear and drove off, the tires kicking up gravel, while his eyes darted to the rearview mirror. Relief washed over him as images of the dog receded into the distance. Hugging the steering wheel, he wiped the sweat from his brow, his breath shaky. "That was close. You can bet I won't do anything that stupid again," he muttered, a hint of a nervous chuckle escaping his lips. He drove less than two miles when he received a call from Lieutenant Dawson again, telling him they had another sniper shooting."

"Can you return to the scene with me," Cassie said. "I could use your help to find what we may have missed. I'll explain more when you get here."

"I'm on my way to New Haven. It'll take an hour to get there. When I do, I want to first look in on Kiara. Do you think there's a connection between this shooting and the one at the beverage company several days back?"

"I'm not sure. At first, I didn't think they were connected. The shooter at the beverage company made perfect hits. In this incident, the shooter's shots weren't accurate because he missed killing his targets. I'll meet you at the hospital. We could go to the scene after we leave there."

CHAPTER
29

hen Sam entered Kiara's hospital room, he recognized FBI supervisor Dell Haskins standing next to Kiara's bed on one side and a Hispanic female that Sam didn't know on the other. Sam first shook hands with Dell, exchanged greetings, and then switched places with him at the side of Kiara's bed.

"How are you doing, Kiara?"

"The shoulder hurts when the drug wears off, but I'm doing okay. The nurse said they would start rehab on the shoulder later today. I'm not looking forward to it. Are you getting any headway finding Travis?"

"I haven't worked on that since your injury."

"Why? What have you been doing then?"

Sam whispered his answer. "Trying to find the person who shot you."

"Any luck?"

"Some."

In return, Kiara gave him a puzzled look but thought Sam didn't want to say too much with others in the room. She changed the subject.

"Sam, this is Mariela Moreno, my friend I told you about."

Sam reached over the bed to shake Mariela's hand, assuming this was Kiara's lover and knowing she wanted to keep it between them. "A pleasure to meet you, Mariela."

Mariela nodded in kind with a smile and shook Sam's hand.

Haskins stepped behind Sam and asked if they could speak privately. They walked into the hall outside the room.

"I had a conversation with Alan Davies. He told me it was his understanding that you are working with us only on the Travis Thornton case and not investigating the guy who shot Kiara. He feels that it's his office's job to investigate the shooting of an FBI agent in New Haven, and I agree with him. However, Davies is pissed you're working on both cases."

Sam maintained eye-to-eye contact with Haskins, whom Sam respected. Sam nodded, agreeing that Davies had concerns but disagreed with them.

"Listen, Dell, regarding the Thornton case, Kiara and I have updated you whenever we have made progress. I shouldn't have to apprise Davies, too. Regarding the shooting, I'm Kiara's partner working on a case assigned by the Boston FBI office. You could count on the fact that I'll find the bastard that shot her, and I'm sure you would do the same if she were your partner. I hope you understand where I'm coming from, and I believe you know I'll find the shooter. I'm here under your supervision and will report any progress on the shooting to you. Kiara is a Boston agent—your agent—not Davies. For one reason or another, Davies opposes my work on any FBI-related cases in New Haven. I guess he feels New Haven is his domain, and all FBI investigations should be under his control, not Boston's. He has a point, but his dispute over who should have control should be with you, not me."

Dell had a predicament, knowing Kiara's shooting was exclusively under the FBI's jurisdiction, but he also knew Sam had an extraordinary talent for finding suspects. He put himself in Sam's shoes, knowing he would do as Sam was doing and work the case to find the person who shot his partner regardless of what agency had the jurisdiction.

Dell, a personable, sensible supervisor with an infectious smile, nodded affirmatively. "I understand your position. I probably would do the same. Nevertheless, I expect you to update me on everything, even if you think it's unimportant. I need to know what you accomplished at the end of every day. In turn, I'll keep Davies up to speed. Can you do that?"

"Yeah, but I don't want other agents interfering with my inquiries. They'll only mess things up. Let me do my thing, and I'll get results."

"Okay. You have my backing to do what you are doing, but keep me informed every step of the way. I'll handle Davies. Understand?"

"I do. Thanks, Dell. Any info on Jarrett and Martin yet?"

"Nothing yet."

"I have another name for you to check. Thomas James Townsend. He operates a business called TJ Realty in Scarsdale, New York. He's connected to Kiara's shooter, not the Travis Thornton investigation."

"Okay. I'll get back to you on what we learn."

"Do me a favor. Would you ask Davies to assign security agents to Kiara's room?"

"You think there's a connection between the confrontation you and Kiara had with Lamartino's son and her getting shot?"

"We shouldn't rule it out. Let's not take any chances that the Lamartino family won't retaliate against her and me for shooting one of the family members."

"I'll speak to Davies about the security before returning to Boston. Keep in touch."

Sam entered Kiara's room, walked to Kiara's bedside, and took her hand. "I'm getting close to finding who shot you, so I hope you get well enough to work with me when we arrest the guy. You won't need to use your arm. I'll be at your side every minute."

"What about the Travis case?"

"Once we get the shooter, we'll return to finding Travis. I promise."

"Kiara, remember what we've been talking about?" said Mariela Moreno.

"We'll talk about it in private, okay?" said Kiara, who then turned to Sam. "I'd like for us to focus on finding Travis. That's our mission here. We can arrest the guy who shot me later. Can we do that, Sam?"

"Whatever. I have to leave now and give Cassie a hand on another matter. I'll visit again tomorrow. So get better and get ready."

Sam and Cassie left the hospital.

"Sam, let's leave your car at the PD. You can ride with me."

"Okay, I'll follow you to the PD."

"You promised Kiara you'd find her shooter and Travis. Can I also count on you to find the shooter involved in my investigations?"

"I'll do what I can. Let's go see what we can find."

CHAPTER

30

L ieutenant Dawson pulled over to the side of the street a distance from the first shooting site. She led Sam into the wooded state park until they reached the location where the police determined the shooter had fired his weapon.

"Did you find any evidence at the shooting scene?" asked Sam.

"No, and we searched for more than an hour."

"Was it the same area used in the beverage company shooting?"

"No. It's about the distance of a football field from the other site here. The shooter hit two kids just outside the high school athletic field: no deaths, but serious injuries to the hip near the groin area on one kid. The shooter hit the other kid in the right arm, his strong arm. We recovered the spent bullets at the school, but not the cartridges."

"You're satisfied that your team thoroughly searched this area and found no spent cartridges?" said Sam.

"Yes."

Sam studied the school down the hill from where he was standing. "The guy had to be a great shot to hit those two kids from here. I'd have to believe the gun had a scope set perfectly for the distance. The shooter had to be skilled with weapons or a practiced user. Regarding the AR-15 your detectives took from the Callahan house, did the examiners find any indication the rifle ever had a scope fixed to it?

"The examiner reported the gun did have scratch marks on the upper receiver, presumably made by a scope, but we didn't find one at the house during our search."

Let's focus on the brush along the path on the way out. Look for broken branches, anything dangling that doesn't belong there, such as torn pieces of cloth—anything out of place. Also, if you spot branches pushed aside or it appears someone stepped on the ground cover leading in another direction, let me know. We'll follow it and see where it brings us."

Sam and Cassie deliberately strolled the path back toward the road, fixating on the bushes, tree branches, and dense ground cover. Cassie took the left side, Sam the right. More than halfway back to the road, Cassie stopped when she spotted bush branches broken and pushed aside. She also noticed someone trampled the ground cover leading to the left.

"Sam, take a look at this area. Is this what you were talking about?"

"Absolutely. Good eyes, Cass. You found it, so you lead."

"Oh, you want me to clear the way for you so you don't get pricked or scratched," Cassie said jokingly.

Sam chuckled and kidded back. "Exactly. Better you than me. I don't want to rip my pants."

Cassie walked forward into the brush and, after several steps, yelled, "Ouch! Damn it. I got pricked by thorns already. You get in front. This was your idea."

Sam pushed his way past Cassie and asked to see her scratch. A tiny blood droplet oozed from the broken skin on a fingertip. He reached into the pouch on the small of his back and took out a small container of Band-Aids. He wiped the blood with tissue from his pocket, kissed her boo-boo in fun, saying, "All better, now," and applied the Band-Aid. Cassie slapped his arm softly, giggling, saying, "Thanks, Daddy." They both laughed and moved forward. They stumbled and swaggered about thirty yards before approaching a ten-foot-tall rock ridge maybe twenty-five yards long.

Using his phone's compass, Sam recognized the rock formation stretched towards the direction of the road. "Let's inspect this ridge. Look for anything unusual or out-of-place road."

They inspected the rock formation where it met the ground. They didn't see anything unusual until Cassie pointed to broken tree branches and leaves that didn't look natural placed against the rock wall.

"Cass, you should do the honors of clearing the brush from the rock."

"I don't think so. There could be a snake behind it. You do it."

"I thought you were a trained cop with a gun. You shouldn't be afraid of some small animal that might jump out and attack you," said Sam, chuckling again. "Come on, Cass, you found this path. Someone could have hidden something behind those branches. It could be evidence. You should be the one to find it. "

Cassie scowled at him. "If there's something scary behind the branches, I will get even with you big time."

"Come on, lieutenant. I'll back you up."

"All right, I'll do it." Cassie grabbed a thick, broken tree branch about eight feet long on the ground. She stepped closer to the branches against the rock wall and pulled them aside. When the area was clear of the leaves and tree limbs, Cassie and Sam stared at what they saw hidden inside a small cavity of the rock formation.

"What the hell is that?" said Cassie.

Sam focused on what was inside the hollow space. "It looks like a dark blue tarp. I hope it's not a body. Pull it out and unwrap it. It could be something connected to your case."

Cassie hesitated with tensed lips before dragging it out in the open. She stood gaping at the tarp, exhaled, and looked at Sam to check it out.

"Don't look at me. Unwrap it."

"I'm afraid of snakes. Suppose one is inside. You unwrap it, Sam."

Sam shrugged his shoulders and gave her a curious look before saying, "I think you should do it. You led us here, so you should get the credit for finding evidence if that's what it is."

Cassie hesitated, went down on one knee, and cautiously unwrapped the tarp to reveal what was inside.

"Oh, my God!" cried out Cassie.

CHAPTER

31

An astonished Cassie gazed at Sam, her eyebrows raised and mouth wide open. "I don't believe it, Sam! It's the M4 and ammo! We found it! You're amazing!"

"Whataya mean? You're amazing. You found it. It's your case. I'm here only to assist."

"I wouldn't be standing here if you hadn't shown me the way through the maze of bushes. I thought we had reached a dead end at this ridge."

"That's not what we're telling your unit. You found what most likely is the weapon used in the shootings. I'm only tagging along. I'll be back in Boston soon, and no one will ever remember my name."

"I'll remember it. Besides, we're a team and found the weapon together."

"Call in your forensic people. You should bring in your whole unit for additional help searching the area residents and businesses with security cameras again. You might find something that didn't seem important the first time you checked. Maybe a second look will be more meaningful. By the end of the day, you might know who hid the M4 after shooting those kids."

Cassie called for a forensics team and detectives to come to the scene. While she called, Sam followed the trampled ground cover to where it exited the park.

"I'll wait on the road and direct the forensics team to you. Yell out if you encounter a bear or coyote."

"Funny, Sam. Be careful not to step on a rattlesnake on the way out."

"Touché," Sam said with a grin.

Sam gradually walked toward the road, inspecting the ground, bushes, and trees, registering whatever he observed. Before exiting the woods, Sam stopped and spotted a shuffled, bare dirt area with imprints of an object he couldn't distinctly identify. He analyzed the markings and patterns in the soft dirt until he figured out what it could be. He heard a vehicle approaching and quickly moved out onto the road and hailed down the forensics van. Two men exited the van, with one saying, "You're lucky we were close by— otherwise, you'd be waiting a while for us to get here."

Sam led them first to what he had studied, asking what they thought caused the markings in the dirt. After carefully examining the patterns, one forensic technician told Sam his opinion, which confirmed what Sam believed the shapes were. Sam then had the techs follow him to where Cassie waited.

After initialing the chain of custody form and releasing the evidence to the forensic team, Cassie followed Sam toward the road. On the way, he pointed out what probably made the imprints in the soiled dirt. They walked onto the road, waiting for the search team to arrive. While waiting, Sam had questions about the result of the initial neighborhood search for cameras conducted by her department following the previous shooting at the beverage company.

"Not much help, Sam. We had two teams headed in opposite directions from the park. Not many homes had security cameras pointing toward the road, and none at what we thought was where the shooter exited the park. Ten houses had a doorbell camera, some not providing good images. Only four had premium units that provided a clearer image of vehicles—two north and two south of the park. The shooting occurred during the late afternoon or early evening commute hour, and the traffic was quite heavy. We couldn't distinguish license plates, only the makes of some vehicles. It didn't help us identify the shooter. Since Callahan's residence is south of the park, we focused on pickups or cars similar to what Callahan's wife drives. We concentrated on the vehicles moving south and found one similar pickup and color; there were no cars and only two bike riders."

"Were the doorbell cameras on the street where the Callahans reside?"

"Yeah. There were two on Callahan's street, one before and one after their house. The one before had the better camera unit, and the other was no help. But, viewing the videos during the selected time frame, we couldn't identify a vehicle similar to Callahan's that drove by the house before the Callahan home."

"I assume there was no pedestrian traffic or anything else seen during the time frame."

"No pedestrians, only two kids on a bike." Cassie saw her team's vehicles approaching and waved to signal them to a stop. When Detective Matt Kendrick saw the smile and glow on Cassie's face, he immediately asked, "You look like you found something?"

"We did. We found an M4 and ammo hidden in a rock crevice inside the woods, about forty yards from here."

"Great work, lieutenant. Hopefully, forensics will find prints on the gun so we can solve this case."

Cassie led the officers to the rock formation, where the forensics team took photos and tagged the M4 as evidence. Once the team finished, they left for their office to examine the weapon. Cassie directed the four detectives and four uniformed officers to approach the same neighbors north and south of the park with security cameras, using the agreed-upon time frame of the school shooting.

"Sam and I will take the two neighbors on Callahan's street."

Sam reminded Cassie about getting the sock and coffee cup to the DNA specialist for an examination.

"It won't take long to look at two short videos. We could drive to the state lab right after we finish."

Two police vehicles drove off, heading north and two heading south. Sam rode with Cassie to the street where Callahan lived and stopped at the house before his. When the home's resident opened the door and learned the lieutenant wanted to view the doorbell camera video again, the owner invited them inside. Cassie and Sam viewed the footage during the designated hours and saw a car similar to that driven by Callahan's wife and one kid on a bike. They noted the times the car and the kid passed by the house. Cassie asked the owner to send her a copy of the video segment to her phone.

Cassie and Sam then left the house and drove to the second resident's home, three houses past Callahan's, to view the doorbell camera. While viewing the doorbell video at the second resident's home, they didn't observe the car or bike pass by, meaning the vehicle and the biker had reached their destination before reaching the resident's house.

After leaving the second house, Cassie and Sam drove to the Meriden state lab to drop off the sock and coffee cup. Cassie introduced her friend, Lalita Cheng, to Sam. Cheng said she had a time-sensitive project she was working on and didn't have time to chat. So Cassie and Sam left the lab and drove to the PD, where the other neighborhood search officers were arriving. They met in the detective's unit and reported they found nothing that helped to identify the shooter.

"Well, Sam and I observed a car similar to what Callahan's wife drives from the house before Callahan's. So, Matt, you, and Ted should interview Callahan's wife to determine if it was her car, who was driving it that day, and at what time."

Sam chose not to give any input until the detectives interviewed Callahan's wife.

"Let's get something to eat, Sam. I'm starving, and I know where to get some delicious food," said Cassie.

CHAPTER
32

C assie asked Sam if he preferred seafood, Italian, or Asian. Sam said he liked all three, but his preference would be Italian.

"There's a fantastic Italian restaurant a short distance from here. I'll call in a takeout order for two special dishes, and we can share both. I have a delicious dessert that'll keep you asking for more."

"I thought we were dining at the restaurant. I don't want to put you out. Besides, I was planning on completing research on Kiara's shooter tonight."

"You're not putting me out. It would be more relaxing at my place. We can talk openly without worrying about who might hear our conversation. We had a good day and should celebrate with champagne."

"Yeah, we should celebrate finding the M4. Champagne sounds good to me. It will help me sleep later at the hotel since their foam-filled pillows are uncomfortable. I prefer feather pillows."

"You're in luck. I have feather pillows at my place. You can spend the night rather than driving back to the hotel. What would you do there anyway, watch TV and fall asleep? Boring. After enjoying a good meal and champagne, we could enjoy dessert and talk shop. You'll be happy you stayed. I promise."

Sam liked the idea of dining with Cassie, but it left an uneasy feeling of being alone with an attractive woman. He guessed Cassie was in her mid-forties, in fantastic physical shape, and a personable, charming redhead. Sam saw that Cassie was all business around her colleagues but friendly and fun to work with as a partner. They lightheartedly needled and teased each other like long-lasting friends. He appreciated Cassie inviting him for dinner, but proposing that he stay the night caused apprehension. He didn't want to put himself in a position of getting lured into a sleepover in the same bed.

"Come on, Sam. I'm hungry and prefer not to eat alone tonight. Besides, it's my birthday, and I don't want to celebrate it alone."

"Oh, happy birthday," said Sam, thinking, *I can't turn Cassie down on her birthday.*

"The restaurant has rigatoni Bolognese, chicken piccata or marsala, lasagna, and eggplant to die for. Choose one, and I'll choose another. We can share and enjoy both."

Sam was hungry, and the selections Cassie mentioned were indeed tempting.

"Uh, I'd have to get my overnight bag from Kiara's car parked at the PD if I stay the night. I assume you have two bedrooms."

"Yes, there are two bedrooms."

"Well, all the selections you mentioned sound great. You pick your two favorites."

Cassie feverishly glimpsed at Sam with a devilish thought and a smile. Cassie decided on the chicken piccata and lasagna.

When they got to Cassie's place, Sam was impressed. Her white ranch-style home was relatively new and in an upscale neighborhood where most houses were similar, probably built by the same builder. They entered through the two-car garage into a combined kitchen and living room area with several extra-large windows and dressed with fine furniture. Cassie had the walls painted a neutral light tan—a separate dining room located in the front room. Down the hall to the left of the living room was a laundry room and the main bedroom. A second bedroom and guest bathroom were on the opposite side of the living room and kitchen.

Cassie placed the food on the kitchen counter and mentioned she had worked long hours and needed a shower. "Sam, you're welcome to take one, too. Everything you need—towels, soap, and shampoo—is in the bathroom. I'll show you where everything is in the bathroom. We can eat first, then shower. Follow me."

Cassie took out two towels in the bathroom and pointed to the shampoo and body wash tubes on a shelf in the shower stall.

They returned to the kitchen, where Cassie warmed the food in the microwave while getting a bottle of champagne from the refrigerator. Sam had begun reading the newspaper articles he photographed from the barn apartment in New Preston. He became engrossed with the story he read while he sat in the dining room. Cassie was about to put Sam's dinner plate in front of him, but he seemed captivated by what he was reading on his iPad.

"Dinner's ready, Sam. Can you put the iPad aside to make room for your dinner plate?"

"Sorry. I'm reading about a murder back in 2014. It's fascinating. I'll finish reading it later."

"That's if you have time."

"What do you mean?"

"Oh, nothing. I'm just preoccupied with celebrating what we found and my birthday. I'm on a high about both," Cassie said with a devious smile. "There's more food if you're hungry, then we'll have dessert."

Sam gave a toast to Cassie's birthday before sharing half of each meal, sipping the champagne as they ate.

"Your dinner selections were delicious, Cass. The lasagna was my favorite, and I must say, being a wine drinker, you picked a fine champagne. You made excellent choices."

She filled his glass to the top. Once they finished eating and emptied the wine bottle, Cassie said she had a special dessert.

"Oh, no, please. I'm stuffed. Maybe later after the shower."

"Yeah, shower first, then dessert." Cassie nodded with a smirk. "You shower first, Sam. I'll clean up a bit here in the kitchen."

While stepping into the shower, Sam had the hot water flow on his neck and back with his eyes closed, enjoying what felt like a warm water massage. He imagined lying on a beach with the warm sun reflecting off his body. Unexpectedly, he heard the shower door close and opened his eyes. He was astonished to see Cassie with a suggestive smile standing before him.

"What—" Before he finished his sentence, Cassie grabbed the back of his head and brought his lips to hers. She kissed him passionately, holding him firmly against her. Sam was not expecting or wanting romance, but he couldn't resist what would follow as Cassie whispered, "It's my birthday. Let's have fun and celebrate it."

CHAPTER
33

While waiting outside the apartment building in Bridgeport for Antonio "Tonio" Acosta to arrive home, Alex maneuvered his car in a slow, deliberate loop around the lot. The twilight sky cast long, creeping shadows across the vehicles, making them appear like lurking predators. He scanned each car, their darkened interiors concealing any potential threats. None of the vehicles looked familiar. Satisfied, he reversed into a spot directly opposite the front entrance of Tonio's building, a single door with a window panel at the top giving Sam a clear view of the mailboxes inside. The position was perfect for surveillance, a strategic and inconspicuous vantage point.

Acosta's silver Camaro arrived about an hour later, the sporty car's sleek form cutting through the dusk. Tonio backed into a space three cars from Alex. The Camaro's engine purred briefly before falling silent. With his lean frame and perpetually smug expression, Tonio sat there for several minutes, his window down, engaged in a heated conversation. His voice tinged with annoyance, carried through the still evening air.

"Yeah. I just got home. No, I don't need company. My girlfriend will be home in about an hour, and I don't want an audience when she arrives. Okay, okay. If you and Bones want to sit outside and watch in case the creep shows up, be my guest. But I'm not bringing out food or beer for you.

Buy what you need before you get here. No, I can handle myself. Besides, I put a second deadbolt on the door and always keep my gun within reach. The guy won't stand a chance if he attempts anything. And, hey, with you two guys standing guard, you could nail him before he gets to the front door. Right?"

Luck was on Alex's side; he had the passenger window cracked enough to catch Tonio's words. He now knew Tonio's buddies, Gil, and Bones, weren't at the complex yet. Tonio ended the conversation, exuding an air of irritation, and exited his Camaro. He walked to the front door and entered the building.

Alex, using binoculars, watched Tonio through the glass window, noting the apartment number on the mailbox he opened. Tonio fished out his mail, unlocked the inner security door, and vanished into the dimly lit hallway. Tonio had mentioned his girlfriend wouldn't be home soon, and with Gil and Bones still en route, this was perfect timing. He decided to make his move. Alex's heart rate quickened, seeing lights flicker in a third-floor apartment. Alex caught a glimpse of Tonio moving past a window.

"The last of the four," Alex mumbled. He had confirmed the apartment number from the mailbox and drove to the building's rear entrance. The old building had recently been outfitted with a metal plate to thwart credit cards or screwdrivers, efficiently bypassing the unsecured keyed front doorknob. However, the metal plate didn't prevent a seasoned lock picker from opening the door or breaking the window to gain entrance. Alex deftly picked the lock with practiced ease, slipping into the building unnoticed.

Wearing his facial disguise, a nondescript cap, and voice changer— he made his way into the building: it was dim and musty, with the smell of stale food and mildew. Alex opened the heavy fire-coded door to the back stairwell and ascended to the third floor. He paused outside Tonio's apartment, listening intently. From within, he heard the mundane sounds of Tonio's evening routine—the rush of water and a muffled flush. Alex used his tools to pick the deadbolts, the lock surrendering without a fight, and cracked the door open, slipping inside.

The apartment was sparsely decorated, a bachelor pad with little personality—a stark contrast to the man who occupied it. Alex's rubber-soled shoes made no sound as he moved across the carpeted floor, heading towards the glow of the bedroom light. He leaned against the wall, peering around its corner. Tonio's back was to him, oblivious while changing his clothes.

"Time to move," Alex breathed, his voice barely more than a sigh. He moved with the grace of a predator, his Taser poised. A creak in the hall's wooden floor betrayed his presence. Tony spun around, eyes widening in alarm, but it was too late. Alex fired the Taser, sending Tony to the floor, his body convulsing as the electrical current coursed through him.

"Uh . . . what the hell . . . ?" Tony moaned, his voice spawning pain and disbelief.

Alex swiftly zip-tied Tony's ankles and wrists while Tony shuddered on his back. He watched as Tony's eyes glimmered with recognition and fear. The man's bravado was gone, replaced by a look Alex relished: pure terror.

"Who are you, and how did you get in here?"

"Speak softly, or I'll zap you until you do. You can call me Alex. I'm sure you know why I'm here. You should have invited your murdering buddies Gil and Bones up to babysit you."

"They'll check back with me and come running if I don't answer. When they do, they'll torture you, then cut you into pieces."

"I'm sure you all would enjoy that. But, unfortunately, I'm the one who will torture you and then cut you into pieces."

Alex's voice was cold, his words calculated to instill fear. "You'll be dead before your girlfriend comes home. What a shock it'll be for her to see your bloody body parts all over the bedroom floor. But, of course, if you decide to play nice and tell me everything I want to know, I'll let you live another day. Sound fair, asshole?"

Tony spat defiantly. "Screw you."

"Oh, you prefer to get tortured before you die." Alex grabbed a pillow from the bed, placing it ominously on Tony's knee. "You know that your friends are walking with canes now. However, I'm taking out both your knees and your ankles. Hmm, you may never walk again. Your girlfriend will drop you like a lead weight. I'll count to three before I start ruining your life. Oh, by the way, this is Bones' gun. One, two, th—"

"Okay, okay, don't shoot. Whataya wanna know?"

"Good choice, Tonio," said Alex, accentuating Tonio's name. "I don't want to stay here all night, so the quicker you answer truthfully, the sooner I'm out of here. That way, I won't have to hurt your girlfriend if she arrives while I'm still here. I'd have no choice but to hurt her. So, answer as fast as I ask the questions. If you lie—I'll shoot your knees apart. Understood?"

Tony nodded, his face pale.

"Who tells your crew what houses to hit?"

"I don't know. Gil knows the guy and gives him a cut."

"So, Gil's the boss?"

"He thinks he is, but he just has the connection to the guy who knows what houses have loads of cash inside."

"I'm sure you know who feeds you guys the alarm codes. Don't lie to me, Tonio, or your first knee will explode."

"I don't know who the guy is, but I think he works with the guy who picks the places to hit."

"Is he one and the same person?"

"Only Gil would know that."

"Other than Zee, who else has murdered those in the houses you rob? Tell me the truth. I know more than you think."

Tony hesitated, his eyes darting as if searching for an answer. "Gil shot a kid who tried hitting him with a fireplace iron and then shot the kid's father. Other than that one time, nobody killed anyone other than Zee. That guy is a wacko."

"What town were you guys in when Gil shot the father and his kid?"

"I'm pretty sure it was in Stamford, or it could have been Westport."

"Where do you keep your stolen cash and diamonds?"

"Hey, man, I need that money for my wedding and honeymoon."

"You won't have a wedding if you don't tell me where you're hiding it."
Alex pressed the gun to Tonio's knee.

"Don't shoot, man. You know, you're just like us, only robbing the robbers."

"Well, should I pull the trigger?"

"Bones told me you didn't take all he had. Could you leave me enough for a ring and a honeymoon trip?"

"I could do that. Tell me so I can leave before your girlfriend arrives."

"There's Clorox wipes containers in the bathroom cabinet. I hid the money inside."

"Where's your gun and cell phone?"

"The gun is under the other pillow on the bed, and I left the phone on the coffee table in the living room."

"Turn over on your stomach."

Alex taped Tony's mouth shut and patted his back pockets, ensuring he had no weapons. He found Tony's gun under the second pillow and his phone on the coffee table. Alex located two oversized Clorox containers in the bathroom, one had a wipe conspicuously sticking out of the top. He ripped off the lids, revealing a stash of twelve thousand dollars and a black pouch containing ten nearly flawless diamonds. Alex stuffed ten grand in his black go-bag, leaving the diamond pouch with the distinctive logo.

As Alex returned to the bedroom, Tony's cell phone rang, its shrill tone startling him. The name "Frank" blinked on the screen. He didn't answer, letting it ring until it went to voicemail.

"Tonio, it's Bones. I don't see Alyssa's car out here. What's up? Damn it, answer your phone, shithead. Is everything okay up there? Come on, man, pick up your phone."

Bones shrugged his shoulders with a curious look at Gil. "Whataya wanna do, Gil?"

"Tell him we're coming up," shouted Gil. "Grab your gun. If the guy is holding Tony hostage, we're gonna tear him a new asshole."

CHAPTER
34

Gil wanted to cover both entrances, so he had Bones drive around the back of the apartment building to have Bones enter the rear door. "Wait till I get in the driver's seat. I'll call you when I enter the building. Wait for me on the third floor. With these bum knees, climbing the stairs will take time."

Bones hesitated. "Gil, I won't be able to jimmy the door with that metal piece they added."

"Use your head, dummy. Just break the glass and open it from the inside. Whoever manages this place certainly never robbed anyone before."

Bones nodded, gripping his gun tightly, and exited the car. He lurked toward the door, scanning the shadowed hallway for residents.

Meanwhile, Tony's girlfriend, Alyssa, arrived and parked across from the front entrance. She gathered her purse and a thick work file and headed to the front door.

Back inside, Alex gripped Tony's phone, knowing that Tony's associates were about to breach the apartment building. He had to leave immediately. Clutching his bag, Alex darted into the living room. He decided to hide the two guns under the couch cushions. He then went to the door, hoping to avoid running into Tony's buddies.

Oblivious to the danger, Alyssa climbed the last step to the third-floor landing. She held her keys, ready to unlock the apartment door. She fiddled with the key to get it upright, then aimed it at the keyhole. The door suddenly swung open. She jumped back with wide eyes and a howling mouth, her breath catching in her throat as a stranger emerged, causing her to drop the keys.

Alex nonchalantly mumbled, "Nice to meet you, Alyssa. I'd stay longer, but I have what I came for. Tonio is waiting for you in the bedroom." He picked up her keys, handed them to her with a forced smile, and bolted down the hall toward the back exit.

Momentarily speechless, Alyssa watched the man she assumed was a burglar dash away before quizzically saying, "Who's Tonio?" Incensed, she fumbled for her cell phone, dialed 911, and hurried into the apartment. Not finding Tony in the front rooms, she frantically rushed to the bedroom and gasped at the sight of him cuffed and gagged on the floor.

"Nine-one-one, what's your emergency?" came the calm voice of the operator.

With a quivering voice and tears welling up, Alyssa reported, "When I got to my apartment door, a strange man came out, pushed me aside, and ran. He, uh, scared the crap out of me. I found my boyfriend tied up on the bedroom floor." She provided her name and address, urging the police to respond quickly before the intruder escaped through the rear door. While Alyssa relayed details to the operator, Tonio, who managed to turn onto his back, grunted and shook his head, signaling her not to involve the police.

"The local police are on their way," the operator assured her.

At the front entrance, Gil limped into the apartment building lobby with the aid of two canes, having broken the glass to unlock the door from the inside. He pressed the security buzzer for four apartments, hoping someone would buzz him in through the locked interior door. The buzzer sounded, and Gil entered the stairwell. He eyed the stairs with frustration, knowing there was no elevator in the old, three-story complex. Gripping the handrail and holding both canes in his other hand, Gil painstakingly began the climb, cursing under his breath about the old bastard responsible for his busted kneecaps. He was breathless after only eight steps, each a small victory and a painful reminder.

Meanwhile, as Alex hurried down the stairwell, Bones had already entered the back door. On the first landing, Alex heard the creak of the heavy stairwell door opening. He peered over the railing and saw Bones, gun in hand, entering the stairwell. Panic surged through him. He spun around, raced to the second landing, and sprinted toward the front entrance. He flew down the stairs, not pausing to check for anyone in his path. As he rounded the last flight of stairs, his heart nearly stopped at the sight of Gil laboring a few steps down.

Gil, seeing Alex, nervously fumbled to reach for his gun in his waistband. His eyes opened wide with fear, sweat forming on his forehead. He wanted to kill Alex so much, but anxiety encompassed his whole being; he became unsteady and dizzy. Alex, driven by sheer survival instinct, barreled down the steps and purposely shoved Gil, sending him tumbling backward. Gil's canes clattered to the floor, where Gil had landed on his back, crying in agony over the sharp spasms curdling inside. He cursed Alex, who had slammed into him. Hearing police sirens growing louder, Gil desperately struggled to get up, scanning for his gun, which lay tauntingly out of reach on the steps above.

Alex stomped on Gil's knee with force before racing out the front door. He hustled around the building to his car, feverishly shedding his disguise. He opened his trunk, threw his disguise gear and black bag into it, and slid into the car's front seat. He yanked the police two-way radio from the glove box, placed it on the passenger seat, and reversed out of the parking spot with his headlights off. With the window slightly open, the wail of approaching sirens filled the night. Fearing a police blockade at the front entrance, he sped toward the complex's back buildings, his mind racing for a rear escape route.

As he drove past the last building, relief washed over him upon seeing a lit back exit. His relief was short-lived though, as the police radio crackled with the dreaded news.

"3415 to 4239, I'm one minute out. What's your status?"

"I arrived at apartment building one, about to head up to the third-floor apartment 3A. Come in through the rear entrance and be on the lookout for any person or vehicle attempting to leave. If I need assistance, I'll let you know."

"Roger that. Coming up on the back entrance now."

CHAPTER
35

pprehensive, Alex nervously slammed the shift into reverse, his heart throbbing as he backed into a tight parking space between two hulking SUVs. Sweat beads trickled down his forehead. He could feel the tension in his knuckles as he released his tight grip on the steering wheel. With a heavy sigh, Alex slumped low in the front seat, hoping the police wouldn't focus on his vehicle. The two-way police radio in his hand buzzed too loudly, so he turned the volume down, his hands nervously shaking.

Bones, panting with adrenaline coursing through his veins, reached the third floor and noticed the door to Tony's apartment was slightly ajar. He waited, his breathing ragged, glancing back and forth until he heard Gil cursing from the stairwell. When Gil saw Bones above him, he yelled, "Get down here and help me, for chrissake!" His voice echoing off the walls.

Bones helped Gil stagger up the remaining steps, his legs trembling from his effort. They both paused at Tony's apartment door, Gil leaning heavily against the wall, his breaths coming in short gasps. They moved with the caution of predators, with Gil motioning towards the hallway as they crept toward the source of voices in the bedroom.

Gil peered around the corner of the wall, his senses on high alert. He could hear the low, pained moans coming from the bedroom. Bones moved stealthily forward, with Gil limping a few paces behind. At the bedroom door, Gil signaled Bones to take the lead, their guns clutched tightly in their hands. They burst into the room with their weapons and instinctively pointed their guns at Tony's girlfriend, who screamed in terror. Her eyes were wide with fear; her face, a shade of rosy pink moments before, turned ghostly white as she stared at the intruders.

On the floor, Tony lay cuffed and groaning, his face contorted in pain. Gil's face flushed with embarrassment, cursed under his breath for scaring Alyssa.

"Bones, cut Tonio loose—I mean Tony—and get him on his feet," ordered Gil, his voice barely concealing his rage.

Tonio excitedly yelled. "Alyssa called the cops!" They heard sirens and a vehicle screeching to a stop outside.

"Shit. Hide the guns," said Gil. Gil opened a chest drawer. "Put it in here, Bones."

"No way, Not in my drawer, asshole," said Tonio, his tone full of anger. "Find someplace in the living room."

The apartment buzzer sounded. "That's the police," said Alyssa as she rushed to let them in.

"Let's join Alyssa in the other room," said Tonio. Gil and Bones quickly hid their guns under the couch. Seconds later, two police officers entered the apartment, seemingly surprised to see three men and a woman standing in the room.

"We need to see identification from all of you," said an officer.

Outside, Alex's anxiety spiked. The tension knotted his stomach as he peeked to see the police cars circling the complex like vultures. As he peered over the dashboard, his pulse quickened when he saw a police car turning the corner away from him.

"4239, could you come up to apartment 3A and assist?" a voice snapped over the radio.

"Roger that, 3415. I'm a minute out."

"HQ to 3415. I'm sending additional units to assist."

"Copy that."

"3415 to HQ, request wants and warrant checks on Peter Gilinsky, Frank Bonarz, Antonio Acosta, and Alyssa Higgins. Over."

Minutes later, the desk officer responded. "Move away so no one hears what I say."

"I'm out of hearing range now."

"No wants or warrants on Higgins. Hold Gilinsky, Bonarz, and Acosta—they're persons of interest to the district attorney. I'm sending additional units to assist. Confirm, you're in building one, on the third floor, apartment 3A, correct?"

"Correct."

"So, when the other units arrive, search and arrest them and bring them to the PD?"

"Roger that."

"What's your take on Higgins? Any indication she's protective of the three men?"

"No sign of it, only toward her boyfriend, Acosta."

"Good. While you wait for the units to arrive, take Higgins aside and question her privately. It seems odd that the two men showed up as the burglar left the apartment. Ask Higgins if they were expecting the two men and whether they were armed. If they were, knowing that the police were on the way, they might have hidden their guns. Be direct with Higgins. Convince her if she allowed the guys to hide guns in her apartment, it would leave her in control of them, thereby, in violation. We could charge her with aiding and abetting."

"Ten-four."

Hearing the radio chatter, Alex knew he had to act fast. His escape would be tricky with additional police closing in. He started the car, its engine softly purring as he maneuvered towards the rear entrance with his lights still off. His heart leaped into his throat when he heard more sirens in the distance and saw flashing blue lighting up the sky on the back road. Anger surged through him. "Damn it," he whispered, a chill running down his spine. "The police have the place surrounded. I'm cooked."

CHAPTER
36

Alex returned to his hiding spot between the two SUVs, shutting off the engine and slumping low in the seat. He watched with bated breath as a police car cruised past, its floodlight sweeping over the parked vehicles. He waited until the car moved on. Alex listened intently to the ongoing police communication.

After communicating with HQ, an officer asked Alyssa to follow him into the hall.

Gilinsky shot a wary glance at Bones, who frowned and shifted uncomfortably.

"Officer, are we free to go? You've got our information. We only came to visit Tony. It's the burglar you should be after, right?" Gilinsky's voice carried a hint of desperation.

"We'll need more information first. Hold tight," said the officer.

"Yeah, but we know nothing about the guy who broke in here," Gilinsky insisted, his tone edging towards irritation. "We can't give you any further information about him. It's late, and we've got work in the morning. We can't stay here all night."

"It'll just be a few more minutes," the officer said calmly. "So relax."

Alyssa followed the officer into the hallway. The officer told Alyssa the two guys who came into her apartment were wanted by the authorities.

"If they came into your apartment with guns and then hid them after knowing you called the police, the guns would remain in your control. So you know, we're arresting these guys, and before we take them to the police department, we will do a cursory search. If we find any guns, we'll have to arrest you for aiding and abetting since you've accepted control of the weapons."

"What? I don't want control of any guns."

"Tell me the truth. Did those two guys have guns, and if so, did they hide them in your apartment? If they hid them, tell me where the guns are so I can take them out of your apartment."

"Oh, boy. I don't want to get Tony's friends in trouble."

"Better them in trouble instead of you for helping them."

"I, uh, I'm not helping them."

"You don't want the guns to remain in your apartment. We're arresting them, and they won't be coming back here. Those guys may have used the guns in a crime. We'll get a search warrant. We'll arrest you if we find any illegal guns under your control."

"Okay, okay, I'm so nervous. You should check the couch, but don't go right to it. I don't want those guys to think I told you."

"Okay, I'll work it so they don't think it was you. Thank you, Alyssa. You did the right thing."

The officer walked back into the living room with Alyssa tailing behind.

"3437 to 3415. Ron and I have arrived and request you buzz us in at the inner security door."

Once 3415 pressed the front door security button, the two officers entered the third-floor apartment in minutes. One officer then faced the three men and asked if they were armed. They all answered no. The officer asked the other officers to search the three men and the room for weapons. Anywhere these guys could get quick access to, including all the furniture and tables. If you find any, don't put your prints on them."

"This is bullshit," said Gil angrily. "We're not armed—if you find any guns here, they don't belong to Frank or me."

A searching officer took only a minute to find a semiautomatic pistol under a couch cushion and a second gun under another cushion. The officer looked under the couch and reported he found two more handguns. The senior officer said he'd call in forensics. He then faced all three men. "I'm placing you under arrest. So, each of you put your hands behind your back."

"Come on, man. We didn't do anything," said Gil. "We only came to visit Tony, so why are you arresting us? You should be looking for the guy who broke into Tony's home and tied and gagged him. He probably hid the guns knowing the police were on the way."

The three other officers searched and handcuffed all three men, including Acosta.

"Why the hell are you arresting me?" asked Tony. "I'm the victim. That other guy broke into my home and threatened to kill me."

"Officer, Tony lives here with me. He's not with these guys. He doesn't even have a gun," said Alyssa.

"Sorry, ma'am. My supervisor informed me that these men are wanted by the District Attorney's Office. We're taking them to the police department for questioning." The officer then dictated the right to remain silent to the three arrested men.

The three men continued to argue that they had done nothing wrong and threatened to sue the officers for false arrest. Gilinsky argued the loudest. Bones bickered some but was more concerned about his letter to the DA. He worried what his friends would do to him if they learned he ratted them out.

"3415 to HQ. We have the suspects in custody. I recommend you call in a forensic team to collect four guns found near the suspects."

"Ten-four. I need one officer to remain there to secure the apartment for the pending search."

"Roger that."

Outside, Alex relaxed with a wide grin, relieved knowing the police arrested the three men. He pounded the steering wheel triumphantly, satisfaction gleaming in his eyes. Alex was euphoric. Everything fell into place, especially after forcing Bones to write a confessional letter to the DA. It worked perfectly. He exited the rear complex, expecting the police to arrest Zee in the coming days. That left only one more payback call to make: a final visit to Detective Leon Mackey for the last but most meaningful retaliation.

Alex sped into the night toward the city. The city lights blurred as he accelerated toward home. He felt a serene calm, knowing his quest for justice was nearing the end.

CHAPTER
37

S am woke up with glossy eyes, staring at the alarm clock on the end table next to the bed. It was after eight o'clock. He slowly sat up, scanning the unfamiliar bedroom in the dim light. The walls were a soft lavender, and the air smelled of jasmine. He sensed movement on his left and turned to see Cassie smiling at him, her wavy hair cascading over her shoulders.

"Good morning, Sam. What a birthday night. How did you sleep?"

"What sleep?" Sam grumbled, rubbing his temples. "It's after eight, and I wanted to start early, but that's not in the cards now."

Cassie's smile widened with a glint of mischief in her eyes. "Wow. You sound disappointed. I thought maybe you were shy at first, but I have to say you were amazing."

"Well, I, uh . . ." Sam mumbled, feeling a wave of embarrassment wash over him. He glanced around, trying to find an escape. He abruptly sat up, bolted out of bed, and nearly tripped over a discarded shoe as he hurried into what he thought was the bathroom.

"Are you looking to wear my clothes today, Sam?" said Cassie, her laughter bubbling over.

Sam emerged from the closet, seeing Cassie smiling and pointing toward the bathroom door. With a sheepish grin, he slipped into the bathroom and turned on the shower. She followed him into the bathroom.

"Ladies first," he said, gesturing toward the shower.

Cassie's smile turned sultry, her movements graceful as she entered the shower. A scream followed as the icy water hit her skin. She moved away from the cold water, glaring at Sam.

"Oh, trying to wake me up for more," she kidded. Cassie grabbed Sam's arm and pulled him into the cold shower, saying with gritted teeth, "Turn on the heat."

As the water warmed, Sam accepted his defeat. He sighed resignedly, surrendering to Cassie's playful persistence for a quick encounter. When he finally stumbled out, breathless and disheveled, Cassie wrapped herself in a towel, her eyes twinkling with satisfaction.

"I'll prepare breakfast," Cassie offered, a mischievous smile on her lips.

"No! Let's have breakfast on the run," Sam shouted from the bedroom, hastily drying himself. "I want to stop by and see how Kiara is doing before work."

"You don't have to answer this, but do you and Kiara have a thing going on, Sam?"

"No. Of course not," Sam replied quickly. "We're partners, and someone shot her while I sat in the car rather than being with her. I have to make things right and ensure she's recovering, that's all."

Cassie's expression softened as she emerged from the shower, her cell phone ringing on the end table. She rushed to answer it, her demeanor shifting to one of business.

"Hi. What's up?" She listened intently before ending the call. "That was my friend at the state lab. She has the DNA results on the sock and cup. I'm going to bring the M4 to her. I want her to examine the weapon now that the forensics team has finished their examination. They only found partial prints, not enough for identification."

"That was fast," Sam remarked about the examiner completing the DNA analysis.

"Let's pick up the weapon and head to the state lab," Cassie said, moving with purpose.

"Sounds good. We can get breakfast on the way," Sam agreed, grabbing his clothes.

*   *   *

Cassie parked her car in front of the state lab building in Meriden, her earlier playful mood replaced by a focused intensity. She gave Sam an alluring smile before stepping out of the vehicle. Inside, the sterile, off-white-walled lobby buzzed with activity. Cassie's friend, Lalita, a petite Asian woman with a sharp gaze, greeted them and led them deeper into the lab's intricate corridors.

"It's a pleasure to meet you again, Lalita," Sam said, extending his hand. "Thank you for completing the DNA testing so quickly."

"You're welcome, Sam. I'm sorry we didn't have time to chat before. I was under pressure to finish another examination. Cassie tells me you are an ATF agent. You are the first ATF agent I have met here. I see you brought a gun for me to examine. Is this gun from a case you're working on?"

"It's a gun from a case Cassie and I are working on. I should mention that you are the first DNA specialist I have met. I hope we will continue our friendship."

"Maybe when we finish our investigations, Lalita can join us for a celebration dinner with champagne," said Cassie.

"Yes. I would love to celebrate with you and Sam."

"It's settled then," said Sam.

Lalita handed the DNA report to Cassie. Cassie held the report for her and Sam to review together. From the report, they learned that the person who wore the sock and drank from the cup was the child of Alexis and Jon Donnelley. As murder victims, the police added their DNA into CODIS, the Combined DNA Index System used by law enforcement to find DNA matches from victims to possible suspects.

"I might be able to examine the weapon later this afternoon, but I need a DNA sample from your suspect," Lalita said, flipping through her notes. "Has he been arrested recently or served in the military?"

"Mark Callahan served in the Army Special Forces," Cassie answered. "We have his service record and a Coca-Cola can from which he drank. I hope you can examine it for fingerprints, too. We only found partial prints. It could solve an important case by identifying the killer through matching prints or DNA. We're looking to nail the guy who killed two people and injured two kids. Right, Sam?"

"Right," Sam said. "We need a positive DNA and fingerprint match first."

Cassie frowned but nodded. "I'm counting on you, Lalita." She thanked her friend, grabbed Sam's arm, and led him out of the lab. As they walked to the car, Cassie finally said, her voice tinged with frustration. "Who else would kill Briggs's son and assistant, then shoot two kids? I don't see any other possible suspect."

"It could be Mark or someone in the Callahan family," Sam suggested cautiously.

"Like who?" Cassie snapped. "Not his wife, possibly his brother, but why?"

Sam remained silent, sensing her frustration. When they reached the hospital, Cassie parked outside the entrance in a no-parking zone. A security guard began waving at her, pointing to a no-parking sign. Cassie flashed her badge, her tone authoritative.

"We'll be out in twenty minutes. Keep an eye on the car, please."

The guard sighed and returned to his post near the hospital door.

Inside, Sam held the door open for Cassie and followed her through the bustling lobby. Cassie stopped suddenly to face him.

"I'm sorry, Sam. You were right. Cases like this often create obstacles. If it isn't the prosecutor needing more evidence, it's the defense attorney throwing roadblocks at us. I still think Mark Callahan was behind the killing at the beverage company. He's the only one with a motive. I can't see his wife or brother having any reason to kill anyone, let alone shoot two middle school kids."

"I agree with you about the wife and brother," Sam said carefully.

"You do? You think someone other than Mark did the shooting?"

"I have a hunch. When we finish visiting Kiara, I'll explain. But you might not like it if I'm right."

CHAPTER
38

Sam and Cassie walked to Kiara's room, their footsteps echoing in the sterile, modestly lit corridor. Sam's jaw tightened as he noticed the absence of security agents outside her room. The stark tan door stood ajar. Sam stepped inside, his heart pounding, when he saw Kiara's empty bed, the sheets undisturbed. He approached the partially open bathroom door and rapped on it, the sound reverberating through the silence. No response. Pushing it halfway open, he peered inside, finding only emptiness staring back at him.

"She's not here. She must be in physical therapy. Let's check there," Sam said, trying to mask his rising unease.

As they made their way to the nurses' station, the fluorescent lights cast harsh shadows, accentuating the tension on Sam's face. He identified himself to the nurse at the desk, a woman with tired eyes but a cooperating smile.

"Patient Kiara Rivers—is she in physical therapy? She's not in her room. Also, why isn't there any security outside her room?"

The nurse flipped through a logbook with practiced efficiency, looking with a hint of confusion. "I'm unaware of any security detail. Let me check her schedule." After scanning the log, she said, "Miss Rivers is scheduled for physical therapy at eleven. I'll call to see if they took her early." She dialed the number, spoke briefly, and said, "Kiara Rivers isn't in PT yet. She's due at eleven."

Sam's frustration mounted. "Where could she be if she's not in her room or therapy? Is she scheduled for anything else today?"

The nurse shook her head, her expression puzzled. "No, she should be in her room."

"What's the protocol for a missing patient?"

"I'll call her name on the PA system. If she doesn't respond, I'll alert security to search for her."

"Will the PA announcement reach the cafeteria, gift shop, or other nonmedical areas?"

"Yes, she should hear it if she's anywhere in the hospital. I'll also page her assigned nurse. She might know where Miss Rivers is."

While the nurse used the PA system to call for Kiara and her nurse, Sam dialed Kiara's cell phone. His pulse quickened when there was no answer. He glanced at Cassie, his eyes dark with worry.

"What are you thinking, Sam?" Cassie's voice was steady, a rock amid the uncertainty.

"I'm pissed that Davies didn't assign agents to guard Kiara's room. That's not acceptable."

Moments later, Kiara's nurse arrived, her face fixed with concern. "You called about Kiara?"

"She's not in her room, and we can't find her. Any idea where she might be?"

"She should be there," said the nurse with a frown. "You checked her room already?"

"Yes, and the bathroom," Sam replied tersely.

"Let's check again. Maybe Kiara went for a walk and came back."

The trio returned to Kiara's room, finding it just as empty as before. The nurse opened the closet and frowned. "Her bag is gone. That's strange."

"Have you seen any security agents outside her room?" Sam asked.

The nurse shook her head, her brow furrowed. "No. Should there have been?"

"Damn it," Sam muttered, pulling out his phone. "I'm calling Davies."

"What do you think happened, Sam?" Cassie asked with her voice tight and concerned.

"I think she's in trouble. She didn't answer the page or her phone. Someone might have taken her."

Sam dialed the number for Alan Davies, the FBI agent in charge. His frustration grew as he waited, pacing the floor.

When Davies finally answered, his tone was dismissive. "What's so urgent, Caviello?"

"Didn't Dell Haskins request security for Kiara's room? There are no agents here."

"I don't have agents to spare for guarding a hospital room. They have security at the hospital. Why aren't you watching her? You're her partner."

"Kiara is an FBI agent whom mobsters recently threatened. She's in danger and should have security posted outside her room."

"I know the circumstances she encountered at Yale. My office made the arrest. Remember? However, Rivers is a Boston agent. Boston should provide the security if needed."

"Kiara is missing. Someone abducted her. I'm contacting the US Attorney and Dell Haskins. I recommend you get agents at the hospital now." Sam hung up, his face flushed with anger. "Damn it. Davies is useless."

"What can I do to help, Sam?" said Cassie. "I could put out a BOLO for any suspicious vehicles near the hospital, especially with New Jersey or New York plates, and seeing any suspicious men with a black female."

"That might help, Cass. Thanks. I'm calling the US Attorney."

As Sam searched for Debra Durrell's number, his phone rang. Seeing Kiara's name, he urgently answered. "Where the hell are you, Kiara? We've been looking all over for you."

There was only silence for seconds, then a man's chilling voice, "Agent Caviello, you don't sound too happy."

"Who is this, and how did you get Kiara's phone?"

"Your partner was kind enough to lend it to me."

Sam's heart sank, dread coiling in his stomach. He suspected a member of the Lamartino family. "Listen, Lamartino, kidnapping a federal agent will put you in prison for a long time. If you harm her, you'll pay dearly."

The man laughed, a sound devoid of warmth. "You're the one who will pay. Your partner is fine for now. I want to make a deal."

"A deal with the devil, huh? What do you want?"

"You. I want to trade Agent Rivers for you."

"How do I know you have her? Let me talk to her."

"You'll talk to her once we agree on the trade."

Sam's mind raced, seeking a safe solution. "I'm not coming to New Jersey or New York. Any exchange must happen here in New Haven. She's under a doctor's care here."

"You don't get to call the shots, Caviello. We have what you want. We decide the place and time."

"You're wrong. You want me, you come here. I'm not risking a trap. Take it or leave it. Call me back with your decision." Sam ended the call, anxiety gnawing at him. He paced the room, weighing the consequences of his refusal. Apprehension set in as he called Debra Durrell to brief her on the situation.

"Sam, come to my office. I'll contact Davies and Haskins to report here, too. Bring Lieutenant Dawson with you. We need to act fast."

Sam nodded, his face hardening. "We're on our way."

CHAPTER

39

Sam and Cassie entered Durrell's office. Brian Murphy, Durrell's
assistant, sat with her, his expression mirroring the unease in the room.
With precision, Sam recounted the hospital turmoil, the unnerving
dismissal from Davies regarding Kiara's security, and Sam's audacious plan
forming in his mind like pieces of a puzzle clicking into place.

Davies's cavalier attitude toward safety stirred a storm of disbelief in the
room, evidenced by the tight-lipped exchanges and furrowed brows.

Sam's determination was evident. "What if we could wrestle control of this
mess by persuading Lamartino to make the exchange here in New Haven?"

Murphy leaned forward, his eyes gleaming with cautious optimism. "I
don't think Lamartino would waltz into our hands. We need a hook. A place
that'll lure him in without raising suspicion."

Sam's mind raced, sketching out a blueprint of possibility. He dove
into the details, painting a picture of an isolated city section devoid of
witnesses, with the interstate in the backdrop. Being unfamiliar with the
city's uninhabited locations, Sam could not pinpoint an area.

Cassie's calm and collected voice interrupted, saying, "I know a few city
spots that would work. I can show you on a map, then bring you to where
we can inspect them."

An acceptable plan emerged as they studied a city map and debated its
pros and cons. Each con met with a steadfast solution from Sam, except for

the indescribable locations. But Cassie's assurance and Durrell's rationality anchored them in agreement.

"I'll have to inform the chief. He'll probably send someone from his staff to attend the briefing," said Cassie.

"That's fine. Make the arrangement. Ask the chief to send someone within the hour," said Durrell. Davies arrived with his assistant but remained silent.

It took more than an hour, but once Haskins and the New Haven Assistant Police Chief arrived, Murphy briefed them on the situation. Davies, already present, was the only one who had issues with the plan. He felt Sam's decision to hang up on Lamartino could result in harm coming to Agent Rivers.

"Agent Caviello is trying to lure Lamartino to Connecticut, where we would have control in covering the swap and making arrests," said Murphy.

"What if they don't call back? What do we do then?"

Durrell cut in, saying, "They want Sam, not Kiara. They're using her as leverage to hold Sam accountable for shooting Lamartino's son."

Sam was annoyed with Davis. "The abduction would never have happened if you had assigned an FBI security team to Agent Rivers's hospital room.

"What are you saying, Caviello? It's my fault Lamartino took Kiara?"

"You could say that."

"Okay, enough of the bickering," said Durrell. "Lieutenant Dawson suggested two possible locations for us to use in case Lamartino agrees to do a trade here. Let's drive to the two locations and evaluate them for the exchange."

* * *

Once outside the federal building, Cassie's car became their chariot for her, Sam, Dell, and the chief to the first location. Sam studied the area, visualizing if they could make the trade there among the existing buildings, homes, and streets. Sam thought it was far from perfect. The group then drove to the second location. They traversed the terrain, weighing each possibility against the other until Sam asked to walk the area. He exited the car on Jackson Boulevard.

Sam stood at the corner where Pearl Street ended at the boulevard. He stood in front of an abandoned five-story brick-and-mortar building. A for-sale sign was attached to the front of the structure. His gaze swept the desolate landscape like a hawk hunting its prey. Across the street was a large vacant lot littered with trash. A short distance behind the lot was Interstate 95, with heavy traffic. An exit ramp off the highway and an entrance back onto the interstate toward New York and Jersey were nearby. As Sam walked further toward Hillcrest Avenue, a block away, the stench of discarded rubbish, heavy vehicle exhaust, and noise from the Interstate assaulted his senses. At the corner of Hillcrest Avenue, Sam observed a small vacant building, once a neighborhood grocery store, and an empty lot on the opposite side of the boulevard. A rusty four-foot chain-link fence surrounded the lot, with sections leaning inward.

Across Hillcrest stood what once was a laundromat, which was now vacant and closed. Further down the boulevard was a small one-story building that seemingly held three small stores, also now closed. A vacant lot came next, then an apparent occupied double-decker home. Sam took several photos of the area.

"Sam, if you took a right on either Hillcrest or Pearl, you'd approach Green Street about eighty yards up," said Cassie. "By taking a right on Green and driving about a half mile, you'd reach the entrance for I-95 west to New York and Jersey. What do you think about the two areas?"

"I think this spot is perfect. I want to walk up Hillcrest and Pearl to see what's behind the buildings. Hopefully, they're good hiding areas for cover and arrest teams."

The group was back at the federal building shortly after discussing the two areas. Using the photos taken, Sam sketched the area. He suggested where agents and officers could be positioned in the unmarked vehicles and on foot. The group recommended minor changes that they agreed would work if Lamartino decided to do the trade in New Haven.

"Anybody hungry? There's a cafeteria on the lower level," said Murphy.

CHAPTER
40

S am, Dell, and Cassie joined Brian Murphy for lunch at the building's cafeteria. The weight of their impending mission hung heavy on their mind.

Brian's words sparked a heated debate over strategy for getting Kiara back as they dissected their plan's potential risks and pitfalls. Sam envisioned every possible scenario and every potential move the mobsters could make.

Then, like a thunderclap amid their deliberations, Sam's phone shattered the silence. His heart shuddered into his throat, knowing it was Lamartino. With a signal to Brian that it was Lamartino, he whispered, "Call upstairs. Have them trace the call."

Sam put the call on speaker and waited for another five rings before answering,

"This is Caviello. It goes down my way or no way. I'm not putting my partner and me in harm's way, regardless of what you want. I know of a quiet, no-traffic location here right off I-95. It'll be an easy off and back on the interstate toward New York. I'll text you a map of the area. When you get here, you can check it out and see it's a safe, desolate place for the trade. Then call me, and I'll be there within fifteen minutes."

"It's not your decision to make. If you want your partner back, you meet where we tell you. Otherwise, you'll never see your partner again."

"It's me you want. I'm the one who shot your son. My partner did nothing. She had a gun to her head. The plan is simple. It'll take maybe five minutes. I wait on a street corner in an isolated, abandoned city section. Your team arrives in two vehicles. The first will have my partner, and the second, your men, who will grab me only after I see my partner set free and walk a good distance from the scene. After that, your vehicles will drive off to New Jersey. No cops, no neighbors, nobody watching. Simple and quick."

"You think I'm going to trust you that no cops won't be surrounding the whole area, including the highway? No fucking way, pal."

"Let's put it this way. We do it here with no cops. If we do it in Jersey, I promise there'll be a hundred federal agents and cops watching over me without you knowing. You'll get away free here but arrested the second I give the signal in Jersey. Your choice, pal. Call me back if it's me you want. Just remember, if you harm my partner in any way, I'll hunt you down, and I'll press to have your son imprisoned for the maximum sentence for the attempted murder of a federal agent." Sam ended the call.

Brian's eyes widened in admiration, a silent acknowledgment of the sheer bravery it took to stare down the barrel of such a decision. "Wow," said Brian. "You've got balls, Sam. I hope your insistence pays off."

"Yeah. It makes me sick thinking that I might have put Kiara in harm's way. It better work for Kiara's sake and mine. I don't think I'd be able to live with myself if this goes bad for her. Let's go upstairs and see if they have a location on the call."

The weight of the moment hung heavy upon them all. Yet even as they prepared to move forward, uncertainty gnawed at Sam's gut like a hungry beast. He knew the risks and the stakes, yet he was determined to see it through, although the thought of being wrong tormented him.

Later, as they convened in the US Attorney's conference room, the tension was ever-present. The call had come from New Jersey. Sam's mind buzzed with plans and contingencies, his every thought consumed by the need to ensure Kiara's safety.

Sam wanted added preparations to cover all contingencies. He sent Lamartino's burner phone, a city map section, and photos of the selected area, highlighting the nearby entrance ramp to the Interstate for a quick escape. Sam hoped it would change Lamartino's mind. Sam knew it was a long shot for Lamartino to agree to do the trade in New Haven. But if he did, it would give his team time to surround the area. Even if Lamartino showed up the day before to check the area for police and had his goons watching it before the trade, Sam thought it would still work. It would necessitate a plan to get officers in place covertly during the exchange rather than in place beforehand.

Durrell agreed. She assigned Dell, Alan, and Chief Giles to initiate a plan to get the teams covertly positioned if the situation called for it. She named Murphy to coordinate the operation using her office as the command center. "Brian, Chief Giles, and I will operate from my office."

If Lamartino came to New Haven, the group decided to put the teams close by but away from the designated area, needing only minutes to get into position unseen. All agreed on the plan. It was late, so Cassie and Sam left the meeting. Cassie suggested they stay together at her place. It was much closer to the exchange location, and getting there would take less time if Lamartino called to meet right away.

"I'll do it on one condition. We sleep in separate bedrooms," said Sam.

"It would be better if we were in the same room. If you get a call from Lamartino, I'll be with you to immediately alert my team and Murphy to get his ready, too. It'll save valuable minutes."

She made a good point, Sam thought. "Okay, but no fun time. Only sleep. We'll need the rest if Lamartino calls me at three in the morning."

Disappointed, Cassie understood and agreed, saying she'd take a rain check.

*   *   *

Three days later, on Sunday, Sam tossed and turned in bed. He alternated between sleep and waking with an anxious stomach that churned like a cement mixer, worrying about Kiara. He dozed off again as the first rays of dawn crept through the window blinds. There would be silence throughout the bedroom other than the sound of Cassie and Sam breathing while asleep. Abruptly, the shrill cry of a cell phone sliced through the room's stillness. Sam's body shook. His muscles protested the sudden intrusion while his hand groped clumsily for his cell. Blinking away the remnants of sleep, Sam squinted at the phone's screen, greeted by the ominous words 'No caller ID.' He jolted to a sitting position, surging with apprehension, knowing all too well who was calling. Suppressing a sigh, he braced himself for the inevitable as he glanced at the time: five-fifteen. It was too early for nerves to heighten, yet too late for a peaceful slumber.

Cassie stirred beside Sam, her presence a reassuring anchor in the swirling chaos of his thoughts. With a resigned nod to Cassie, signaling her to call her team with his voice muffled from sleep, Sam answered the call with a defiant growl, "What?"

The voice on the other end, dripped with malice and mockery, saying, "Didn't get enough sleep, uh, Caviello? You must be worrying about your partner."

Sam clenched his jaw, his fingers tightening around the phone as he struggled to maintain his temper. He nodded to Cassie—it was Lamartino—then responded forcefully, "As I already told you, I'm not putting my partner in a no-win situation and having us trapped somewhere in another state. I have to see my partner walk away free in her local environment, near the hospital,   not some dark waterfront, never to be seen again. Let me know when you're serious about the exchange."

The voice on the other end chuckled, devoid of warmth or humanity. "We never wanted to hurt your partner, only you, pal. We checked out your location. It'll do. So, let's do it right now. Be here in ten minutes, or we're outta here."

Sam's heart pounded in his chest, adrenaline coursing through his veins as the reality of the situation sank in. "What? Where? You're here in New Haven in the area I mentioned?"

"Yeah. Now get your ass here before we leave. Understand?"

Sam's mind raced, thoughts colliding in a whirlwind of panic and desperation. "Hey, man. I'm still in bed. It's a twenty-minute walk to get there. I'm not even dressed. I'll need more time, and you know it."

"We're watching the place. My men have the place surrounded. There better not be any cops showing up anywhere near here. I'll give you fifteen minutes. If you're not here, we'll be gone. The clock is ticking."

Sam, with a sinking feeling in the pit of his stomach, said, "Impossible. I need twenty if I run."

Cassie tapped Sam on the shoulder, pointing at her watch, a sharp reminder of the urgency of their situation.

"Well, stop talking and move, Caviello." The phone then went dead.

Determined, Sam swung his legs over the edge of the bed, the weight of success to save Kiara pressing down on him. He slept dressed, asking Cassie to help attach his small secondary pistol to his body.

"I called my team and Murphy, too."

"Thanks, Cass. You'll have to drive me partway so I can get there on time. Remind everyone of our code word, fire."

CHAPTER
41

Sam and Cassie raced against the clock to her car, already outside the garage. Although the streets were quiet, Cassie drove Sam through the tangled one-way streets to get Sam where he needed to be in time for the exchange.

As they neared the rendezvous point, Sam's pulse quickened, his senses hyperaware of every shadow, every fleeting movement in the dim light of dawn. The skyline, bathed in the ethereal glow of sunrise, cast long shadows along the pavement.

Sam's focal point, the abandoned building, loomed like a specter in the early morning haze, its decrepit façade a stark reminder of the unknown danger that lurked before him. Sam's breath caught in his throat as he surveyed the scene, his eyes scanning for any sign of movement amid the morning's tranquility.

Sam sped to the corner at the end of Pearl Street. When he turned the corner onto Jackson Boulevard, he saw three black vehicles, sleek and menacing, lining the street like sentinels of the underworld. Sam's jaw tightened as he recognized the figures emerging from the shadows, their presence a tangible threat in the peacefulness of the dawn.

One was Geno Lamartino standing between the building and the middle black SUV. With swaggering confidence and the menace of a predator, he waved Sam to come forward to him. But beneath his bravado, Sam sensed the tremor of uncertainty in his eyes. A big bruiser-type guy stood nearby to protect Santo Lamartino's other son, who was average-built, shorter, and younger. Two other bodyguards stood by the rear SUV, one older, partially bald with graying hair and muscular but portly. The other was younger and shorter, with a full head of dark curly hair, bulging arms thicker than Sam's thighs, and a broad muscle-bound chest. He clenched his fist as Sam walked by him.

As Sam faced his adversary, he noticed Geno's smirk widen, saying, "Tough guy, huh? Let's see your license, so I know it's you."

"You think I'd bring my wallet? I didn't figure I needed anything where you were taking me?"

"Hmm, right. Turn around and raise your arms high." Geno sifted through Sam's scruffy hair and used both hands to search Sam's body from his head, across his arms, to the ankles for a weapon, then shouted, "He's clean!"

As Sam hoped, Geno missed searching his armpits, where Cassie helped secure his small pistol with Velcro straps under his oversized shirt sleeves. Geno waved at an associate outside the first black vehicle, a four-door Cadillac sedan. On signal, his associate opened the rear passenger door. A woman emerged from the back seat. Her silhouette haunting in the dim morning light. She wore recognizable clothes and had dark skin but didn't turn toward him so Sam could get a facial identification. She began walking toward Hillcrest Avenue, where the mob guy pointed. Sam's heart raced as he called out her name, his voice desperate to ensure it was Kiara.

"Keep walking," shouted the mobster who guided her out of the Caddy. She kept walking without turning.

At that moment, Geno's grip tightened around Sam's arm, pulling him toward the SUV. Sam knew this was the beginning of a battle that would define the outcome. Without warning, he whipped around to the right with his elbow up high, hitting Geno squarely in the nose, causing blood to spray like a crimson geyser. With a savage kick to the groin, he sent Geno crashing to his knees, his bravado crumbling beneath the weight of pain.

But there was no time for hesitation as Sam pivoted and launched himself at the big bruiser guy, reaching for a weapon. With a forceful reaction, Sam wrestled the man's arm, slamming it against the unforgiving edge of the open car door, causing a sickening snap of bone. The man screamed in agony and dropped his gun to the sidewalk. Sam kicked it under the SUV.

The two men from the rear SUV rushed toward Sam. Sam pushed and tripped the big bruiser to the ground in front of them, causing the first guy to fall over him. The younger guy jumped over both men lying on the sidewalk and grabbed Sam's left arm. Using the palm of his right hand, Sam shoved it hard to the guy's face, pushing it into his nose. The guy fell backward, tripping over his partner on the ground. Sam quickly climbed into the back seat of the SUV, closing and locking the door. He reached into his shirt, pulled out his small pistol, and put it to the driver's head, shouting, "Get out of the car, now!"

The driver rushed to exit the Caddy and ran toward the front sedan. Sam quickly exited from the driver's side, yelling, "Fire! Fire!"—the signal for the cover teams to come to his aid. Within minutes, police vehicles with sirens and flashing blue lights began arriving. Agents and police carrying assault weapons from the top of nearby buildings yelled, "Police, everybody on the ground."

The front Cadillac sped from the curb, but the oncoming police cruisers prevented their escape.

Cassie stopped beyond the cruisers. She exited her car and ran toward the woman released from the first sedan. The woman's head was down, walking toward Hillcrest Avenue. Cassie approached the woman and forced her head up for recognition. Disappointed, Cassie yelled to Sam, "It's not Kiara!"

Shortly, police and FBI agents flooded the street. The mobsters tried running in vain, creating a chilly, emotional scene of apprehensive chaos. No one fired a weapon, but the clicks of handcuffs closing sounded one after another.

Hearing Cassie's cry that Kiara was not the bait, Sam's impulses screamed, despondent over the deception that unfolded before his eyes. Angry, knowing the operation was a betrayal, he became more defiant and determined to find Kiara and bring her back safely. Sam clutched his feverish stomach, churning with gurgling sounds of vomiting. He hid behind the black sedan, holding back any gagging and internal expulsion. Sam took shallow breaths as his eyes caught Geno leaning over with his hands cupping his groin. Sam's face crumpled with anger and clenched teeth as he fixed his scowl on Geno. He was boiling over with rage, clenching his fists as he marched toward Geno. Sam forcibly slapped his face more like a hammer punch and threw him to the ground, demanding answers. Nearby, Alan Davies rushed toward Sam with two agents. He interjected Sam's fury, his voice a sharp rebuke, shouting, "What the hell are you doing, Caviello?"

Sam's frustration simmered momentarily, his resolve unwavering in the face of another adversary. "What does it look like? It was just a love tap on the cheek of a family member. Maybe you'd rather kiss him.

"That's insubordination, Caviello."

"Lamartino tricked us. They didn't bring Agent Rivers to trade, only a fake substitute."

"Well, beating suspects is not protocol!"

Aggravated, Sam stepped toward Davies, almost nose to nose. His eyes bore down, displaying intolerance for Davies's arrogance. "Oh, you want etiquette, courtesy, and good manners. Let me watch you handcuff and arrest this monster with politeness if you even know how to." Sam moved to the two young agents with Davies. "One of you take a photo of your boss trying to cuff this mobster for the morning newspaper."

Sam watched Davies ask one of his agents for their handcuffs since he didn't carry them. He then struggled to get Geno's arms around his back to cuff his wrists together. Davies yelled at his agents to help him. Sam shook his head in disgust at what he saw and walked away toward Cassie, who held the arm of the decoy. Cassie advised Sam that the woman claimed Geno

Lamartino had paid her five hundred dollars to play a role in a movie scene. "You want to talk to her?"

"Nah. It would be non-productive. Have the FBI interview her. I need to make a call. Sam walked where he had privacy and called an ATF colleague for the second time.

"Hey, Sam. Sorry, I couldn't answer when you called before. I haven't heard from you in more than a year. What's up, my friend?

"You still on the FBI Organized Crime Task Force in New Jersey?"

"Yeah. It's going great. Why?"

"You still working the informant I gave you?"

"Yeah. He knows his shit, man. He's helping out a lot. I hope you're not calling to take him back, are you?"

"No. My partner, a female FBI agent, was abducted by the Lamartino family. Are you guys working that crew?"

"We are, but we haven't received any intel on them kidnapping an FBI agent."

"They recently took her. I need to find her before something bad happens to her. They took her to get to me. I know Sunday's probably your day off, but I need your help to find her. I want to meet with you and the CI. I need to know everything you know about Santo Lamartino, especially how I can get close to him. I won't get you involved, but I don't know the territory, like where the guy hangs out and where he lives."

"When are you planning to come here?"

"Today. I'll call you when I can break away from an arrest. I want to meet somewhere close to where Lamartino will be."

"Well, the guy is a creature of habit. He frequently spends time with his floozy on Sunday nights and leaves her place around midnight to head home to his wife. Nice guy, huh?"

"That's perfect. Text me where to meet you and DJ, somewhere private near the floozy's place. I'll text you what I need. Have that stuff with you when we meet. It'll take me a couple of hours to get there."

"How many guys are you bringing with you?"

"I'm coming alone."

CHAPTER
42

D riving to New Jersey was a bear on a Sunday afternoon. The end-of-weekend traffic was always heavy, a relentless river of headlights and brake lights stretching into infinity. The usual number of maniacs on the road made it treacherous as they weaved in and out of traffic lanes, hell-bent on getting wherever they were going before everyone else.

Sam hadn't been able to leave New Haven until nearly midafternoon. Durrell had wanted him to help interview those arrested, but Sam's mind was set on getting to New Jersey sooner rather than later. Before leaving, Sam had briefed Durrell on getting background on Santo Lamartino, though he kept the more precarious details of the real reason to himself, knowing she would disapprove of his plan. Sam did tell Cassie his mission but left out details; discretion was his ally. After gathering a few essential items, he set out for New Jersey.

Navigating the interstate, Sam drove cautiously, maintaining his speed and glancing at his rearview and side mirrors, vigilant against the chaotic ballet of vehicles around him. Every honk, every sudden lane change was a potential catastrophe. He arrived safely at the meeting place, a hole-in-the-wall pub a few miles from the residence of Lamartino's girlfriend. It was nearly five-thirty when Sam stepped inside the very dark dive. The place smelled of stale beer and desperation, where one might not leave the same way they went in, if at all. He scanned the room, his eyes adjusting to the dim light until spotting his colleague waving from a back booth. Sam gave his colleague, Rodrigo "Rod" Perez, a bump hug and the informant, Dontrell Jiles, or DJ, a fist bump.

Rod wasted no time providing extensive background on Santo Lamartino, noting his marriage with three sons, two of whom were part of their father's criminal enterprise.

"His youngest son, Gianni, wanted no part of the family business. He went his own way and graduated from college and law school. What didn't sit well with his father was when Gianni got a much younger black woman pregnant. Santo forbade him from marrying her. Word on the street was Santo paid her off to end the relationship. Furious, Gianni changed his name to Jonathan Martin and started fresh. He's now a professor at Yale."

"I'm familiar with Professor Martin," said Sam. "But let's stick to what you know about Santo and his mistress. How do I get into her place without being seen by his muscle?"

DJ leaned in, lowering his voice to a whisper. "I can help you with that, Sam. I've snooped around that place repeatedly for Rod and the task force."

Sam outlined his plan but made it clear he didn't want them directly involved, only needing DJ to assist him in getting into the house and warning him if Santo's men arrived. Rod felt apprehensive about Sam's plan, heavily weighed down by unspoken risks.

"How long will this take once you're inside?" said Rod, concern etched on his face.

"No idea. The shorter, the better. I want to be out within twenty minutes, give or take a few. I need DJ to drive me to the house, show me how to enter unseen, then leave with the car. I'll call you to return it when I leave the house."

Rod sketched the floozy's house interior on his notepad, a crude but functional blueprint as they talked. "I'll stay nearby until you're out."

"How do you know about the inside?" Sam asked, eyebrows raised.

"I've been in the house before, but that's between us," DJ replied with a sly grin.

Sam wasn't surprised. He glanced at his watch—it was almost six. "When does Santo usually arrive at his girlfriend's place?"

Rod checked his iPad, tapping a few keys. "He's not there yet. Let's grab a bite; it might be a while."

"You've got a camera on the house?" Sam inquired.

"Of course. The task force set it up months ago. If he shows up, we'll know."

Over a hasty meal, Sam filled in Rod and DJ on his partner's abduction, the trade-off Lamartino demanded, and the disastrous outcome of the attempted exchange in New Haven. A few minutes past six-thirty, Rod glanced at his iPad. "Santo's driver just pulled up in front of the hussy's place. He's going inside now."

"How long does his bodyguard stick around?" Sam asked.

"He doesn't. He comes back to pick up Santo when he's called."

"Well, that's a break. DJ, walk me through how to get in and out of the house without being seen."

DJ, with pointers from Rod, briefed Sam on the best way to infiltrate the house. "Rod and I have the necessary items you asked for. But Sam, whatever you do, don't get caught."

"Right. You guys have been a great help. I'm jittery just talking about it, but Lamartino forced me to do it this way. Wish me luck, and Rod, I owe you."

*   *   *

DJ led Sam through the backyard of a neighboring house on a rear parallel street. The six-foot chain-link fence separating the properties stood as a silent sentinel. With finesse, DJ released small metallic s-hooks that held together a section of the chain link fence he had previously cut. He then pulled back the section like opening a secret door. DJ secured it open with the s-hooks to keep it from snapping back.

Handing Sam a device to unlock a sliding glass door, DJ gave him a firm handshake. "Good luck, man." He then disappeared into the night, driving Sam's car to rendezvous with Rod. The plan was hazardous, and every minute phase had to work for success.

With a night vision device strapped over a black full-face mask, Sam moved silently across the backyard. The back deck loomed ahead. Sam softly stepped onto the deck. He approached the glass slider door, his heart pounding against his chest. Testing the handle, he found it unlocked. A stroke of luck or a careless oversight—either way, Sam took it as a good sign. He slid the door open just enough to slip inside, moving the curtain aside cautiously.

The room inside was a combination living room, dining room, and kitchen, dimly lit by a sliver of light from a partially open bedroom door. Sam took a moment to orient himself, noting the layout from Rod's sketch. He didn't need the night vision device but had to move carefully to avoid bumping into anything that might give him away.

Creeping forward, he passed a cushioned armchair, its arm draped with a coat. From the bedroom, the unmistakable sounds of giggling and sexual moans mingled with the squeak of a bed. Sam knew Santo and his mistress were inside, possibly indulging in more than each other's company. He pulled out his phone, set it to video, and positioned it low on the open doorway to capture the compromising scene. The footage would be Sam's leverage, a potent bargaining chip against Santo if needed.

Two minutes in, a phone rang in the bedroom. Sam's pulse quickened. Santo's gruff voice broke the rhythm of moans. "Shit! Who the hell is calling me now?" Santo picked up the phone to see who was calling, muttering, "Ah, shit. I gotta take this, sweetie. I'll be right back for more."

As Santo headed to the living room for privacy, Sam quietly moved from the bedroom door and hid behind the cushioned chair. His heart pounded like a drum in his chest, the thrill and terror of the moment blending into a potent adrenaline cocktail. He held his breath, the weight of his mission pressing down on him.

CHAPTER
43

S anto opened the bedroom door barefoot, wearing his pants and a sleeveless white T-shirt. His feet made no sound against the cold, tiled floor as he entered the dimly lit living room. He closed the bedroom door softly behind him. The only illumination came from the pale glow of a single kitchen counter night lamp. Santo sank into the worn, cushioned chair, its creak breaking the heavy silence.

"Yeah, what's up, Skip?" said Santo, holding his phone to his ear. "I'm busy, so make it quick." His voice was gruff, annoyance engraved into every word.

The voice on the other end of the line was frantic, loud enough for Sam to hear. The caller complained about the woman giving him trouble, warning him about being arrested. Skip wanted to know what he should do.

"Jesus, Skip. Put a sock in her mouth or slap her around until she shuts up. You're in charge there. Don't call me again. I'm busy." Santo hung up, exhaling in frustration as he attempted to rise from the chair.

Before he could stand, Sam's hand yanked him back down by the shoulder.

"What the fu—" Sam cut his protest short as he pressed a cold gun barrel against his temple, his voice a deadly whisper.

"One sound from you, and you're dead. Your life ends here on your squeeze's chair, not at home with your wife."

"I don't think you know who I am, pal," Santo spat back.

"I know who you are all too well, Lamartino," Sam replied slowly, his voice changed to a foreign accent made to disguise his identity.

Santo's body quivered under the threat, realizing his usual bravado was useless without his bodyguards.

"Whisper, or I'll pull the trigger."

"What do you want? Money. Just name it." Santo's voice was barely a whisper now, fear overtaking his usual arrogance.

Sam leaned in closer, his breath hot against Santo's ear. "Call Skip back. Tell him you decided to take care of the woman tonight, once and for all. Say you're driving to him. When you arrive, you'll beep the horn. Tell him to take the woman out to the car and put her in the back seat with her head covered and wrists tied. Got it?"

"Yeah, yeah, I got it. What're you gonna do with her?" trembled Santo.

"The same thing I'm gonna do to you if you don't do as I say." Sam's words dripped with menace.

Still trembling, Santo tried to negotiate. "I need her to make a trade, man. I'll pay you five grand to let me keep her."

"That's pocket change compared to what I'm getting."

"I'll double it."

"You got twenty-five grand in cash on you? Hmm, I doubt it." Sam's tone was mocking him.

"I can get it at my house."

"What, you think I'm stupid? I'm not going anywhere with you except where I tell you." Sam spoke slowly in broken English. "Make the call now." Sam cocked the gun, the metallic click making Santo jerk with fear.

"Easy, man, I'm calling him." Santo's hands shook as he reached for his phone.

"Give me your phone first." Sam scrolled through the recent calls, selected the last incoming call, and handed it back to Santo. "If you make one mistake, you're a dead man."

When Skip answered, Santo repeated the instructions, his voice hollow and submissive. He ended the call.

"You did good. Now, give me your phone." Sam pocketed the phone and motioned for Santo to put on his coat, having already checked the pockets for weapons.

"Who are you? You don't sound like a cop." Santo's voice was a mix of curiosity and fear.

"I go by many names, none of which you know, but a cop? Ha, that's a good one. Now get off the chair, and let's go see Skip."

"I need my shoes, man. I'm barefoot."

"No shoes. Button up your coat and pants and move to the rear slider."

"I have to tell Gina I'm leaving." Gina had turned up the sound on the TV, oblivious to what was happening.

"I'll let you call her from the car." Sam slid the door open and pushed Santo out onto the deck. The cool night air was cold against Santo's bare feet. Sam shut the door quietly behind them and forced Santo off the deck, pulling his own phone out to call DJ.

"I'm out," said Sam to DJ and ended the call.

Sam pushed Lamartino through the fence opening. He undid the ties holding the fence open, allowing it to swing back to its closed position. Sam still had the gun pointed at Santo's head.

"Move to the street. Don't make a sound." Sam's voice was low but threatening.

They remained behind a large shrub near the road until Sam heard DJ dropping off Sam's sedan as planned. DJ left in Rod's car. Sam pushed Santo to the street, forcing him toward the awaiting vehicle. They moved in unison, two shadowy figures in the darkness. Sam opened the car door and motioned Santo to sit in the passenger seat. Sam moved around the front of the car with his eyes on Santo and entered from the driver's side.

"You see the plastic ties hanging over your left shoulder from the headrest?"

"I see them," Santo replied, his voice trembling.

"Buckle up and then put your right hand into one of the open sections. Then, pull the strap down to tighten it around your wrist. That'll keep you from doing anything stupid while we're driving."

Once Santo cuffed his wrist, Sam's tone softened, but only slightly. "Now sit back, relax, and tell me how to get to Skip's place. So you know, my friends are close. If you don't take me straight to Skip and the woman, I'll have to torture you until you do. That'll be fun for me. Ha, ha, ha."

Santo wasn't laughing. His mind raced with fear, believing this guy was crazy enough to do what he said. As they drove, Santo gave Sam, whom he assumed was a demented killer, the most direct directions to where he kept the kidnapped agent. The drive was silent, but Santo worried about his well-being throughout the ride, the minutes stretching into an eternity. It was an eternity for Sam as well. Sweat permeated through the mask he wore.

"When you go around the next curve, turn right after the large boulder just off the road."

Sam made the turn. The car bounced over a deteriorated blacktop riddled with potholes. Each jolt sent a loud bang through the undercarriage, making Sam worry about the front tires surviving the impacts as they approached a desolate, dilapidated warehouse.

"This can't be where Skip lives. What is he, homeless?" Sam's voice was incredulous.

"I brought you to where you wanted to go, not to say anything about where Skip lives or doesn't live."

Sam made a U-turn to keep the passenger side facing the building. He started beeping the horn until a door creaked open. A tall, thin man in his fifties emerged, pushing a hooded figure bound at the wrists. Sam cut the plastic tie, freeing Santo's hand, then lowered the passenger side window.

"Tell him to stop and remove the hood so you can see her face." Sam's tone was commanding.

Santo complied, his voice fractured. Once Sam recognized it was Kiara, he ordered Santo to have Skip cover her head again and put her in the back seat.

"Don't answer any questions. Tell Skip you'll call him in the morning."

"What's going on, boss?" Skip asked, his voice tinged with confusion as he placed Kiara on the back seat.

"I'm taking care of business. I'll call you in the morning." Santo's voice was flat, devoid of emotion.

Sam closed the window and slowly drove off. In the rearview mirror, he saw Skip shrugging his shoulders, his arms raised in bewilderment.

"Take a left," Santo instructed, trying to regain some semblance of control.

Instead, Sam exited right and stepped on the gas.

"Where're you going, man? You're going the wrong way. Aren't you taking me back to the house?" Santo panicked.

Sam didn't respond, his eyes fixed on the navigation screen as he memorized the warehouse's location.

"There's another plastic loop over your shoulder. Put your right arm into it and tighten it around your wrist."

Sam slowed to crawl and pointed his gun at Lamartino's face. "Do it now."

Santo complied with the orders. Sam put the gun on his lap and used his fingers to expand the map on the screen, searching for a suitable stopping point.

"Where are you taking me? If you bring me back to Gina's place, I've got ten grand stashed there. It's yours." Santo's voice was desperate now, grasping at straws.

"Ha. You take me for a fool. You'll know where we are going when we get there." Sam's reply was cold and final.

Santo fell silent, the fear tightening his chest. He concocted the thought that the masked man was going to kill him where no one would find his body.

"Name your price," said Santo, his voice tattered.

"Quiet while I think."

Not long after, Sam saw what he was looking for on the navigation screen. Two miles further, he turned right off the road.

Santo panicked. "What? Wait? Why are you stopping here? This is a frigging cemetery, man. What's going on?"

CHAPTER
44

Santo wiggled in his seat, his stomach churning and his heart thumping, matching the rhythm of his frantic breaths. Every nerve in his body tingled with fear as he glanced around the desolate cemetery, the moon casting eerie shadows among the gravestones like spirits lurking in the night. He couldn't shake the chilling thought that he might never leave this place alive, his body forgotten among the silent dead.

Sam cut the plastic tie around Santo's wrist and exited the car. He trotted around the car's front end to the passenger door, opened it, and shouted for Santo to get out.

Santo could hardly breathe. His chest heaved with the weight of desperation. Sweat formed on his forehead, stinging his eyes as it cascaded down his cheeks. He wiped the sweat away with his coat sleeve. Panic clawed at his insides, and he let out a pitiful whine, pleading, "Come on, man, I've got a wife and kids who count on me. Please." His voice shattered with fear, the words failing as he strategized his next move, inching ever so slowly toward the open car door.

"Get out of the car, or I'll drag you out."

Impatient, Sam grabbed Santo's arm with a vice-like grip, pulling him out of the car. Santo, who outweighed Sam by forty pounds, immediately realized that it was now or never—fight or flight. Summoning every ounce of his weight, he rammed into Sam with the force of a bull, lifting him off his feet and slamming him to the ground with a bone-jarring thud. Sam gasped, winded, struggling to regain his breath as Santo lunged for Sam's gun in his hand; the cold metal glinted in the moonlight, just out of reach.

Sam's reflexes kicked in, propelling his gun inches out of Santo's reach. Not wanting to escalate to lethal force, Sam balled his left hand into a fist and delivered a crushing blow to Santo's face, then again with his right hand, forcing Santo back. Sam pushed and lifted his upper body, shoving Santo off him with both hands.

Santo scrambled to his feet and screamed for help with only the dead in earshot. He ran in the darkness, blind, for a way to escape. He took off scampering as his unfit body protested. His bare feet pounded the rough stone pathway, sharp stone bits biting into his soles, each step a painful reminder of his peril.

Behind him on the ground, Sam chuckled at the sight of Santo's ungainly escape, his legs jerking up and down as if dancing a frantic jig. Rising slowly, Sam brushed off his pants, took a deep breath, imitated a mock chase, and yelled, "I'm right behind you, Santo!" He watched with amusement as Santo stumbled towards a grassy section, finally finding some relief from the punishing stones beneath his feet.

Sam retrieved his gun and shifted back to the car. He opened the rear door and spoke softly, "Okay, You could get out now."

"No. Leave me alone," Kiara's voice trembled with fear, her body curling away towards the middle of the seat. "I'm a federal agent. If you hurt me, you'll spend the rest of your life in prison."

"I'm not going to harm you, Kiara," said Sam in his usual voice. "I'm taking you back to New Haven. Now get in the front seat, please."

"What?" Kiara's confusion and fear were apparent, her covered face withered and confused.

Sam leaned in, his expression softening as he pulled off his mask and hers. "Look, Kiara. It's me."

"Sam?" she cried, her voice a choked whisper. Tears welled up and spilled over, leaving wet trails down her cheeks. "Sam," she sobbed, "You came for me."

"Yes, but I don't want your kidnapper to know it's me. Let me free your hands, then move into the front seat." He gently untied her hands, his movements deliberate and calming. Once Kiara was in the front seat, Sam put his mask back on and glanced over his shoulder to shout at Santo again. "I'll find you, Santo!" He shed the mask, slid into the driver's seat, and carefully drove out of the cemetery, the car's tires crunching softly on the gravel path.

Meanwhile, Santo huddled behind a massive headstone, his entire body trembling. He panted heavily, coughing occasionally, as he brushed tiny pebbles from his aching feet. Santo's mind raced, knowing he had to move, but became paralyzed in fear of the deranged killer chasing him. Santo's heart fluttered faster than a hummingbird's wings as he peered cautiously around the edge of the headstone.

Seeing no one, he forced himself to his feet and started jogging toward the road.

His steps were unsteady. He tripped over a low headstone, crashing onto another flat gravestone with the palm of his hand, hearing a crackle of bones breaking, screaming in pain.

"Ah. Damn it," cried Santo, clutching his hand. He rolled to his side, rubbing the injury, waiting for the pain to subside. Exhausted and defeated, he collapsed in front of another headstone, his heart hammering wildly. The absurdity of dying from a heart attack in a cemetery wasn't lost on him. He let out a bitter laugh, seeing another gravestone opposite him inscribed, 'Pray sinner for forgiveness or eternally suffer in hell.'

Calming his nerves, Santo took a cautious peek, ensuring the coast was clear before scrambling towards the road. When he finally reached it, he leaned heavily on a wooden guardrail, gasping for breath like a man who had just finished a marathon. Minutes later, headlight beams cut through the darkness, coming from a curve to his left. He limped onto the road, arms waving frantically. His coat flapped open, revealing a soiled white T-shirt and battered, bare feet.

The approaching pickup truck swerved as its driver, distracted by the radio, suddenly noticed the barefooted figure. He jerked the wheel, narrowly avoiding a collision, but the side mirror brushed Santo, knocking him to the ground. The driver, eyes wide with alarm, glanced back and saw the man struggling to rise. Guilt gnawed at him, but knowing he had been drinking, he hesitated to call the police or offer the guy assistance. He backed up with the window down, yelling, "You okay, buddy?"

"Yeah. I'm okay," lied Santo, trying to explain why he was on the road. "I just fought with a friend. He got pissed and left me here. I need to get home, but I'm stranded. I'd appreciate a lift. I'll give you fifty bucks. It's about a fifteen-minute drive."

The driver eyed him skeptically. "You don't look like you've got two cents, never mind fifty bucks."

"Looks can be deceiving. I have a friend only fifteen minutes from here. I'd be grateful if you could drop me off there. I promise I'm not homeless. Please."

The driver, feeling a mix of sympathy and guilt, finally nodded. "I guess I can do that much. Hop in."

As they drove, Santo asked to use the driver's cell phone to call his friend, instructing him to be ready with fifty dollars. Skip was waiting outside the old warehouse when they arrived. Santo handed the promised fifty and thanked the driver, who drove off with a satisfied smile.

Santo used Skip's cell phone to call his bodyguard. "Vinnie, a hired killer, took the FBI agent from the warehouse. I need you to gather Ron, Joey, Marty, and Frank and find the bastard. Kill him, and bring the woman back to me. The guy's in a tan sedan with Massachusetts plates, probably heading past Saint Marks Cemetery, heading toward the turnpike. Check gas stations, diners, and anywhere he might stop. Have the guys and you meet me at the warehouse. I'll have a photo of the woman. Get here quick."

CHAPTER
45

S am's fingers danced nervously over the navigation screen, eyes glimpsing between the digital map and the darkened road ahead. The dashboard glow cast his face in a cool, ghostly blue. Symbols for gas and food flickered up ahead, promising a brief reprieve. Three miles later, the neon lights of a gas station glimmered through the twilight, reflecting off the damp pavement. Sam's cell phone buzzed insistently on his lap. He snatched it and glanced at the caller ID. It was Rod.

"Hey, everything went down as planned. I have the package. We'll talk later, Thanks." Sam pulled into the lot of an old-style diner adjacent to the gas station.

"Why are we stopping?" Kiara's voice was fragile, barely audible over the engine's hum.

"I'm hungry, and I need coffee. You hungry?" Sam's tone was gentle but firm, trying to mask the urgency simmering beneath the surface.

Kiara's eyes darted around, unfocused and glazed with fear. "Can't we, uh, stop when we get to Connecticut?" She sounded incoherent, the words tumbling over each other.

He parked the car between two large SUVs. It was a calculated move. Staying out of sight was crucial now. He reached beneath the seat, his fingers brushing the cold steel of his badge and a leather case containing his knife. Sam shoved the case into his sock, his badge into his pocket, and tucked his gun securely into his belt. He turned to Kiara, his eyes softening as he saw her huddled in the passenger seat, her lips trembling and eyes wet with tears. Her breaths came in shaky gasps like she was cold.

Sam's heart ached at the sight of her; her vulnerability starkly contrasted with the fierce determination he knew she always had. "What's up with you, Kiara? We're going home."

Kiara lunged forward, wrapping her arms around Sam, clinging to him as if he were her lifeline. "I thought"—sniffle—"I thought you were someone who was going to kill me. I was so scared, Sam. I"—sniffle—"thought you were going to leave me and Santo dead in the cemetery."

Sam held her tightly, feeling the rhythm of her fear pulsating against him. "I can't imagine what you went through. But you're safe now. We're going back to New Haven. We'll find Travis and get you back to Boston."

Kiara tightened her grip on him, her body shaking with quiet sobs. "You saved me. I don't know how to thank you."

Sam pulled back slightly, looking her in the eye. "You just did. Now, try to get a hold of yourself. Everything's back to normal now. We're a team again. Let's get inside. I have to pee bad."

Kiara's grip loosened, and she looked at him, her face breaking into a small, shaky smile. "You have to pee?" She giggled, a sound so unexpected it almost startled Sam.

"Don't make me laugh, or I'll pee my pants," Sam chuckled, feeling a strange, lightheartedness bubbling up despite the tension.

Kiara's giggle turned into full-blown laughter, causing Sam to join in. "Okay, okay. I have to pee, too, so let's go pee," she said, still laughing.

Sam reached under the seat, pulled out his smaller pistol, and handed it to Kiara. "Take this, just in case Lamartino's goons are nearby."

They stepped out into the cool night air. Sam popped the trunk, throwing on a nondescript jacket and retrieving a black pea coat, a ski cap, eyeglasses, and a New Jersey license plate.

"What's all this for?" asked Kiara.

"The coat, glasses, and hat are for you. I want you to look different from those bastards who held you. The license plate has magnets; it's to cover the Massachusetts plate. Lamartino's men might be on the lookout for us."

"Didn't you take his phone?"

"I did. But if Santo makes it to the road and flags down a car, he could ask to use the driver's phone to call for help."

Kiara shook her head in agreement.

"Let's get inside and use the restroom," said Sam, putting on a New York Giants cap. "We can order sandwiches and coffee to take with us or have them here."

"I'm starving. Let's eat here," Kiara said, her voice firm with the first hint of decisiveness since their escape.

The diner had a single unisex restroom. Sam had Kiara go in first while he ordered two sandwiches and coffee. As Kiara emerged from the bathroom, Sam noticed a man slipping into it just as she left. *Figures. I hope that guy's not in for the long haul. I gotta go bad,* Sam thought, squeezing his thighs together.

Kiara took a seat next to him at the counter. Sam's eyes scanned the diner, sipping his coffee. A lone guy sat at the counter's far end, two men occupied a booth, and a man and woman with two kids took up another booth by the window. Sam noted the positions of the exit signs, calculating possible escape routes. He then noticed Kiara staring at him.

"What?"

"Are we meeting the backup team here?" she asked.

Sam glanced towards the restroom as the man exited, then excused himself and hurried into it. When he returned, Kiara was still watching him intently. "Where are we meeting the backup team, Sam?"

Sam didn't want to discuss her rescue. He focused on his sandwich, chewing slowly, buying time.

"Well. Are we meeting them here or later?"

"I had help from a colleague in New Jersey and his CI. They provided minor support. No one could know that they helped me."

"Who were you talking to when we stopped here? You said things went down as planned."

"That was my colleague checking on the status."

Kiara seemed puzzled by Sam's reluctance to share details, figuring he had to have backup from New Haven. She sipped her coffee and finished her sandwich. "I'm still hungry. I'm getting another sandwich. You have to pay. I don't have any money."

Sam's gaze flickered to the diner's front window, scanning for any signs of Lamartino's men. Kiara followed his gaze, sensing his unease. Sam's focus returned to his food, concerned about potential threats.

Oblivious to the tension, Kiara savored her second sandwich, her eyes occasionally darting to the window, expecting to see someone join them, maybe Sam's backup crew. They both asked for a coffee refill. Kiara occasionally snuck a peek at Sam.

Sam's watch ticked away the seconds, not answering Kiara. She cradled her coffee cup, wondering why Sam wouldn't answer her. He rose to use the restroom again, his movements purposeful, his mind whirring with plans.

Once he returned, Kiara was still sitting there, her eyes searching his face.

"We'll be leaving in a few minutes," said Sam. "Do you need anything else for the ride?"

"No. Are we meeting your colleagues now?"

Sam shook his head. "No. We're not meeting anyone."

"Then who are the four guys in the two cars that just arrived?"

CHAPTER
46

Sam stood to peer out the window, catching a glimpse of four Mob flunkies huddled in two cars, their eyes scrutinizing those in the diner. The harsh glow of the diner's neon sign flickered, casting ominous shadows that whirled across their faces. Sam's anxiety elevated. He became despondent over having to deal with these gangsters again. He swallowed hard, his mind racing with ways to protect Kiara. He turned to face Kiara.

"Kiara, get low and move around the counter into the back kitchen."

"Why?" Kiara's eyes widened with alarm, her fingers gripping the counter's edge.

"Don't argue. Just do it, please. I'll follow you in there."

Sam pulled his badge from his coat, flashing it to the waitress, who eyed him suspiciously. "Ma'am, I need you to follow us into the kitchen. Now."

The waitress, her name tag reading "Laura," glanced at him, a crease of worry forming on her forehead. "What's going on?" she asked as they joined the cook, Kurt, who was Laura's husband. The odor in the kitchen lingered with the scent of frying bacon and onions.

"There are four Mafia men about to walk in here. They're after the woman I'm with. We need to hide her. I don't want a shoot-out in your diner."

Laura's eyes widened, disbelief etched on her face. "You're joking, right? I don't want any trouble in . . ." Her voice trailed off as the bell above the door jingled, and the four men entered, their presence looming like a storm cloud. Laura took a step back, her eyes flustered seeing the intruders.

Sam leaned in closer to Laura; urgency seeped into his tone. "I need a place to hide her right now. Somewhere they won't think to look."

Laura shrugged, her face pale. Kurt, wiping his hands on a stained apron, spoke up. "I've got a truck out back. It's a four-door. She could lie on the floor in the back. There are blankets and boxes to cover her. The windows are tinted—they won't see a thing."

"Perfect. Let's get her out there before those guys come in here."

Sam peeked through the swinging kitchen door, his gaze landing on the men showing a photo to the diners. Sam asked Laura to act normal and go back to the counter. "If they ask about the woman in a photo, tell them she came in to use the bathroom and then left. Say you didn't see any car. If they ask why I was back here, tell them I'm the diner's owner, checking the place before obtaining money to deposit in the bank tomorrow."

Laura nodded, her face set with determination. Sam and Kurt quickly ushered Kiara through the rear door, placing her on the truck's back floor and covering her with blankets and boxes. The chilly night air stung Sam's cheeks as they hurried back inside, locking the vehicle behind them.

Laura greeted the four men with a forced smile. "Do you need a menu?" she asked, her voice steady despite the fear in her eyes.

One of the men, a hulking figure with a scowl etched into his face, thrust a photo toward her. "Has this woman been in here?"

Laura studied the photo, her hand trembling and clammy. "Yeah, she looks like the woman who came inside to use the bathroom and left in a hurry."

The other men showed the photo to the remaining customers. Each person shook their head, denying they saw her. Sam reentered the dining area, picked up his coffee cup, and took a simulated sip, his eyes glued on the intruders.

"What about you, pal?" the stocky man asked, shoving the photo in Sam's face.

Sam glanced at the photo, his brows knitting together in a frown. "Laura, is that the woman who came in just to use the restroom?"

Laura nodded, playing along. "Yes, I believe it was."

"Why is there another coffee cup next to you?" the man pressed, suspicion dripping from his voice.

Sam thought quickly. "I asked for a refill. Laura brought me a fresh cup like she often does. I'm the owner here."

The man turned to Laura, who confirmed Sam's story with a nod. "Who's in the backroom?" he demanded.

"The cook, my husband, Kurt," Laura answered, her voice tight.

"Mikey, check the restroom," the mobster barked, then added, "I want to talk to Kurt."

Laura stepped aside, her pulse quickening as the big man pushed past her into the kitchen. Sam watched, holding his breath, as minutes ticked by. Finally, the man returned after seeing Kurt cooking, checking out the kitchen area, and returning to the front. His gaze swept over the counter before he turned to his companions. "Check the cars in the lot, then the gas station next door," he grunted.

A collective sigh of relief swept through the diner. Sam motioned to Laura for two bottles of water to go, keeping an eye out the window as the men checked on the cars parked at the restaurant. They then walked to the gas station, went inside, exited about 10 minutes later, and walked out carrying bags of snacks and six-packs of beer. They drove off, their taillights disappearing onto the highway.

Sam paid for the sandwiches, coffee, and water and left a big tip. "Thank you," he said to Kurt and Laura, his voice heavy with gratitude. "You've been a huge help."

When getting Kiara from Kurt's truck, she clung to Sam's arm, her body unsteady as they walked to their car. Sam opened the car door for her. She sank into the seat, still trembling from the ordeal.

"We have a two-hour ride to New Haven," Sam said gently, handing her water. "Try to relax, maybe take a nap."

"Can I borrow your phone to call Mariela? She must be worried sick,"

"I don't want my phone records showing calls from New Jersey. I'll let you use it when we get closer to New Haven."

Kiara's gaze bore into him. "You didn't have a backup team, did you?" Her voice wavered. "Why didn't agents from New Haven or Boston help you?"

"Going alone was the best option. I didn't want to put anyone in jeopardy of losing their job. It's better if you don't know the rest. I'll be the only one to answer questions about what happened tonight from our supervisors and the attorneys."

"Sam. You kidnapped Lamartino at gunpoint, didn't you?"

Sam's silence spoke volumes.

"You did, didn't you? I can't believe you."

"Don't ask questions you don't want the answers to," Sam said, his voice low. "You're my partner and my friend. Do you think I'd let those bastards get away with what they did to you? No fucking way. Lamartino was lucky he didn't do anything stupid."

"I was so scared, Sam. Every minute, I thought they were going to kill me. And then you showed up, and I didn't know what to think. When you told me it was you, I thought you were a mirage, an angel sent to bring me home." She sniffled, tears rolling down her cheeks. "I'll never forget what you did for me. You are the best friend I ever had."

Sam chuckled, a warm, comforting sound. "You're going to make me cry," he teased, trying to lighten the mood.

Kiara swatted his shoulder playfully. "Always joking, Sam."

"I appreciate what you said, but you're safe now." Sam took a deep breath. "I never did anything like this before. It was nerve-racking for me, not so much for my safety but yours. I don't want to talk or think about it anymore. Try to relax and not ask questions. I need to calm down, too." Sam looked to see Kiara nodding her head in agreement. "The less you know, the better. Your boss and the attorneys will ask you what happened tonight. You won't have much to tell them." He paused for his words to sink in. "Let's get to New Haven. I don't want to stay in New Jersey longer than necessary."

*   *   *

As they neared Milford, Sam called Cassie. "I've got Kiara. She's okay. We're about thirty minutes from New Haven. Brief Durrell and meet us at the hospital."

He ended the call and handed Kiara his phone so she could call Mariela. Kiara chatted with her girlfriend until arriving at Yale-New Haven Hospital. Sam was relieved to see Cassie and Brian Murphy waiting there. They clapped their hands together, applauding as Kiara and Sam exited the car. Cassie hugged Kiara and Sam, her eyes brimming with relief.

Brian hugged them both as well. He informed Sam that Durrell paved the way for Kiara to be readmitted without any hassle. "She'll call you later."

Inside, a nurse escorted Kiara to her room, promising a doctor would check on her soon. Moments later, Dell Haskins, still in New Haven following the failed trade for Kiara, arrived with two FBI agents. He immediately requested a private word with Sam.

Outside the room, Dell was serious, his expression stern. "Tell me what the hell happened tonight, Sam."

"I'm tired and groggy, Dell. I need to sleep before coherently describing what happened. I'll give you a short version now. After the stunt Lamartino pulled on us, using a substitute for Kiara, I couldn't chance they would never release her or hurt her. So, I went to New Jersey to get help from a colleague and an informant to find Santo Lamartino. When I found him, I convinced him to turn Kiara over to me and brought her back here."

"Oh. You convinced a New Jersey Mob boss to turn Kiara, whom he kidnapped, over to you, a federal agent. And Lamartino said, 'Hey, no problem, Sam. I'll let you have Kiara back, and you don't owe me a thing.' Is that what you're telling me?"

"Pretty much so. Yeah."

"Sam. Listen . . ."

"I know what you're going to say, Dell, but you wouldn't have approved it if I told you what I planned to do to get Kiara back. I did what I had to do before any harm came to her. Nobody got hurt. Lamartino doesn't know who I was, and there is no way for him to find out. There'll be no repercussions from it. Kiara is back safe and unharmed. Let it go at that."

"I can't accept that. I need to know how it went down. My boss, the US Attorney, and others will want full details."

"For some, what I did could be considered crossing the line. But what I did was morally, ethically, and just. Brian Murphy told me that Durrell wanted to meet with me. I assume she'll ask the same question. I'll explain what happened exactly the way I'm explaining it to you. If I give her more, you'll know about it. I'm sure she'll brief you on what she learned. Let's focus on Kiara's well-being, not what I did to get her back. Right now, I'm dead tired and need to sleep before meeting with Durrell in the morning. We'll take it from there. After that, I plan on finishing my job here by arresting Jonathon Martin, or should I say Gianni Lamartino, for lying to us. His arrest could lead us to Travis. When it does, I'll find the person who shot Kiara."

Dell sighed, unable to voice his approval. "We'll talk again after you meet with the US Attorney."

As Sam started to walk toward the exit, Dell, shaking his head in disbelief, called out to him. "You're some agent, Sam!" He paused, shaking his head. "Don't repeat what I said, but thanks for bringing Kiara back safe. Outstanding job."

Sam tipped his head, saying, "Thanks, Dell. Would you assign an FBI security team outside Kiara's room?"

Dell nodded with a silent promise. Sam walked away, relieved that he brought Kiara back unharmed. More so, he was fortunate to be alive.

CHAPTER
47

As Sam navigated the dimly lit streets toward his hotel, the soft hum of the car's engine was interrupted by his phone ringing. He answered the call, seeing Durrell's name flash on the screen. Durrell proposed they meet for breakfast and promised to text him the details in the morning.

After a hot shower, Sam set the alarm for five-thirty and collapsed onto the bed. The day's tension melted away as sleep claimed him within minutes. In the morning, the alarm's shrill ring jolted him awake at dawn. Sam rolled over twice, not wanting to get up, but remembered Durrell scheduled breakfast with him. He showered again, shaved, and dressed. As he tightened his shoelaces, his phone buzzed with a text from Durrell detailing the time and place of their breakfast meeting.

Unfamiliar with the restaurant, Sam did a quick Google search and discovered it was an upscale venue on the nineteenth floor of a luxury hotel, boasting panoramic views of the city's historic green. To match the setting, he opted for a jacket but skipped the tie, aiming for a balance of casual and classy.

With time to spare before meeting Durrell, Sam drove through the morning haze to Yale University's Cooperative residence for professors and administrators. He hoped to find Gianni Lamartino, known more familiarly as Professor Jonathon Martin. The streets were quiet so early in the morning, the calm before the city's academic bustle. He parked outside the apartment building and entered its marbled lobby. Approaching the visitor's desk, he introduced himself and asked for Professor Martin.

"He's not in. He left around fifteen minutes ago," replied the desk receptionist, a young man with tired eyes.

"Was he alone?" Sam inquired, his tone probing.

"No, I think he was with two students."

Sam pulled out his phone and showed a photo of Travis. "Is this one of the students?"

The receptionist squinted at the image. "Yeah, that's one of them."

Sam then showed a photo of Julian Jarrett, which he had obtained from campus police. "And this one?"

"Looks like him, yeah."

"Did they mention where they were going or when they'd return?"

The receptionist hesitated before replying, "I heard one of the students mention Panera, but I'm not sure if that's where they went."

Sam thanked him and walked briskly to the nearby café. Checking his watch, he saw it was nearly seven and called Kiara.

"Hi, Sam. I have a special visitor, Mariela. She wants to say hi." Kiara's voice was light, and the familiar warmth in her tone was evident.

Mariela's voice sounded sincere. "Thank you for bringing Kiara back safely. She spoke so highly of you. You're her best friend, so now you're mine, too."

Sam smiled at the genuine affection. "I appreciate that. You have my friendship as well."

Mariela handed the phone back to Kiara. "Did you sleep well, Sam?"

"I conked out as soon as my head hit the pillow. Hope you managed to get some rest, too."

"I wish. I tossed and turned, haunted by memories of that cold, damp warehouse. But waking up to Mariela by my side made it all bearable."

Sam's tone grew serious. "How did it go with Dell? I'm sure he grilled you on your escape."

"It was okay. I told him I couldn't remember much because of the drugs. I only briefed him on what happened after you found me. He wasn't thrilled but didn't push for more. He mentioned arranging security for me."

"Good to hear. I just visited the Yale Cooperative Apartments. The desk clerk told me Professor Martin left earlier with two students. I showed him photos of Travis and Julian, and he identified them as the two students. So, it appears Travis is alive and well. The desk clerk overheard one of the students mention a café, so I'm heading there now. If they're at the café, I'll follow them back. If Travis and Julian return to the apartment with Martin, we'll go there with Lieutenant Dawson and a detective to get Travis. Are you up for that? We could ask Dell to send an agent with us."

Kiara had her phone on speaker. Mariela, overhearing the conversation, interjected, "Kiara needs rest. She can't work so soon."

"Kiara will be safe with me. It won't take more than an hour. I'll bring her back to the hospital afterward," Sam reassured.

"It's okay, Mariela. I'll go with Sam and come back in time for the physical therapy. You can wait for me," Kiara insisted, her determination clear.

"You two sort it out," Sam said. "I have to meet with Durrell soon. I'll call you later."

Disguised in a baseball cap and sunglasses, Sam entered the café. He scanned the patrons and spotted Martin with Travis and Julian at a table in the rear. The two youngsters had smiles on their faces as they spoke like they were good friends. Sam left the restaurant, crossed the street, and hid behind a parked car. When the professor and students finally exited the café, Sam followed them discreetly to York Street, watching from a distance as they entered the apartment building. Sam waited until it was a few minutes before nine to meet with the US Attorney. Satisfied that Travis and Julian hadn't left the building, Sam drove to meet Durrell.

Arriving at the restaurant ten minutes late, he found Durrell already seated. Sam followed the host to her table. She greeted Sam with a hug, a gesture that caught him off guard, but he awkwardly reciprocated.

"Good morning, Deb. Sorry, I'm late . . ."

"No problem, Sam." Durrell interrupted. "It gave me time to enjoy the view of the city's central park. How are you? Did you sleep well?"

"I was out like a light. I set the alarm because I didn't want to oversleep."

They sat at the table adjacent to a large window overlooking the city green.

Durrell's gaze softened. "You had a critical mission. First, I want to thank you for rescuing Kiara. I'm just a bit disappointed you didn't trust me with your plan. I could have provided support."

Sam sighed, leaning back in his chair. "I couldn't be sure anyone would approve of my strategy. I didn't want to put you in a tough position if things went wrong. I wasn't certain my scheme would work out, but I couldn't let anyone hurt Kiara. Some will say I crossed a line, but I did what I believed was morally and ethically right."

Durrell's eyes sparkled with curiosity. "Tell me how you did it, Sam. It stays between us. I'm worried about Santo Lamartino. He's dangerous and may seek revenge."

"He doesn't know it was me. I wore a full face mask and used a foreign accent. He thought I was a hired assassin."

Durrell's eyebrows shot up. "You had the Mafia boss. How?"

Knowing it would stay between them, Sam recounted his daring plan, detailing how he coerced Lamartino into releasing Kiara with the help of an informant. He described the tense journey from the mistress's home to the warehouse, the final confrontation at a cemetery, and the aftermath at the diner.

"I've never done anything like this before. It was tense and exhausting. I hope I never have to face anything like that again." Sam confessed, his voice sincere.

Durrell leaned forward, her expression earnest. "What you did was courageous, Sam. The pressure and fear of failure must have been immense. I was impressed with your work on the Harrington case, but this—this is something else."

Sam interrupted gently. "Thanks, but to change to a matter of importance: I saw Travis and another student dining with Professor Martin this morning. I followed them to Martin's apartment. They didn't leave while I was there, so I think they might still be inside."

"We should have a surveillance team there."

"I'm working alone, and Kiara's in the hospital. Davies and I don't see eye-to-eye. He doesn't trust my methods, and I don't think he understands what it takes to do the job."

"What about Dell? He has agents with him."

"He assigned them to stand guard outside Kiara's room."

Durrell pondered for a moment. "I could call Davies to set up surveillance."

"That would just give him the credit for finding Travis. Kiara should get the recognition for finding him, not Davies. She went through hell and back."

Durrell nodded thoughtfully. "It's not about who finds him; it's about the senator knowing her son is safe."

"I'll check the security cameras at the building to see if they left. If they're still there, I'll get Kiara and head to the apartment building with support from Dell and Lieutenant Dawson. Kiara deserves to finish this case. It's her victory, and she needs recognition after what she went through."

Durrell considered Sam's words, understanding the importance of closure for Kiara. "There will be no legal consequences toward you from my office, but Lamartino won't forget this. You've taken down his sons. He might try coming after you."

"I'm ready for whatever comes next, Deb."

"I know you are. Let's reschedule breakfast. You should go and get Travis. That would put the senator at peace. I'll call Dell to have agents with you for backup. Let me know how it turns out."

Sam agreed. He left the restaurant with a new resolve in his step. He called Kiara to get ready to find Travis and bring an end to their investigation.

CHAPTER
48

Kiara stood by the mirror, her mind racing with anticipation. The hospital room starkly contrasted her current appearance as if she had entered another unknown world. Her sharp eyes glinted under the fluorescent lights as she turned to face the room's door, which swung open.

Sam's silhouette filled the frame. His expression displayed urgency but controlled calm. The two exchanged a silent nod, a language forged through days of working together.

"Got the approval from Haskins," Sam said, his voice low and measured. He quickly briefed Kiara and the two FBI agents stationed at her door, stressing their gear's importance. "It's a low-risk operation, but keep your vests on and bring extra ammo and plastic cuffs," he said. The seriousness in his eyes contradicted his words, hinting that no mission was ever totally without danger.

As they made their way to the vehicles, Kiara slipped on her vest and cuffs before sliding into her car. The other two agents followed in a separate vehicle. The drive was swift, the city streets a blur of grays and blues under the morning sky. They arrived at the apartment building, where Cassie Dawson and Detective Matt Kendrick stood by the entrance, their stances radiating readiness.

Sam parked the car close to the building; the engine ticked as it cooled. Just as he was about to step out, his phone rang. He glanced at the phone's screen, noting the absence of a caller ID. His brow furrowed as he debated whether to answer. Finally, curiosity won.

"Yeah, hello," he said, his voice tinged with caution.

The voice on the other end was raspy and sounded defensive and anxious.

"Whatever happened to your partner wasn't my doing. I had nothing to do with it."

Sam recognized Santo Lamartino's voice. Sam kept his response steady, masking the surprise.

"I don't believe you. You must have had something to do with it."

"I swear it was not me," Santo insisted, a note of desperation crept into his tone. "Some masked guy found where she was kept and took her. That's all I know. I swear."

Sam's mind raced as he processed the information. He chose his following words carefully. "I can't talk now. I'm about to arrest your son, Gianni. He lied to us about a Yale student's whereabouts. His parents are worried sick, not hearing from him for weeks. I saw Gianni with their son and Julian Jarrett having breakfast this morning. Jarrett and maybe Gianni are scamming their son out of his money."

A heavy silence followed. Sam could almost hear Santo mumbling to himself on the other end. "Are you still there, Santo?"

"Yeah," came the reluctant reply. "If I convince my son to turn the student over to you, will you promise not to arrest him?"

Sam's eyes narrowed. "He may be involved in the scheme with Jarrett."

"You may not know Jarrett's real name. It's Jeremy Barrett, and he is Gianni's son."

"I didn't know that," said a surprised Sam. "Are you sure? Jarrett is nineteen years old."

"Yeah. My son knocked up some young girl at school twenty years ago. It's been almost that long since we've talked. He wanted no part of the family business. For personal reasons, I didn't want him involved with this girl and didn't want her to have my son's child."

"You mean you didn't want her as your daughter-in-law and to have her child," said Sam, emphasizing her child.

"Whatever," Santo grumbled. "My son got pissed when I paid her to break it off with him. I've got a reputation to keep. Gianni switched schools, finished in New York, and never talked to me since."

Sam's mind was quick with the following query. "If he's pissed at you, what makes you think he'll listen to you?"

"He still talks to my wife. You've arrested two of my boys. I'd consider it a favor if you didn't arrest my only other son. If you arrest him, he'll lose the job that he loves."

Sam considered the proposal. "Don't have your wife call him. It might cause him to do something stupid and get him arrested. I'll do this as a favor," Sam, figuring he may need one in the future, "providing your son doesn't interfere and cooperates with us. It's up to him to avoid arrest." With that, Sam ended the call, his mind already on the mission ahead.

The lobby of the apartment building was a maze of shadows and dull lighting; the air smelled of disinfectant. Kiara and the agents moved towards the elevator, their footsteps echoing in the nearly deserted space, other than a maintenance guy washing the floor. The desk clerk, a young man with weary eyes, looked up from his school paperwork.

"If you're visiting a resident, you have to sign in," he said, a pen poised in his hand.

Sam flashed his badge. "We're with the police. We need directions to the stairwell."

The clerk's eyes widened, and he quickly pointed down the halls. "Two stairwells. One on the west side, one on the east side."

"If you lived in apartment 708, which stairwell is closest?" said Sam, his tone all business.

The clerk hesitated, then said, "The east side. I'll show you."

Sam nodded to Kiara and the FBI agents to head up to the apartment while Sam and the detectives followed the desk clerk to the stairwell.

The clerk led Sam and the detectives down the hallway to the stairwell door, a fluorescent light flickering overhead.

"Is the exit door at the end of this hall the only rear exit out of the building?" Sam asked, his gaze sweeping the area.

"Yes," the clerk replied nervously. "There's another exit on the other side of the building, but this is the only one here."

Sam thanked the clerk and asked Cassie and Matt to cover the west side stairwell. He stepped into the stairwell landing, positioning himself strategically to intercept any would-be escapees from the floors above.

The clerk returned to his desk and performed his duties with a sense of obligation. He picked up the phone and dialed the number for apartment 708. "Mr. Martin, you have visitors," he said, logging the visit in the book with trembling hands.

The elevator doors slid open on the seventh floor with a soft chime. Kiara and the agents stepped out, moving swiftly toward apartment 708. The hallway was quiet, the muffled hum of the city barely penetrating the thick walls. A door creaked open near the end of the hall, and a shadowy figure peeked out, eyes widening at the sight of the agents.

In a flash, Jarrett and Travis bolted from the apartment to the exit sign, their footsteps pounding down the stairwell.

Sam's phone buzzed. He answered Kiara's call, her voice urgent and breathless. "Travis and Jarrett are heading towards you!"

"I can hear the footsteps," Sam replied. "Bring Martin down with you. When you exit the elevator, turn right and head towards the stairwell."

Standing in the middle of the bottom stairs, Sam pulled out the photos of Travis and Jarrett, memorizing their features. Moments later, the sound of rapid footsteps grew louder. Travis and Jarrett burst onto the last set of stairs, their faces contorted in panic, seeing Sam holding a badge, resting his other hand on his holstered gun.

"Hey, Travis!" Sam called out, his badge gleaming under the stairwell light. "We've been looking for you for weeks. Your mom has been worried about you."

The two young men froze, their eyes wavering around in desperation. The chase had ended, but for Sam, the real challenge began.

CHAPTER

49

Sitting at a cluttered desk, Alex sifted through the heap of material he had amassed on Detective Leon Mackey. The files spread across the surface revealed every mundane and noteworthy detail about Mackey's life. From his address on a quiet street in Stratford to his twenty-year tenure as a decorated Bridgeport police officer, no stone was left unturned. Once a promising young officer, Mackey had transitioned to the Bridgeport Judicial District State's Attorney's Office, earning several commendations along the way—from the police department and the State's Attorney's Office alike.

Mackey's past painted a picture of a life spent in service. In his youth, he was an average student who played football at Stratford High School, a compact five-foot-ten-inch offensive lineman with a solid build of slightly over 200 pounds. He wasn't fast but fiercely protective of his quarterback and ball carrier, a trait that would later define his approach to policing. Straight out of high school, he joined the Army National Guard, balancing a second shift at a machine shop while attending Housatonic Community College.

Now, at forty-eight, the man reflected in Mackey's high school yearbook photo was almost unrecognizable. His once-thick, light brown hair had thinned to mere wisps of gray that sparsely covered his crown. The sharp features of his younger self had softened, weighed down by years of stress and disappointment. Over the past few years, his once-sterling record of solving cases had waned, overshadowed by a new generation of bright, ambitious investigators. Following a painful divorce, Mackey had become increasingly withdrawn, trading his social evenings for solitary hours at a local bar in Stratford, where he would nurse a burger or steak sandwich and a few beers. His belly, now swollen to an uncomfortable two hundred thirty-five pounds, was a testament to his growing indifference to exercise and the passage of time.

Mackey had begun searching for a way out, disenchanted with his job and nearing retirement eligibility. He applied for Assistant Director of Public Safety positions at two nearby community colleges, hoping to escape the grind of his current role and secure additional retirement benefits.

On this particular day, Mackey was reviewing the criminal records of suspects in a recent robbery case. He meticulously added information to the case file before calling it a day. As he left the office, he made a detour to his old haunt at the Bridgeport PD, yearning for a familiar face and camaraderie.

Walking into the detective's unit, he saw three young detectives and a uniformed officer huddled around a desk, whispering. The room fell silent when they noticed Mackey. The detectives quickly dispersed to their desks, their expressions carefully neutral.

"Time to hit the road and solve some cases, boys," one detective announced, his voice carrying a forced bravado. The two detectives hurriedly gathered their files and walked past Mackey.

"Hey, Mackey, if you're looking for your buddy, Harry, he went to Stamford to hide at his usual tap house—oops, I mean to work on a case," said one detective with a grin as he passed Mackey's desk.

Mackey's face twisted with frustration. "Smart-ass," he muttered under his breath.

The uniformed officer in the corner made a phone call, his eyes glancing towards Mackey intermittently. When the call ended, he approached Mackey with a nod of recognition.

"Hey, Mike, what's all the commotion about?" Mackey asked, trying to mask his unease.

"Big arrest the other night involving the guy wanted for assault. You know, the one in the sketch the DA circulated."

The officer piqued Mackey's curiosity. "They arrested the guy, huh?"

"Uh, no. Not the guy in the sketch. They arrested three guys who were after him."

"I thought you said an arrest involving the wanted guy in the sketch." Mackey's confusion deepened, a knot forming in his stomach.

"Yeah. That guy got away. But they pinched three other armed guys."

"Do you know who the three were?" Mackey asked, his mind racing.

"I don't know, and the arresting officers aren't saying a word. DA's orders."

"Shit," Mackey whispered, trepidation eating away at him. He had a sinking feeling about who the three men arrested were; if so, his arrest could follow. Mackey needed a drink. Desperation gnawing at him, he headed to his favorite bar, the weight of the arrests pressing heavily on his psyche.

Mackey pushed open the creaky door of the local pub, the faint scent of whiskey and fried food hitting him as he entered. The dim light inside contrasted sharply with the afternoon sun outside, casting long shadows through two windows across the worn wooden floor. He glanced around, spotting Ron, the burly bartender with a perpetual five-o'clock shadow, busily arranging an assortment of complimentary crackers and pretzels for customers to enjoy with the drinks. Mackey shuffled over and grabbed a handful before taking his usual stool at the bar.

"Bourbon with a beer back," he muttered to Ron, who nodded knowingly and poured the first of several shots. Mackey downed the bourbon, the warmth spreading through his chest, but it did little to ease the knot of worry in his stomach. His mind was a whirlpool of anxiety about the three men arrested. He needed to find out their names. Each attempt to reach Gilinsky's new burner phone ended in frustration, the line cutting straight to voicemail. A cold dread settled over him, fearing that

Gil, Bonarz, and one of the other crew members might be behind bars. That would spell disaster for him.

Nearly three hours later, Ron's patience had run thin. "That's enough drinks, Mack," he said, pulling away the shot glass. Mackey scowled, but Ron's stern gaze tolerated no argument. Irritated and slightly unsteady, Mackey slid off the bar stool and stumbled into the harsh fading light of dusk.

The parking lot was a minefield of cracks and potholes. As Mackey trudged toward his dented sedan, he caught his foot in a jagged hole and pitched forward, crashing down onto his left knee and wrist. Pain shot through him, a sharp, burning sensation. "Damn it!" he spat, struggling to his feet. He clutched his throbbing knee and shook his hand in a futile attempt to alleviate the pain.

Blinded momentarily by a car's headlights, Mackey squinted and took a few steps, only to trip on another pothole and crash down on the same injured knee. Someone ran from a car entering the parking lot and stopped to help him.

"Hey, Mack, it's Vince from the bar. You all right, man?"

"Yeah, yeah, I'm fine," Mackey grumbled. "Tell your boss to fix these friggin' potholes. It's like an obstacle course out here."

Vince reached down and helped haul Mackey up by his armpits, his grip firm but gentle. "You live just down the road. Let me drive you home. Leave your car here and pick it up tomorrow."

"I'm good. I can make it," Mackey insisted, but his legs betrayed him, wobbling precariously. Vince held on, steadying him.

"Come on, one step at a time. I'll take you home." Vince guided Mackey to his car. He eased him into the passenger seat and slid behind the wheel. The drive to Mackey's place was a blur of passing streetlights and the engine's hum to Mackey, who slumped in his seat, half-conscious.

At Mackey's modest ranch house, Vince helped him to the rear door. Mackey fumbled for his keys, his hands clumsy and uncoordinated. The keys slipped from his grasp and clattered to the ground. Vince retrieved them, unlocked the door, and guided Mackey inside. He laid him on the bed, carefully removing his shoes and propping his legs onto the bed. Mackey mumbled incoherently, a guttural growl rumbling from his throat.

"There lies Bridgeport's finest. What a joke," Vince muttered under his breath, a smirk curling his lips. He left the house, leaving the keys on the bedroom end table and neglecting to lock the door. As he pulled away, the alarm company called since no one shut off the alarm when entering the house. But Mackey was dead to the world, sprawled across the bed, snoring louder than the clamor around him. The alarm company, suspecting a break-in, dispatched local police to the scene.

A few miles away, Alex was cruising towards Mackey's home. His heart pounded with anticipation, the culmination of his long quest for vengeance just within reach. Today would be the final chapter, the ultimate reckoning. As he neared the cul-de-sac at Fitch and Boyd Circle, Alex saw blue and red emergency lights flashing from police vehicles. Alex slowed his car, peering at the scene through narrowed eyes. Officers stationed four police cars around Mackey's house, their lights casting a strobing glow on the curious neighbors gathered outside. Alex wondered if they had come to arrest Mackey or if something more sinister had occurred—a heart attack, perhaps, or even a desperate act of suicide.

Whatever the reason, Alex knew tonight wasn't the night for redemption. He drove past, feeling frustrated, but a sigh of relief calmed him. Perhaps, just perhaps, it was a sign from his mother, a message that his mission was complete and it was time to move on to live a life of normalcy. A sense of peace settled over him as he gazed up at the star-filled sky; a warm, loving sensation banished his anxiety and left him smiling for the first time in years.

CHAPTER
50

Jarrett calmly announced, "As you can see, Travis is alive and well, but he doesn't want to talk to his mother just yet."

"Is that right, Travis? You don't want to tell your mom you're okay?" said Sam, his eyes glaring at both men. "Would you rather she and your dad think you're hurt or dead?"

"Don't answer him, Travis. Let's leave and get something to eat," Jarrett urged with his hand gently resting on Travis's shoulder.

"So, what are you, Jeremy, Travis's boss or kidnapper?" Sam's gaze remained steady on Jeremy.

"Neither. We're in a hurry, and for your information, my name is Julian," Jarrett snapped back defensively.

"That's what you told Travis. However, your real name is Jeremy Barrett, and Yale University has banned you from being on campus property because you allegedly scammed money from two students here. I've called the campus police, who are en route. And I'm sure Travis's mother plans to bring charges against you for holding him against his will," Sam countered with authority.

"That's bullshit. I'm not holding Travis against his will. I'm protecting him."

"Really. What are you protecting Travis from, keeping his own money?" Sam pressed, his eyes narrowing further.

"Murder charges," Jeremy blurted out, desperation showing in his face.

Sam smirked, then turned to Travis. "Is that true, Travis? You murdered someone?"

Travis hesitated, confusion clouding his features as he glanced between Sam and Jeremy.

"Uh, we're late for dinner. Let's go, Travis," Jeremy interjected, attempting to divert attention and move past Sam.

"Sorry, Jeremy. Travis is not going with you. Travis is staying here with me," said Sam, blocking Jeremy's path.

Jeremy looked back at Travis, frustration evident in his eyes. "You don't have to stay here. Let's go eat."

"Travis, if you are in trouble, you know your mom and your dad, an attorney, will support and help you no matter the issue," said Sam, his voice calming yet resolute. "If your trouble stems from being with Jeremy, then I assure you, it's probably a scam to get money from you. That's his gig. How much money have you given him?"

"That's none of your business. Travis, let's leave now," said Jeremy, pleading.

Travis didn't move. He mulled over Sam's words, wondering if the agent was right about Jeremy scamming him.

The stairwell door creaked open. Kiara, flanked by FBI agents and local police, entered the room with Professor Martin.

"What's going on here, Sam?" said Kiara.

"Jeremy claims Travis murdered someone. I don't believe him. I think Jeremy came up with a scam to convince Travis he did something he didn't do. I'll prove it if Travis answers one question. Travis, did you recently give Jeremy a large sum of money?"

"Don't answer, Travis," Jeremy interjected hastily.

"I gave him ten thousand dollars for an attorney," Travis admitted quietly, his eyes avoiding Jeremy's gaze.

"What's the attorney's name, Jeremy?" Sam pressed, his tone accusatory.

"That's my business," Jeremy shot back defensively.

"Call the attorney right now so I can verify you gave Travis' money to him." Sam persisted.

"It takes time to find the best lawyer for him. I haven't found one yet," Jeremy hedged.

"You're not looking for any lawyer. You're keeping the money. I'm arresting you for lying to a federal agent. Turn around and put your hands behind your back."

In a panic, Jeremy shoved Sam, attempting to go around him and escape, but Sam reacted swiftly. He tripped Jeremy, sending him sprawling face down on the cement floor. With practiced efficiency, Sam knelt on Jeremy's backside, grabbed his wrists, and handcuffed him behind his back.

Meanwhile, Kiara approached Travis, her demeanor calm and reassuring. "Travis, your mom and dad will be relieved to know you're safe. Let's get you out of here."

Sam had the FBI agents take custody of Jeremy, then pulled Jonathan Martin aside for a private conversation.

"I planned to arrest you, Professor, for lying to us and aiding Jeremy in his schemes," said Sam. "But your dad called me. He asked me not to arrest you, fearing it could jeopardize your job here at Yale. He told me you wanted no part in his business and haven't spoken to him in years. He also told me that Jeremy is your son. So, here's the deal: If you cooperate with us and answer our questions truthfully, I'll recommend that you not be charged, so hopefully, you won't lose your job. It's your choice."

"He's my son. I disapproved of his past indiscretions, but I had no idea about any scheme he had against Travis," said Martin, with a conflicted expression.

"Well, you have much explaining to do to convince the US Attorney about what you knew and didn't know. You're coming with us to the courthouse."

CHAPTER
51

K iara, Sam, and the FBI agents escorted Jeremy Barrett to the federal courthouse, where they handed him over to the US Marshals for holding pending arraignment. Meanwhile, they convened with Debra Durrell and her Assistant, Brian Murphy. The agents briefed Durrell and Murphy on their investigation, detailing Barrett's background and the alleged false accusations he made against Travis. Sam recommended not charging Jonathan Martin, provided he cooperated truthfully.

"Did you inform the senator that we found Travis?" said Durrell.

"No. We want to interview Travis about a murder accusation Barrett made before contacting her. I don't trust anything Barrett says. It could be another one of his scams," said Sam.

"Are you and Kiara planning to continue with the alleged murder claim?"

"Our mission was to find Travis. Now that we have him, our job is done. The local FBI office can take the lead on the follow-up investigation. Kiara and I will now focus on the person who shot her. We'll interview Travis and leave Barrett's interview to the FBI.

"Okay. Talk to Travis and let us know what he has to say. Brian and I will discuss your findings and recommendations. If you feel confident in his statement, we'll inform the senator and have her speak with her son," said Durrell.

Sam and Kiara entered the interview room, where Travis waited nervously. Kiara started the interview by asking Travis about his relationship with Jeremy Barrett and the person he knew as Professor Martin. She then prompted Travis to recount Barrett's accusation of murder.

"I don't remember anything about a murder," Travis said, his voice shaded with confusion. "Julian—or Jeremy, whatever his name is—wanted to go to a new nightclub in Bridgeport. He invited me along, probably because he needed me to cover the cost of a car rental. His friend Tyrese joined us."

"What do you know about Tyrese?" Kiara inquired.

"Tyrese is a Yale student majoring in Social Studies. He's a big, muscular guy with tattoos. He seemed like a nice guy."

"Do you know his last name?" Kiara pressed gently.

Travis paused, struggling to recall, then said, "Griggs. Tyrese Griggs, that's it."

"Okay. So you rented a car. What happened next?"

"We went to this nightclub, Vandell's Lounge, I think. The place was packed with people. Julian took us around to meet his friends. He ordered drinks and put them on my tab. I don't like to drink, but Julian insisted I have one. It wasn't long before I got bored and wanted to leave, but Julian kept pushing for more drinks," Travis sounded frustrated. "Julian wanted me to mingle and meet people. I wasn't interested."

"Okay, then what?"

"Julian introduced me to some guys near the DJ booth. I don't remember their names. He kept pushing me to hook up with one. I refused, things got heated, and one of them got aggressive. Tyrese stepped in. A fight broke out—I got knocked out. Next thing I knew, I was in the car with Julian and Tyrese, heading back to New Haven."

"So, no murder?" Kiara asked.

"I don't know. I didn't hit anyone, but Julian said I pushed a guy who cracked his head on the DJ's platform. They told me he was dead. Then they dragged me out of there."

"Sounds like a setup," Sam said. "Security footage should clear things up. When did Jeremy start asking for money?"

"The next morning. Julian said I needed a lawyer before the cops came for me. Tyrese backed him up. I panicked and paid."

"Listen," Sam said, steady and firm. "You need to talk to the U.S. prosecutor. Tell him everything. If needed, the FBI can use your statement for a warrant to get the lounge's security footage."

Travis exhaled, tension easing. "I'm disappointed in Julian—or Jeremy, whatever, but I'm more worried about the FBI arresting me."

"They won't if you're telling the truth," Kiara assured him. "They'll find out what actually happened."

"Your parents are on your side, no matter what," Sam added.

Travis still looked torn, his thoughts a mess. "I can't believe this. I liked Julian. I thought he cared."

"Jeremy's a con artist," Sam said bluntly. "He used you. Your parents never will. How much money did you give him?"

Travis hesitated, realization sinking in. "I don't know. Too much. I feel like an idiot."

Kiara placed a hand on his shoulder. "You're not. Jeremy played you. Your parents love you—trust them, not him."

With their support, Travis agreed to make his statement. Afterward, Debra Durrell had him call his mother. Kiara and Sam waited as he spoke with her.

When he finished, he looked content. "I told my mom I was sorry for not calling. She and my dad are driving to New Haven—we're having dinner together."

Kiara smiled. "That's good. You did the right thing."

Travis managed a small smile. "Yeah. I'm lucky to have them."

Sam and Kiara exchanged a subtle fist bump as they left the courthouse. "We found Travis. Now, maybe, he'd start finding himself," said Kiara.

*   *   *

After leaving the federal building, Travis returned to campus, planning to begin catching up with his studies and reconnecting with his friends. The word of him back on campus buzzed through Yale with its usual energy, but for Travis, it was a new beginning. He faced a crisis and emerged more assertive, with a newfound appreciation for his family's support and true friends.

His relationship with Addi remained on his mind. He knew he needed to have an honest conversation with her about everything that had transpired. When he gained the courage to call her and apologize, they agreed to meet and talk at their usual spot.

As Travis headed towards the library, he couldn't help but feel upbeat. The future was uncertain, but for the first time in a long while, Travis felt confident about who he was and would take his time before deciding what he wanted in life.

CHAPTER
52

O n the way to their car, Kiara walked with Sam, holding his arm. Sam smiled, saying, "I'm impressed, Rivers. You talked to Travis more like his mom than an FBI interrogator."

"Was that a zing, or are you joking with me again?"

"No joking this time. You did better than I would have done. You've come a long way since we started working together."

"That's a zing," she retorted.

"Maybe a little. But we're a good team. We can tease and jest with each other while still dealing with serious matters. I think you understand now how I feel about victims. We in law enforcement should help those victimized, especially kids, not only nail the bad guys."

"I've heard you say that dozens of times. You embedded helping victims into my memory bank. Now, let's talk about more immediate things—like my need for coffee. You're driving, so the first stop is a café where they have—"

"I know, your favorite latte," Sam interrupted, rolling his eyes playfully.

"Hey, you're learning from me now."

They laughed as they entered the G-ride. The late afternoon sun cast shadows across the parking lot, painting everything in a warm, golden hue. The afternoon traffic was heavy. Kiara led Sam to a quaint café tucked away on a quiet street corner. The freshly brewed coffee and baked goods aroma greeted them as they entered. The ambiance was cozy, with soft lighting and rustic wooden furniture. They settled into a booth by the window; Kiara ordered her usual latte, while Sam opted for a coffee with cream, no sugar.

As Kiara sipped her latte, a satisfied smile spread across her face. "I'm ecstatic we finally found Travis. You kept your promise, Sam." Her eyes locked onto him, a mischievous glint in her gaze.

"What's up, Kiara? I see that shifty grin," Sam asked, his eyebrows raised in curiosity.

"It's not what you think, Sam. I just remembered when my boss assigned me to this case. I thought it was because of my success working with the gang task force. But when he told me you had explicitly requested me as your partner, I never expected that. I didn't even know a senator was pushing for you to join the FBI's investigation. Some of my colleagues were upset that you got assigned to the case. However, a few agents thought differently, knowing you did a heck of a job rescuing Ena and the state police detective's daughter."

"Mm-hmm. Anything else?"

"A few agents joked you must be clairvoyant. I don't believe in that, but there is a mystery about you, Sam. It's like you have a sixth sense."

Sam chuckled. "Uh-uh. Everyone tries to label my work as psychic nonsense or a scam. I can't read minds or predict the future. Call it a hunch, a gut feeling—whatever you want. But those feelings are usually on target. That's all there is to it. Right now, I'm determined to find the guy who shot you. Let's get back to work after you've had your fill of latte. I want to find the guy, or whoever it was."

Kiara's eyes narrowed as she picked up Sam's slip about 'the guy or whoever.' She was about to ask him about it when her cell phone rang.

"Hey. Hi, Mariela. We just finished at the courthouse. Sorry it took so long. Sam and I are celebrating over coffee. I should be back at the hospital in about fifteen minutes." Kiara listened for a few minutes, then ended the call. "My apologies, Sam. Mariela has to head back to Boston. She got called to be at work tomorrow. I promised her I'd drive her. I can continue with my physical therapy on my own. Right now, that's a priority: not catching the guy who shot me. Besides, FBI policy prohibits me from working on the investigation since I was the victim,"

"I know, but I thought we could work around it."

Kiara took a breath. She looked Sam in the eye, wanting to be honest with him, and said, "I have a lot to think about regarding my career with the FBI. We can talk about it another time. I'm driving back to Boston in my car. I could try getting you another one from Davies or Dell."

"Forget about asking Davies."

"Are you sure? You're here on an FBI assignment. I should be able to request a car from the local office."

"Thanks, but Davies said the local agents will investigate your shooting, not me. But I'm determined to finish the case and get the person responsible for injuring you."

"I'm sorry for leaving you without a car, Sam. You could drive back with me, get your car, and return to finish the case."

"Don't worry about me finding a ride." Sam dialed the local ATF office about borrowing a spare vehicle, only to be told there were no spares. He then called Lieutenant Dawson, explaining his situation. Dawson agreed to meet him at her office.

"Drop me off at the PD. Lieutenant Dawson agreed to help. As I said several times, when you help the police, they will return the favor when needed."

"Dell will insist an FBI agent participate in the investigation if you believe an arrest is imminent."

"I'll call Dell when it comes to that. I'm sure we can work something out. Get some rest and be careful driving to Boston."

"I'll be careful. So, are we good, Sam?"

"Yeah, of course. We're good."

CHAPTER
53

When Sam entered the bustling detective unit, his gaze immediately fell upon Cassie, eagerly summoning him to her back corner office. Sam noticed a cluster of detectives huddled around Detective Kendrick, their faces illuminated by the glow of a large screen. With a quick nod to Kendrick, Sam made his way to Cassie's office.

"What's going on, Sam? Did your car break down?" Cassie's voice carried a tinge of curiosity.

"No, nothing like that. Kiara and I tracked down Travis Thornton. We had him call his mom. The senator and her husband are coming to New Haven to see him. Everyone's ecstatic. But there's a downside—Kiara's taking some time off in Boston, and that leaves me without a partner to finish investigating the guy who shot her."

Cassie's brow furrowed in bewilderment. "How do you do it, Sam? First, you led me to the M4 hidden in the park, and now you find Travis, whom the FBI couldn't locate for weeks. You're like a magnet for finding people."

"I've just been lucky with my hunches."

Cassie rolled her eyes playfully. "Where can I buy those magical hunches of yours?"

"If I knew, I'd bottle and sell them," Sam quipped, swiftly changing the topic. "What's happening with the detectives?"

"Matt's setting up an iPad to review footage from the doorbell cameras on a projected screen. They're trying to identify any connections to Mark Callahan and the recent shootings at the beverage company and the school. So far, no luck."

"While we wait, could you call the DA? I want to meet with him in the morning regarding the arrest of three men who attempted to chase down the wanted person depicted in the sketch the DA circulated. I'd appreciate it if we worked together on that investigation."

Cassie agreed and made the call. The DA, Lamar Irving, was intrigued by why the lieutenant called on behalf of an ATF agent regarding the arrest. He agreed to meet in the morning.

"We're ready, lieutenant," Kendrick said from the doorway.

"Let's watch the video, Sam," Cassie said, leading him back into the squad room where the detectives assembled.

Everyone had their eyes focused on the footage of vehicles passing by various security and doorbell cameras around the time of the shootings. The images showed a mundane parade of cars and pedestrians, none of whom attracted their attention.

"We didn't see Mark Callahan's truck," Kendrick said, rubbing his temples. "Just a sedan like the one his wife drives. We plan to interview his wife about her whereabouts. What did you see that we missed, Sam?"

Sam's eyes scanned the room, sensing a collective frustration. He turned to Cassie, hoping she'd caught what he had.

"The only thing I noticed was the kid on the bike. Is that what you think is important?"

"Exactly," Sam replied. "And you saw him during both incidents."

"What? Are you suggesting the kid is the shooter?" Kendrick's voice was skeptical.

"I'm not saying that," said Sam. "But he's definitely a person of interest. I would check with the school to see if there were any issues between the two kids shot and Callahan's kid. If it turns out there was, you might have your shooter."

"Wow," Kendrick said, shaking his head in disbelief. "That's a stretch. I can't imagine a fourteen-year-old capable of such precision with an M4."

"You'd be surprised what young kids can do," said Sam firmly.

Cassie felt Kendrick had a point but trusted Sam's instincts. "We also got a call from the New Haven ATF supervisor. ATF traced the M4 through the Army. They reported that they assigned the M4 to a soldier killed in action. The gun was never recovered and was considered lost."

"That often happens in war zones," Sam remarked. "Soldiers sometimes bring back souvenirs they find, including weapons."

Just then, Cassie's phone rang. After a brief conversation, she hung up. "That was Lalita at the state lab. She found additional prints on the M4. We should head over there. Matt, call the school and arrange to meet with the principal about any incidents between the kids shot and Callahan's kid."

Cassie and Sam drove to the Meriden state lab, arriving forty minutes later. On the way, Sam brought up his need for a partner to finish the case against Kiara's shooter.

"The missing person guru needs a partner with a car," Cassie teased. "Am I right?"

"One hand washes the other. Can you help me?"

"We might be able to work something out," she replied with a coy smile.

Sam smirked. "Why do I feel like there's a catch?"

Cassie's smile widened. "Not quite. Think of it as a friendly quid pro quo among friends."

"Should I guess what kind of quid pro quo you're referring to?"

"No need to guess. I'd be happy repeating the night we celebrated my birthday," Cassie hinted.

"Ah, that was my guess. You know, you never did tell me your age."

"You're not supposed to ask a woman's age."

"Right. So, is that the only way to work this out?"

"No, I'll be your partner. But I hoped you'd be my partner in another way again. It's a win-win."

Sam didn't answer her request but said, "I'll guess you're thirty-six."

"Trying to get on my good side with that compliment, huh, Sam?"

They arrived at the lab, where they were greeted by Lalita in the lobby, who led them to her desk, saying, "I found two partial fingerprints on the M4 that your department missed—one on the bottom left of the collapsible stock and one on the magazine's right side. They don't match the previous prints, but the DNA closely matches Matt Callahan—probably a family member."

Cassie beamed. "Lalita, you're a magician. Thank you so much."

"Agreed," Sam said. "It's not often prints get missed during forensic examinations. You're good at what you do."

Lalita provided her report to Cassie. Cassie smiled while leaving the lab. She drove back to New Haven. On the way, she called Kendrick to check on the school situation.

Kendrick said he was at the school meeting with the principal and would see her back at the office. Cassie and Sam arrived at the PD and waited for Kendrick and Detective Ted Porter to arrive. When they arrived, Kendrick looked somber.

"Well, I have to admit it could be the kid. I spoke with the principal and gym teacher, who informed us that Jeffrey Callahan had fought with Jake Horton, a known bully. Horton and the other kid involved in the fight were the two kids who got shot at the school."

"Callahan's kid probably was pissed that his dad got laid off, blaming the owner's son. Unfortunately, the woman with the son was collateral damage," said Sam. "He probably felt invincible after that shooting, so it was easy for him to get even when he got bullied by nailing the bully and his friend at the school."

"We'll try interviewing the kid, but my guess is the Callahans won't allow it and will lawyer up," said Kendrick.

"We have partial prints on the gun that closely match Matt Callahan's. Perhaps the other partials found are a match to his Kid, Jeffrey. Cassie said. "Talk to the DA and see what he wants to do."

"Why not have a female detective work undercover as a lunch monitor at the kid's school?" said Sam. "When the kid has lunch, have the detective retrieve his tray and whatever he drinks from. Have Lalita conduct a DNA analysis comparing it to what she found on the M4."

"Good idea," said Matt. "I'll talk to the DA and get it approved. Thanks, Sam." After the detectives left for the day, Cassie suggested getting takeout and having dinner at her place.

"I need time to prepare for our meeting with the DA," said Sam. "Not to mention, I'll need a whole night's sleep."

"I promise you'll get to bed early."

"Another night, maybe, but not tonight. Sorry. I have a ton of work to do about a murder years ago. I'm trying to figure out if there's a connection between the murders and Kiara's shooter."

*   *   *

In his hotel room, Sam read every newspaper article that reported on a murder in Westport and the nearby communities. What he learned told a heartbreaking story of a home invasion by four masked men who murdered Alexis and Jon Donnelley and their two teenage children. The police questioned a suspect, Geno Alonzio, who an unidentified witness claimed was one of the killers.

However, three persons, two men and a woman, came forward as alibis for Alonzio and swore he was with them at a bar miles away during the home invasion. Based on the alibis established by a detective, the prosecutor had no choice but to release Alonzio without charging him.

The more Sam read the articles, the more insight he gained to connect the dots in solving the cold case investigation. He searched online for background information on the Donnelley family. As Sam read the background of Jon Donnelley, his wife, Alexis, and the children, Sam said in a loud whisper, "That's it! I've solved the mystery. I not only know who shot Kiara, but why."

CHAPTER
54

The following morning, Sam was up early. He went to the lobby for the continental breakfast and coffee. He brought his iPad with him to show Cassie the news story of the arrest of three men in Bridgeport. He filled a bowl with cereal, added a banana, and sat at a table with his coffee. While he studied the news story, Cassie called and said she'd be there to pick him up in ten minutes. He asked her to come inside and have a coffee and a muffin, his treat. When Cassie arrived, she sat at Sam's table, saying, "Morning, Sam. You're buying me breakfast, huh?"

"Well, not exactly. Let me know what you want, and I'll get it. It's complimentary with the room. If anyone asks if you're a guest, let me answer."

"Oh, I get it. You don't want to pay extra for me."

"Something like that, yeah," Sam said with a smirk. "Should we confirm our meeting with the DA?"

"The DA or his receptionist won't be in their office at seven-thirty-five? It's more like eight-thirty, nine o'clock. I'll call after you fetch my breakfast and coffee, cream, one sugar."

"You're sweet enough. You don't need sugar."

"Thanks. That's a good way to start the morning with me, Sam, but add the sugar. Can you get it now?"

"Yes, ma'am. I'll hop right to it."

Sam returned to the table with coffee, orange juice, two muffins, and a banana.

"I didn't want two muffins," Cassie said with a smirk.

"Hey, the other muffin is for me, not you."

They both chuckled.

While she sipped her coffee, Sam placed the news story on his iPad in front of her to read. After reading the article, she asked why it was important.

"It's connected to Kiara's shooting."

Cassie looked at Sam quizzically, saying, "How's this connected to Kiara? I don't get it."

Sam took the time to explain the connection. He began by briefing Cassie on the Donnelley family murders seven years earlier. Sam added, "Now the police arrest three men, one of whom was bound and gagged by an unidentified man wanted by the district attorney. That man is the same guy in a sketch circulated by the DA, the same man who shot Kiara. You'll understand more when we meet with the DA."

Sam saw it was eight-twenty. He asked Cassie to call the DA's Office and tell him they had information about the guy in the sketch to get his attention.

*　　*　　*

The early morning sunlight glinted off Cassie's windshield, driving to the DA's Office in Bridgeport. The sun's penetration cast a golden hue over the car's interior, causing Sam to lower the visor and put on sunglasses. His brows furrowed in concentration while detailing his extensive research on the Donnelley murders in Westport, which had haunted the town for years.

"An unidentified witness placed Geno Alonzio at the scene and fingered him as one of the murderers," Sam explained. "The prosecutor didn't charge him. Evidently, an unnamed detective vouched for Alonzio's alibis, saying Alonzio was miles away at a bar during the home invasion."

Cassie's knuckles whitened as she gripped the steering wheel, her eyes darting from the road to Sam, absorbing every detail. "You think the detective was in on it?"

With a grim smile, Sam nodded, "I do."

They arrived at the courthouse, an imposing building, a silent guardian of justice. Cassie mentioned it's a historic three-story Romanesque masonry building with a six-story tower in front capped by a conical roof. Sam admired the tower for a moment before they entered the front entrance. They arrived at the DA's Office for their nine o'clock appointment. The receptionist asked them to have a seat. Sam was anxious for the meeting to start. His fingers tapped his knee in unison with the clock ticking on the wall above the receptionist's desk. Ten minutes later, Irving, a burly man with a stern demeanor, finally appeared. His handshake was firm, his eyes piercing, as if trying to read the motives behind their visit.

Inside his office, dark wood paneling and a towering bookshelf lined with a library of legal writings gave the space an air of authority. Irving gestured for them to sit, his eyes never leaving Sam's face, trying to place him from prior meetings.

"Why the sudden interest in our suspect in the sketch we circulated?" he asked, his tone guarded.

Sam leaned forward, his voice low and determined. "I'm certain the man in your sketch is the same person who shot my partner in New Haven. The descriptions match perfectly. Your office had reported the guy assaulted Peter Gilinsky in Derby?"

Irving's eyebrows knitted together, his lips thinning into a hard line. "We haven't identified him yet. He's assaulted others other than Gilinsky. We had no apparent connection until the recent arrest of Gilinsky and two others. Do you know who he is, Sam?"

Sam's eyes gleamed with the fire of a hunter closing in on his prey. "I chased my partner's shooter and wrestled him to the ground. When he landed, his hair and beard got partially dislodged. During the struggle, one of his sneakers and a sock came off. He managed to grab his sneaker and ran, but I kept the sock. We had it analyzed for a DNA match, but he was not in the CODIS system for an identification." Sam didn't disclose what the DNA analysis revealed. "If we can make a connection to the three men you arrested, we might break the cold murder case wide open."

Irving's curiosity was piqued, though skepticism lingered in his frown. "So you know the guy wore a disguise, and you think there's a link between him and an old murder case?"

"Yes, the shooter wore a disguise, and I'm sure he has a connection to the three guys arrested. Knowing their identities could be the key to solving several home invasions and murders seven years ago."

What Sam had said got Irving's attention. He was clearly intrigued but cautious. He deliberated for a moment before deciding to indulge Sam's request. He handed over a file containing the names of the three suspects. Sam scanned the list. His suspicions were confirmed when he saw the names. He passed the file to Cassie, who noted the names with a sharp intake of breath.

"Do you have any evidence these men were involved in home invasions and murders?" said Sam.

Sam's question hung in the air, heavy with implication. Irving's eyes widened in surprise, his mouth momentarily slack. He rubbed his chin thoughtfully, clearly weighing his following words.

"I have information from an informant, but it's unverified. I'm intrigued by how you've managed to link these men to these crimes, including the shooting of your partner."

Sam leaned back, his expression resolute. "It's all about connecting the dots. The shooter is the missing link to solving the Donnelley murders, not as a suspect, but the one who puts Gilinsky and his crew at the murder scene."

Irving's eyes widened, and he leaned forward, a new intensity in his gaze. "You've got my attention, Sam. How do you tie the shooter in New Haven to a years-old home invasion in Westport?"

"If I could see the information you received from your informant, it might help," Sam said, meeting Irving's gaze with unwavering determination.

"We know there's a connection between the shooter and the three men you arrested," said Sam, suspecting the DA knows more about those arrested. "Do you have additional information on the three guys, including a fourth Gilinsky crew member named Geno Alonzio? If you do, it fits perfectly to complete the puzzle."

Irving was stunned by what the ATF agent had postulated. Irving had to know more from Sam, measuring the risks against the benefits of disclosing more to him. He called his investigator to discuss further disclosure. The DA and his investigator exchanged whispers before Irving handed Sam a letter, redacted but revealing enough to set Sam's pulse racing. "This letter implicates Geno Alonzio and Peter Gilinsky in the Donnelley murders," Irving said, his voice a low murmur. "It names Acosta and Bonarz as part of the crew. You can take notes, but no copies."

Sam's eyes scanned over the letter, his mind racing. "Whose name did you blacken out?" he asked, pointing to the obscured section.

Irving's face hardened. "It names a detective involved with the crew. We can't risk his name getting out before we verify his involvement."

Sam nodded, scribbling notes. "Have any of the men talked?"

"Not yet," Irving replied, his frustration evident. "We'll be offering a deal to Bonarz this afternoon."

"Good," Sam said, meeting Irving's gaze. "This information is invaluable. We're getting close to the truth. Cassie and I plan on interviewing who I believe is the person in your sketch."

Irving's eyes narrowed. "What? So you do know who he is?"

"I'm relatively certain, but I'll know for sure after the interview."

"I expect you'll keep me in the loop. We need to nail this guy."

"I will," Sam agreed. "Just one more thing—was Gilinsky an alibi for Alonzio?"

Irving looked to his investigator, Art Shannon, who nodded, saying, "He was one of the alibis."

Sam's lips tightened. "Just as I thought."

"Hmm. It seems you know more than you're telling us, Sam."

"No, sir. It was a hunch that if Alonzio was the only suspect, I wondered if one or more of the other crew members could have been an alibi for him. I don't have all the answers yet, but it behooves me to verify my instincts. I will stay in touch and get your office involved when I have ironclad evidence to make arrests. Thank you for sharing this information with us. We'll be in touch."

On the drive back to New Haven, the city skyline rose in the distance. Cassie finally broke the silence. "You know who shot Kiara?"

Sam nodded, his jaw set with determination. "I'm certain. We'll make the arrest soon. But first, let's grab lunch in New Haven. I have a lot to tell you."

CHAPTER
55

During lunch, Sam summarized everything he had painstakingly researched and learned regarding the spree of robberies and murders in Westport that pointed to the three men recently arrested by the Bridgeport police.

"They were arrested while attempting to capture the guy in the DA's sketch. Kiara told me it was the guy in the sketch who shot her. The question I needed to answer was why he shot her."

With a ruffled look, Cassie listened intently to the sheer scope of what Sam was revealing. It gave her pause, asking, "What do the robberies in Westport by the three men have to do with the person who shot Kiara?

From what Sam had read in the newspaper article and notes he took from the desk of the woman's apartment in the barn, he told her there was a witness who claimed Geno Alonzio, or Zee, as his cohorts call him, killed two of the four Westport family members. Sam then told Cassie who he believed was Kiara's shooter and why Kiara was shot. It then became clear to Cassie what the connection was between the three men arrested by the DA and the shooter.

"Alonzio was released when the investigating detective found three alibis for him," explained Sam. "Since Alonzio was the only suspect, it was conceivable that one or more of the robbers involved in the Westport murders were the alibis. We need to find Alonzio, the fourth guy involved in killing the family members."

"So you think the guy in the sketch only shot Kiara to avoid being arrested?"

"That's my theory," said Sam. his fingers tapping rhythmically against the table, connecting the dots for her.

Cassie's mouth and eyes opened wide, surprised at Sam's suppositions.

"I wanted to be sure before identifying the shooter. It's embarrassing if later it turns out I was wrong. Anyway, that's only half of what I wanted to tell you. The other half might be hard for you to accept as a law enforcement officer."

"I hope it's nothing illegal."

Sam recounted the shooter's background in vivid detail, painting a picture that made the hairs on the back of Cassie's neck stand on end. The identity, motivations, and dark undercurrents of the shooter's actions were laid bare. Sam gave Cassie ample time to digest this barrage of information.

Then, in a calm tone, he revealed his plan—a strategy that, if executed, would lead to two starkly different outcomes. Cassie's mind raced, grappling with the moral and ethical implications. She knew one option would be challenging to pull off, but there was logic in Sam's proposed expectations.

"I understand the dilemma, Sam, but you'll need the prosecutor's approval," Cassie said firmly.

"I don't like overthinking and waiting until it's too late to act," said Sam. "I'll call the DA to see if they had any luck interviewing Bonarz or the other two suspects. Depending on what he says, we'll decide how to confront the shooter."

Sam dialed the DA's number, the sound of each ring amplifying the tension inside him. Finally, the receptionist answered and transferred the call.

"Any news on your end, Sam?" asked the DA.

"Nothing yet. Any breakthrough with Bonarz or the other two?"

"Bonarz was the one who wrote the letter to us. He claimed the guy in the sketch broke into his apartment and forced him to write it at gunpoint.

Since Gilinsky seems to be the gang leader, we'd prefer not to offer him a deal. We figured Bonarz and Acosta would give us all we needed to prosecute Gilinsky. We questioned Bonarz and offered him a deal for his cooperation. He swore that only Gilinsky knew the identities of the guy who selected the homes to rob and the alarm installer he used. But Bonarz said he once overheard a telephone conversation Gilinsky had with a guy he called Jimbo, complaining about the installer, Fitzy. Bonarz didn't hear what the complaint was about. He thinks Jimbo might be the one who picks the houses to hit. Gilinsky likes keeping control by not telling the crew from whom he gets his information. Regarding Fitzy, we know it's Sean Fitzgibbons who has moved to a new address in New Rochelle. My investigators are on their way to interview him."

"Did the name Thomas Townsend come up? It's a long shot, but he might be Jimbo. His middle name is James. If Bonarz hasn't heard the name Townsend, mention it to Gilinsky. It might get his attention thinking you know about him. Did Bonarz seem willing to testify against Gilinsky and the others for a deal?"

"Yes, but he wants the same deal for his friend Acosta. We told him we'd consider it and get back to him."

"Does Bonarz know where Alonzio is?"

"No. Bonarz described Alonzio as a creepy, sex-obsessed misfit who creeps women out. Bonarz doesn't know where he's hiding."

"When will you talk with Gilinsky?"

"My investigators will be questioning him next. Gilinsky likes to think he's untouchable: that none of his crew would betray him. We plan to tell him we have a witness willing to testify for a deal. We'll also hint one of them is Townsend, the name you gave me, which might rattle him."

"Ask Gilinsky where he thinks Alonzio is and if he has a girlfriend. If we get a lead, the lieutenant and I will move on it," said Sam, already plotting his next steps.

"We will. I have to take another call, Sam. Anything else?"

"No. Good job so far. If I find anything significant, I'll call you."

"Okay. Talk later, and thanks for the tip on Townsend."

As Sam hung up, he found Cassie's piercing gaze fixed on him. "You were on the call with the DA for a long time. Fill me in, Sam. I'm your partner now, remember?"

With a sheepish smile, Sam gave her a detailed rundown of his conversation with the DA. "Let's wrap up here and head up north."

"I'm having another coffee first," Cassie said, with a stubborn resolve that Sam had come to admire.

"No problem."

Cassie took her time, savoring her coffee while Sam, unable to sit still, reviewed his notes again, trying to come up with anything he missed in the investigation. It was nearly twenty minutes before they left the diner. When back in Cassie's car, Sam's phone rang. The DA's name flashed on the screen.

"Sam, my investigators talked to Gilinsky. When they mentioned a deal for his cooperation, he remained cocky and defiant. But when they brought up Townsend's name, Gilinsky became a meek, mousy listener. Gilinsky said he'd only cooperate if we agreed on no jail time for him. The investigators laughed, saying the prosecutor wouldn't agree with the idea of no prison time. He then said he had nothing further to say. However, when asked about Alonzio's whereabouts, Gilinsky called him a nutcase. He didn't know his whereabouts, but he mentioned Alonzio frequented two escorts, who went by the names Daisy and Ruby. I thought you'd want to know."

"Thanks, Lamar. We'll look into it. Maybe we'll get lucky," Sam replied, glancing at Cassie with hope.

Knowing Cassie had deep roots in New Haven, Sam asked, "Are you familiar with any prostitutes named Daisy and Ruby working in New Haven?"

"What do prostitutes have to do with our case?"

"Geno Alonzio is still MIA. He's known to frequent prostitutes named Daisy and Ruby. Could you contact your department's vice unit to see if they know who they are and where we could find them? If we get an address, we could check it out."

"I'll call the unit and see what they have on them. Are we still planning to arrest the shooter today?"

"One thing at a time. If you can get an address on the escorts, we can check it out quickly. If it's a dead end, we head north."

Cassie made the call, her fingers drumming impatiently on the dashboard as she waited for an answer. After what felt like an eternity, the vice squad captain returned with the information Sam had hoped for.

CHAPTER
56

C assie meticulously jotted down notes while the captain briefed her on the two escorts. She requested the captain to send over photos of the women. The images arrived on her phone moments later, and she told Sam the addresses were close by, one in Fair Haven Heights, the other across the Q River.

Using GPS navigation, Cassie maneuvered through the city streets until they reached the apartment complex in Fair Haven Heights. They discreetly parked away from the apartment in building four and entered the entrance foyer. Cassie repeatedly pressed the buzzer for Lyla Banks until a wary female voice answered.

"UPS with a package," Sam improvised smoothly.

"Just leave it," came the hesitant reply.

"I need a signature."

Reluctantly, Banks came to the door. The door clicked open, and Sam wedged his foot in to prevent it from closing completely. Cassie stepped forward, displaying her badge.

"We're looking for Geno. Is he here with you?"

"I don't know any Geno. You've got the wrong apartment," said Lyla defensively.

"Sure you do, Daisy. That's the street name you use as an escort, and Geno is your steady client. We need to verify he's not hiding in your apartment. We'll follow you inside."

"Do you have a warrant?" Lyla shot back defiantly.

"Geno's wanted for murder and robbery. Harboring him makes you an accessory," said Sam. "We could get a telephonic search warrant for your entire apartment. We'll stand outside your door until we receive it. When we do, we'll search every nook and corner of your apartment. That will take hours. If we find drugs or anything illegal, we'll arrest you, take you to headquarters for processing, and then to court for arraignment. You'll get held overnight. The quickest and easiest way is for you to let us make a three-minute look to verify Geno is not in your apartment. If he's not, we leave."

The threat seemed to sway Lyla. "If I let you look, you'll leave in a few minutes?"

"We'll be quick. No more than five minutes," said Cassie.

Lyla hesitated but led them to her apartment. "I do have a visitor, but it's not Geno." So be nice when I let you inside."

The apartment was small but tidy, a faint scent of perfume lingering in the room. Sam and Cassie swiftly swept through the living area, then moved into the bedroom, where they surprised a man lying in bed waiting for Lyla to return.

Sam had a photo of Alonzio and knew the guy in the bed was not him. However, for whatever it may have been worth for the NHPD for identification, Sam grabbed the guy's trousers sprawled on the floor to check for a weapon and identification. He handed the guy's license to Cassie.

"Hey, whataya doing? You have no right to search my pants!" shouted the man in bed.

"Just making sure you're not armed or wanted by the police, pal," said Sam as he felt the trouser pockets again.

Cassie remembered the name and returned the license to Sam, who threw it to the guy in bed.

"Stay where you are while we check through the house," Sam told the guy.

Cassie and Sam did a quick but thorough search of the apartment but didn't find Geno. Satisfied, they thanked Lyla and swiftly departed, returning to their car.

"Let's move fast to Ruby's place. Daisy might call to warn her that we're coming to her place next," said Sam.

Cassie drove to Ruby's apartment with the emergency lights flashing but no siren. They reached the smaller apartment complex consisting of two buildings, with two stories each. Cassie drove around the buildings looking for apartment 6A. The apartments were numbered A for the first-floor apartments and B for the second-floor. As Cassie passed apartment numbers 1A and 2A, Sam scanned ahead, shouting, "A guy's leaving an apartment further down! Step on it! He's moving pretty good for a guy with a limp. It looks like he's heading for the woods. Pull up as close as possible to him, and I'll jump out to grab him."

Cassie accelerated, pulled ahead of the guy a few yards, and stopped. Sam leaped out and shouted, "Police! Stop!" His command stopped the guy in his tracks. Sam secured the suspect against the hood of their car, shouting for him to put his hands on his back at the waist. The guy complied, allowing Sam to handcuff and search him for weapons. Sam recovered a gun tucked into the man's belt at the waist while calling out, "Gun!"

Sam handed the firearm to Cassie and completed a body search, finding a wad of cash, a cell phone, and a wallet inside the guy's pants. Sam gave the money and phone to Cassie. He opened the wallet and pulled out a driver's license in Geno Alonzio's name. Sam handed the wallet and license to Cassie, saying, "It's our guy, Cass. I'll park him in the back seat. Call the DA to tell him we'll bring him to the PD in New Haven for processing. Have the DA send his guys to pick him up. That way, we don't have to drive to Bridgeport."

"The DA sends his gratitude for finding the last of the crew. He's sending two investigators to the PD to take custody of him," said Cassie.

"I'll call my squad to be available to help with the processing at the office. It'll take a while. Maybe we should call it a day and head north in the morning. Unfortunately, our overtime budget is limited."

"I prefer not putting it off. I don't want the shooter to skip town."

"Are you saying you have a gut feeling that the shooter will leave the area?"

"You could say that."

"And you say you're not psychic."

"I'm not. I'm being cautious."

"Hmm. It seems your hunches are always on the money."

CHAPTER
57

W hile processing the prisoner, District Attorney Irving, flanked by his two investigators, strode into the room to take custody of Alonzio. Curious, Sam asked Irving if his investigators had ever identified the security company that installed the home alarms in Westport."

Irving, his graying hair meticulously combed, replied, "Studying our files from years back, we had interviewed three installers. They all claimed they showed homeowners how to set the alarm code. They used the standard code 1234 for testing and instructed the homeowners to change it. We couldn't prove otherwise."

Sam's voice carried a hint of urgency when he asked, "Did all the installers work for the same company?"

"No," Irving said, shaking his head slightly. "Fitzgibbons was the only self-employed alarm contractor recorded in the cold case files. Fitzgibbons had claimed he lost his records regarding who he worked for or what houses or businesses he had installed alarms. The other two were full-time employees of a nationwide security company, and the company's records didn't reflect contracts that their employees installed alarms at the homes that got robbed. None of the installers had criminal records, including Fitzgibbons."

"Did you collect DNA at the home invasion scenes?"

"Only at the Donnelley residence. We found blood stains on the bedroom floor. According to Bonarz's letter, Alonzio was in the bedroom and killed the mother and daughter there. The former DA never arrested or charged Alonzio because he had alibis, so they never collected his DNA. We'll collect it now. If it matches, we've got him for murder."

"Did you interview the alarm installer, Fitzgibbons?

"My investigators reported Fitzgibbons is sticking to the story he gave investigators seven years ago. I told them to bring him to my office for further questioning. If he doesn't cooperate, we'll arrest him."

"Maybe offer him a deal for his testimony against Gilinsky and Townsend."

"That's our plan, Sam," Irving said, turning to his investigator. "Get on that, Art. Is there anything else we can help you with, Sam?"

"Yeah, did you serve search warrants at the homes of the four men, including the unnamed detective?"

"The affidavits for warrants have been approved. We'll execute them later today or in the early morning hours."

"I guess that's it," said Sam, his voice exhibiting relief.

Cassie and Sam left the PD. On the way to her car, Cassie received a call from Detective Kendrick. She listened intently, her eyes narrowing as she did. After ending the call, she briefed Sam.

"The detectives went to interview the Callahans. Callahan's wife answered the door. She said her husband wasn't home. He was interviewing for a job. Matt asked to talk to her son, Jeffrey, but the wife refused and told them to leave. The prosecutor authorized an arrest warrant for Mark Callahan for possession of the M4 and murder. Unfortunately, we don't have identifying prints or DNA for his son yet."

"It's a shame when a fourteen-year-old might have committed murder," said Sam with concern. "Did the DA approve of having a female officer pose as a teacher's aide at Jeffrey's school during lunchtime?"

"Yes. We're finalizing getting the chief's approval and the school's cooperation so the undercover can act as an aide. If we get Jeffrey's prints and DNA and we get a match, we can arrest both father and son. It'll be interesting to see Mark Callahan's reaction to his son's arrest."

Sam's voice reflected regret. "I don't like the idea of convicting a kid of a violent crime. I'm more for helping kids, not destroying their lives. But, if the kid committed murder, he has to be held accountable. Let's head north and arrest the shooter."

"I have a better idea," Cassie said, a mischievous glint in her eyes. "Let's go to my place and celebrate. You could bring me up to speed on your arrest plan since I'm your partner now."

Sam chuckled, shaking his head. "I should have known you wouldn't forget about a repeat of your birthday night. He checked the time, realizing it was later than he thought. "I need to call Kiara to make sure she made it to Boston okay."

The phone rang several times before going to voicemail. He left a brief message, his heart heavy with concern.

Seconds later. Sam's phone buzzed. It was Kiara. "Hi, Kiara. How are you?"

"I'm good. We made it back safely."

"Great. How is Mariela? Is she happy to have you back?"

"Very much so. I'm happy to be back, too."

"Lieutenant Dawson and I just arrested Geno Alonzio in New Haven. Alonzio and the others have a connection to the person who shot you. The lieutenant agreed to help me confront the shooter."

"Remember, this is an FBI case, Sam. Dell will want an FBI agent involved."

"I'll call Dell and work something out." Sam ended the call, his mind racing to devise a plan. He stared into space, pondering his next move.

"Hello, Sam, come back down to earth and talk to me. Are we having fun tonight, or what?"

"Sorry, Cassie," said Sam, his face set with determination.

"Did Kiara make it to Boston okay?"

"Yes. She needs time to think about her future with the FBI. We should find the shooter now, or we might miss our chance. Are you still willing to help?"

"Of course," Cassie said, her eyes full of resolve. "I understand you want to find the person who shot your partner. I'm your partner now and won't back out to help you."

"Thanks, Cass. I'll try to make it up to you."

Cassie's eyes sparkled. "Wow, I didn't expect that. If you follow through, I'll make it an extraordinary evening."

"You've already done that," Sam replied with a smile. "Let's get outta here and make the arrest."

CHAPTER

58

Cassie and Sam pulled into the gravel-strewn parking lot of a weathered diner, the kind that seemed to defy time with its faded neon sign flickering 'Open' and the scent of fried bacon and peppers hanging in the air. They hoped for a quick meal before what promised to be a long, grueling day that may extend into the evening. The late afternoon sun cast kaleidoscope beams of light through the diner's dusty windows.

Inside, the booth they chose had cracked vinyl seats and a burned-out fluorescent lightbulb above them. It had a clear view of the highway, a perfect vantage point for someone so bored they counted vehicles passing by on the road. As they slid into the booth, Sam's fingers were already dialing Dell Haskins to brief him on his arrest plan and request an FBI agent to replace Kiara for the arrest.

Haskins listened to Sam's request before answering, "Sam, there's an FBI office in New Haven. You can call the SAC and ask for assistance. Kiara's shooting happened in New Haven, so it's going to be their case to prosecute. Boston is two hours away."

"No way am I calling Alan Davies," Sam retorted, his tone concealing dissatisfaction. "Davies made it clear he doesn't want me working this case. He has it in for me, continuously lecturing me on his conceived policy and procedures, none of which he understands. He's critical of everything I do and disapproves that I was assigned to work on an FBI investigation in his state.

You and I already aired this out at Yale Hospital. I thought you understood why I have to work on this case. You said you would do the same if you were in my shoes. Besides, I'm surprised you don't consider it your office's responsibility to track down the shooter of a Boston agent, regardless of where it happened. Kiara was in New Haven working on a Boston case when someone shot her."

The tired-looking waitress approached, her steps slow and deliberate as if each movement required a concerted effort. She refilled their coffee cups with an unsteady hand, dripping lines of brew down the side of Sam's cup. She left without a word, shuffling her feet back to the counter.

Sam turned his focus back to the call, his voice a low murmur in the quiet diner. "I don't need an army of agents for the arrest, Dell. He explained why the arrest would be a low-key arrest. There won't be any confrontation,"

"Sam, it'll take hours for one of our agents to get there," Dell said, sounding exasperated.

"The credit for the arrest belongs to Kiara and the New Haven detective who's been working with us. All I need is one agent to represent your office during the arrest."

"That'll piss off the New Haven SAC," said Dell, his voice sounding impatient, not wanting any political fallout between offices.

"Can you get someone from the Hartford FBI office?" Sam countered, tapping his fingers impatiently on the table. "The arrest location falls under Hartford's jurisdictional area and is not far from their office. It'll take the agent about the same time as the detective and me to get there ourselves."

"How do I explain it to my boss and the agent-in-charge in Hartford?"

"They only need to know a New Haven Detective and I are handling it. If you can't get a Hartford agent, I'll proceed with what I've got."

"This is an FBI investigation, Sam, not your solo crusade," Dell insisted, sounding frustrated.

"I'm not alone. The New Haven lieutenant is with me. They have jurisdiction over a shooting in their city. The lieutenant can call in the entire detective division if needed. I'll call you with a report after the arrest."

"Hold on, Sam." Dell took a deep breath. He wanted an FBI agent involved in the arrest. "Let me check our roster for an agent who lives west of Boston. I'll call you right back."

"I don't expect any problems. With one FBI agent, the lieutenant, and myself, the arrest should go smoothly. You and I worked together before, Dell, so trust me on this."

"I'll be in touch," Dell said, ending the call with a click.

Cassie had been listening intently, her eyes widening at the intensity of the conversation. "Wow. That was some phone call. I've always wanted to talk like that to the FBI. Is he going to help?"

"I expect he will," Sam replied, a small, grim smile tugging at the corners of his mouth. "Let's eat and get on our way."

They ordered a chicken sandwich to share, swapping out fries for veggies and adding a side salad. Sam made another call as they waited for their food, this time to ATF Agent Jennifer Clarkson, who worked for him at the Hartford office. The phone call was brief but decisive; Jennifer agreed to assist with the arrest and to meet up for a briefing beforehand.

"I need another favor, Jen," Sam said, lowering his voice. "Once we make the arrest, I'll need a ride. I'll explain everything later."

Their meal arrived just as Sam's phone buzzed with a call back from Dell. The waitress tipped the plate she brought to their table. Sam caught the sandwich sliding off the plate, eased it back on the plate, and helped her carefully put it on the table.

"I'm listening, Dell," said Sam.

"Sam, Becca Vaillans, a Hartford FBI agent, will assist you with the arrest. She's a rookie with less than eighteen months on the job, so keep an eye out for her. Good luck with the arrest, and call me with the results." Dell provided Agent Vaillans's cell number before hanging up.

Sam felt a sense of accomplishment and contentment. "We've got an FBI and an ATF agent onboard, Cass. We'll brief them at the back of the post office, then head to the suspect's residence."

"If you need extra help, I have Detectives Kendrick and Porter on standby."

Sam and Cassie finished dinner. While leaving the restaurant, they got a whiff of roasted meat mingling with the scent of grease-stained air.

"Remind me not to stop to eat at this place ever again," said Sam.

CHAPTER
59

While driving Cassie's car, Sam crawled past the driveway at 44 Shore Hill Road, his eyes looking for signs of the BMW or the Mustang convertible. The houses in this quiet, rustic neighborhood sat back from the road, hidden behind manicured hedges and towering oak trees that hid the late afternoon sun. The air was crisp with the scent of pine and birds chirping within the trees. Sam couldn't see either car as he drove past, so he headed to park behind the post office to stay out of sight.

Once Agents Clarkson and Vaillans arrived, Sam briefed Cassie and the agents. The tension was evident by those gathered for an arrest at the dimly lit lot. Agents always prepared for an operational arrest, knowing they were risky since anything unexpected could happen. Sam detailed his plan, provided assignments, and had everyone wearing body armor, carrying additional loaded ammo magazines, and having their weapons locked and loaded. Sam headed to the subject's residence in Cassie's sedan while she and the two agents followed behind in Clarkson's SUV, all three anxious but focused.

Sam pulled up in front of the barn, its weathered brown paint peeling under the relentless assault of time and heat from the sun. The front and rear sliding doors were open, framing the shadowy interior. The suspect's blue Mustang, its sleek body glistening under the harsh fluorescent light, faced the open rear door, ready for a quick getaway. Sam noticed the BMW was missing, a detail that set his nerves on edge, thinking the suspect might not be there.

The other officers parked on Sam's right side, hidden from the open barn door. Moving with the stealth of shadows, all three officers exited their vehicles, their boots crunching softly on the gravel as they surreptitiously positioned themselves along the barn's rear corner. The suspect's Rottweiler began barking as soon as it sensed movement outside.

Curious and cautious, the woman Sam believed was Kiara's disguised shooter stepped outside her apartment. Her sharp, hazel eyes narrowed with a piercing stare towards the barn's open front door, where she spotted Sam leaning casually against his car. Her face tightened with a cold, annoying stare.

"You again? What are you doing here?" she said in an irritated voice.

"I'm here to talk and hopefully help you," said Sam calmly.

"Help me? There's nothing you could do to help me," she snapped, defensively crossing her arms.

"I have information that will benefit you. I hope you will return the favor by providing details that will help me?"

"There's nothing you could tell me I would care about, and I have nothing to give you in return. You made the trip for nothing. You should go back to where you came from and leave me alone."

Sam began slowly stepping toward her. The dog's growling intensified as it scratched at the closed apartment door, eager to confront the intruder.

"What are you doing? I want you off my property now, or I'll call the police and have you arrested."

Sam continued his measured walk toward her.

"If you come any closer, I'll let my dog out, and you won't like what he'll do to you."

"That won't work, Elli," Sam said, his voice taking on a more assertive edge.

The woman's eyes widened with surprise and anger at hearing her name. She opened her mouth to refute him but then decided not to engage in a futile argument. Instead, she pulled out her cell phone, her fingers trembling as she began to dial. "I'm calling the police."

"No need to," said Sam, pulling open his lightweight jacket to reveal his badge clipped to his belt.

Elli's face drained of color. "You're the police? You lied. You said you were a reporter."

Sam took a step closer, his eyes locking onto hers, trying to convey sincerity and urgency. "The police arrested Peter Gilinsky, Frank Bonarz, and Tony Acosta thanks to the letter you had Bones send to the DA. I arrested Geno Alonzio a few hours ago. The police plan on arresting the detective soon."

Elli gasped—her eyes fluttered, and her jaw dropped in stunned silence. Although she already knew of the arrest of three of the men, she panicked that Sam knew of her involvement. However, when Sam included Alonzio's name among those arrested and the detective, Elli felt a wave of euphoria filled with gratification. But as she processed the information, a glimmer of fear ignited in her eyes, growing into a severe panic. She wondered if Sam was there to arrest her.

Sam continued, his tone softening slightly, hoping to gain her trust. "The police haven't arrested the detective yet, but they know he's connected to Gilinsky and his crew. I'm confident he'll go down with the others." Sam took another step closer, his movements slow and deliberate, like a predator trying not to spook its prey.

Her voice trembled, betraying her inner turmoil. "Are you here to arrest me?"

CHAPTER
60

Before Sam could answer, a dark sedan pulled up alongside the car Sam had driven. Sam's eyes narrowed as he recognized it was the BMW Elli had driven. Sam watched as a man in his mid-to-late-fifties stepped out of the car. The guy gave an air of authority while walking with measured confidence, his eyes gazing first at Elli and then at Sam.

Sam immediately positioned himself between the man with wavy, graying hair and Elli. Sam's hand hovered by his jacket that covered his gun. "Who are you?"

The six-foot-two, stocky man, wearing a tailored brown plaid sports coat over dark brown trousers, glanced at Elli, his brow creased in concern. His head tilted toward Sam, hinting for Elli to identify her visitor.

"He's the police, uncle," murmured Elli, her voice barely above a whisper.

"The police. Why are the police here?"

"Ask him," said Elli.

The man's face tightened as he faced Sam. "What's this about? My niece hasn't done anything wrong."

"Who are you?" said Sam, his command evident.

"I'm Elli's uncle and guardian," the man replied, his tone defensive.

"Yeah, I heard her call you uncle, but what's your name, and why are you here?"

"I'm here visiting my niece. Is that against the law?" The man's eyes flashed with irritation as he started to step past Sam.

Sam stepped in front of the uncle to stop him. "Answer my question. What's your name?"

"That's none of your business. Now step aside."

Grabbing Elli's uncle by the arm, Sam twisted it behind his back. Elli's uncle tried turning away from the hold, causing Sam to shove him against the barn's wooden wall.

"Augh! For chrissake, that hurts! Let me go!"

"I can arrest you for threatening a federal agent. Now answer my question. What's your name?" Sam's voice was demanding and unyielding, pushing the man's arm up higher, eliciting additional pain.

"Yow. Okay, okay. It's Thomas Townsend."

"Uh-huh," muttered Sam, figuring it was Townsend. He kept Townsend against the wall, his free hand patting Townsend's back belt area. His fingers brushed against a hard lump where Sam found and pulled out a gun.

"I have a permit for that," said Townsend, gasping for air.

Ignoring him, Sam slipped the gun into his back pocket and continued to search Townsend, his fingers moving until he felt another bulge in Townsend's chest coat pocket and pulled out a leather travel pouch.

"What are you doing? That's my business papers. You have no right to search me. I'm a respected businessman. I'm going to sue you for unnecessary roughness," said Townsend, his voice outraged.

Sam leaned into Townsend, keeping him pinned as he rifled through the pouch. "I'm authorized to verify your identity," he said, pulling out a passport. "I see you have a passport. Oh, wait, looky here. You have three passports, all in names other than Townsend."

Sam pocketed the passports and unfolded a set of documents stapled together. He quickly scanned the papers, his eyes narrowing. "These are realty sale agreements for 44 Shore Hill Road."

Sam handed the documents to Elli, who took them, hands shaking. Without studying the documents, she looked first at Sam and then her uncle, her face a mask of confusion and anger. "Why are you hurting my uncle?"

"Let me go, officer. I answered your question," said Townsend with a strained voice. Townsend tried to twist away from Sam's grip, but Sam tightened his hold, forcing him to stay still.

Angered, Townsend swung his left elbow at Sam's head, but Sam blocked the blow with his left arm, then pushed Townsend's right wrist higher, making the man cry out in pain.

"Ow! Stop! You're going to break my arm!"

"Bring your left hand to the small of your back, and I'll relax holding your arm," said Sam with a low growl filled with restrained fury.

"Stop hurting him, please!" screamed Elli, her voice breaking with fear and anger.

Townsend relented, lowering his left arm. It allowed Sam to cuff his wrists together. A shiver flowed down Elli's spine, witnessing her uncle arrested and handcuffed.

"Why are you arresting him?" Elli's voice was high-pitched with panic. Her uncle had arrived innocently, but the scene had erupted into chaos. She feared what Sam might do to her if she didn't cooperate.

"There's a reason why I'm arresting him, Elli. The district attorney believes your uncle is the mastermind behind all the robberies, including the theft and murder at your family's home."

CHAPTER
61

Townsend's voice cracked with desperation, echoing off the timeworn wooden walls of the aged barn. "That's bullshit! Don't believe him, Elli! He's lying! I had nothing to do with any robbery!"

"The DA's investigators arrested Sean Fitzgibbons, the guy who installed the alarm system, not only at your parents' home but at many others that got robbed," said Sam, his voice stern and unwavering. "Fitzgibbons worked for your uncle. Your uncle provided the alarm codes to Gilinsky and his gang."

Elli's eyes bore into her uncle with a fury that could melt steel, her gaze sharp and unrelenting. Her usually bright hazel eyes turned cloudy with tears of rage and disbelief. Elli's jaw clenched so tightly that a vein throbbed visibly at her temple, and her cheeks flushed with anger and betrayal. Her voice trembled as she finally spat out, "Is this true, uncle?"

Townsend's gut churned like a ship in a stormy sea, his heart pounding with a sickening rhythm. Beads of sweat formed on his forehead, glistening under the dim light of the overhead bulb. He remained silent, his mind racing with thoughts of escape ever since Sam mentioned Fitzgibbons and Gilinsky. The weight of his deceit hung heavily on his shoulders, dragging him into an abyss of panic.

"Looks like your uncle is selling this property, Elli," said Sam. "Look at the documents. Those papers you hold are the sales agreements."

Elli's fingers trembled as she leafed through the documents. Her lips were pressed into a thin line, her voice dripping with anger and disbelief. "Uncle, my mother left this property to me, not you! You can't sell this property!"

"It's his real estate company handling the sale. Pretty convenient, wouldn't you say?" said Sam sarcastically. "Look at the agreement again. There's another agent's name on it. I suggest you call that person to demand he put the sale on hold. Tell him you are the property owner and will sue if the property gets sold. Among the documents I handed you is a plane ticket for Cuba tomorrow."

"I have business in Cuba," said Townsend, his voice barely above a whisper.

"I bet you do, but the ticket is not in your name," said Sam. "Not to mention, Cuba is also one of the few countries that doesn't have an extradition agreement with the US."

"Elli, your mother named me the executor of her will. I planned on giving you half of the sale proceeds." Townsend's voice wavered, the words sounding hollow even to his own ears. "I'm only taking what's coming to me for all the money I spent as your guardian, including nearly a hundred thousand dollars in education expenses."

"That's not for you to decide. You can't justify taking half of what my mom left to me alone." Elli's voice was like ice, her anger freezing the air around her.

"He's not just taking half. He's taking all of it, Elli," Sam interjected, his tone filled with disgust. "He's taking everything he can to a safe haven in Cuba where no one will find him."

"Hey, I provided plenty to you, Elli. More than most children get," Townsend stammered, his desperation profound. "I gave you financial security and a home with the love Marge and I gave you."

"I don't want this property sold. I'll fight you in court," said Elli, her voice firm and unwavering.

"It's too late. The seller and buyer already signed the agreements." Townsend's voice was a weak attempt at authority, but it lacked conviction.

"I think you're wrong about that, Townsend," said Sam, a smirk playing at the corner of his lips. "You're not going anywhere but jail. The DA will ensure that your complicity in robberies and murder will be enough to void any sale agreement you signed and put you away for a very long stay in prison."

At this point, Sam signaled his backup team. The three officers marched in, their faces set in grim determination. Elli's heart raced, her initial fear that they had come for her subsiding only when she saw their focus was on her uncle. She had always known that her quest for vengeance carried the risk of capture, but she also knew Sam had done what the authorities failed to do for seven long years—facilitate the arrest of the thugs who had killed her family.

Elli was confused with conflicting emotions. The realization that her uncle might have played a role in her family's death was a bitter pill to swallow. His deception in trying to sell her property and his plans to flee the country were more than she could bear. Tears streamed down her cheeks as she turned to Sam, giving him a nod of gratitude for his help and advice.

Elli had no choice but to accept her fate. She knew the police were now aware of her actions against the four men who had robbed and killed her family. She also sensed that Sam was trying to help her get justice for her family. She decided to cooperate fully with whatever questions he had.

Sam had Agents Clarkson and Vaillans secure Townsend while he and Cassie interviewed Elli in her apartment. He first called the DA to update him on Townsend's arrest and the documents found in his possession.

"Great work, Sam," said the DA. "You've done enough to help bring charges against an organized criminal enterprise operating in the state for years. Fitzgibbons agreed to cooperate after we offered him a deal. You might not know that Fitzgibbons connected Townsend to a group in New York responsible for similar robberies."

"Good to know, and thanks. We'll transport Townsend to New Haven PD for processing before turning him over to your investigators. I'll call you once we have him there. But first, we need to interview the suspect who shot my partner."

"Holy shit! You're arresting him, too?"

Sam moved far away from Elli and Townsend, ensuring they couldn't overhear. "Well, the shooter is not a he but a she. She's the daughter of the Donnelley family that Gilinsky and his crew murdered.

"Oh, my God, Sam. I'm . . . I'm speechless. I don't know what to say."

"Don't say anything yet. I want to meet with the US Attorney to discuss leniency for any charges she'll face."

"What? Why would you do that?"

"She was only fourteen at the time. That might remind you of who the witness was that accused Alonzio of murdering her mother and sister."

The DA paused before saying, "Oh, yeah. I know what you're thinking. We can deal with that when we meet. Good job, and thanks. We'll talk more later."

Sam ended the call and turned to Elli. "I need to ask you some questions privately," he said gently.

She nodded, her eyes still filled with tears. She tied her dog, Rusty, to a pole outside her apartment door, then led Sam and Cassie inside. Rusty growled at Sam as he walked past. Sam's eyes glowed with concern, figuring the dog remembered his sent.

"Will it be safe for the agents with the dog out here?" said Sam, a hint of apprehension in his voice.

"Rusty, down. Be good," Elli commanded. "He'll behave. He's well-trained and only barks and growls at trespassers. He won't attack or bite."

You could fool me, Sam thought. He remembered how the dog had chased him through the woods, snapping at his heels with a ferocity that made Sam shiver.

Elli sat at her dining table. Cassie and Sam sat opposite her. Elli took a deep breath, her hands clasped tightly in her lap before asking a question.

"Is Sam your real name?"

"This is Lieutenant Cassidy Dawson from the New Haven Police Department," Sam began, his tone professional and reassuring. "I'm ATF Special Agent Sam Caviello. The agents outside are FBI Agent Becca Vaillans and ATF Agent Jennifer Clarkson."

"I've heard of ATF. They investigate gun crimes, not murders and robberies. Am I right?"

"You are. The FBI and local police handle murders and robberies. ATF gets involved when criminals illegally possess or use firearms to commit violent crimes. My involvement started when my partner and I worked on an unrelated case in New Haven. That's where my partner, a female FBI agent, was shot outside a Starbucks café."

Elli's eyes widened in shock, her hand covering her mouth, whispering, "Oh, my God."

"I was waiting for her in a car across the street," said Sam. "When I heard the shot, I saw the shooter running and tackled who I thought was a man, but it was you. You clocked me in the head with a gun."

"That was you? I thought you looked familiar when you followed me to the café in town. I'm so sorry," said Elli with a frown. "I apologize for hitting you, and I didn't want to shoot the agent. I regretted shooting her. I couldn't sleep for days, knowing I should have run when I saw she didn't have a gun."

"You gave me several stitches, I might add." Sam pushed back his hair to show Elli the scar. "When we wrestled, your wig and fake beard shifted enough for me to recognize you were probably a woman. You might remember I took your sock. Your DNA was on it."

"How did that connect me to the people who murdered my family?" Elli's voice trembled, her body tensing with the weight of Sam's revelation.

Sam avoided mentioning the news clippings he found in her desk drawer. "Gilinsky complained to the police about a guy who shot him in the knee. Based on his description, a police artist sketched the assailant and circulated the drawing to local departments. I later recognized that the person in the sketch who wore a disguise was you. I did some digging, gathered background on your family's murder, and eventually read the letter you had Bonarz send to the DA."

Elli's face drained of color, her head bowing in defeat. Believing the intricate plan she had meticulously crafted for years would give her invincibility had crumbled. She had thought her disguise was foolproof, but now she realized how fragile her illusion had been. The female FBI agent's intervention shattered her hope of a clean escape.

Agent Clarkson opened the apartment door, whispering a need to use the bathroom in the house.

"The door is unlocked," said Elli.

Clarkson apologized for the interruption and left.

Elli finished what she was saying to Sam. "I didn't want to shoot the agent. That was a terrible mistake. I would never kill anyone, not even those creeps who murdered my family. I purposely aimed for her shoulder so I could escape before she arrested me. I had to keep my promise to my family to get justice. I can't apologize enough for hurting the agent. I hope she's okay."

"She's recovering," Sam replied, his voice softening.

"I'd like to meet her to apologize in person. I'll tell you whatever you want to know, especially about my uncle's issues with my father's success. Ask your questions."

Suddenly, a loud, vicious barking erupted outside the barn. Rusty's growls echoed menacingly through the wooden structure.

"What's going on out there?" said Sam, rising from his chair, worrying about his partner's safety.

CHAPTER
62

While Sam and Cassie interrogated Elli in her cramped apartment, Townsend plotted his escape. He constantly considered ways to break away and flee the country. Townsend knew he couldn't survive spending years behind bars. It made his skin crawl; he'd rather die than let that happen.

Townsend had watched Elli loosely tie Rusty's leash to the wrought iron post outside the apartment. Rusty was a gift to Elli from Townsend years ago. Townsend had trained the dog to obey him implicitly before giving him to Elli. He formed his plan when he observed the agents entering Elli's apartment. He waited a few minutes for Elli and the agents to get settled inside, then put his plan into action.

"Agents, I need to use the bathroom. I can't hold it any longer. I'm a nervous wreck about being arrested. Please. If I crap my pants, it'll stink up the place. I promise I won't do anything stupid."

The two agents exchanged a glance, their faces reflecting annoyance and suspicion. Agent Clarkson finally spoke, her voice edged with skepticism.

"There's no bathroom out here in the barn, and we can't disturb Agent Caviello."

"There's a bathroom in the house. Please. You'll be right outside the door. I can't go anywhere. There's no window in the guest bathroom."

Clarkson sighed, her patience wearing thin. "I'll have to check with Agent Caviello first."

"For Christ's sake. Are you two trained agents scared of me? I have a fractured hip and can hardly move," said Townsend, hoping to play on their pity. "Please, I'm about to crap my pants."

"I'll check with Caviello."

Clarkson tapped on the apartment door and cracked it open, saying, "Townsend needs to crap. Is there a guest bathroom inside the house?"

Elli responded, saying the back door was open. So Clarkson and Vaillans were to escort Townsend into the house. Before they started, Townsend abruptly turned toward the barn, shouting, "Rusty, come boy! Come, Rusty!"

"What are you doing, Townsend? Keep moving to the house," said an irritated Clarkson.

Rusty's ears perked up, barking, his powerful body straining against the leash as he tried to break free.

"Come, Rusty, come!" Townsend yelled repeatedly, his voice growing more urgent.

"Stop calling the dog, or I'll take you back to the barn where you can shit your pants," snapped Clarkson, her eyes darting nervously between Townsend and the agitated dog.

Rusty pulled harder, his barks growing more frantic, until finally, with a sharp yank, he broke free from the post. The dog bolted toward Townsend, barking ferociously, his teeth bared in a menacing snarl. The agents instinctively backed away as Rusty approached them, his growls filling the air with a threatening rumble.

Townsend seized his chance when the agents backed away, focusing on the dog. He moved toward the house, the pain in his hip forgotten in the adrenaline rush. Reaching the door, he turned his back to the door, twisted the knob with his cuffed hand, and shoved it open. He entered and slammed it shut, locking it behind him.

Breathing heavily, Townsend dashed to the kitchen. He pulled out the drawers as utensils hit the floor and echoed through the quiet house.

Townsend found a box cutter and quickly lay on the floor. Grimacing in pain, he contorted his body, maneuvering his handcuffed hands over his uplifted feet with his knees against his chest. He brought his hands in front of him. He sliced through the plastic cuffs with the box cutter, freeing his hands.

He got to his feet, scanned the drawers, and found a cell phone and a portable charger. Grabbing them, he hurried to the main bedroom. The sound of the front door banging open sent a jolt of fear through him. He forced open the bedroom window and climbed out, tumbling to the ground with a heavy thud. Ignoring the pain, Townsend scuffled to his feet and limped toward the woods, the dense foliage offering a potential escape route.

Townsend cautiously scaled over an old farm stone wall, its weathered stones shifting under his weight and off balance. Behind him, the agents stormed through the house with their guns drawn and their faces displaying frustration.

*   *   *

Rusty's frantic barking shook Elli from her conversation with the agents. She rushed out of the apartment, Sam and Cassie hot on her heels. Outside, the scene made Elli's heart leap into her throat. She screamed, seeing Rusty snarling at the two female agents with their guns drawn. "Rusty, no! Come, Rusty! Come!" Elli shouted, her voice trembling with urgency.

Rusty hesitated, his gaze switching between the agents and Elli. Hearing Elli's commanding voice, the dog finally vaulted toward her, his tail wagging, seeking acceptance, and leaving the agents to sigh with relief.

Clarkson pointed to the house, yelling, "Townsend's in the house!"

Sam ran to the house, yelling for Cassie to cover the front entrance. With their weapons drawn, Clarkson and Vaillans followed closely behind Sam. Inside, the kitchen was a scene of hurried disarray. Drawers on the floor revealed some contents strewn across the floor, including the box cutter.

Elli entered the house, her face pale with fear. Pointing to the drawers, Sam intensely asked her what items were missing.

Elli inspected the open drawers. "He took a cell phone and charger."

"Great. Just what we needed," Sam muttered under his breath.

"In the bedroom!" shouted Vaillans from down the hall.

Sam rushed into the bedroom, his eyes immediately locking onto the wide open window.

"I saw him running into the woods," said Vaillans.

"Stay near the barn and watch his car," said Sam to Vaillans and Clarkson. "He might circle back,"

Sam climbed out the window, landing lightly on the ground. Cassie, appearing around the corner of the house, gave him a questioning look with her arms in the air.

"Townsend went into the woods. Follow me, Cass," Sam vaulted over the old, crumbling stone wall, the rough stones scraping against his shoes. Cassie followed, her movements more cautious but no less determined. Together, they plunged into the dense woods, their pursuit of Townsend taking on a desperate urgency.

CHAPTER
63

Townsend trotted forward until he came to a neighbor's cottage, a quaint structure of faded white paint and creaking wood, on the same side of Shore Hill Road. The cottages here, each clinging to a bygone era, were few and far between against the encroaching wilderness. The house he approached belonged to an older gentleman whose name Townsend had forgotten. The empty driveway and the absence of a garage suggested no one was home.

He rang the doorbell and knocked with the force of a man desperate to elude his pursuers. The house remained silent, the echo of his knocking absorbed by the dense foliage. A rustle of leaves behind him signaled the agents' pursuit, giving Townsend a spike of anxiety. He pressed his shoulder against the door and shoved it open with a grunt, the old wood giving way under his weight.

Purposely leaving the door ajar, Townsend sprinted through the house, a shadow moving quickly past dusty furniture and faded curtains. He burst through the rear door, locking it behind him with a swift twist of his wrist. Townsend hurried past an old shed into the sheltering woods. He hoped the agents would waste precious minutes searching the cottage, giving him the lead he desperately needed.

Knowing the back roads like the veins on his hands, Townsend remembered a nearby lake with its small airport and a car rental station. That would be his gateway to freedom. He planned to retrieve his rented car, return the rented BMW at the airport, and disappear to his office in New York in an Uber. If needed, he'd print a new e-ticket and catch a flight to Cuba, a final, desperate attempt to escape his pursuers.

Cassie, a fit fifty-year-old with a petite frame packed with muscle and determination, struggled to keep pace with Sam. Sam maneuvered through the woods with the agility of a deer, barely touching the ground as he ran. When he reached a clearing, he paused, his breath misting in the cool air. Ahead, the old white cottage stood with its front door open like a gaping mouth. He waited for Cassie, who emerged from the forest, her cheeks flushed with exertion.

"We have to be quick," Sam urged, leading her into the cottage. They moved with purpose, checking each room, but Townsend was gone. The absence of a basement left them only one option: the rear door. Sam pointed towards it, his body taut with urgency.

"Everything okay, Sam?" Cassie asked, concern lacing her voice.

"Yeah. Townsend used this place as a decoy. He's still on the run." Sam's voice was tight, a coil of frustration ready to snap. Out the rear door, Sam pointed to the shed, then moved with Cassie through the back woods, their pace unyielding.

"Sam, you're losing me. I'm not as fast!" Cassie called out, her breath ragged.

Sam slowed, scanning the ground for signs of Townsend's passage. He moved with precision, listening intently. Leaves rustling ahead made him veer right. "We're close. Let's move."

Sam moved quickly, but Cassie, in her haste, stepped on a loose rock. She stumbled, grabbing at a branch that snapped under her weight, sending her sprawling to the ground.

Hearing her fall, Sam turned back. "Are you okay?"

"Yeah. Tripped on a rock. Sorry."

"No problem," Sam helped Cassie to her feet, saying, "It looks like an opening up ahead. We might see him there."

Townsend had reached the edge of the woods, crouching in the field's tall grass as he eyed the barn to his right. The field stretched out like a forgotten quilt, patches of wildflowers dotting the tall grass. He hurried along an old stone wall. Townsend wiped the sweat from his brow and crept to the open rear door, his pulse hammering in his ears. Townsend scanned the inside area, but Elli and the agents were nowhere in sight.

A bark from Rusty inside the barn shattered the silence. Townsend cursed under his breath, "The frigging dog could smell a fart from a half mile away." He heard Elli's muffled shouts, "Rusty, quiet! Lay down!" The dog whined before falling silent in reluctant compliance.

The barn, a relic of his childhood, loomed before him, a fortress of memories and regrets. His father had turned this place into a haven, a sanctuary away from the world's chaos. Now, it was a potential trap. He remembered the joy of growing up here, but bitterness tightened his chest as he recalled how his father had left the property and the family's jewelry business to his sister, Elli's mother. The sting of being left with the leftovers still stung him.

"Move, stupid," Townsend muttered, his legs trembling from the impaired hip. He glanced around the barn's corner, peeking inside to ensure the agents were not lurking there. He didn't notice Agent Clarkson staring at his BMW on the right corner of the open front barn door. His body tensed with fear. His hands were clammy and cold. He squatted down to stay hidden by the Mustang and moved to the apartment door. He peered into the window and saw his papers on the desktop. Rusty raised his head, sensing Townsend at the door. The dog whimpered but didn't bark. Elli was at the sink, staring out the rear window.

Townsend quietly slipped inside unseen. Rusty didn't move or make a sound other than wagging his tail. Townsend snatched the papers off the table, stuffed them into his jacket pocket, and then began searching Elli's desk drawers. His fingers trembled as he rifled through the contents.

"What are you doing, uncle?" Elli's voice, soft yet firm, caught him off guard.

"I'm innocent, El. The agents have it wrong," Townsend whispered. "I need to get to my car and leave without being seen. I'll clear this up with my attorney." Townsend's voice was urgent, bordering on frantic. "Where are the agents?"

"I don't know. I've been in here with Rusty since they searched the house."

Townsend didn't have time for games. "Did they all chase after me?"

"Only two," Elli admitted with a hint of regret.

"I had no part in what happened to your mom and dad, El. I loved Alexis. She was my sister, for chrissake." His voice cracked, whispering denials.

He found what he was looking for in another drawer.

Elli's eyes narrowed. "What are you doing with that gun? You'll get yourself killed if the agents see you with it."

"I need protection. I can't go to jail. I won't survive it. Where are the other agents?"

Elli sighed, frustration evident on her face. "I don't know. They could be anywhere."

"Call them here. Tell them you saw someone out back. I'll slip out the bedroom window and make a run for it."

"No, uncle. I can't. They're trying to help me. If they realize I helped you, I could be in serious trouble. Besides, if what they say is true, you should face up to what you did."

Townsend didn't have time to argue. He grabbed the gun.

"Not that one. I took it from one of the killers."

"What killers? Never mind, I gotta get outta here."

He took the other gun in the drawer and headed to her bedroom. He opened the window and peeked left and right to check the surroundings. Elli followed, tears streaming down her face. Townsend turned to face her, strolled back, and hugged her.

"I shouldn't tell you this, but I want you to believe I had no part in what happened to your mom and dad." What he whispered to her caused her to shake her head in disbelief, causing tears to stream down her cheeks again. Townsend kissed her forehead, then struggled to exit through the egress window.

He snuck to the barn's front corner near where he parked his car, several feet from the two vehicles driven by the agents. The rear of his BMW was just a few feet from the sedan. His path to freedom lay before him but was fraught with risk. He peeked around the corner to ensure the coast was clear. He didn't see anyone out in the open but knew they were nearby, waiting for him. He took a deep breath. His heart raced in desperation as he suddenly dashed toward the agent's car.

CHAPTER
64

Sam and Cassie emerged from the shadowy tree line, stepping into the vast expanse of the open field. Sam's gaze swept across the horizon, his sharp eyes catching every subtle movement. His right arm twitched, a familiar shiver running through his hand—a premonition, the sensation he had learned to heed.

"He's in the barn," Sam stated with certainty, his voice barely above a whisper.

"He is? I didn't see him go in there," replied a confused Cassie.

"He's in there. Let's move," Sam insisted, his tone leaving no room for doubt.

As they hurried toward the barn, Cassie's mind buzzed with curiosity. Sam's uncanny ability to pinpoint their targets had baffled her. She needed an explanation of what happened when his arm trembled. She was sure there was a connection to what guided him somehow.

Reaching the back of the barn, Sam quickly called agents Clarkson and Vaillans, whispering, "Be on alert. Townsend is in the barn. He could be armed if he managed to get into the apartment."

"You think Elli would give him a gun, Sam?" Cassie asked, her eyes scanning the area, searching for any signs of movement behind her.

"No, but he might know she has guns in the house and grab one."

"You know she has guns in the apartment?"

Thinking fast to cover he had been in the apartment, Sam answered, "She had to have a gun when she dealt with Gilinsky and his crew members."

Agent Clarkson crouched low inside the barn, her eyes trained on the BMW and the apartment door. She hadn't seen or heard Townsend enter, whispering, "How does Sam know he's in the barn?" The barn was silent, save for the distant droning of insects.

Sam and Cassie moved stealthily to the barn's open door. Sam peered inside, seeing no movement. He then signaled Cassie to cover him as he entered the apartment door.

Hearing movement, Clarkson gazed at the Mustang behind her, tension coiling in her muscles, turning and aiming her gun in the car's direction. She held her breath with her finger on the gun's trigger until she saw Sam enter the apartment door. "Phew, I almost shot at Sam," she whispered, sliding her finger off the trigger, exhaling, and refocusing on the BMW outside.

Agent Vaillans was positioned near the house's rear porch, ducking low against the side of the house. Her eyes fixed on the BMW's driver's side door, every muscle primed for action. Both agents were poised to act at the slightest sign of Townsend.

The moment Sam entered the apartment, the dog started barking furiously. Elli appeared from the bedroom, quieting Rusty with a wave when seeing Sam in the apartment. Clarkson, startled by the barking, swung her gun again toward the apartment door but relaxed when she saw Cassie there.

Inside the apartment, there was a stark contrast to the distressed scene outside, where the agents were in an agitated state of suspense. Elli, her face pale with worry, pointed toward the bedroom. "My uncle took a gun from my desk. He went out the bedroom window."

"He's aiming to get himself killed, for Pete's sake," said Sam, frustration showing on his creased face.

"Please don't kill him," said Elli, pleading, her voice breaking. "I'm mad as hell at him, but he's still my uncle. Put him in jail if he's guilty, but don't kill him, *pleeease*."

"Let's hope he doesn't do something stupid," said Sam.

Sam noticed the window was open wide. He immediately contacted Clarkson and Vaillans, informing them that Townsend was heading toward the BMW. As Sam rushed to exit the bedroom, he saw the apartment door ajar, with Cassie standing just outside.

"Elli pushed past me in a hurry, heading outside," she explained.

"We have to stop her." Sam brushed past Cassie.

Townsend's heart pounded as he measured the distance between the agent's car and his BMW. At the agent's rear bumper, he peered between the vehicles, seeing no one. His stomach churned, and his nerves wound tight like a spring. Sweat dripped from his forehead, stinging his eyes as he gripped his gun with a trembling hand. He darted out between the two cars when, unexpectedly, his peripheral vision caught movement—a figure to his right shouting, "Stop." Townsend spun and fired spontaneously.

CHAPTER
65

Townsend turned away and recoiled at the BMW's back bumper. His snarling frown revealed his gross mistake of instinctively firing his gun at who he thought was an agent. His face crushed into folds with tightened lips and rutted brows, mumbling "Damn it" after seeing his niece, Elli, fall to the ground. "What the hell was she doing?" Townsend's hand quivered as he clutched the BMW's bumper, emotionally whispering, "I didn't mean it, El."

Sam bolted out of the barn as a gunshot sounded, just as Elli dropped to the ground. His heart surged with fury and fear. He crouched low, cautiously approaching her, scanning for any sign of Townsend.

Townsend rubbed his eyes clear, trembling, breathing heavily, his heart beating like a racehorse. He nervously glanced around the BMW's driver's side, seeing no immediate threat. His mind, void of logical thought, only that of escaping, prompted him to move toward the driver's door. Townsend felt now more than ever he had to get to the driver's seat and get away before the agents grabbed him. Squatting along the side of the BMW, Townsend reached for the car's door handle, his hand wildly trembling. Suddenly, a voice shattered the tense silence.

"FBI! Don't move, or I'll shoot!" shouted Agent Becca Vaillans. Her voice quivered, the reality of the situation weighing heavily on her.

Townsend couldn't see Vaillans, but with his gun slipping in his clammy hands, he fired blindly in the direction of the voice. The bullets buzzed by Vaillans wildly, missing their mark. Desperation clawed at Townsend as he wrenched the car door partially open. He fired again in a last-ditch effort to keep the agent at bay. The bullet slid off the side of Becca's helmet, skidding slightly off to the right, hitting and breaking the house's back door window.

Despite the chaos and the concern that the bullet hit her, Vaillans aimed her gun, her heart hammering her chest as she pulled the trigger. The bullet struck Townsend dead center in his chest. His eyes widened in shock as he gasped for breath, his head bashing against the car. He fired one last futile shot in the air before his butt slid down the BMW to the ground. His eyes gazed at the blue sky until his eyes became glossy and full of white light, then blind to the world as his breath surrendered his existence.

Sam, still tending to Elli, heard the shots. He called out, laced with concern, "Becca! Are you okay?"

Momentarily stunned by her actions, Becca Vaillans stared at Townsend's lifeless body. The weight of her actions crashed over her, leaving her breathless and shaken. "I'm all right," she squealed. "Townsend is down." Becca's hand felt the side of her helmet. She was concerned that the bullet might have penetrated through. Not feeling it did, she removed the helmet to verify there was no hole. She sighed heavily, thankful Sam had insisted she wear the helmet.

Sam let out a relieved sigh. He turned his attention back to Elli, who was bleeding profusely from her left side. Cassie crouched beside him, helping to find the wound. Blood had soaked through Elli's blouse, staining her torso. Sam lifted her torso, then raised her blouse to reveal the entrance and exit wounds. He quickly retrieved two bandages from his first aid pouch, his hands moving with trained agility.

"Cassie, call 911 for an ambulance and the state police. Ask the state police to call for a coroner." Sam spoke softly to Elli, saying, "An ambulance is on the way. Stay awake and alert. You're going to be okay. I'm here with you."

"My uncle?" Elli's voice was weak, her eyes pleading for answers. Vaillans now stood with Clarkson, their expressions somber. Seeing Sam look at her for confirmation on Townsend, Vaillans shook her head, gesturing Townsend was gone.

"I'm sorry, Elli, but your uncle made the fatal mistake of shooting at our agent. Sam paused, then glanced at Becca, asking, "Did you retrieve his gun?"

"No," she said, shaken by her failure to do so. "I'll go get it." Clarkson interrupted. "I'll get it," recognizing Vaillans was trembling and not herself.

Elli's eyes welled with tears, her voice barely a whisper. "He said he would never make it in jail. I tried to stop him."

"He chose his fate, Elli. He chose death over living in hell," Sam gently said.

"Can I sit up?" Elli asked, her voice tinged with pain.

"It's better if you wait for the EMTs," Sam advised, his expression full of concern.

Clarkson returned with Townsend's gun. Sam asked Becca to fetch a pillow from the house to make Elli more comfortable. When Becca returned with a pillow, Sam saw her cheeks were pale; she had a solemn gaze in her eyes.

"Are you okay, Becca?" said Sam.

"Uh, a little down, but I'm alright," said Vaillans, her voice shaky.

"Don't dwell on Townsend. You had no choice. You did what you had to do—what the FBI trained you to do. I have to make some calls. Stay with Elli and keep her awake. I'll be right back."

Sam reassured Elli before stepping away to call Dell Haskins. As Dell answered, Sam explained the situation, detailing the events with a steady voice. "Would you call and brief the Hartford agent in charge and Davies?" He ended the call without waiting for Haskins to question him.

Sam moved to a more private spot to contact the Bridgeport DA, updating him on Townsend. "Townsend shot his niece, Elli Donnelley. Our agent had no choice but to put Townsend down when he started shooting. Elli is seriously wounded. We called the state police and for an ambulance. I can't talk," Sam gave him the location address and then called to brief the US Attorney Durrell in New Haven and asked for a later meeting with her to discuss the situation with Elli Donnelley.

"I won't be in the office until Wednesday. Will that work?"

"Yes, but let's meet at one o'clock. It's a long ride from Boston." Sam ended the call after recommending what officials she should invite to attend.

"Sam, Elli is asking for you!" shouted Becca.

Sam rushed to Elli's side. "I'm here, Elli."

Trembling and cold, Elli's hand reached for Sam's head, pulling him closer. She whispered a fragment of her uncle's secret about her mother, her breath cold against his ear. She coughed again, her grip slackening as her eyes fluttered shut.

Sam frantically checked her pulse, his fingers trembling. He found no pulse. Panic surged through him. "I need help here!" he shouted. He began administering CPR, his movements desperate but precise. "Does anyone have a portable defibrillator?" His plea hung in the air, unanswered.

"I hear a car in the driveway!" said Becca. She dashed to the driveway, her footsteps pounding against the gravel.

Moments later, she returned, breathless. "It's the state police! They have a defibrillator, Sam!"

State Trooper Tyrell Franklin rushed in and knelt beside Sam with a calm demeanor. "We meet again, Agent Caviello. You're lucky I was close by." Looking at Clarkson, Franklin uttered, "Keep what you're doing until I get the defib ready." Once he set the defibrillator, he said, "Hit the red charge button."

Elli's body convulsed as the electric shock coursed through her, her chest lifting from the ground in a jolt. The silence that followed was deafening.

Sam had backed away, his face a mask of anguish and hope. He glanced at the sky, where a cloud had shaded the bright sun.

"Still no pulse," said Franklin.

Sam closed his eyes while crossing his fingers, whispering, "Come on, Elli. Stay with us. It's not fair for you to die now."

Franklin increased the charge, his expression grim. "Again," he commanded. Clarkson pressed the button, and Elli's body arched higher with the second jolt. Unexpectedly, Sam's face felt intense warmth. He opened his eyes only to be blinded by a radiating glow from the sky illuminating the area surrounding Elli; the magnitude of light was reminiscent of a photographer's bright flashbulb going off.

"I've got a faint pulse," whispered Franklin, his voice a lifeline of hope. Sam breathed a sigh of relief, whispering, "Thank God."

A distant siren grew louder, heralding the arrival of the ambulance. Within moments, two EMTs arrived, their faces set with determination as they rushed to Elli's side.

Sam watched as the EMTs worked, a silent prayer forming on his lips. Elli had endured the nightmare of her family's murder for years, clinging to the hope of justice. She deserved a chance to live beyond the shadows of her past. He gazed at the sky again, wondering what the glow of light came from while thinking maybe it was a sign from above.

Cassie approached Sam, softly asking, "What the hell was that, Sam?"

"What do you mean?"

"That jolt of sunlight that blinded us when Jennifer pressed the defibrillator button."

"I don't know, but whatever it was, it brought Elli back to life."

Abruptly, Sam's phone vibrated. The caller ID flashed with a number from the New Haven FBI office. Sam grimaced, anticipating a bureaucratic wrath. He ignored the call until a moment later, his phone buzzed again. He reluctantly answered the call and listened to Davies' tirade for as long as he could stand it.

"What the hell kind of rogue operation are you running, Caviello? You've violated so many protocols I've lost count! You're in Connecticut, not Boston. You failed to keep this office, specifically me, informed of your actions. Cease your operations immediately until agents from my office arrive. Expect me there as well."

"That's unnecessary," Sam interrupted. "I've already notified the Hartford and Boston FBI offices, the state police, the State DA's Office, the New Haven Police Department, and the Connecticut US Attorney's Office. Representatives from each are either here or on their way. The scene is secure. No need for you to be here."

Davies's voice grew harsher. "Oh, I need to be there, Caviello. I'm ordering—"

Sam cut him off. "Right now, I need to focus on the scene here. We can discuss this later." Sam hung up without waiting for a response, the receiver's finality echoing in Davies's ear.

"Everything okay, Sam? You look pissed," said Cassie, her eyes reflecting concern.

"Who, me? Not at all. I'm at peace with my actions." Sam forced a smile, though tension still lingered in his features.

"Well, Townsend's certainly at peace now," Cassie said with a wry smile.

"We should all be at peace now that the situation is over. We did our best, and we're all safe. That's a win in my book."

"I need to call my office," said Cassie, walking away.

Alone, Sam took a moment to breathe in the crisp evening air. The sky was now a canvas of light blue, streaked with vibrant red, orange, and pink hues as the sun began to set. He let the warmth of the setting sun wash over him, a contented smile spreading across his face. Closing his eyes, he allowed himself a brief respite from the day's events, especially the uncanny brilliant flash of light that mesmerized him and others as the defibrillator hit Elli a second time. It seemed creepy, unnatural. He took a deep breath, wiped away the thought, and returned to the challenges that lay ahead: Townsend's death, Elli's recovery, and the aftermath of the operation. Despite the chaos, he felt a profound sense of accomplishment. He had completed his mission in Connecticut and was ready to return to Boston. A sense of fulfillment and anticipation fueled his journey, hoping an extended vacation would soon begin.

CHAPTER

66

artford's FBI Assistant Agent-in-Charge Mike Conway, who is responsible for the geographical area of New Preston, arrived within the hour. Boston FBI Supervisory Agent Dell Haskins arrived at the chaotic scene about an hour later. State Police Captain Ed Reyes and Sergeant Tyrell Franklin coordinated efforts with the arriving coroner. New Haven Detectives Matt Kendrick and Ted Porter joined Cassie at the scene. The only conspicuous absence was that of Alan Davies and his team.

Sam wasn't eager for another scathing critique from Davies, so he discreetly approached Dell Haskins and Mike Conway, saying, "I've got an urgent meeting with the Mass State Police. I'll be leaving here momentarily. I hope you guys don't mind taking charge of the scene from here."

Summarizing the tumultuous events, Sam detailed Townsend's escape and desperate return for his car. "During Townsend's movement to his BMW, he shot his niece, Elli Donnelley, who he had mistaken for us. When Townsend continued to his car to escape, Agent Vaillans ordered him to stop. She had no choice but to return fire when Townsend fired several shots in her direction. Her shot was fatal." Sam's voice softened as he praised FBI Agents Vaillans, Detective Dawson, and Kiara Rivers, underscoring their bravery and recommending them for a well-deserved commendation.

Regrettably, Davies and his team arrived. Davies searched and saw Sam with an expression of frustration evident on his face. Sam immediately asked Dell. "Can you brief Davies? My ride to Boston is about to leave.

Not waiting for a response, Sam, holding his go-bag, signaled to Agent Clarkson it was time to leave. They rushed to her car. Sam heard Davies shout his name, which echoed through the air for everyone to hear. Ignoring Davies, he shut the car door, saying to Clarkson. "Drive, and don't stop for anyone."

*   *   *

The landscape blurred into a hazy palette of greens and browns in the rural community as Clarkson's car sped away from the scene. She glanced at Sam, her face an expression of curiosity and concern. "What's the deal with Davies? He seemed pretty angry."

Sam sighed, leaning back in his seat. "He's the new FBI agent-in-charge in New Haven and not thrilled that I'm conducting investigations on his turf. A US senator specifically requested I get assigned to assist the FBI in finding her son, who went missing while attending Yale University. During the investigation, an unrelated suspect shot and wounded my partner, FBI Agent Rivers. Davies declared his office would lead the investigation because it happened in New Haven. But Rivers was my partner—I had to be part of the investigation to find her shooter."

"Did you find out who shot her?"

"Yes. Elli Donnelley. I had Agent Vaillans arrest her for Rivers and me."

"What? Elli? Why would she shoot Rivers?"

"It's a long story. I'll explain on the way. But first, let me know how you and your daughter, Jalissa, are doing. Then, fill me in on what's happening at the Hartford ATF office. After taking some needed time off, I'll be back there."

Clarkson's eyes lit up. She launched into an animated recount of the past months, her daughter's milestones, and the bustle of work in Hartford, subbing for Sam while he was on assignment. Her voice was a soothing counterpoint to the adrenaline-fueled chaos Sam had just left behind. She detailed several significant cases the Hartford ATF team was working on, and her pride in their achievements was evident.

"I'm thrilled you're coming back to Hartford, Sam. It's been nearly a year. Everyone will be thrilled. How long's your vacation?"

Sam grinned. "Hopefully, a year."

Clarkson laughed. "Get out of here. A year?"

"I'm kidding. Maybe a few weeks, a month. I haven't decided yet. But you can tell everyone I'll be back soon."

"Good to hear," Clarkson said with evident skepticism. "There was a rumor going around that you weren't coming back. The guys were pretty bummed."

"What rumor? From where?"

"Headquarters. The word was Boston's ASAC is transferring, and you're up for the job."

Sam chuckled. "That's not happening. I have zero interest in that position. I prefer staying in Hartford or continuing to work in the field. But who knows? We'll see."

Clarkson changed the subject, asking, "I don't mind driving you to Boston."

"That's not necessary. You've already done more than enough. Drop me off at the state police barracks in Sturbridge. A trooper will drive me the rest of the way."

"Seriously? How'd you pull that off?"

Sam smirked. "Let's just say I've got a few good friends in high places."

CHAPTER
67

S am directed Jennifer to the state police station in Sturbridge. Parked in front of the state police facility were three state police cruisers and two unidentified vehicles. The police barracks, a two-story age-old red brick building, had been there for over twenty years. As they pulled into the parking area, Sam saw a trooper with his back to him chatting with a civilian. The trooper's broad shoulders with hash marks and sergeant stripes on his sleeve designated years of service and rank. Sam thanked Jennifer for the ride, her smile comforting before he stepped out and approached the big, burly trooper.

"Hi, I'm Agent Sam Caviello. Are you waiting for me, sergeant?"

The trooper turned slowly, revealing a face that brought a rush of memories flooding back. "Yeah, and it's about time you showed up," he replied, a teasing edge in his voice.

"Holy shit. Jim Markham. What are you doing in Sturbridge?"

"This is my new home now. I'm the night shift commander, for now anyway."

They shook hands, their grips firm, and embraced with hearty slaps on the back that spoke of shared history and mutual respect.

"Uh, did you put on a few pounds, pudgy?" Sam teased, a grin tugging at his lips.

"It's all just extra muscle from sitting on my ass behind a desk."

"Did you get selected to drive me to Boston?"

"Hey, I volunteered, man. It's great seeing you again."

"It's great seeing you, too. You're not telling me this is a prize assignment you volunteered for?"

"It is. My shift ends at midnight. If we leave now, I'll get home early tonight. I live a short ride from Boston. Not to mention, I'm chauffeuring the guy who was most responsible for me getting promoted to sergeant."

"I was?"

"You spoke highly of me to Major Burke. You can't get much higher than him. He later privately thanked me for helping you find Al Madari, the terrorist leader you nailed cold to the tree. The major later asked me to apply for the sergeant position. I did, and low and behold, I was promoted two weeks later. Thank you very much, Sam."

"I'm sure it wasn't only what I said to Burke. He recognized you for what you did to help find that terrorist who killed a lot of troopers during the raid. It was a well-deserved promotion."

"Maybe, but thanks for your input. Let's get on the road. It's getting late. Plus, I want to hear how you lost your car."

The drive to the entrance ramp for I-90—the Mass Pike, as it's called—was short. After Sam threw his bag in the cruiser's back seat, he sat buckled up in the passenger seat. The day's events weighed heavily on him. Arresting Alonzio, dealing with Townsend's arrest and escape, and Elli getting shot had drained him to the bone.

"Okay, Sam. Did your car get stolen, or did you forget where you parked it?

Sam chuckled. "No. I needed money to buy dinner, so I sold it to a guy looking for a ride to Ohio."

"Right. Now tell me what really happened."

"I drove to New Haven with my partner, an FBI agent, who had to return to Boston."

"So she stranded you without a car. Nice partner."

"Nothing like that. The agent got injured and needed time to heal back in Boston. The agent offered to get another car for me, but I hooked up with a New Haven detective to finish the case we worked on. I got a ride to Sturbridge from an ATF agent I worked with in Hartford."

"I often think back to the day the FBI and the state police raided the farmhouse where the terrorists held those two hostages," said Markham. "You and Detective Juli Ospino were the ones who found where they hid after shooting a female trooper in Revere. I remember you were against raiding the farmhouse until we could gather more intel about the farm. All hell broke loose when the FBI and our guys hit the place. No one, except you, thought the terrorists were ready for us. The booby-trapped farmhouse killed the SWAT team members when they hit the door. We lost twelve agents and troopers that morning, including your partner, Detective Ospino."

Sam's heart clenched at the mention of Juli. Her name brought a flood of memories of her he had tried hard to suppress. He and Juli had shared a connection beyond mere partnership—a budding romance cruelly cut short by her untimely death. He turned away from Markham, staring out the window, lost in thoughts of what might have been.

Forty minutes into their drive, a sudden crackle from Markham's two-way police radio jerked Sam back to the present. The alert was a harsh reminder of the dangers still lurking out there.

"Attention all units. Be on the lookout for a dark gray Nissan Rogue hijacked in Hartford by a Hispanic male suspected of shooting two men in Hartford. The suspect is five-ten, average build, wearing a black hoody and blue jeans. He is armed and dangerous. The vehicle he hijacked had a four-year-old child in a booster safety seat in the rear. A trucker on I-84 spotted the Nissan on I-84 heading east toward the Massachusetts border. Proceed with caution." The message ended with a repeat of the stolen vehicle's description and license plate number.

"Just what we need. Another carjacking crazy driving off with a kid in the back seat. I hope they nail this guy before anything happens to the kid," said Markham. Markham continued his tale of how the terrorist leader escaped from the farmhouse with Sam in pursuit. "You chased the bastard through the woods, forcing him to leave behind the two hostages while he ran to the road where a crony was waiting for him in a van. That left you in the middle of the road without wheels. Again, I might add."

"That's when I came in for the rescue like I'm doing now," said Markham, trying to lighten the mood. He glanced at Sam, hoping to coax a smile from him, but Sam seemed to focus on the traffic ahead.

"Hey. You okay, Sam? Did I say something I shouldn't have?" Sam didn't answer but concentrated on the traffic ahead of them. "What the hell are you looking at anyway?" said Markham, a hint of curiosity in his voice.

"A dark-colored Nissan Rogue passed you seconds ago."

"No way. You're kidding, right?"

"I wish. I don't need to get involved in another chase. Step on the gas, and let's check it out. Hopefully, it's a different Rogue."

"It better be; otherwise, we might not get to Boston tonight."

Sam shook his head, hoping it was not the right Rogue. He had enough tension for today. He didn't need any more.

Markham floored the Ford Explorer. The engine roared as they quickly closed the gap to the Nissan. Sam squinted at the license plate. Markham did the same.

"Oh, shit. Just my luck. It's the carjacker." Markham grabbed the mic and spoke with a tense urgency. "All units, this is 4458. I'm in pursuit of the Nissan Rogue carjacked earlier in Hartford with a young child in the rear seat. I recently passed the exit for Grafton on I-90 East. Request backup. I have an ATF agent as a passenger. We're in pursuit."

Markham received confirmation from responding troopers. He turned to Sam, saying, "You're armed, right Sam?"

"I am. My vest is in the bag on the rear seat."

"Well, get ready to put it on fast. I'm going to pull the bastard over. I doubt he'll voluntarily pull off to the side of the road."

Sam had already called Kiara to let her know he'd arrive in about an hour, but now it seemed like it would be much longer. Markham activated the cruiser's emergency lights and siren, but the suspect showed no signs of slowing down. Instead, he accelerated, speeding away.

Markham pushed the Explorer harder, edging closer to the Rogue's rear bumper. He tried to pass, but the suspect swerved wildly, clipping the cruiser's front end and speeding ahead. Markham stayed on him, the two vehicles locked in a dangerous dance as the suspect zigzagged across the lanes between cars to prevent the cruiser from passing.

"Be careful, Jim. You don't want anything happening to the kid."

"I'm not letting this creep escape. One way or another, I'll force him to stop before we get into heavy city traffic."

"Try swaying to his right, attempting to pass him. When he turns right, swing back to the left, floor it, and try passing him."

Markham nodded and executed the maneuver. He swayed right, baiting the suspect into turning right. Then, with a quick flick of the wheel, Markham swung left and accelerated, passing the Nissan. The suspect reacted by swinging left, smashing into the cruiser's rear side as he tried to block the pass. The Explorer fishtailed into the Rogue, forcing it toward the inside lane. Markham continued steering right, pushing the suspect car toward the guardrail. The hijacker attempted to regain control, but Markham's relentless push left the hijacker no room to maneuver. The Nissan's rear end hit a guardrail and then skidded to a halt. Markham stepped off the gas pedal and maneuvered to the Nissan's backside, where traffic moving toward them could see his emergency lights flashing.

The carjacker bolted from the vehicle, firing three shots at the cruiser and hitting the windshield. Markham and Sam crouched down behind the dashboard. The carjacker grabbed the child from the back seat and fled into a wooded area off the side of the road.

Sam and Markham remained low in the seats as further shots hit the windshield. They saw the suspect disappear into the woods with the child clutched in his arms. Sam exited, threw open the rear door, and reached for his bag in the back seat. He quickly slipped on his armored vest and placed extra ammo magazines into his rear pocket. Since it was nighttime, Sam pulled out a night vision device and a flashlight. Markham had a hard time strapping his undersized vest around his potbelly. While Sam vaulted over the guardrail, Markham stumbled as his foot caught the rail's top edge. He fell face down, hitting the ground hard.

"Everything okay, Jim?"

"Yeah, I just need to turn in this vest for a smaller size, ha."

As they both moved to the tree line, the suspect shot at the officers from the woods. Markham fell backward onto his butt and toppled down the slight incline, cursing in pain.

CHAPTER
68

Sam dropped to the ground, his heart thumping against his chest. He crawled toward a tree for cover, staying low. The forest around him seemed to breathe, shadows shifting with each rustling leaf, but his trained eyes saw no movement ahead. He yelled to Markham, his voice a tense whisper.

"Are you hit, Jim?"

Markham grunted with anger. "The nitwit got my vest. He'll pay for this."

Sam couldn't help but throw in a quip despite the gravity of the situation. "At least you have that extra flab—uh, muscle as a cushion now."

Markham snorted, a sound more from irritation than humor. "Oh, you're a jokester now." He cursed under his breath, struggling to push himself up from the ground, his bulk not making it easy. As he rose, his eyes narrowed in the dim light, catching sight of something unusual. "What the hell is that on your head?"

"It's a night vision device," Sam said, not breaking focus.

"What, you carry that around to see your way home in the dark?"

"Touché," Sam retorted. "Let's get this creep before he hurts the kid."

Sam adjusted his night vision lenses, the world around him shifting into a surreal landscape of green and gray. He moved quickly, his steps almost silent as he treaded through the dense forest, each tree trunk a potential shield from the lurking danger.

"Are you with me, Jim?"

"Yeah, somewhere behind you, but I can't see a damn thing."

"I see you on my left. Let's stay apart, with me on your right. Keep cover behind trees as we move forward."

The forest seemed to close around them, the air heavy with the scent of damp earth and leaves. A distant cry reached Sam's ears—a child's cry. His heart clenched, and he moved forward swiftly, trying to minimize their distance. But a careless step on a dry branch gave away his position, the snap echoing like a gunshot in the silent woods.

Hidden in the shadows, the suspect reacted instinctively to the sound, firing blindly in Sam's direction. Through the night vision lenses, the muzzle flash was a blinding explosion of light, a phenomenon called haloing, forcing Sam to close his eyes and turn away. The bullet whizzed to his left, splintering the bark of a nearby tree and sending sharp wood fragments into his face.

Sam hit the ground, feeling the fragments hitting him like slivers of metal. *Whoa, that was close,* Sam thought, his adrenaline spiking. He ducked back behind the tree, his mind racing. *If not for these lenses, those bark bits could have blinded me. Come on, man. Stay covered.*

Sam quickly scanned for Markham, spotting his partner's lumbering form, giving away his position with each noisy step. Sam winced, realizing their approach had been too risky, especially since his partner lacked vision. He waited until Markham was parallel with him. He softly spoke for him to keep cover before moving, darting from tree to tree in quick, controlled bursts.

Ahead, the child's whimpering grew louder, hinting Sam was getting closer. He pressed on, determined to close the distance to the suspect. Each step was a gamble. As he got closer to the child's cries, Sam spotted the child alone, sitting against a tree, quivering with tears streaking his grimy cheeks. He saw the carjacker moving to a distance to his left. Sam quickly moved the kid to another side of the tree to avoid the carjacker from seeing them.

Sam removed his night vision device without wanting to frighten the child further. "Hi. You're okay now. I'm with the police. My name is Sam. What's your name?"

"Robbie," the boy whispered, his voice trembling.

"Hi, Robbie. I'm going to take you to your mom, okay?"

The boy nodded, his eyes wide with fear. Sam quickly fashioned makeshift foot loops from plastic cuffs attached to his belt. "Did your daddy ever give you a piggyback ride, Robbie?"

Robbie nodded, a small smile breaking through his tears.

"Good. I'm going to give you a ride now. Put your feet in these loops, and hold on tight, okay?" Sam guided the boy's feet into the loops and hoisted him onto his back, pulling his hands across his shoulders with his fingers hanging onto the inside edge of Sam's vest. "Hold on tight, Robbie."

Meanwhile, Markham struggled through the underbrush, his breath coming in heavy gasps. He knew he needed to get back into shape—trekking through these woods was no place for a man who'd let himself go soft. But there was no time for self-pity as he pushed on.

The young carjacker heard leaves shuffling and twigs snapping from Markham's direction. He sensed an opportunity. He shifted his position after sighting Markham's silhouette coming toward him. He figured if he took out one officer, the other would focus more on rescuing the child, allowing him to escape. He crept silently, his twenty-twenty vision fixed on Markham's slow, labored movements. The carjacker silently moved and hid behind a wide tree trunk.

Unaware of the danger, Markham paused to catch his breath before moving to the next tree, not knowing who was waiting on the other side of it. He felt the suspect nearby somewhere in the darkness.

The carjacker took a deep, silent breath and tightened his grip on his gun. He took a short, quiet step around the tree and saw Markham's backside silhouette leaning against the tree, breathing heavily. Even in the dim light from the moon, Markham's broad body was impossible to miss. With a calculated move, the carjacker edged closer, positioning himself for the deadly shot.

Not far from where Markham hid, Sam's heart skipped a beat as he tightened his grip on Robbie. Robbie squirmed on Sam's back, constantly grabbing near Sam's ears, dislodging the night vision goggles Sam used to keep an eye on Markham's movements. He desperately repositioned them against a tree, ultimately revealing the ominous scene through the eerie green-tinted light—the hijacker creeping up on Markham. Sam had to act quickly.

The carjacker paused when hearing leaves rustle in the background. He glanced behind him and saw only darkness. The carjacker felt the rush of impending conquest as he stretched his arm around the tree and nudged his gun closer to Markham's head.

Through the ghostly green hue of his night vision, Sam saw the carjacker reach around the tree with his weapon aimed directly at his partner and friend. Panic surged inside Sam's soul. He could feel the cold sweat trickling down his back—the moment's gravity pressing down on him like a physical weight. Sam was concerned about the distance, but there was no time for caution, no room for error. He had to make a choice—a life-or-death decision. He kneeled and placed his gun arm elbow on his knee to steady his aim.

The carjacker, eyes burnished with a twisted sense of triumph, nudged his gun against Markham's head. "Sorry, man," he whispered, his words a chilling threat of imminent death, putting pressure on the trigger.

CHAPTER
69

arkham felt the cold, unyielding steel of a gun barrel pressed against the back of his head. The weight of impending death pressed on him, his heart beating like a wild drum in a funeral march. He closed his eyes, visions of his wife's gentle smile and his children's laughter flashing before him. Just as despair threatened to consume him, a deafening boom split the air, the brutal sound of a gunshot echoing through the quiet night. In a state of unconsciousness, Markham perceived the cracking of bone, then the heavy weight of a thud, resonating like the pounding of a death toll.

For a moment, the world was still, the quiet pierced only by the rustling of leaves as Sam rushed to the tree. Then, a troubled voice shattered the eerie calm.

"Jim? You okay, buddy?"

Markham's mind swam in a sea of confusion, darkness pressing on the edges of his vision. He blinked against the blurriness, his eyes slick with tears he didn't remember shedding, trying to discern if he was still living or among the dead.

"Jim, talk to me, damn it!"

The voice was urgent, familiar, a lifeline in the encroaching void. "What? Sam, is that you?" Markham rasped, dragging his sleeve across his face. He swayed right, his foot hitting something on the ground. His eyes shifted there where he saw the carjacker sprawled lifeless among the swell of leaves. Beyond the body, Sam emerged from the shadows, a child clinging to his back.

"What the hell?" Markham gave a huge sigh of relief. "Holy shit, Sam. I thought I was a goner. Where did you come from? "

"Sorry, Jim. I had to be sure before—I mean—hell, you know what I mean." Sam replied, his voice steady but with a tremor of adrenaline.

"That shot sounded like it came from a distance. Where were you?"

"Uh, you don't want to know," Sam said with a wry grin, the tension easing from his shoulders as he gazed, admiring his friend. He took a glance at the young guy dead on the ground. Sam's stomach growled and churned, distraught for taking a life. He knew it would haunt him for days.

Markham's legs felt like jelly as he stepped over the fallen body, his heart still hammering from near death. He reached out a trembling hand to shake Sam's but found himself pulling Sam into a fierce embrace; the child crunched in his grip. Tears flowed down his face, his weakening voice whispering, "Thanks, man. Because of you, I'll get to hug my wife and kids tonight."

"Hey, you'd have done the same for me. Let's get out of here and get you and this little guy back to your families."

Abruptly, as if someone flipped a light switch, bright beams from flashlights pierced the darkness, forcing Sam and Jim to shield their eyes.

"Police, keep your hands up in the air!" came the authoritative bark of multiple police officer voices converging on them.

Markham cleared his throat and yelled, "It's Sergeant Markham and an ATF agent! The suspect is down, and we have the boy. We're all good here." He turned to Sam, offering a weary but grateful smile. "Like you said, buddy, let's go home."

*   *   *

Sam leaned against the guardrail, watching as a swarm of state police officers and detectives descended on the scene. EMTs were already attending to the boy, checking for injuries, and offering reassurances. Sam, exhausted and eager to return to Boston, pulled out his phone and called Kiara, who picked up almost immediately.

"Are you in Boston, Sam?"

"Sorry, no. I hitched a ride with the state police in Sturbridge. We got a bolo call for a carjacker with a kid in the back seat just past Worcester. We ended up in a chase, and the suspect took off into the woods with the kid. The trooper, the kid, and I made it out okay, but not the carjacker."

More troopers arrived, offering congratulations to Markham for rescuing the child. Sam scanned the crowd and spotted Major Jack Burke arriving.

"Kiara, I have to go. The state police honcho arrived. I'll call you later and explain in more detail."

Major Burke joined the police assembly and took Markham aside to get his story. While Jim briefed Burke, he glanced several times in Sam's direction. Burke patted Markham on the shoulder, then marched directly to Sam with a stern but approving expression.

"I'm not surprised by what you did here, Sam. Even hyping Jim for saving the kid's life."

"He did. It was a team effort, Jack. Jim was a real hero, forcing the carjacker into a guard rail and into the dark woods where we surrounded him. I hope you recognize him for his heroic efforts here. The important thing is that the kid is safe, and we all get to go home tonight. "

Burke nodded affirmatively, saying, "It looks like letting Jim drive you to Boston was a good call on my part."

"Thank you for that. However, I still need to get to Boston. It's been a long, trying day."

"Give me a few minutes. A lieutenant will be here soon. I need to get some order here, and then I'll drive you myself. I'm sure you know we'll need to take your gun for examination since the shooting resulted in the suspect's death. Did you contact your boss yet?"

"No, I'm not sure I want to call him this late," Sam replied, pulling out his phone.

Burke recognized Sam was exhausted. "Let me speak to him first. I'll make sure he understands what happened."

Sam selected his boss's number and handed the phone to Burke, who gave Sam's boss a concise report of the events, praising Sam's heroic actions and promising a full report would follow. As Burke spoke, an EMT approached and waited patiently until the call ended.

"Excuse me, Major. Would you like to call the boy's mother? He's unharmed, just shaken."

"Yes, I'll make the call. But first, I need to inform the Hartford and Connecticut State Police that we have the boy, and he's safe." Burke handed the phone back to Sam. "You sure you won't reconsider working for me?"

"Maybe in a few years when I retire. We'll see."

"All right. Give me a few minutes, and I'll drive you to Boston." Burke walked away with a phone pressed to his ear.

After the scene began clearing, Burke drove Sam to Boston. They talked without pause, their camaraderie forged through shared investigative conflicts with mutual respect. Sam had worked temporarily under Burke's command against terrorists in the Boston area, an undertaking that had deepened their professional relationship into a genuine friendship.

"What investigation were you working on in Connecticut, Sam?"

Sam outlined a senator's request for him to get involved in an FBI investigation that turned into more than he wanted to handle. "It postponed my vacation and my return to Hartford," said Sam, a note of weariness in his voice. "If I'd been on vacation, I wouldn't have had to deal with what turned out to be more than anyone expected."

"You sound like the cases wore you out. Did your investigation end successfully, or were things left undone?"

"The one investigation turned into multiple others, each one connected to the other with successful outcomes. Every investigator involved pulled their weight and delivered what was needed to succeed. Yeah, I'm worn out, but there was satisfaction in all of it. The kind of satisfaction that comes only after hard, dedicated work, where exhaustion is just a reminder of the price we pay for success."

"Well said. You want me to drop you off at your son's place?"

"Wherever is convenient for you."

"I live in Newton, and we're past there now, entering Boston."

"You can drop me at the nearest T-line. I need the fresh air and a walk."

"No way. I'll take you to your son's apartment. It's the least I can do."

When Burke pulled over at the apartment building, he offered his hand for Sam to shake. Sam gripped his hand firmly. "Thanks for the ride, Jack. It's great to see you again. Rumor has it you'll be the next state police superintendent. If that's true, congratulations. They couldn't have picked a better trooper for the job."

"Thanks. It comes with a mountain of responsibility and stress, but I can handle it. My offer for you to join me is still open, now more than ever."

"I'll keep it in mind. Stay healthy, Jack."

Sam exited the car, his tactical bag slung over his shoulder, entering the apartment lobby. He called Kiara while heading to the apartment.

"I'm so glad you called, Sam. How did everything go?"

"It was chaotic but successful enough. How are you holding up?"

"I'm managing. Spending time with Mariela is helping."

"I'm at my son's place and could use some rest. Can we meet tomorrow? We could discuss the case, especially about the woman who shot you."

"A woman?"

"Yeah. Who would have thought? If you agree, I'd like to discuss leniency on any charges brought against her."

"Leniency, huh? That's a switch. I assume you have good reasons for that."

"I do. The woman was just a child when she witnessed her entire family murdered. She made a promise to get justice for her family. She suffered for so many years before finally starting her quest for retribution against the killers. When you confronted her, she hadn't completed her operation and purposely aimed to only wound you so she could escape arrest and finish her mission. She wants to meet you to apologize.

"That's unexpected. It sounds like we have a lot to talk about. I also want to discuss my future with the FBI with you."

"Well, that's unexpected, as well. We should meet with Dell in the morning to finalize everything for the case file."

"Okay. The briefing might be my last. Call me in the morning."

"I'm looking forward to our talk."

CHAPTER
70

Kiara and Sam met at the Boston FBI office at nine o'clock sharp. Dell Haskins, the agent-in-charge, Austin Taylor, and all the agents currently in the office greeted Kiara with a symphony of congratulatory applause that resonated through the office. Taylor's briefing lauded Kiara and Sam for their exceptional investigative success, hinting at an upcoming formal recognition commemorating their success.

Motioning for Dell to follow him, Taylor escorted Sam to a secluded room, where the stark lighting and sterile tan walls reflected the gravity of their discussion—Taylor's need for a detailed report on Sam's investigations. With a steady voice, Sam dictated his statement from notes. His voice, clear yet somber, resonated in the room, every word a testament to his and Kiara's meticulous work.

Meanwhile, Kiara prepared her statements in a separate office. The cool metal of her pen felt reassuring against her fingers as she scribbled down the details, each stroke a reminder of the resolve that had driven her through her darkest days of being shot and kidnapped. From her written statement, she dictated what someone would later type on FBI investigative reports.

Kiara and Sam reconvened in a small conference room, where the scent of freshly brewed coffee and bagels awaited. While drinking coffee, they examined their statements, ensuring they were consistently aligned. The tension eased as they reviewed and edited the drafts, the camaraderie between them unmistakable. After an office assistant typed the final versions, they signed their statements with a sense of finality and accomplishment. They made copies for each agency and themselves.

After wrapping up at the FBI office, Kiara and Sam met with Donna Ranero, the Supervisory Assistant US Attorney in Boston. With its mahogany furniture and soft, golden lighting, her office exuded a sense of gravitas. They briefed her on their investigative triumph and outlined the loose ends that still dangled ominously.

Next, they made a quick stop at the ATF office. The sterile, bustling environment contrasted sharply with the gravity of their mission. Sam submitted his report to the agent-in-charge, who had it faxed it to ATF Headquarters in DC for the Director's review. The clicking of keyboards and the hum of conversation provided a stark backdrop as Sam casually requested a four-week vacation starting the following Thursday. His boss, caught in the whirlwind of agency duties, barely paused before granting the time off. Sam held back from asking about the swirling rumors regarding the open position for assistant special agent-in-charge, preferring to leave some mysteries unsolved for now.

With their responsibilities concluded, Kiara and Sam agreed to reward themselves by meeting at a cozy restaurant on Revere Beach. Leaving Boston's cityscape, the sun's amber glowed against the city's mosaic of brick and concrete. Sam drove directly to Revere while Kiara stopped at Mariela's apartment to change clothes. The beach's gentle waves provided a soothing soundtrack as Sam studied his favorite scene before finding a spot on the restaurant's outdoor patio waiting for Kiara to arrive. Beachgoers were in large numbers, scurrying between the beach and restaurants for burgers and beers.

Kiara arrived at Revere Beach about forty minutes later. The afternoon sun glinted off the ocean, its golden rays dancing on the waves as though nature itself were in celebration. Sam squinted against the light, sliding on his sunglasses as he spotted her crossing the street.

Kiara moved toward Sam with an ease he hadn't seen before, as though the weight she usually carried had finally been lifted. Her red floral print Kami dress fluttered lightly in the warm breeze, hugging her figure just enough to accentuate her confident stride. But it wasn't just the dress—it was her hair, long and wavy, cascading freely over her shoulders. Kiara reached him with a broad smile, her cheeks flushed from the sun and perhaps something more. She tugged a lock of hair behind her ear, almost self-consciously, though the expression in her eyes told a different story.

"Wow. Is this the new you?"

"You look surprised," she teased, tilting her head slightly, her voice playful but soft.

"Not surprised, just blown aware by the new look. You look amazing, like a swanky, high-end attorney," Sam was stunned—not because she looked beautiful, though she did, but because this moment felt like a declaration. Kiara had kept her hair neatly bound, always polished and professional as if to shield herself from being anything but controlled, serious, and capable. This was different. Letting her hair down wasn't just about style; it was about freedom.

"I needed a change," said Kiara, as if to dismiss the significance of her new look, but her voice wavered just enough for Sam to catch it.

"It suits you," he said, his tone sincere. And it did—because this wasn't just a change in appearance. It was a glimpse of the woman beneath the layers of discipline and duty. She was radiant and unguarded, standing before him. "I have to say, you look hot."

"Are you making a move on me, Sam?" she teased, a playful giggle escaping her lips.

"I assume you're kidding. If you're not, let's go to my place," Sam shot back, his grin broadening. They both erupted into laughter, the often shared humor they enjoyed while working together.

"I knew you'd have a good comeback. You're fun to be with, Sam," said Kiara, her voice light with an undercurrent of genuine affection.

"I try to lighten things up at times. How are you feeling after resting back in Boston?"

"Well, I've been busy. I talked to my two lawyer friends. They're excited about starting a firm together. It has brought a new outlook and excitement to life for me. After everything—getting shot, kidnapped, and having to answer to multiple bosses—I'm seriously looking forward to a new career."

The waiter arrived for their order. Sam ordered champagne to mark the occasion. When the champagne arrived and poured, Sam gave a toast. "Well, you look and sound inspired to start a new career. I'm happy for you." Sam raised his glass to celebrate her new beginning.

He then settled into a comfortable rhythm, updating Kiara on the latest developments with Elli Donnelley and the thugs that had shattered so many lives.

"I've thought about Elli. I can't even begin to fathom the pain Elli endured, seeing her family murdered and reliving those nightmares. I admire her bravery in confronting those killers. I think recommending leniency is the right thing to do."

"Does that mean you don't want to meet Elli? She wants to apologize to you personally."

"I don't want to relive or be reminded of what happened in New Haven. I've decided to follow your recommendation. I don't need to meet with her or Durrell. I'll call Durrell with my thoughts, and I trust you to represent both of us at the meeting."

They both smiled unconsciously, the relief and joy of returning to Boston evident in their expressions. They ordered a light meal: Kiara opted for a Caesar salad, while Sam chose a codfish sandwich.

"Can you wait until I return from vacation to discuss your leaving the FBI?" Sam asked.

"Mariela's opposed to me staying with the FBI. She doesn't want to worry daily about whether I'll come home safely. My friends in Virginia are eager for me to join them in starting a law firm. I'm excited about it and have no misgivings about leaving the FBI."

"Is Mariela willing to move to Virginia?"

"We haven't decided where we'll set up the office yet, but wherever we decide, it's pretty much a done deal. Besides, Mariela's company has a huge office near DC. Hey, let's not talk business anymore. Tell me about your upcoming vacation and what's next for you when you return."

The conversation drifted to lighter topics, their laughter mingling with the waves crashing on the shore. The sun cast a warm glow over the beach and their futures, as yet unwritten but bright with promise.

CHAPTER
71

D riving back to the apartment in East Boston, Sam's fingers drummed on the steering wheel when his cell phone rang. It was his son, Drew, calling.

"Hey, how are you?" said Sam with excitement.

"I'm fine, Dad. Just wanted to let you know I'm coming home earlier than planned."

"That's great news! When are you leaving?"

"Hang on a sec, someone's calling me." The line went silent, punctuated by the hum of the car engine. Three minutes later, Drew's voice returned, sounding frazzled. "Sorry about that. It's wild here trying to wrap everything up before we leave. I should be in Boston on Wednesday night. Can you pick me up at the airport?"

"Of course. I'm so glad you're coming back early. Are you planning to take some time off once you're home? I was thinking of a trip to the Caribbean for at least ten days. We could go together. My treat."

"That sounds great, but let me get back to you on Wednesday. Send me the details about where you're planning to go. I'm being paged again. Gotta run. Talk soon. Love you."

"Love you, too, Drew. Stay safe. Bye."

Sam took a quick shower at the apartment, the warm water washing away the day's stress, and settled into a leather armchair with his laptop, scrolling through luxurious Caribbean resorts. He found a stunning beachfront villa and booked it, imagining the feel of sand between his toes and the sound of waves lapping against the shore.

*   *   *

Wednesday couldn't come soon enough for Sam. The minutes ticked by with agonizing slowness. His phone buzzed with a text from Drew confirming his arrival time at Logan Airport and giving him a go on vacationing together. Sam's heart lifted, knowing his son would join him for this much-needed escape.

It took more than two hours to drive to New Haven. Sam decided to stop at the hospital for a short visit with Elli before meeting with the Durrell. Elli's eyes opened wide, surprised to see Sam enter her room. Sam stood close to her bed, mentioning he was pleased she was recovering well. He told Elli he would recommend leniency for any criminal charges made against her, but it would be up to the prosecutors to determine her fate.

"Thanks, Sam. I appreciate it. Is Agent Rivers with you? I wanted to apologize to her."

"Agent Rivers went through hard times during the investigation, and like you, she needed time to heal. But she did send a message. First, she wanted to know why you used the name Alex.

"I used it in remembrance of my mom, Alexis. She forced me into the safe room that saved my life."

"More importantly, Agent Rivers understood the horror you went through witnessing what happened to your family. She praised your courage to face such evil murderers that resulted in uncovering evidence needed to get a conviction and imprison them for a long time. She also recommended leniency on any charges against you. You kept your promise to your family to get justice. For that, Agent Rivers and I commend you.

We wish you well and to put the past behind you. We hope you live a happy, safe, and successful life."

"This might be foolish to mention, and you probably didn't sense what I did when I got shot by my uncle. But when I was near death on the ground, a bright light appeared. I saw my mother's image. She touched my cheek with her hand. I felt her warmth and saw my mother surrounded by a huge white halo smiling at me—then a jolt went through my body. I thought she lifted me into her arms and brought me with her."

Sam was speechless regarding the flash of light he witnessed, but he saw no image.

"All during the times I confronted those killers, my mom was with me. I felt it. She protected me until I kept my promise to get justice for her and my family."

With tears rolling down her cheeks and her emotions preventing her from speaking, Elli held out her hand for Sam to hold.

Sam wasn't sure how to respond, but he needed to support her somehow. With a smile, he grasped her hand and whispered, "It was divine justice."

*　　*　　*

Entering the US Attorney's office just before one o'clock, Sam got receptive greetings from Debra Durrell, her assistant Brian Murphy, Lieutenant Cassie Dawson, DA Lamar Irving, State Police Captain Ed Reyes, and FBI agent Dell Haskins. Sam appreciated the welcome but felt it more deservingly belonged to Agent Rivers, Lieutenant Dawson, and especially Elli Donnelley.

"Sam, before we start, Kiara called regarding leniency for Elli Donnelley."

"Kiara needs time to participate in physical rehabilitation after being shot and therapy after being kidnapped with threats on her life. She needs time to heal," said Sam.

The room was silent, every eye fixed on him, the gravity of his words sinking in. Sam continued. "Kiara wanted me to tell all of you that she forgives Elli and admired her courage to face her family's killers. What she accomplished in identifying and exposing the crew responsible for dozens of home invasion robberies and several murders was remarkable. Kiara and I believe that Elli has suffered enough since childhood. She now deserves all of life's love, respect, and happiness, void of continued nightmares and fear."

Everyone there knew the truth of Sam's words and felt the depth of Elli's sacrifices. They recognized the system fell short of getting justice for her family. There was a collective understanding in that silence—a recognition of a brave soul who had performed the unimaginable and now deserved peace.

"I believe everyone present agrees with you, Sam. We will continue to discuss how best to handle what charges, if any, Elli might have to face. One option might include a local charge of an unintentional firearm discharge in city limits. With no prior criminal history, Elli would be eligible for the accelerated rehabilitation program. The program could result in the eventual dismissal of the charges without the need to plead guilty."

Durrell reviewed her notes, then said, "Many of you have updated news on the investigations Kiara and Sam worked on. I'll start with what the FBI learned from interviews and reviewing the security camera at the Vandell's Lounge in Bridgeport. The security footage confirmed what Travis told us: A yet unidentified man knocked Travis unconscious, and then Tyrese Griggs pushed that guy, knocking him to the floor. The FBI verified the guy wasn't hurt. I informed the senator and Attorney Ranero of the good news."

Lamar Irving spoke next. "Regarding what Elli whispered to you after being shot by her uncle, we interviewed Townsend's partner, Davis Moore. He confessed that he provided the alarm codes to Gilinsky but not for the Donnelly home. Moore admitted being romantically involved with Elli's mother and would never have put her or her family in jeopardy. He was unaware of how Gilinsky got the alarm code for the Donnelly residence but believed Townsend probably gave him the code, believing no one would be home that night. We've also executed search warrants at the four suspects' residences, including Detective Mackey's, finding ample evidence to keep them behind bars for a long time. Tomorrow, my office will indict Gilinsky and his crew. We anticipate long sentences for Gilinsky and Alonzio, with shorter ones for Bonarz and Acosta, who cooperated and will testify against both of them. I want to thank Sam, Kiara, and Elli for helping to solve the Donnelley murder case and several similar cold cases."

"Lamar, please include Lieutenant Dawson and Agent Rivers for commendations," said Sam.

"Come on, Sam. Without your help, we wouldn't have solved those cases," Cassie interjected.

"I simply assisted you and Kiara. Kiara led the way in finding Travis, and you for discovering the M4 hidden in the park that made the case against Callahan."

"What about you and Kiara rescuing that young female trooper from five armed militiamen?" added Captain Reyes.

"I merely assisted Kiara and the trooper in that situation."

"Okay, Sam," said Durrell. "Your partners will get the recognition they deserve, but so will you."

Cassie then chimed in. "To bring Sam up-to-date, a detective working undercover as a teacher's aide recovered the soda can and tray used by Jeffrey Callahan during lunch. The DNA technician, Lalita Cheng, compared the DNA found on the M4 to the can and tray and found an exact match for the kid. I believe Jeffrey Callahan was the shooter who killed two people at the beverage company and injured two middle school students. Once his father learned of the DNA match, he confessed to both shootings, claiming his son only helped carry the weapon into his truck. He claimed he hid the gun at the park, not his son. But it's clear to me that Jeffrey was the real shooter. The DA hasn't decided what, if any, charges he'll bring against Jeffrey."

"Well, I think we covered everything for today," said Durrell. "Unless there's anything else, we'll end the meeting. We'll reconvene soon to discuss the prosecution strategy. Thank you all for your hard work."

As the room emptied, Durrell requested that Sam stay behind. Sam was eager to get on the road to Boston. He was impatient to see Drew and begin a vacation. When everyone left the office, Durrell's serious expression became warm.

"Sam, Alan Davies from the FBI lodged a formal complaint this morning. He feels that his office had primary jurisdiction over the investigation of Agent Rivers's shooter, not you. I spoke with Austin Taylor, Dell Haskins, and the FBI ASAC in Hartford, and they all supported your actions. Without getting into details, Davies dropped his grievance."

"Thanks for having my back. I appreciate your support. Is there anything else? I have a long drive ahead."

"I just wanted to congratulate you personally. Your work in finding Travis and solving the other cases has been outstanding. You deserve a vacation. Enjoy it, relax, and come back refreshed." Durrell stepped around her desk and hugged Sam warmly, a gesture of appreciation and a safe journey. "Don't forget. I owe you a breakfast."

EPILOGUE

Cassie waited in the sterile, fluorescent-lit receptionist's room, her fingers drumming impatiently on the armrest of a cushioned chair. The faint hum of office chatter seeped through the thin walls, but it did little to distract her from the knot of anticipation tightening in her chest. When Sam finally emerged from Durrell's office, a tired smile on his face, she felt an inexplicable relief wash over her.

They walked out together, the late afternoon sky casting a long shadow from the federal building on the city's pavement. Cassie knew Sam was bound for Boston, a departure that felt too final after their recent whirlwind of shared success. Her voice betrayed a shade of desperation, asking if he had time to grab lunch and toast their investigative successes with champagne."

Sam shook his head slowly. "I wish I could, Cassie. My son is flying back from Ukraine. I need to be at the Boston airport to pick him up. I'll come back after my vacation. We'll celebrate properly then. I promise."

Cassie bit her lip, disappointment warring within her. "Today was . . . intense, Sam. I've never worked a case resulting in such a bond of trust and friendship."

A nostalgic smile crossed Sam's face. "The bonds formed during difficult, high-stakes cases are special. In our case, it's a testament to the lasting friendship and respect for each other." He offered a playful grin, trying to lighten the mood. "You are a brilliant, dedicated detective and beautiful, of course. It was a pleasure to work with you. I'd team up with you anytime."

Cassie smiled despite the lump in her throat. "You're a special person, Sam." On impulse, Cassie moved closer and hugged Sam tightly. "I'll miss you. Don't forget your promise about dinner."

"I won't," Sam assured, squeezing her back gently before stepping away.

Cassie watched him walk toward his car, a solitary tear slipping down her cheek. Sam turned, blew her a kiss, and waved, his silhouette fading into the afternoon light as he drove away.

*　*　*

Sam drove almost mechanically to Boston, where the city lights sparkled from the setting sun. He kept his travel at the speed limit, the road ahead a blur of dark asphalt and white lines. Coming out of the Williams Tunnel for the airport, his phone vibrated against the dashboard, the screen lighting up with a familiar number. He answered the call.

"Hello," he answered.

"Hi, Sam, it's Donna Ranero."

Sam's shoulders tensed. "What's up?"

"I'd like you to stop by so we could talk."

Sam frowned, a pang of irritation surfacing. "It's late. I'm on my way to the airport to pick up my son. He's returning early from his assignment in Ukraine. We're leaving for the Bahamas in the morning. What's so important that it can't wait until I return? Am I in trouble?"

"No, nothing like that."

"Well, I can't meet with you now or tomorrow. It'll have to wait until I'm back in ten days."

Donna's silence stretched uncomfortably. "The senator called, thanking you and asking me to express her gratitude for finding her son."

"That's nice of her, but that's not why you're calling, is it?"

"No," Donna admitted. "She mentioned you to the president. He wants to meet you."

Sam's mind raced. "What for? To thank me? Or is it something else?"

"The senator didn't say, but he wants to meet you personally."

Sam sighed deeply. "I'd be happy to meet him after my vacation."

Donna backed off, sensing Sam's frustration. "I understand, Sam. I'll try to find out more and get back to you. Enjoy your vacation."

Sam disconnected the call with a heavy sigh. He had just reached the airport. His son's flight must have arrived early—he was waiting outside the terminal, a backpack slung over one shoulder and a large suitcase by his side. Sam stopped and rushed out of the car to embrace him. He felt the weight of worrying lift off his shoulders with his son safely back home.

As they drove from the airport, Sam's phone rang again.

"Sorry to bother you again, Sam," said Donna. "The senator will arrange for you to meet the president in DC upon returning to Boston. You'll have dinner with the senator and her husband the night before."

Sam gritted his teeth. "What's this about, Donna?"

"I don't know, Sam. I'm just relaying the message. Call me when you're back. Enjoy your time off."

Disconnecting the call, Sam exhaled sharply, frustrated, his curiosity gnawing at him. He tried brushing it aside while focusing on the road ahead.

"What the hell is that all about, Dad?" asked Drew. "What have you been doing lately to get the president's attention?"

"I have no idea and don't want to think about it. We'll be in the Bahamas tomorrow, drinking piña coladas on the beach. My only wish is for us to relax, leave the job behind, and enjoy our time together in paradise. Eleven days later, it's back to the grind."

ACKNOWLEDGEMENTS

My gratitude to ATF, the agency where I worked for nearly thirty years. ATF provided a lasting community of friends and colleagues with whom I served, including special agents, industry operations investigators, and administrative professionals. The men and women of ATF dedicate their lives to serving and protecting the great citizens of the United States.

Special thanks to Editor Erin Clyburn for her tremendous insight and constructive overview of my story. She went above and beyond what I expected, providing exceptional feedback that highlighted the story's strengths, pinpointed areas needing improvement, and identified which areas to exclude. She addressed key elements such as point of view, character development, voice, settings, and plot lines. Erin recognized and suggested areas to strengthen the story's tension and areas for descriptive amplification. I place Erin in the top tier of book editors.

I'm grateful to my coach, Geoff Affleck, and his team for mentoring and guiding me through the challenging process of launching and promoting my books, including the complex steps of self-publishing and optimizing sales. I couldn't have done it without his expertise.

Once again, I would like to extend my thanks to author Wayne Miller, my friend and former colleague, for his ongoing input, editing tips, encouragement, and sharing his marketing ideas.

My wife, Donna, spent hours proofreading my book and provided suggestions that made sentences and paragraphs more readable and meaningful. Her tiresome editing is much appreciated, with love as always. To her and my son, Paul, thank you for the everyday support and encouragement I received while writing.

To my friends, relatives, former classmates, and ATF colleagues, thank you for reading my books. I appreciate your praise, encouragement, and support for my stories.

ABOUT THE AUTHOR

Stan Comforti is a retired federal law enforcement officer with over twenty-nine years of experience, first as a Federal Air Marshal and then as a Special Agent with the Bureau of Alcohol, Tobacco, Firearms and Explosives (ATF). As an ATF field agent, he worked on many high-level federal investigations against felons with guns, gang members, drug dealers, gun dealers, arsonists, and killers. His work included many undercover assignments. He later became a field office supervisor for several years, until he was appointed to a Division Level Operations Supervisor position. During his supervisory roles, Stan also led the ATF Boston's Special Response Team (SWAT). Following his retirement, he began writing fictional crime thrillers based on his vast experience investigating federal crimes. In late 2023, he published three crime thrillers: *A Cry for Help, Chasing Terror, and Finding Ena,* which have garnered positive reviews and a growing readership.

THE SAM CAVIELLO FEDERAL AGENT CRIME MYSTERY SERIES

Book 1: *A Cry for Help*

Book 2: *Chasing Terror*

Book 3: *Finding Ena*

Book 4: *Divine Justice*

Available at Amazon and other book sellers.

If you enjoyed this novel please leave an Amazon review.

Connect with the author at stancomforti.author@gmail.com, or visit StanComforti.com. You also scan the QR code to reach his website

www.ingramcontent.com/pod-product-compliance
Lightning Source LLC
Chambersburg PA
CBHW030245120726
47903CB00005B/1626